I've travelled the world twice over,
Met the famous: saints and sinners,
Poets and artists, kings and queens,
Old stars and hopeful beginners,
I've been where no-one's been before,
Learned secrets from writers and cooks
All with one library ticket
To the wonderful world of books.

© JANICE JAMES.

THE TYCOON

Sweeping from the Philippines, through Kenya, Spain and England, this is the final part of the trilogy of the Aitken family begun with THE EXPATRIATES and THE SILK KING. The year is 1977 and the nightmare which is to last four years has just begun for the Aitken family. Caught up in the political upheaval of the Philippines, Hugo Aitken is imprisoned for anti-governmental activities a few weeks after the disappearance of his Filipino wife, Linda. Marking each day on the wall of the cell, Hugo fights to retain his sanity—unaware that Linda is just yards away in the same prison.

MARY WELLS

THE TYCOON

Complete and Unabridged

ULVERSCROFT
Leicester

First published in Great Britain in 1988 by
Severn House Publishers Ltd.,
London

First Large Print Edition
published June 1990
by arrangement with
Severn House Publishers Ltd.,
London

British Library CIP Data

Wells, Mary
    The tycoon.—Large print ed.—
Ulverscroft large print series: general fiction
I. Title
823'.914[F]

ISBN 0-7089-2229-5

Published by
F. A. Thorpe (Publishing) Ltd.
Anstey, Leicestershire
Set by Rowland Phototypesetting Ltd.
Bury St. Edmunds, Suffolk
Printed and bound in Great Britain by
T. J. Press (Padstow) Ltd., Padstow, Cornwall

For Andrew

Part One

1977

1

I'M staring out of the window at the late afternoon sun shimmering on the pool, in the club where businessmen like myself delouse themselves both inside and out after a day's work in Manila. I am standing here to avoid watching Linda who is brushing her hair at the dressing table. Each time she lifts her arms her shoulder straps tighten and roll into thin black ropes which bite into her flesh.

"I don't want to go." I'd rather be in that pool, I'm thinking moodily.

"Why don't you want to go, Hugo?"

Her voice has that patience you never hear in Western women. A voice that says, whatever makes you comfortable, Hugo. Never says, give me your reasons and I will negate them with my fine feminine mind.

"It's a waste of time."

I make the mistake of turning round. She is standing watching me in her black petticoat with her rounded limbs and

3

abundant black hair cascading down her back.

"There's a man coming from Canada to interview Papa." She's speaking in that nervous tone that makes the words run together and seep away at the end of a sentence.

I knew, and I was interested, but I didn't want to be interested. I wanted her to dissolve into great gusts of Filipino rage so that I could categorically refuse to go. Just a few words about my tight, safe little country where everything is so comfortable . . . or our colonial attitudes . . . that would have done the trick. But she didn't.

"It will be just like all the other get-togethers. Nothing will come of it."

She turned away. For a moment her back stiffened like Filipino backs do when their owners are angry.

I hate Filipino politics. I hate the way the Fat Cats prey on these disorganised excitable people who trust too easily. I despise myself for my Anglo-Saxon attitudes, and know that I wouldn't love them so much without their guilelessness. Ten years of my life wouldn't be too much to give up to see them a fun-loving democ-

4

racy again, but I can't see it happening. If there was an alternative to Marcos and that Medusa—the lovely Imelda—and *if*, by the remotest chance, it was done through the ballot box and not the gun—all Marcos had to do on the day was to hand out Green Shield stamps. Those smiling unlived-in faces can't hold a thought for more than a moment.

Linda was standing beside me now, talking about the Canadian as if he was the Second Coming. A chap's face hovered in my mind and I toyed with the idea that I'd seen him on the telly when I was last in America. She leant against me and my arm crept around her shoulder. That was when my resolve started to weaken. We kicked the subject to and fro and the hostility started to diminish. I gave in. Oh God . . . all this trauma after seven years of marriage.

Half an hour later I was phoning her mother to say we were on our way and Linda was hanging round my neck and laughing and biting my ear.

Then I instructed Francesca, our amah, to wait by the phone until we rang to say we had arrived safely. This was all done with a certain sternness to give the impression I was still the head of the household, which I so rarely am.

But sternness evaporates when I talk to Francesca. She stands in front of me and listens with total concentration, her hands held together, resting on her black apron. She came to live with us four years ago, when Sylvie was born and I bought this expensive house for Linda. She knows all about the streets of Manila. She knows that people disappear on the way to a restaurant. She knows about the vacuum in families when the military pass by. We are her family—replacing the one she so rarely sees, who gobble up her salary and slave at the sugar. But she is happy as long as she has someone to love and she loves us.

Soon Linda and I were driving through the manicured loveliness of Forbes Park where everything is rich and exquisite, every blade of grass cut with scissors by cheap lackies. When we came to The Wall guards in navy blue changed the position of their guns and raised the barricade and we drove into the district of Makati. We passed Rustans—the Harrods of this privileged area, owned by the First Lady, but we're not supposed to know that.

The rush hour was over so I covered the eight miles to downtown Manila in ten minutes. Tinkle town was still its normal sordid self and I drove through the long straight boulevards at top speed heading for the Doc's suburb.

You would be surprised at the Doc's district. It's a slum and the house is very ordinary. He doesn't have to live there but he won't leave his patients. When they receive the knock on the door they rush for him. He finishes what he's doing, washes his hands, reaches for his linen jacket and strolls down to the barracks. He doesn't budge until they've told him where the missing person has been taken. He is the only person I know who goes into that place without a lawyer. Sometimes he waits all day. My Ma-in-law sends the driver with food. He talks to the soldiers. He knows their names, their families. He knows so much that I can't understand why he isn't arrested.

Well, I do understand. He's conquered fear—and this makes the bully-boys uneasy and deprives them of their most

7

potent weapon. They can't make him out, but I can. He's got a heart condition and he doesn't care. After a few drinks he raises his fists and shouts, "What about our bargain God? Me and Marcos—two for the price of one!"

He's quite something, my Father-in-law.

The house was in its usual state of turmoil when we arrived. I say house in the loosest of senses—more a roof over a multitude, all on the move, all talking at the tops of their voices. Children rush about falling over cables. Aunts, uncles and cousins congregate in the middle of the floor to talk as if they never meet and move a fraction when a camera rolls by. Elderly ladies in cardigans sit round the edge of the room and make space for more ladies. Neighbours arrive with their own chairs and sit close to the cameras until they are moved. My Mother-in-law was closing curtains in a half-hearted way until she saw us, then held out her arms with delight as if she hadn't seen us for years. In fact we only met yesterday when we brought Sylvie to stay. Sylvie is the light of my life.

8

My eyes start to sort out the clutch of small people darting in and out of passageways, and come to rest on the dark head bossing her cousins about. She rushes across the room, grabbing my knees as I sink into a chair.

"Have you missed me?" I stroke her curls as she scrambles on my knee.

She ponders. "No."

I twist my neck towards my Ma-in-law's laughter behind me.

"I asked for that, didn't I?"

"We're making a film." My daughter's voice is hoarse with excitement.

"I know."

It crosses my mind, as it always does on these hopefilled occasions, that a certain discretion is lacking. Doing something that the government considers illegal would—one would think—constitute getting the children to bed early. I raised an eyebrow at Linda's mother.

"They're cover," she murmurs.

My English caution isn't satisfied. "What will you do if someone comes?"

Her sang-froid is admirable. "Tell them we're making Home Movies." She strolls towards the decibels of noise in the middle of the room. Children help move furniture against the walls and collide and dissolve into laughter. The cameras roll towards the three chairs in the centre of the room and suddenly, unbelievably, there is silence.

Hands gesticulating, slightly shorter than his wife, the Doc strolls into the room deep in conversation with a tall middle-aged man with a grey crew-cut. He stoops to catch the Doc's words but his eyes are on the cameras. He interrupts to call instructions to men called Joe and Buck, and jots notes on his clipboard. He looks vaguely familiar and I think I've seen him on CBS.

Then the lights are out, leaving two spotlights glaring harshly on the chairs. The producer says something and the Doc and the Canadian sit on the chairs. A clapperboard snaps and it is unnervingly quiet.

The North American voice launches into a spiel about the political situation in the Philippines. He pauses and looks round the room at the fascinated faces—crowding in doorways, children on laps, thumbs in mouths; the cameras pan around, following him.

"It is difficult for viewers, in what appears to be a relaxed family atmosphere, to appreciate the risks Doctor Marquez is taking tonight, when he agreed to allow this film to be transmitted from his house."

Again he paused. Suddenly I was seeing the film through the eyes of people sitting comfortably in their homes in the West. I held my breath in case he went over the top—but he was good, with a lifetime's experience behind that delivery.

". . . not to put too fine a point on it . . . the door could crash open any minute and all these people would be taken away and it would be unlikely that we would see them again . . ." He turned to the Doc. "Doctor Marquez, I can only ask what makes you do it?"

I didn't catch the Doc's reply because I was busy scanning the room for the least crowded exit and frantically wondering how I was going to get Sylvie out when the knock came. My attention returned to the Doc and my moment of fear passed.

"There is someone here who can answer your questions better than I can."

The cameras swung towards the kitchen

door, and there, walking towards the third chair smiling like a cheeky school boy, charisma blazing like a beacon, was our man—our hope for the future—Benigno Aquino.

The place was in uproar. People standing on chairs, cheering, clapping, shouting—"Ninoy! Ninoy!" It was deafening and there was a lump in my throat. The cameras moved in close and he sat down next to the Canadian.

"Well it's evident you are among friends, Mr. Aquino. But some people would say yours is the most corrupt country in Asia. What would you say to those people?"

The friendly voice started to reply, but I hadn't got over the shock of seeing him. He was in prison. What was he doing here? How on earth had they managed this? I looked around for the coral dress Linda was wearing and stared at her transfixed face on the other side of the room. She'd known! And she hadn't told me!

"Corruption, like communism, is a movable feast—" Ninoy looked well, stimulated, not like a man who had spent years in prison.

"It's influenced by geography and culture. Is a child corrupt when its parents give it sweets and it cries for more? Or are the parents corrupt, are they buying affection? Is a young man corrupt because he does favours to obtain money to feed his family? Or should he maintain a high moral stance and watch his family starve?"

But these allegories were not what the interviewer wanted.

"Mr. Aquino—I was at a fire in the slums of northern Manila yesterday. The firemen stood in the street haggling over the price of water whilst the shacks burned to the ground."

"That is corruption—yes. The chiefs of the fire department demand their cut from the firemen. This graft goes right up to the Minister. If men don't pay they lose their jobs. What can they do?"

"And who is to blame for the kidnappings, the lootings, the rioting? I've seen police stealing from the looters."

"These are all symptoms of an evil regime."

I was holding my breath. Sock it to them Ninoy!

"And is it true to say that the proceeds

13

finance the New People's Army, the Communist Party?"

"The question you should be asking is why do we have the NPA and the communists after being a democracy for years?"

"And you are going to tell me."

Ninoy leaned back in his chair enjoying the cut and thrust.

"Mr. Hennessy, humour me. If your country—a democracy only eight years ago—suddenly found itself in the grip of a family like the Marcos who were backed by a cabinet—no, a whole government—intent on getting on the gravy train *and* all those people were in a position to influence the police and the army, what would you do? May I suggest that you would gather in friend's houses and devise schemes to overthrow the authorities? But before you could accomplish any change you were picked up one by one. Then your children, incensed by the injustice—infuriated by the disappearance of parents, teachers, lecturers—might form themselves into groups. Maybe even call themselves communists, although they had never read a book on Marx in their lives. And when they in turn disappeared and possibly turned up dead in a swamp, what would *you* do Mr. Hennessy? Would you still look for labels?" The producer made winding up signals and the presenter cast his eye over his clipboard.

"How would you correct the situation, Mr. Aquino?" Ninoy looked serious, like a man who knew his time was running out.

"Marcos must go. And it would be better if the USA pulled out. The indiscriminate confetti of American dollars will only breed another Marcos."

"But the Americans need the country for their bases." Ninoy shrugged. "Bases or a communist Philippines? That is the core of the question, Mr. Hennessy. Do you know how much American Aid ends up in the Marcos' Swiss accounts?"

The Canadian shook his head.

"No. Nobody does. But when the lady wears diamonds in her shoes for a charity function . . ." He shrugged.

"Thank you, Mr. Aquino."

The interviewer neatly brought the programme to a close. He'd liked that bit about Imelda's shoes. It would slot in nicely with her "Let's be kind to the poor" chats. The Doc and Ninoy stood up, and disappeared through the door, leaving a vacuum.

Everyone milled around searching for the person they wanted to talk to and the cameras were trundled away creating a corridor amongst the turmoil. I searched along it, looking for Cory, Ninoy's wife, but the space filled up like a tide coming in. So, with Sylvie still hanging round my neck, I steered us towards the drinks table.

The interviewer was there first, sipping a whisky. It's strange how alone a man can look in a crowd. He was the definitive picture of culture shock. A man who has crossed too many time zones too fast, who has read up Asia on planes and is still unprepared.

Because I recognised myself in that look —trotting round the world selling the company—I spoke to him.

"Is this your first visit to our torn little country?" His eyes swivelled in my direction and I saw that the interview had drained him.

"Yes it is. I'm a sprog in South East Asia."

16

"A sprog?"

"Air Force slang for someone who's new to the job." He was sinking that whisky fast. I negotiated the bottle with one hand.

"Canadian Air Force?"

"No. RAF in the Middle East. Then I became the expert on that area. The Asian chap is ill. They sent me to get a new viewpoint."

I noticed his accent. "You're English. My wife thought you were Canadian."

"I emigrated to Canada after the war, then moved on to the States. Not many people spot it these days."

"Do you like it?" I eased Sylvie's stranglehold on my neck.

"There's been some good opportunities, but I rather wish I'd been able to stay in Africa."

"I was born in Africa."

His eyes lost their vague look and he asked, "Which part? I'm sorry, I didn't catch your name?"

"Aitkin—Hugo Aitkin. I was born in the Sudan—my father was in the Political Service before Independence."

I tipped the whisky bottle over our glasses, then noticed the slightly stunned look on his face. Another one who had come across the Empire Builder; everyone's come across my father.

"Your father was David Aitkin?"

"That's right. I suppose you knew him?" I felt slightly interested but not enough to listen to another chunk of nostalgia.

"Yes. I knew him. And I'm beginning to think I knew you."

I laughed in that wary way people do when they are in the dark. We both gave our glasses unnecessary attention.

Suddenly he asked "Did Sarah go back?"

I stared at him. "You mean to Kenya?" Sarah's my mother.

"Yes."

"Yes—she went back."

He became aware of Sylvie. "Is this your daughter?"

They stared at each other across the generations and Sylvie asked in a penetrating voice, "Who is this man, Papa?"

"A friend, Poppet . . . shall we find Mama?"

Her arms tightened. She has an unerring instinct for the unusual.

"Why don't we get out of here . . . go for a drink or something?"

"Good idea. We're off to Hong Kong in the morning."

Ma-in-law appeared at the first wail and extricated those arms expertly with promises of unthought of goodies.

Then we were out of that tangle of people and into my car and at the last minute Linda rushed out of the house and fell into the back with Hennessy. Then we left that horrible district behind and, driving along Roxas Boulevard, I saw the garishness through his eyes. Girls in tight skirts bursting out of their tee shirts like over ripe fruit, tottering along the sidewalks clutching overfed US sailors. The men's hands wandered over them in a way that would have had them arrested in their home towns.

Linda chatted to Hennessy in that fast staccato way, pouring out information about anti-government groups at the university where she works. She caught his attention. I watched through the mirror as he took out a notebook and started scribbling.

Suddenly she caught sight of a man in a doorway. She grabbed my shoulder saying, "Wait—wait just a minute—" Opening the door, she was across the pavement like a shot.

I gave a small moan and dropped my head on the wheel.

"She's very involved isn't she?" Hennessy commented.

"Too much . . . she takes such risks . . . When she leaves home I often wonder if I'll see her again."

"Oh surely that's an exaggeration!"

"That's what they all say when they've got their return ticket in their pocket!"

The noise from the traffic behind became cacophonous.

Linda rushed back, urging me to go on, insisting she could get herself back home. She turned away before I could remonstrate. Returning to the man it was clear she was trying to persuade him to do something he didn't want to do.

Depressed I could see it was going to take time. These wonderful enthusiasms have been going on too long. Helplessly I watched as they disappeared down an alley like something in a "B" movie, then I let in the clutch and pulled out into the hostile traffic.

The military are instucted to keep away from tourist spots, so it was a relief to get inside the Manila hotel. The place is glutinous with wealth and another world from the violence on the streets. I could see Linda was still on Hennessy's mind as we sat swallowed up in the vast chairs.

"Your wife is Doc Marquez's daughter, isn't she?"

I nodded. "We met seven years ago when I was promoting the company in the Philippines."

He considered this then said, "I heard about your father's silk industry. How is he?"

"He died in '63."

"Oh—I'm sorry to hear that." But he didn't sound sorry—just conventional.

"He must have been only in his fifties . . . illness?"

"No. An accident . . . soon after the Malaya Emergency ended."

The conversation dried up until he asked "Did Sarah marry again?"

"No she didn't." I wasn't going to talk about Klaus so I waded in with the questions game. "You were in the Sudan, I suppose, when you were in the RAF?"

His eyes crinkled into a beguiling smile that must have eased the tension for many an interviewee. "You don't recognise me, do you Hubert?"

Hubert! Nobody calls me Hubert any more.

"Perhaps you remember my wife—Frances. You were seven at the time."

Seven! My mind lurched back to a ship leaving Liverpool in those dark days after the war. A frightened kid, until I met a young woman with blonde hair who was frightened too. Then—a kaleidoscope—and she was in and out of our house by the Nile. At the club, by the pool, in the Equatorial South with us on holiday. Always with my father. Then I remembered. No wonder this chap wasn't breaking an arm and a leg over my father's death.

"Peter!"

"The same."

Incredulously I stared at the grey hair that used to be blond. At the khaki clad officer Abas used to call the captain.

"You taught me to drive!"

After the third drink Hennessy tore himself away from the past and asked, "What made you settle in the Philippines? I thought you Aitkins were a fixture in Malaysia."

"Policy changes in Kuala Lumpur. They like to employ their own. We've got a manager running the place now. Our headquarters are in London, but someone has to supervise the purchase of raw materials. I was looking for a new base when I met Linda and Manila seemed a reasonable place then."

This concentration of questions lowered me somewhat. It seemed to dilute my life into a series of chances. I felt as impermanent as a kite in the wind. With firmness and authority I turned to my interrogator and said, "Now tell me about Frances. Where are you living? How many children have you produced?"

2

IT was after one o'clock before I was back in the car driving towards Makati, my head swimming with whisky and *temps perdu*. Hennessy had talked and talked, weaving a spell of the past in that engaging way people do, who earn their living with words. All at once his eyes glazed over with fatigue and I'd packed him off to bed.

Now it was wonderfully quiet with only the chattering of the cicadas and the whoosh of the tyres to come between me and my thoughts. Peter had clarified what had been in my mind for some time—the fact that it was time we moved on. When Linda and I talked about it somehow *mañana* always prevented us from reaching a decision. But tonight, when I got back, I'd have it out with her. Charles, my partner, would be pleased if we returned to England. Poor old, over-worked Charles.

When I arrived at The Wall the guards

looked agitated as they raised the barrier, but I was too tired to take much notice. It was only when I turned into our drive that something seemed different. No lights were on and I couldn't hear Francesca's radio. Our private guard didn't hasten to chat to break his nightly hours of patrolling. But then he often had a quiet kip under a hedge.

Inside the front door is a second door with double locks on it. I stared at it, my keys suspended in my hand. The inner door had been smashed open with a fire axe. The chain from one of the locks swung silently to and fro. Slowly I pushed the door open trying to fight the shock and stared at a scene of destruction.

The hall is tiled and circular. All the contents of the upstairs rooms had been thrown down from the balcony above so that the floor looked like a gigantic bazaar. Burglars! But why should burglars slash the curtains to pieces? Why should burglars grind broken glass into everything with muddy boots?

Stunned, I walked through the archway into the drawing room trying to take in the slashed sofas and chairs, their stuffing erupting.

"Francesca!"

My voice echoed hollowly in the empty house. I trod on something sharp and bent down to see what it was. A triangle of glass had pierced the sole of my shoe. As I tried to pull it out my eyes gravitated towards the floor and came to rest on reddish brown stains. Bending forward I gingerly put my finger on it. Sticky, half dried, rancid blood . . .

I sank into one of the ripped chairs, shattered with the shock. Whilst I was levering away at the piece of glass I noticed blood stains on the arm of the chair. I got up again in a hurry, then saw that my desk had been ransacked. Drawers had been overturned onto the carpet and showers of papers cascaded from the top of the desk to the floor. I tried to recall what I had brought home from the office, but my mind was in a turmoil.

"Francesca!" I called again.

I couldn't budge the glass in my shoe so I took it off and limped through the hall and into the kitchen. The contents of the fridge were on the floor. Wrappings had been torn off the food. Even the ice cubes had been smashed. Cupboard doors hung open; upside down drawers and their contents were scattered everywhere.

Silently I continued into the utility room where we stored junk, and stood staring at the tiles leading to the amah's room along the passage. A trickle of blood seeped under Francesca's door.

She was crouching in the little space between the end of the bed and the wall. I noticed her legs first because they were sticking out at queer angles, then her hands clutching her chest covered in blood. She watched me like a small, cornered animal with a bleached face. The fear in her eyes slackened as she recognised me. A tiny moan escaped, and one hand fell onto the bed. I stared at the hand in horror, searching for the nails, but the fingers were only bloody stumps.

Blood from her chest wound dripped onto the tiles and I knelt in it and slid my arm round her back. When I tried to lift her an unspeakable small rattle forced its way upwards and escaped from her mouth. My stupid attempt to move her caused the blood to flow more freely and I watched in horror as it pumped and spurted, draining the life out of her.

After that I didn't dare move again. So together we sat and I talked about Sylvie. I remembered a lullaby she sang when my child was fractious. Because hearing is the last faculty to go in the dying I tried to keep talking. Her eyes never left my face. Once she choked, then her eyes returned to me. I knew she was dead when her eyes became fixed but I still didn't move, just in case . . .

There were fragments of light in the sky when I accepted the fact that this was no burglary. Burglars don't pull out old lady's nails. Burglars don't search through papers. Only skilled military do that.

It is five o'clock—the time when people die—and I am dialling the Doc's number, and my arm is still numb. The ringing was an empty sound and seemed to go on for a long time. Finally he answered.

"Sorry to wake you." My voice is terribly normal. "We forgot to give you Anna's present. I wanted to catch you before you left."

I could hear his stertorous breathing.

28

Anna, Linda's sister, is the key to our carefully worked out code. She lives in Hong Kong and her birthday was three months ago. The In-Laws keep a bag packed and make a bolt for it when things get heavy with Marcos. The present was our code for Sylvie.

"Then you'd better meet us at the airport, Hugo. You can bring it with you." His voice sounds just like mine.

"On second thoughts—could Linda have brought it over yesterday?"

"Don't worry, we'll look for it." But I felt sure he'd got the message. If Linda was with me I would have asked her about the present.

"Anything else? If not I'll get my head down for an hour or so." He was telling me they would be on the seven o'clock flight.

"Is Linda going with you this time?" I had to be sure he understood that Linda wasn't with me.

Then I heard the anxiety in his voice. "No—not this time."

"I didn't think she would. There's a new intake at the university."

I listened as he put the receiver down.

There were two clicks instead of one. With fingers depressing the bar I unscrewed the mouth piece, then the plate at the bottom of the telephone. Inside, amongst the pieces of metal was a round stud-like nut. I chucked it out of the window and put the thing together again.

After that I sat in the least damaged chair and switched on my music. The strains of Mozart pushed away panicky thoughts about Linda. An hour later I had a shower and the fierce tattoo of the water dinned into my head that Francesca could have saved herself if she'd told them where we were; and if she had they would have burst in whilst we were drinking and congratulating ourselves and we would have been arrested and Ninoy killed.

Later I sifted through the spilt papers to see what they had found. It was only a gesture because we never kept anything important in the house. Then I sat at the desk and concocted a bland note for Linda which said—in essence—beat it, and stay away.

I had to go and see Francesca again before I left. She was lying on the bed where I had left her, face turned to the wall as if sleeping, but her cheek was cold. I pulled the thin blanket up to her neck because she feels the cold since she grew older.

When I returned to the drawing room I couldn't find my Walkman. Now I couldn't wait to get out of that house. Panicking, I returned to the bathroom and chucked cold water over my face and head. On my return I found the Walkman down the side of a chair. Picking up a handful of tapes and my wallet and passport I left by the kitchen door. The memory that will stay with me is broken glass crunching under my shoes.

The security forces were milling around the airport when I arrived—eyes everywhere moving from one passenger to the next in that inhuman way of theirs. Mama Marquez and Sylvie were standing near the indicators, surrounded by small pieces of hand luggage. The Doc was talking to Hennessy whilst the team milled about with one eye on their equipment.

Sylvie spotted me and shot across the departure lounge shouting, "We're going to Auntie Anna's . . . we're going to Auntie Anna's!"

"I know, Pet." Hand in hand we made our way to the others whilst I searched frantically for Linda.

"Is Mama here?" She shook her head vaguely. She's used to her mother's absences. The In-Laws shook their heads very slightly as we approached. The men in green watched but didn't move. They were probably looking for a couple—a European man and a Filipino woman—and I was thankful that the crew's departure coincided with ours.

"I can't come until I've found her," I muttered to the Doc. "Hasn't anybody seen her?"

He shook his head. "No one since last night."

With one eye on those carbines I started to tell him about Francesca and the state of the house, then the indicators whirled and chattered over our heads and the boarding sign came up. Mama picked up Sylvie and we edged towards the gates. Peter and the Doc followed with the cases and the crew drifted after them. On the far side of the gate Sylvie suddenly realised

32

I wasn't going with them. She started shrieking, her arms out towards me, "Papa! Papa!"

I was through those gates like a shot and her arms were tight round my neck. An airport official dragged at my sleeve.

"Mama and I will be coming tomorrow, my darling."

Her little body was shaking with sobs. "You promised . . . you promised." What did I promise? In God's name, what did I promise?

"Look." I struggled with my back pocket and pulled out the universal wallet. "Buy yourself a present in Hong Kong—and one for Mama—" The sobs turned to breathy gulps and she stared at the money I was holding out, then she buried her head in my shoulder and muttered, "Don't want a present . . ."

"Yes you do." Patiently I waited as other passengers pushed past.

Reluctantly her head came up and she looked into my eyes . . . eyes like Linda's. "Can I go to Lane Crawford?"

I sighed and added more notes to the ones she was clutching. The most expensive shop in Hong Kong. The official's hand became insistent.

"Of course you can."

I transferred her and the loot to her grandmother, then slowly faded away behind the barrier. The distance between us became a great gulf. Peter turned and made the thumbs-up sign and I watched as the team took it in turns to distract her. Then they turned a corner and I was staring at a blank wall.

Aimlessly I wandered away, full of thoughts about the folly of staying in this dangerous country for so long. For too long I'd fooled myself that I was staying for Linda's sake, but the truth is I stay for myself, for the smiles and the people who greet me on the streets. The rest of the world has such lonely streets.

3

THE obvious place to start looking for Linda was her university, the Ateneo de Manila. In the past when sudden curfews were put into effect and she was caught in the city she had spent the night there. As I passed the spot where we had left her talking to the man on the previous evening, a cleaner came out of a closed restaurant nearby with garbage. My foot hovered over the car brake and I couldn't decide whether to stop and question him. Slowing down I stared at the low forehead and blank expression as he stood blinking in the sunshine and thought that I wouldn't get anywhere there.

The campus was still fairly empty as I strolled across the grass towards the office she shares with her Head of Department. I tapped on the glass of the open window and stood there blinded by the piercing sun. The room was a mass of shadows and I could only vaguely see the two big desks facing each other.

35

Edgardo Herrera came over, beamed and said, "Hugo, my friend . . ." and waved me in. As he walked towards me I thought, not for the first time, how niggardly nature had been with his legs. Sitting behind his desk he seemed tall with the dignity commensurate with his position. I stepped over the window sill and clasped his outstretched hand in a sincere handshake.

"How are you on this beautiful morning?"

"Fine . . . fine." Then, as an afterthought, "How are things with you?"

"Fine . . . fine."

Edgardo was a man who listened with care to the conversations of English speaking friends, then used their phrases liberally to illustrate his familiarity with the language. His most recent acquisition was "fine' and this gnostic response accompanied the most banal statement.

"Coffee?" I nodded. "Fine."

This exchange had given my eyes time to adjust to the change of light and one thing became clear. Linda was not in the room. I slumped into her chair and watched Edgardo busy himself with the coffee arrangements.

He was brisk and deft with the small man's efficiency. But I had never been sure of him; when his genial smile relaxed his mouth was thin and drooped at the corners. He needed recognition like the rest of us need oxygen. For some time I'd felt the Principal of the college should guard his back. Constantly I'd urged Linda to be circumspect, not to confide in him, not to mention names. But circumspection is not Linda's strong point. She thinks the best of people too easily.

"You are so cautious, Hugo. Edgardo is a fine man—an honourable man."

Sometimes she makes me feel old and jaded with my hard earned knowledge of the human lot.

Herrera returned to his desk and placed a silver tray of perfect impeccability between us.

"You have come to tell me she's not well this morning." I nodded noncommittally.

"I knew it! She had a headache yesterday. She's had a lot of headaches recently. Only yesterday I said, Linda, go

37

to a doctor my dear. You are quite white these days. Your eyes are pale."

I nodded and said something about her over doing things. At least it was clear that she hadn't been in since the previous day.

"Can you cover for her?"

"Oh yes—no problem." His self-confidence jarred.

"But you have a new intake today?"

He nodded vaguely. "There's not much work for the first few days . . . new books, timetables . . ."

"Which books are you doing this term?" I asked, stretching out the conversation.

"Trollop, Iris Murdoch and Norman Mailer," he replied with pride, as if he'd written the books himself.

I smiled admiringly. Mailer! Herrera never let anyone forget that he'd done a postgrad course in America. He handed me a small cheroot and stirred his usual cup of black. I stirred my large cup of white and we smiled at each other like brothers.

"How is the world of commerce, Hugo? I suppose you are off on your travels again quite soon?"

"Yes. Hong Kong tomorrow for a few

38

days. My partner is arriving from London."

I stared out of the window and wondered how commerce was myself, recalling Charles' urgent voice on the phone. In theory Charles is supposed to be in charge of sales in Europe and America but this division of labour doesn't work out because there is so much to occupy him in London. So we often meet in Hong Kong, because we are all paranoid about the phone in Manila. Half the business men here go to Hong Kong to use the phone. I met a chap on the Space Programme once who told me he never used the phone until he was inside Jardine Matheson's office. Now we smile at each other when we meet like a couple of Secret Agents.

I stood up saying, "I must be off, and leave you to your affairs. Sorry about Linda—she's bound to be alright tomorrow."

"No hurry—give her my love. You must come to dinner, dear chap—just as soon as she is better."

His Malay face was transparent with unasked questions and I wondered why he was always so interested in the company. But you can never tell what goes on in academic's heads—perhaps he liked the sound of my voice.

I returned the way I had come, keeping an eye open for Linda's students. When I was half way across the lawns I heard the patter of Herrera's little feet behind me.

"Hugo." He pulled up beside me and I caught a look that, for want of a better word, was cunning on his face. "Just before you go, the word, Ellipsis, what is the derivation of that word? Would you happen to know?"

I shook my head. "Edgardo, I'm in textiles—not syntax."

These questions are intended to focus on the blinding light of his intellect. Linda calls him a Gerund-Grinder. I looked at my watch and he drifted away. Ellipsis . . . a figure of syntax by which a word or words are left out or implied. Why had he picked that word?

Then I caught sight of Lyla and the problem vanished. She was standing under a tree near the gates, her lovely face, like a tinted magnolia, crumpled with distress.

"Lyla! Whatever's the matter?"

She struggled with the need for respectful behaviour and anxiety to have some disaster removed from her world.

"Mr. Aitkin, may I speak with you?"

"Sure,—what is it?"

"Mr. Aitkin, have you seen Linda since late last night?"

"What time last night?" I enquired carefully.

Misunderstandings arise and spread like smoke with these girls.

"Very late last night, midnight." She almost whispered the last word.

"It was about ten o'clock when I last saw her, Lyla."

Her hands rushed up to her face and those great eyes latched themselves to my face in horror. Carefully I took her by the shoulder and directed her to a bench. One wrong word in a situation like this induces hysterics or unbreakable silence.

"Where is she?"

She moaned. Caught in a trough of despair.

"Tell me."

"I thought she would be home by now." She started to twist a piece of hair.

Firmly I removed the hair from her

hand and pulled her round to face me. This didn't seem the time to be pandering to the primitives.

"For God's sake—when did you last see her?"

Those great brown eyes settled on me again as if drawing strength.

"Last night—" she swallowed, "we were coming home from a disco."

"Yes—"

"—in a jeepney."

I sighed.

"She'd been running. We stopped to give her a lift. She talked about a man who was an informer—"

"Yes."

"Suddenly—" Lyla's eyes became enormous, "out of nowhere were soldiers. The student who was driving put his foot down and drove like a madman. She was shouting at us to put her down or we would be caught too. We got to a quiet lane and we thought we had lost them so we slowed down and she scrambled out. We shouldn't have done that Mr. Aitkin —we shouldn't have left her."

She was in tears now, and I felt a cold fear creeping over me.

"Where was this?"

"I don't know. It was so dark."

I was furious that they had left Linda in the middle of nowhere at night, but one has to be so careful with these Filipinos. One edgy comment and she might go home and commit suicide.

"Come on. We're going to find your friends—they might remember."

We went to the library, but it was empty at that hour. Then to the canteen where a few blank faces stared at us. We chased from one lecture hall to the next, but none of them housed Lyla's colleagues. Baffled we came to a halt in a corridor.

"Could they be in the bar at this hour?"

The question was too much for her, so I took her hand and rushed her round the streets near the university. In and out of bars, standing in doorways staring, even venturing into unlikely toilets. Finally defeated, I stood on the pavement writing down my office number and the In-Laws' number and instructed her to ring at any time of the day or night, because it would comfort me considerably to know where my wife was before leaving for Hong Kong. Then I got into a taxi and told the driver the In-Laws' address, only remembering my own car left in the university car park when we were nearly there.

The reason for my trip was to see Moleta, the Doc's assistant and Linda's cousin. The two surgeries are in an extension or annexe built onto the side of the Doc's house. When the taxi had driven away I walked round to the back and came across the usual queues of ragged women and children overflowing from the waiting room. Dolefully, they stared as I pushed through.

Moleta looked up from a fecund stomach lying on the couch and said, "Oh, it's you, Hugo . . . won't be a moment."

I sagged against a wall and waited until the lady had scrambled behind a screen with her clothes. She was a T'boli woman —all eyes—full of agitation in the capital.

Moleta washed his hands, then got out a packet of fags, drawing the smoke deeply into his lungs. I allowed him a moment of tranquillity. A small boy pushed his head round the door, sucking his thumb. His mother tiptoed round the screen and I said, *"Paalam—salamat"* and her brown eyes crinkled into a fawn like smile.

44

Ash was sprinkled liberally on the floor as Moleta asked, "What's up?"

"Trouble. The amah's dead, the house ransacked, and Linda's missing."

"Is that all?" Tiredly he grinned through the smoke and I had to grin back. I'd take refuge in a sick joke if I had his job.

"Have you seen her since the interview?"

He stared at nothing, hordes of people tripping through his mind, and I tried to remember how old he was. About eight years younger than me, yet he looked fifty.

"Have you asked the aunts?"

"No. If I do that it will be all over the neighbourhood. She's probably holed up somewhere, keeping her head down. I thought Roilo could look for her. He knows all the places." Roilo is Moleta's brother—a law student who has been in trouble with the authorities for political activities—and now earns his living as an enquiry agent for a law firm in the business quarter.

"Good idea. You're off to Hong Kong tomorrow, aren't you?"

"Yes—early."

45

"Come round for supper. He'll be here this evening." Then looking at his watch, "I must get on." He put his arm round my shoulders, easing me back into the waiting room. "Don't worry, I'll keep him at it while you're away. She'll turn up, you know Linda." He stood in the street waving as I walked along the dusty passage to the front door. At the corner I turned to wave but he was surrounded by agitated women who had settled on him like moths.

Popping my head into the living room, my hand on the door knob ready for a quick getaway, I asked if there were any calls for me. Huddled in groups, the aunts questioned each other, adjusted cardigans, questioned each other again, then shook their heads. A variety of voices gave reasons why I should stay. Smiling firmly, I fought off their blandishments and backed away in case they overwhelmed me.

"I'll be back for supper tonight." Mollified, they returned to their discussions.

I collected my car and finally arrived at my office where I passed the afternoon sorting papers for tomorrow's trip. Then I compiled lists for my secretary. Time whizzed by. At six o'clock on the dot I gathered together my briefcase, my business suit on a coathanger in a cellophane bag and my greatcoat with my music in the pocket. Then I went down in the lift to the garage under the building and laid them neatly on the back seat of the car. I made sure that the light was gone and night was masking the city before I slid into the driving seat and started to drive in the direction of Forbes Park.

Some weeks ago I had noticed a section of The Wall where the bricks were crumbling. After several false sightings I found the place with the help of a torch and parked the car some distance away under some trees. Once over The Wall I moved from shadow to shadow, keeping a healthy distance from the guards, and finally arrived near the edge of a neighbour's estate where I could get a good view of our house.

An open jeep was parked in a strategic but not conspicuous position near our drive. The driver and his oppo looked tired, as if they had been there for a long time. Their eyes swept over the road, the club and the general scenery in a perfunctory way but I was well concealed by the hedge surrounding a tennis court.

Twenty minutes later another jeep arrived driven by a solitary army officer. He stood questioning the men for some time, then retreated a few yards to get a better view through the windows of the house. I circled the estate on foot for nearly an hour but there was nothing unusual afoot—even the club was quiet because it was a weekday evening—and everyone was battened down inside their fortifications.

Later that night, after a well-earned dinner, I discussed tactics with Roilo in a corner. I had prepared a list of phone numbers and places where he could contact me in Hong Kong. Although he slipped into his role of private eye happily enough, he got distracted easily, calling to people and then forgetting to lower his voice. The aunts looked round curiously and tried to listen to our conversation. I kicked him and he looked hurt. Somehow, I was losing confidence in him and wouldn't have been surprised to find that he'd left the list on a table with his drink.

I found a spare bed, had a few hours' kip and was back at the airport by seven. The early morning news broadcast was bombarding the cabin as we wrestled with luggage in over the seat racks. The news-reader was recounting a sweep by the military in northern Luzon. He quoted a general who stated, "We had to destroy the village to save them from the Commu-nists." What folly! Alice in Wonderland!

4

BY nine-thirty I was in my office in Kowloon reading a message from Charles, which said ring him at the Lee Gardens hotel. Momentarily I was relieved that he wasn't staying at the Peninsula, as expenses were at an all time peak in the current audit. The telephone account alone would have solved a Third World country's Balance of Payments Deficit.

Twenty minutes later I could hear him talking to the girls in the outer office and concluded that he had walked over from his hotel.

As he loomed in my doorway, he was in the process of removing the jacket of his business suit which he then shook and placed over the back of a chair.

"Bloody flights! How do you stop your suits getting creased?"

"I wear a track suit."

Charles is more serious than he was when we lived in Singapore. He is confident and prosperous but his smiles are less frequent and he is only relaxed in the bosom of his family.

"How was the flight?"

"Terrible!"

"You got here quickly anyway."

"If I sit down I succumb to jet-lag." A wan smile appeared.

"How are Penny and the girls?"

The smile spread and settled and I thought, that marriage is your strength. "Fine."

Oh God . . . not another one!

"The family's fine, but something funny's going on with the shares—best not discussed on the phone."

"How do you mean? Charles—your hair's receding."

He frowned and stood up to look in the mirror, his fingers seeking out the thinning centre on the crown.

"Rubbish!"

But Charles' hairline had been sacrificed to the company little by little as the years went by and it was nasty of me to mention it.

I lit a cigarette without thinking and Charles stared at it as he sat down, then tipped a box of matches onto the desk and started separating them into groups of ten. He's trying to give up.

"About the share movement?"

"The market's very volatile. Someone's buying up the small shareholders." He averted his eyes from my fag.

It must be quite serious, I thought, because we've had these problems before since we went public eight years after my father's death. How bemused he'd be with our current difficulties compared with the one-man-band he'd known when we only had the Silk Farm in Malaysia.

"Is it Liang again?"

In those days there were four partners; my father and I, Charles, our lawyer, and Klaus, our Industrial Chemist. Now there were only the two of us because Klaus had turned out to be a wrong 'un—influenced by Liang—the old enemy.

Charles shifted his gaze from the matches and replied, "Oh no. I had a bit of news the other day. He's living in Beijing with his new wife and concubine. The government's paying him a substantial pension."

"My God. They look after their own!"

The chunk of rock that passed for Liang's Chinese face swam into my mind. He was sent down for fourteen years for assorted fraud, but only served three. That bugger could bribe Saint Peter! He came into our lives because of the Silk Farm, which, for his own convoluted reasons, he was determined to acquire. After his release we had terrible troubles with the suppliers and this was one of the reasons I had stayed on in Asia. Charles put every type of enquiry agent on to him, but nothing turned up; not surprising if he was behind the Bamboo Curtain. Finally we decided to go public to raise capital . . . and I trotted round the world making everyone that mattered offers they couldn't refuse and things settled down—until now.

"Haven't you any idea who's buying?"

"Vague little companies with holdings that are always a dead end. Obviously nominees."

But my mind was still on Liang. "If he's getting a pension, it proves it was all a destabilising ploy."

"Looks like it. But that's yesterday's news. Policies at the top have changed now and old Chinese businessmen go home to

53

die. We'll never know the whole truth. Let's leave him in the capable hands of his ancestors. And that can't come a day too soon." We grinned at each other.

"What have you done about the shares?"

"I've bunged all the small sales into a computer to try and find a common factor."

I had a vision of brigadiers and ancient widows tumbling about amongst the machinery.

"It couldn't be a take-over?"

He shrugged. "Hard to say. There's so much cash floating about, the city's awash with it. Insurance, Pension Funds, you name it."

Then I *did* start to feel anxious. It's no joke owning a Group like ours; you can never take your eyes off things for a moment. The days when we only worried about paying bills and completing contracts are long gone. Out there is a world full of predators and one never knows from which direction they are coming.

"They can't touch the silk, can they?"

Sometimes he looks at me like a teacher

with a pupil that could do better. "Hugh —you know that is limited to you, me, Sarah and the children. It was *always* excluded from the deal."

I just wanted to hear him say it. I knew very well that a trust had been formed to look after Sylvie, Charles' girls and E-Woh when the Great Reaper intervened.

"It must be one of the big textile groups." Our subsidiaries flickered through my mind. Wool, nylon, dye works, dress and shirt factories, and thousands of franchises throughout the world with our trade mark, a multi-coloured butterfly.

"It's not just the grabbers. There are the asset-strippers creeping out of the woodwork looking for tax losses."

Charles stood up and reached for his jacket.

"Come on. I need a decent lunch after all those bits of muck on plastic trays."

Instantly I felt better. Whilst Charles is hungry the world is still rotating on its axis and things can only improve. Wasting no time, we made for the lift at a brisk pace.

Mentally I slotted our lunch at the Peninsula into the category of morale booster for Charles and by the time he'd finished his Sweet and Sour and Soy Prawns it was beginning to work.

"One thing did show—and that was that the acquired shares were all undervalued. They hadn't caught the punter's imagination, for some reason."

He leant back in his chair, sipping his white wine and said, "And here's another thing you're not going to like. Another thing that links this buying—" He paused for maximum effect.

"The broker was offered thirty per cent above the quoted price."

"What?" A Chinese waiter picked up our wine bottle and examined it unnecessarily . . . the word broker had caught his attention.

"That's not quite as bad as it sounds because, as I said, they had slipped in value."

I called for another bottle, and we both stared out of the window, towards Natham Road, looking at the hotel's brown Rolls Royces waiting for customers.

Charles continued, "I can only connect it with the publicity we attracted about the Leicester shirt factory."

Our shirt factory is the star in our galaxy and won an award last year—added to which it shows the highest ratio of profit of any of the works. We ploughed in masses of capital for modern technology because of the Multi-Fibre Agreement. This agreement safeguards the amount of imported raw materials from under-developed countries and makes our fore-casts much more accurate.

I dragged my eyes away from the traffic below and asked, "Are you saying you think someone has his eye on the patents and would run down other things to get it?"

Charles shrugged. "It's all guesswork at the moment."

"Is there any new opposition?"

"The Koreans, but it's rubbish."

"What about the Israelis?"

"The stuff's good, but it's only a trickle compared with Leicester. They can't touch us on deliveries. Besides, the shekel's unstable."

I thought of the work we had put in to get cutting to delivery down to three weeks. I recalled a po-faced Middle

Westerner who had been manoeuvring for ages to get a piece of the action.

"What about that bible thumper in Indiana, the chap who prays for guidance before a deal. He's been trying to get in on the act?"

"He's had a heart attack, and passed things over to his sons."

We exchanged brief grins, then Charles said, "You're looking a bit peeky. Where's Linda? I've got that information about schools for Sylvie. Penny's been rushing around giving them the once over."

He opened his briefcase and put some brochures on the table.

"She wasn't able to come."

I had a superstitious reluctance to voice the events of the last days but there was no avoiding it so I regurgitated the current drama. His eyes opened wider when I came to the part about Francesca's death, then he said that it was probably a burglary that went wrong.

I leant across the table and said, "Charles, her finger nails—that's no burglary."

"Linda'll be back when you get home. She's pushed off before on these political junkets. She'll walk in, as large as life."

But he looked serious and I was glad to see he hadn't forgotten the dangerous things that occur in South East Asia. Over the brandy he told me a story about a South African sitting next to him on the plane. He was a diamond exporter and came to Hong Kong with his family twice a year. Two years ago he was walking along Natham Road one evening with his daughter, window shopping. Turning to draw her attention to something, he was in time to see the fifteen-year-old being dragged towards alleys in the Old Town of Kowloon. And that was the last he'd seen of her.

"God—how awful!"

"Yes. It's time you came home Hugh."

"I've been thinking about it very seriously."

We arranged to meet at six o'clock in the bar and Charles returned to the office to send some telexes. Chilled by his story of the South African businessman and his daughter, I hurried over to Hong Kong Island to see my little girl.

Anna's flat is a little bit of the Philippines

and a touch of the home from home. It's in an older block in Happy Valley, mostly occupied by Chinese families. They bought the sixth floor flat because it has a roof garden of sorts and, after a disgusting barbecue, during which all concerned get covered in a fine sheen of charcoal dust, they can sit and watch the races.

The lift never works so I leapt up the concrete stairs and fell into a tightly packed, electrically lit room where there appeared to be standing room only. Sitting in the middle of the floor was my beauty, hugging a reluctant cat.

"Papa!" she shrieked. "Let's go to Lane Crawford."

The cat shot out of her arms as if it had a bad case of claustrophobia and made for the door. Anna fought her way through the mob and swamped me with affection and all the other arms dragged me down to cheek kissing level. I felt rather pleased with my welcome.

Judging the moment to a nicety, the Doc grabbed me by the arm and urged me into a passage. His questions about Linda were lost in the uproar and we stood there being jostled by two Filipino maids. We retreated to the kitchen where a third girl was attacking a mountain of dirty saucepans and a cook was beating something to death in a copper bowl.

With his mouth to my ear, he said, "Let's get out of here."

After the flat the streets seemed an oasis of tranquillity and we only met half of the five million inhabitants of the Colony on our way to Central. We called to each other over the heads of the ethnics like a flock of birds and by the time we reached Chater Road the Doc had grasped the essentials of his daughter's disappearance. Sylvie confided in me the details of the obscure toy she intended to buy and by the time we got off the escalator at the first floor of Lane Crawford I thought I'd gone deaf, but that's Hong Kong. I sank into a chair while she ransacked the toy department.

For a six-year-old who clearly knows her own mind, she seemed to be taking an inordinate time to find her heart's desire, so I got up and inched my way round to the rare *objet d'art* department and stood looking at a jade dragon on a plinth that cost half the reserves in the Bank of England.

A voice said, "Hello Hubert, small world. Have you found Linda?" Peter Hennessy stood there hung about with various carrier bags.

I didn't feel I could go over it again on my feet so I suggested having an ice cream. The restaurant is adjacent to the toy department so I waved to the Doc who was supervising Sylvie's search and we plodded over to a spare table. Somehow it was easier to tell the tale over a raspberry ripple. I looked up as I put my long spoon in the saucer and, because he'd gone silent, asked, "Do you think I'm making an unnecessary song and dance?"

He stared at me, then said, "Unnecessary! If it was Frances I'd be doing my nut!"

I was relieved in a strange way, that at last someone had reacted.

"What does your father-in-law think?"

It was hard to explain about the Doc. Hard to tell how he had become numbed by the events of the last years. Hard to talk about the fatalism and culture barriers of a people who hadn't experienced first hand the rights we took for granted. I loved him too much to give Peter examples —like the time I ranted and raved about the bar girls and children sold into prostitution, and how his reply, "How else can they earn their living?" had shocked and appalled me.

"I think I might come back with you."

I stared at Peter unable to believe my ears.

"But haven't you other assignments?"

"The producer was very taken with the Aquino interview. He's considering a series on Dictatorships. You know the sort of thing, abuse of Aid Monies. The CIA backing the wrong leaders. As we are already here I could talk him into returning if you and the Doc could shunt us in the right direction."

"Of course we can." God, I was relieved! The advantages of having a few of your own kind around when in trouble flooded over me. Linda—your feet won't touch the ground when this little episode's over!

"When can we see your producer? I'm going back tomorrow."

Peter stood up and chucked some Hong

Kong dollars on the table. "Let's strike while the iron's hot. He'll be in the bar at the Peninsula. He's already thought of a title—*Paradise Lost*. What do you think of it?"

The film crew had taken over the bar when we got back to the Peninsula and were lining drinks up in a dangerous fashion. The producer caught sight of me and called, "Hugo, baby . . ." in that affable way that Americans have. His rye and ice slurped dangerously as he walked towards us. Peter murmured in his ear then guided him towards a table in the window.

As Peter talked the producer watched me, his profile toughening keenly. I thought now was a good time to phone Charles and retreated to the booths in the corner. I tried the Lee Gardens and the office but he wasn't there. Then, just as I was replacing the phone, he walked through the door and stood looking around. I propelled him to an empty table.

"I got through to the brokers."

Charles still has this habit of picking up

a conversation in mid-sentence. Normally it amuses me but not today.

"Charles—"

"What?"

"Do whatever you think fit. I can't give my mind to it until I've sorted this business out. Now listen, this chap that's approaching is going to help. The minute Linda's back I'll be on the plane to London, and this time it'll be permanent."

"When will . . . ?" But Peter and the producer had homed in on us. I stood up and introduced them. The American greeted Charles like a long lost brother and called him Charlie. Charles looked surprised.

Then the producer became very serious, his face earnest with the effort.

"I think we have a winner here, Hugo. Peter and I would like to quantify some details. Say, do you *know* Marcos?"

I nodded noncommittally and outlined the idea of the documentaries to Charles and their use in unearthing my wife. Charles gave me an old fashioned look as though I was playing hookey. The producer removed a pad from his pocket and neatly itemised questions. Then he announced plans for dinner. Charles looked horrified and excused himself. I stayed put and impressed upon my partner that I would be in the office at eight-thirty.

5

THE past four weeks have been the worst in my life. Peter's team returned to Manila with me, full of plans, keen as mustard—confident that they could manipulate the citizens of this banana republic with no trouble. And what happened? Nothing happened. The producer went to the appropriate ministry to get permission to film and returned very cocky.

"No problem . . . these people have got their priorities in order . . . they understand Uncle Sam." But his face became grimmer as the requests for details in triplicate started to pour in. Finally, he stormed back to the ministry but the Minister wasn't there. Up country on official business. He didn't believe them.

"They're waiting for the rustle of greenbacks." In high dudgeon he flounced back to New York leaving the rest of us to kick our heels. Two of the cameramen took off for Luzon and the others mosied around Manila filming background stuff.

Special Branch were still around our house so I dossed down in my office where I had a camp bed, because I had no heart to look for another apartment. I phoned the Doc every other day. We had agreed that it was too risky for the family to return. He passed his days in Hong Kong thinking of people I should contact but nothing came of it. Charles phoned but the line was very bad from London and I got depressed after his calls. There was no avoiding his implication that I would be better employed almost anywhere than the Philippines. One anxiety superseded another. I slept badly and wondered hopelessly what would happen to the company if Charles got ill.

This morning when I woke I couldn't remember her face. I ferreted around in my wallet and took out a snapshot but she looked like any young woman on a beach playing with her child. Staring at it I had no heart to get up and start another fruitless day. Someone hammered on the door. It was the janitor with the post. I waited

68

furtively, ashamed of the way I had deteriorated. One by one letters slid under the door. I got out of bed and flicked up the blinds, then filled the kettle. The coffee jar was empty. Scooping up the mail I went back to bed. Then this fixation crept over me that if I gave Linda my undivided attention *before* opening the letters I would remember her face.

I concentrated on the day we met. Banging into each other in the street. I'd just come out of a shop—turned to shut the door—and her books were all over the pavement. She bent down first, then looked up at me with that lovely laughter. A passing acquaintance stopped to chat and introduced us—the tiny chances that form our lives . . .

The idyll started to evaporate before Sylvie was born. She discovered politics. Always rushing to meet people. Time for everyone . . . all that energy. One day I found myself not reacting to that ravishing smile. It was for everyone—not just me. Let's face it, she was the world's greatest smiler. I developed this theory that she wouldn't have got involved in politics without that smile and all that energy.

I became morose. I felt one of a crowd. So when the baby was born I turned more and more to her, until Sylvie became my whole life.

Francesca taught me how to fix formulas and change diapers when I got in before Linda in the evenings. As she grew older Sylvie turned to me—not her mother.

"Where's the duchess?" I used to call Linda the duchess. Sylvie's precocious—and that's my fault. Well, what can you expect when a child goes from *Winnie the Pooh* to Browning's *"This was my Last Duchess"*? Once, there was a terrible row when Sylvie told her mother she was too free with her smiles.

"Why are you turning my child against me?" she yelled. I'd give anything to hear that yell now.

I stumbled out of bed and rummaged in a cupboard, convinced I would find a spare jar of coffee. Someone in this Catholic country heard my prayers. Triumphantly I bore it towards the kettle. After a couple of cups of the brown drug I found I had enough strength to open the mail. Invoices —freight and lading documents—bank correspondence. Then my heart missed a beat and jumped and juddered about and the coffee in my mouth went sour. I stared at an official looking envelope with the Ministry of the Interior's mark on it. I ripped it open, but my brain couldn't grapple with the numbers and initials in the boxes on the flimsy form. My eyes were riveted to an oblong space which contained Linda's full name. Attached . . . stapled . . . was a black and white passport photo . . .

Then I remembered her face . . . but not this face. Those lack lustre eyes stared at nothing. The flesh had fallen away from her cheek bones. That lovely hair was now straight and lank and cropped around her ears. Wisps clung to her neck. This was the face of someone who never smiled.

On the bottom third of the form was a scribble in Tagalog, the official language of the Philippines—the language I had never bothered to learn properly because I always had a secretary. It was something like "next of kin" then deteriorated into a scrawl.

I stared out of the window sick with shock. I was staring at the blue sky, and I looked away sharply because I couldn't bear the thought that wherever Linda was she couldn't see the sky. My brain seemed to have shifted into neutral and I knew that I had to get out of that office before it would function again.

I dragged on my slacks and tee shirt and stuffed my wallet and passport and the form into my pockets. I heard my door slam behind me, then I was standing by the elevators watching the numbers change, concentrating on the small arrow pointing downwards. The doors swung back and blank business faces stared at me. I stepped in and turned to face the door, studying those diminishing numbers as if I was about to take an exam. A long time later the doors opened on the ground floor. Across the marble foyer—through the swing doors, strolling in the sunshine like extras waiting to shoot a film—were soldiers in green uniforms.

I let the other occupants jostle me but I didn't move. Then I stabbed at the button with nineteen on it and slowly the doors started to close. A Japanese with a brief-case knocking against his knees made a dive for the doors, calling to his colleagues. The strange language attracted the attention of one of the soldiers. For a long second his eyes hovered over the Asiatics then rose to the Westerner at the back of the lift. He moved towards us but I was stabbing that bloody button and the Japanese watched me in the glass mirror with disapproval.

The lift stopped at the twelfth floor and I shot out. The second lift was in the bowels of the building so I ran for the emergency stairs. There was a rear exit through the basement which housed the boilers. My lungs were fit to burst by the time I had pounded down fourteen flights of concrete. Then I was running along low ceilinged spaces, with enormous pipes just above my head which seemed to be holding up the entire building. In this nightmare world of the civil engineer I thundered towards the double doors crissed-crossed with iron rails. They couldn't be locked . . . it was illegal to lock them . . .

They weren't.

In the alley way outside the door—they were waiting for me.

I didn't give way to total panic during that

ride to the jail—sandwiched between goons stinking of the great unwashed. Even when they wouldn't answer me I thought well this is the worst part. I'm British—my passport's in my pocket—I'll see a superior who can communicate. But I didn't see any superior. And it was lucky that I'd seen those huge walls from the outside so I could brace myself against the shock. But it didn't work when the massive doors crashed down behind me.

I was pitched onto the ground in a desolate courtyard and when I tried to get up they kicked me in the kidneys.

I yelled, "Take me to your bloody leader." But those flat eyes didn't register. Then I was at a small gate and a hulk of a sergeant who had abdicated from the human race, grabbed a handful of tee shirt and pitched me down some filthy steps. I bumped and bounced to the bottom, then I went mad. As he followed my progress I lurched for his ankles and battered at him with strength I didn't know I possessed. Bawling for his backup boys they fell on me like a pack of wild animals. Prisoners rushed to the bars of their cages and the noise was like something in a zoo. I had never heard such a paroxysm of hatred. By the time the cell gates slammed it was almost a relief.

The first thing was the smell. Sweat, sewage, foetid air. In the half light from the window near the ceiling men sat or lay on the floor, knees drawn up, shutting out reality.

Then I was afraid. Afraid I might take someone else's space. For the first time in my life I couldn't walk away. My head started to thump where one of the guards had kicked me and I slid onto the floor by a wall.

A squat looking peasant with a bandana round his forehead said, "Got cigarettes?"

I shook my head and he walked away. As my eyes got used to the light, I started counting. Thirty-three men and two buckets. My head fell back into my hands of its own accord and I drifted into a kind of daze.

I don't know how much time passed but someone was talking to me.

"What . . . ?" I stared up at a consumptive looking man with burning eyes.

"I said take your watch off."

I lurched away. "Not on your nelly, Matey! That watch stays on my arm!"

He smiled mirthlessly. "That's what you think. One thing's for sure. It won't stay on *your* arm. The guards will have it off in a flash. If you give it to me, we can swap it for food."

I stared at him foolishly. "You're Irish."

"That's right. One of the brothers from a mission in the north."

I noticed he didn't specify where. "What were you picked up for?"

"They said I was a Communist."

"And are you?"

The smile became grim. "I am now." He looked at my head. "You'd better let me clean that." I felt my head whilst he was gone and sticky clots of blood came away on my fingers. He returned with a tin mug half full of water and produced a clean handkerchief.

"How long have you been here?" The water in the mug turned a startling red.

"About nine months."

"*Nine* months! But you're British. Have you been charged?"

"I believe I was." He found the question amusing.

"What do you mean, you believe you were? Either you were, or you weren't."

"What's the difference when minds are already made up? There was this farce for months whilst I was still up north. Some question of bail. I was in and out of court like a yo-yo. It was all an excuse to get me in here."

He didn't look like a priest, just another chap in slacks and sweaty tee shirt.

"Have you seen your Consul?"

"Oh yes, lovely fella, but he can't do much for Communists."

"Hasn't he done anything?"

"He brings me clean handkerchiefs." He smiled again at the mute horror on my face. "But not lately. I don't blame him for not coming—there's nothing he can do. I'd probably do the same in his shoes. Why burden himself?"

This Irish logic dried me up. He seemed to have had enough too because he stood up and held out his hand.

"Now—without more ado—the watch."

I unstrapped it and handed it over. The priest walked over to the fearsome looking chap who had asked me for cigarettes and asked him for something. There was some fishing around in a bundle, then he handed something over. The Irishman squatted on the floor and opened a packet, my watch carefully beside him on the concrete. The rest of the inmates watched and laughed lewdly as condoms spilled out of the packet. My timepiece disappeared into a small balloon which was tightly knotted. This in turn was placed into a second, then a third. Finally the packet was tied firmly with a shoelace and lowered into a sewage bucket. With the air of a job well done he returned to the brigand character and the two were soon deep in conversation.

I tried to contain my impatience but after a minute or two I couldn't stand it. Stepping over bodies I approached and said, "Could I have a word, Father?"

He broke off. "I'm a Brother, not a Father." His eyes glittered like a Jesuit soldier-priest and his voice had an edge to it. "Time is something we all have plenty of; go and start learning patience."

I shambled back to my place.

It wasn't long before he returned and the appealing Irish tones were back again. "That fella's a pirate. He's got a lot of clout in here."

In a kind of desperation I asked, "Look —what's the form? When will they send for me?"

He mused, then answered. "It could be today, it could be weeks. It depends if someone upstairs is interested in your case."

"How long did you wait?"

He seemed to be thinking of something that happened a long time ago. "Not for long. But they knew I had been helping the guerillas. Do you know something they want to know?"

I tried to think, but I hadn't adjusted. I still thought of myself as a British citizen.

"They've got my wife, she's political."

"Ahh . . ." I could tell he didn't think that was good news.

"Where are the women kept?"

"There's a women's wing over the other side, but there are other prisons—"

Suddenly I was in the grip of a panicky fear and the cell shimmered and lost focus. My muscles were bunched and knotted and all I could think about was smashing my way out and finding Linda.

His hand was hard on my wrists, his eyes on mine and he said, "Cool it!"

I stared back trying to catch some of his strength.

"What's your name?"

"Jon—Jonathan McMahon."

He was staring at something on the floor, then back at my wound. "Your head is streaming with blood. Can't you feel it running down your neck?"

"I thought it was sweat."

There was a further exchange with the hulk who had cornered the French Letter market and the guard outside accepted some cigarettes. At this point I slipped into the most glorious oblivion.

A stinging cold something was pressing against my head. Unwillingly I returned to full consciousness.

"You need some stitches, but you won't get them. I've cauterised it. Now lie down and keep still." McMahon folded a bit of sacking and put it under my head. Like a lifeline I clung to one of the Consul's handkerchiefs and manoeuvred myself into the prone position. God, the relief.

Much later a tiny light in the ceiling shone in my eyes and the space where the window had been was full of blackness.

The cell seemed steeped in the smell of boiled rice. Someone was trying to shovel some into my mouth but I felt too hot to eat. I drifted off to sleep again as a toothless smile retreated.

The next day I was burning up and I thought—it's cholera. My system isn't used to these dainty conditions. The toothless smile had appointed himself my private BUPA nurse. He sponged me with bits of rag and urged nourishment at regular intervals in a weird dialect. He returned once and leant over me to make a mark on the wall. I moved my head a bit to see what he was doing.

There was a line with another through it. He stepped back, pleased, and ducked his head in a little bow. Then he came back and wrapped my fingers round a piece of charcoal. What humanity . . . what couth . . . you wouldn't find Imelda doing that . . . Days passed—retched up rice and water days—days when I thought I was dying—days when I was afraid I wouldn't—and all the time I was burning, burning, and only the drops of rice water kept me going. Then a terrible clanging as the cell gates slammed and the noise threatened to split my head open. McMahon was pushing pills down my throat, his hand over my mouth to stop me bringing them up and I was suffocating.

Sometimes I dreamt that I was back at school in the sanitorium. More days passed and the fever turned to a weak sweating. Sometimes I watched my father fighting his old enemy Liang in very slow motion. And one morning I woke and knew it was passed.

Carefully I turned my neck and looked up at the wall above my head. Stupidly I stared at the rows of crossed out lines. Stupidly I counted, losing my place, starting again. TWENTY-SEVEN!

I couldn't believe it. I tried to stand up but my legs were jelly.

"He's with us!" McMahon's voice rang round the cell and ricocheted off the walls. His arms were round my shoulders and he sat me up. I fell back like a rag doll. Soup appeared and I kept it down. The bandit brought me a piece of chicken. They were a noisy lot, but when I slept I could hear them trying to be quiet. I don't think I could have slept without that subdued noise.

They started exercising me. Arms under my shoulders. Back and to, to and fro, legs dragging after me like a baby. Cheers encouraging me.

Gradually my strength came back. The guard watched my perambulations through the bars. On the thirty-fifth day they came for me.

The corridor looks an endless distance and I feel as if I've been in hospital for a long time. I shamble along with two goons in front, and two behind, prodding me when I lurched against the walls. As I pass each cell there is an accumulation of noise and it dawns on me that this is the roar of the crowd encouraging me. I am soaking with sweat before they push me through the door.

And that was the first time I saw him. Sitting behind his desk, the sun flickering on his epaulettes, smelling of aftershave. He stands up . . . pulls out a chair.

"Mr. Aitkin—I'm so glad to see you have recovered." He had a nicely modulated voice, the sort of voice I am used to, a reasonable voice.

How quickly one loses one's self respect. Little things do it, the relief of falling into

a wooden backed chair is too important.
The disgust at one's own filth, I couldn't
look him in the eye. He seemed to be
giving me time to adjust—to recover from
the journey from the cell. He shuffled
papers, made small talk, then pulled a
dossier towards him. He looked up and
smiled.

"Your address Mr. Aitkin? Shall I put
down your office, or have you a new
apartment?"

"No."

He wrote something on a form. "Next
of kin?"

My heartbeats were slowing. I tried to
listen to my brain which was trying to get
a warning message through. I gave my
mother's address in Kenya.

He put his pen down and leant back.
"Is that where you were born?" The question was couched in a tone of idle
curiosity.

"No, but I was born in Africa."

"Your parents were missionaries?"

"No. My father worked for the government before Independence."

He picked up the pen again and the
smile faded from those strange eyes.

"Interesting—but I think your Filipino relations are closer kin than your mother." He seemed to be looking past me, but it was an illusion. He had a faint cast in one eye.

I heard myself say, "I'm not answering any questions until I've had a bath."

He stared at me for a moment, then said mildly, "That seems reasonable." He touched a bell. As the two goons escorted me into the yard I thought perhaps he had wanted to get my measure.

In my entire life I'd never seen anything so perfect as that sky. I stood rooted to the ground gulping in the air, feeling the sun on my skin. Suddenly an enormous jolt hit me between the shoulder blades and I was sprawling on the ground. I tried to stand up but a second jolt flattened me and my mouth was full of mud. Then they turned off the hose and stood laughing like lunatics. I turned round and saw the sergeant who had welcomed me to this fun palace, with his fingers on the switch. He was waiting for one word. His minions started to look anxious when I didn't oblige. Suddenly he lost interest and threw the hose on the ground and walked away.

Later a goon forced me on to a stool and waved a cut throat razor in a way I didn't like. Roughly he started to scrape it over my head. After the first involuntary pulling away I thought, Oh shit, it's only hair.

6

IN the early months I used to wonder why the British Consul didn't come. I couldn't stop reacting to footsteps in the corridor. I made bargains with God. I developed strange behaviour patterns such as walking round the cell an allotted number of times before anyone spoke to me. Luck if I did it, bad luck if I was interrupted. Lice. Sometimes McMahon would inveigle a can of paraffin from a goon and we sat in a circle dropping in contributions. Then we would inspect each other's heads. If one little devil had escaped attention—Bad Joss. A clean head —Good Joss.

Sometimes I was bitter, particularly with the Consul, and thought how right my mother was when she called them the Whitehall Farce. Bitter towards Charles, the Doc, Hennessy. They must know I was here. Individually or jointly they could do *something*. McMahon's Irish Consul didn't come any more. Perhaps he'd run out of handkerchiefs, or mislaid the address of the prison. When he stopped coming I started to lose hope. Losing hope is the wrong expression. The outside world faded and ceased to exist. There was no life outside those walls.

When I'd accepted that, I passed the time dreaming. Take gin, for instance. I'd visited a Ginnery in Plymouth once and watched the whole process from start to finish. I considered juniper berries, then spent a happy time combing the world for the product, downing a few with knowledgeable old sports in places like Penang and Bali. After a while I convinced myself I was getting pissed. But I had to be careful with my mind and not stray down dangerous paths.

One morning when it was particularly hot and humid in the cell I decided to go swimming in the sea. Mentally I discarded my sweaty vest and jeans and strolled along the beach feeling the grains of sand between my toes. The sand was really hot so I walked in the shallows and tiny frothy waves lapped around my ankles. In the distance, there was the sea whispering up on the beach, inches at a time for miles and miles. Then the water was up to my calves, my waist. I turned to wave to Linda who was standing watching me a long way away. Then I dived under the water and swam and swam, watching the green depths and the fish neatly avoiding me with effortless grace. After a while I thought I would surprise her so I swam underwater for ages without coming up for air until my stomach touched the sandy shore. I stood up looking for her but she wasn't there. I swung round to see if she was swimming. Nothing. Just an empty shadeless, peopleless beach.

Then I was on those bars, shouting and raging, and gentle hands roughly dragged me away, away from the locked hot metal and the guard's baton beating down on my hands. So I don't go swimming anymore. The water stings my eyes—and we can't have a chap with running eyes, can we?

It was difficult to see a plan in the interrogation routine. There was no pattern or indication when one would be sent for. Some were sent for frequently and thrown back into the cell in a terrible state, their flesh a mass of burns.

McMahon was one of these. They really worked him over, poor devil. But I never got passed on to the heavy boys. It was always Garsales. It crossed my mind that he was trying to create bad feeling between me and the other prisoners. Some did look at me strangely when I kept on walking back to the cell on my own two feet, so I took to goading the goons on the return journey and they were only too glad to oblige with a punch-up. Confidence was restored when I was pitched face first through the door of our little home.

Garsales seemed to enjoy our chats. I wondered if they were putting halucinogenic drugs in the food or if I was suffering from a vitamin deficiency. I became unsure of my own judgement. Whatever he asked me, I answered at great length and with little regard for the truth. My inventiveness often took *me* by surprise. Sometimes I thought I'd gone too far when my tales took on the colour of Scheherazade. Then I'd look up and see his face lost in a bemused trance. One day he asked me if I liked music—and would you believe it the next time he had a tape on his record player. Prokofiev.

He couldn't hear enough about London. Was the city like Metro Manila? Where did the stockbrokers live? Was Wimbledon a good suburb? Could the Prime Minister own shares on the Stock Exchange, as Marcos did? What do they do at the Barbican? Can you walk from the city to Buckingham Palace, Hugo? Yes, he called me by my Christian name.

I humoured him for months, until one day I'd simply had enough. There's a limit to what one will do for a cigarette.

"Garsales, today is the day you get me a lawyer."

He sighed. "Jamie. My name is Jamie."

"I don't care what your name is. I want a lawyer."

His pupils dilated and became fixed. I thought, heavy-boys, here I come. It was now or never. I didn't cringe, but I tried to placate.

"I've been in here for nine months."

I stood up to follow him. He swung round and yelled "*Sit down!*" I did with alacrity.

He paced about that office and I didn't dare speak. There was a conflict going on in his head, that Malay head whose moods swung like a pendulum. He flicked up the blinds and stared down into the yard. He walked over to a wall mirror and stared critically at his hair, raising a hand to sweep it back carefully in a Latin gesture. Then he turned and stared at me.

"Nine months," he echoed as if I had just said it.

I nodded.

Then, in a voice more curious than concerned with the fact, he asked, "What do you miss most?"

"News of my wife."

He snorted irritably. It was the wrong answer.

"What else?"

I was alarmed at his unpredictability. Off the top of my head I said, "Work. The routine of work to break up the day."

"Hmm." He waved at me to get out as if he couldn't stand the sight of me. As an afterthought, he pressed the bell and the goons fell on me like wolves at feeding time.

A few days later the goons slung a galvanised bucket and a mop at me, and jerked their heads at a tap in the yard.

Then they cleared off to their hole to smoke.

I sloshed water about the corridors for a while, then took the bucket outside and threw the water onto the baked earth. I hadn't been outside since the hair cropping incident. The concrete paths around the perimeter looked as if they could stand a wash so I started to mop them. It seemed too good to last. This was indeed party time. I found myself whistling. Prisoners came to the bars and joined in. Soon we were giving a very reasonable rendering of Winchester Cathedral. The guards bawled at us to be quiet but the blokes were well away and I got bundled back to the cell.

Another day they said my lawyer was waiting to see me. How cruel man is. In a small interview room a podgy, disinterested Indian sat in a western suit, the tools of his trade spread importantly before him. He didn't bother to hide his distaste as I walked in. In a high English voice that leaned heavily on past elocution, he asked me questions and laboriously wrote down my answers. I never saw him again.

I continued with my mopping, whistling through my teeth like a loon. The guards thought I was stir-crazy but as the time passed they didn't really see me. Like an old tramp my bucket and I drifted down passageways and through doors that I had never entered before.

The plan was to stay inconspicuous, and to do that I had to stay away from the yard. But I was a welcome distraction to the inmates locked away in their cells. They whistled and cat-called for a tune and it was hard not to oblige. There was a near riot one morning when the entire prison let rip with "I've got a feeling you're fooling . . . I've got a feeling you're having fun . . ." After that I was slung back in the cell and taken off mopping duty for a fortnight.

But the yard was a magnet with its fresh air and sunshine. I could even ignore the post at one end, the size of a man with crossbar with handcuffs attached and the earth in front stained a sombre brown.

All the time I listened for women's voices. At the end of the first year I revised my calendar. I sanded off the days and replaced a line to represent a week—then crossed through four for each month. There were a number of children in the prison—separated from their families—rounded up by the goons when they had a blitz on villages.

The guards let them run in and out of the cells and one, a boy of about five, had attached himself to McMahon. At night he curled up next to him like a cat. He had been watching my artistic efforts, tugging at my trousers, trying to tell me something, but I didn't understand his dialect. I ruffled his hair absently but he flew at the bars as if he could hear something. Then there was a cacophany of shouts and the door was flung open and a body hurtled in.

It took me minutes before I recognised Jon. They seemed to have broken every bone in his body. When I tried to move him dreadful screams came out of his mouth in an involuntary way as if they weren't connected to him. Blood kept surging into his mouth and I tried not to think about internal injuries.

Terrified that he would choke on the blood, I knelt for hours raising his head and shoulders. Surely he was going to die tonight.

I kept on saying, "Hang on in there,

buddy—there's things we've got to talk about."

Once, hours later, he tried to get up like an animal trying to survive. I said, "Keep still you fool. Do you want to go back for more?" But the effort knocked him out.

The brigand produced some brandy from somewhere and Jon managed to keep it down. I must have dropped off because at dawn I jerked awake and found him watching me. His mouth started moving but no sound came out. I bent forward my ear next to it, urging him to try again.

"The film . . . Ninoy . . . shown in America."

Speechless I stared. He continued as if he'd just discovered speech. "Marcos . . . execute Ninoy . . ."

He slumped back exhausted with the effort. Then, as if he'd forgotten something, I felt his muscles tense.

"Linda's here."

All I could think was, she's here, she's here, she's alive. And then the terror of their revenge flooded my mind. Revenge for the world knowing. I looked at McMahon's broken body, and thought almost calmly, that's what they'll do to

Linda—until the last member of the group is dead.

After that the easy times were over.

To get to the Women's Wing one has to go through the Persuasion Block. Even torturers take a break at lunch time, and I was only going to get one chance. I bet you thought they were at it hammer and tongs day and night with relief teams at the ready when one group showed signs of fatigue? Not in this part of the world. Here it's more haphazard. Those that know have told me they all join in when the spirit moves them. Then again, they have a low threshold of concentration and they might slope off for a break, leaving some poor bastard on the apparatus and find him dead when they return. The officers get furious at this sloppy behaviour.

It's hard for me to talk about the women's wing. To begin with it's darker than the rest of the prison. It reminds me of parts of the London zoo. Not the nice new quarters the animals have these days; but the ancient cages of my childhood. The dank unclean, high ceilinged places, always wet with water and urine, where you long to set the animals free. And silent —so silent. One girl to a cell on wooden bunks, staring with unfocused eyes.

I'd thought what I was going to do, but suddenly I forgot the words. I clanged the bucket on the concrete to attract their attention, and in a strangled, toneless voice sang, "Lover—when you're near me— when you're near me SAY YOUR NAME." There was movement like birds. Someone called to another. I mopped furiously. Then I gained momentum. Loudly I whistled then broke into the lyric— "Lover . . . de de de da . . . SAY YOUR NAME." One of the girls was at the bars.

"Hugo—it's me, Lyla—" A door clanged in the next corridor. Footsteps approached.

"Where's Linda?"

Her feeble voice drifted towards me. "Next block."

I chucked the mop down and pushed my hand through the bars.

"Do your family know you're here?"

She clung to my hand and tears started to pour down her cheeks. She pulled my hand up and started kissing it again and again.

"Do they?"

The tears turned to sobs. I heard her shriek before the baton came down on my back. I stumbled and fell over the bucket. For some reason that made me laugh and I shouldn't have done that. On and on those sickening thuds until I was on my knees. The last one I remember nearly smashed my head in and I thought, whoops— another artery gone.

7

A MONTH in solitary lying in my own filth—well, later they told me it was a month.

Then the hose treatment and the inmates cheering me as I tried to get to my feet. Back to the cell. A warning to the others. God! I was pleased to see them.

The toothless peasant escorted me proudly to the wall and presented an up-to-date calendar. I stared at it and my mind got hinged on the subject of walls; walls to keep people in, to keep people out, no walls in paradise.

Later he dragged on my arm—propelling me across that elegant salon, towards McMahon who was lying on sacking, the boy squatting beside him. Then the smell of gangrene was in my nostrils and I turned to look at the others to give me time to adjust my idiot features that function on their own.

His eyes were alive, but the rest of him had died whilst I was in solitary. The hand that was on the boy's head came towards me then wavered as if it had lost its way.

I took it and said, "You're not letting me down, are you Jon?"

A smile hovered over his face, not quite connecting, and he replied, "It will be nice to let go."

The brigand came over with a thimbleful of brandy and said something in his hoarse gruff voice. A communal guffawing filled the air.

"What did he say?"

Jon swallowed several times, then translated, "Imelda says Filipinos are never poor and sick because they have such wonderful hearts."

They were laughing, laughing!

The boy put a rag in a tiny mug of water, then squeezed it and put it in McMahon's mouth. With the concentration of the dying he sucked. When the rag slipped away leaving exhaustion in its wake the boy looked terrified. Jon's eyes were on the child and he struggled to rouse himself. Something in dialect passed between them and an ancient faith shifted the fear. Looking at the boy I thought of Sylvie . . . then struggled not to . . .

I sat beside him as he wafted between life and death. When the light had gone I was sure he'd gone with it, but he rallied and said, "Look after the boy."

After that there were minutes when he wanted to hear my voice. "Linda?"

"I didn't see her, but she's here."

Ever so slightly his head inclined and he murmured, "Then there's a chance."

I talked about Vietnam and how the people had rushed to join up—so proud of their democracy—and light returned to his eyes. And when they came back to the homes the government had promised them —to the apartment blocks built without foundations—to tower blocks without steel reinforcements that collapsed in clouds of choking smog driving out oxygen, the heroes died.

Tears ran down his face and a frightening rattle started in his throat.

"Jon! Shall I get a priest?"

He gulped and the awful rattle stopped. There was a wisp of breath on my face— "Just a coin for the ferryman." And his head fell sideways like a rag doll.

With terrible regret I closed his eyes.

It was forty-eight hours before they let us out of the cell to bury McMahon. After that a lethargy pervaded the jail and the guards didn't bother to lock the cells and prisoners drifted in and out with news of the outside. Marcos and Imelda were busy crating up the contents of the Malacañang Palace prior to doing a bunk. Then Imelda got the bright idea of building walls around the slums so that foreigners couldn't see them and people were employed who hadn't worked for years. Walls round tips like Smokey Mountain. The crisis passed and Marcos and Imelda unpacked.

Finally Garsales sent for me.

I saw at once that he'd changed. He was indecisive and smoked constantly. When I called him a sod he didn't seem to hear me, just pushed the cigarettes across the desk. I shouted at him about Linda and he seemed to think that I was complaining about not seeing her, rather than her terrible conditions.

He said, "It's your own fault, you

should have asked me." As if I hadn't asked him a hundred times!

All caution deserted me and I harangued him like a madman for all the needless, heedless, unthinking bestiality that went on in that fortress. It was only when I paused for lack of breath that I really saw his eyes. They were still like a reptile, turned inwards on his own thoughts, and all my ranting was nothing more than a sudden storm. He pushed his chair back and strolled towards the window, his eyes still and brown, not focussing. I was nothing more than a shadow.

The slow pacing came to a halt by the door. He turned and said, "Come." The hinges creaked, and he disappeared into the corridor.

The uncanny thing was that he didn't send for the goons and I felt naked as I walked behind that pristine gaberdine uniform. Down stairs, through the yard, rusty keys clanging before we were in Top Security. Then the Persuasion block and dread that I was on a one way journey. Higher walls lost in darkness above my head; walls fitting into each other like a maze with no exit. I tried to pull a mental blind down over my eyes, which was a mistake . . . because I allowed the gates to clang behind me without counting them . . .

I knew we were in the Women's Wing because of the smell. Even in prison women don't smell as much as men, but there was an indescribable something hanging in the air which would remind me of that prison for the rest of my life. Suddenly I *knew* I was in the section I'd been in before and terror gripped me as I passed Lyla's vacant cell.

Garsales was walking at a fast clip and we were in another block. I was sweating from every pore in my body before we arrived at the last cell and I nearly collided with him as he bent to unlock the gate.

A girl was lying on a bunk under a filthy blanket. Her eyes were rivetted on Garsales and she was pressing her back against the bricks of the cell wall, kneeling now, the blanket under her chin. A thin screaming started and went on and on.

"Linda, Linda!" I grabbed her, pushing past Garsales, trying to make those eyes look at me. But her gaze never left his face. Then he was in front of me, dragging her off the bench, grabbing her cheeks, twisting her head in my direction.

"Look at him, you silly bitch." But there was no recognition. Suddenly her eyes rolled up and her body went limp and she collapsed on the floor.

"You bugger, you bugger." I tried to pick her up and lie her down on that bunk.

He walked into the passageway saying, "Come on. You can come back tomorrow when she's got used to the idea." He was suddenly bored.

"I'm not leaving her!"

He turned and took a step back into the cell and I watched his eyes dilate. There was a gun in his hand and slowly, so slowly, he raised it and took aim—at Linda.

Then the return journey started and his leather boots echoed on the stone floors. When he unlocked the section gate I stopped mulishly outside Lyla's cage.

"What happened to that girl?"

He returned and read the name on the outside.

"I don't remember."

He didn't send for me the next day, or the

next week. I had no work because I was now classed as untrustworthy. The days dragged by. I started getting terrible pains in my chest and swallowing food was agony. The brigand's brandy nearly made me shoot through the roof and I missed McMahon more than I can say. Once a day we had half an hour in the yard and I was able to check that Linda was still in the Women's Wing. The boy had attached himself to me after Jon's death and we passed many hours playing noughts and crosses on the cell floor.

It was four months before Garsales sent for me again. The first thing he said was, "You don't look well."

He, on the other hand, looked better, calmer, as if he had come to a decision and a weight had been removed.

"How much longer is this going on?"

Sitting on the wooden chair, the room seemed to be divided into two; Garsales with all the aces in his fine carved chair and me on the other side of the desk—a no-hoper.

"It could end quite soon if you co-operate."

"Co-operate! Everyone on that list will

have scattered by now—and you know it!"

When he didn't answer I got desperate. "I'll tell you anything you want to know if you get us out."

Garsales is a master of timing. The pain in my chest twisted like a knife as I forced myself to wait.

Finally he spoke. "As a foreign national you could be deported, but that wouldn't apply to your wife, who is a Filipino citizen."

I was standing up, shouting, "Look, I'll pay you anything, but it's got to be both of us. A Swiss bank account . . ."

Suddenly I doubled over with that knife tearing into my gut. "You'll get nothing if I die of this ulcer."

He pressed the bell for the goons and a wave of hopelessness swamped me as I was prodded out of the room.

But I started getting a milk ration.

Three weeks later he said "How's your stomach? Is the milk helping?"

I laughed mirthlessly and clutched my trousers to stop them slipping down, and tried to tie the tops into a knot.

I heard him say, "I've thought of a way . . ."

"You bet there's a way, and the British Consul will find it!"

"He could do nothing for your wife. What a pity she kept Filipino citizenship . . ."

I couldn't hide the look of defeat. Edgily, like a querulous child I asked, "Are you sure you don't want my money?"

He leaned back in his chair and replied, "I don't want your money Hugo." Then, as if plucking a notion out of the air, he said, "Life is simply a question of geography. Advantaged people live in the West."

I stared at him. "You want to live in the West?"

"That is my intention." He looked pleased that I had caught his drift. Every day is a new day to Garsales—and this one seemed to please him. "The present administration won't last much longer. The Americans will see to that."

"Well, get out. What's stopping you?"

"And what do I do when I'm out, as you say? Do I roam around sponging off my fellow expatriates?"

"You could live on my money." What was I talking about? I felt ill, my mind wouldn't function, and I sounded like a debilitated careers officer.

Luckily Garsales didn't take up my offer. "That would give me no satisfaction Hugo."

Tiredly I asked, "What *do* you want?"

"I want to work for you."

Speechlessly I stared at him, wondering if this was some sort of game.

He continued as if it was the most normal thing in the world. "You are the head of a major concern, one might almost say a conglomerate. Consider . . . somewhere there is a reasonable niche for me."

"Never!"

"I think so." His hand moved towards the bell and mine went out to detain him. Never in my wildest moments had I thought of anything like this.

I heard him say, "It will work out very well, Hugo. I'm a herd animal, a conformist at heart. There's a great freedom in outwardly conforming and I've had lots of practice. Now, go away and think about it." This time his finger touched the bell.

I returned to keeping my calendar on a

daily basis. He waited just the right time —that is to say long enough for me to find prison life unendurable, but not long enough for my ulcer to burst.

When I returned to his office he didn't waste any time. Pointing to his phone he said, "It's a private line. You can dial directly to London." He walked towards the door.

I shouted, "Wait. Linda, too?"

"Of course." His voice suggested that there had never been any doubt about it.

There were whoops of delight when I got through to Charles.

"Hugh! Where are you? We couldn't trace which prison . . ."

I gave him the name of the prison, terrified that we would be cut off. "Listen! Listen . . . don't interrupt . . ."

I gabbled through Garsales' conditions and Charles' euphoria turned to howls of wrath. The line crackled with static and I was sweating.

"Put him down as a management consultant, then send the contract to the Doc in Hong Kong . . ."

The static turned into a roar and Charles' voice died away.

But that wouldn't do at all. For weeks there were daily meetings and the wording of the contract had to be changed to Corporate Managing Executive in Strategic Planning Technology. Salary— £60,000. A car went with the job plus non-contributory pension rights and equity participation. I nearly had a seizure when I read the equity bit! He even included medical insurance coverage. Garsales had done his homework!

I felt like a traitor when I went back to the cell after those sessions. I gagged on the smells. I couldn't stand the heat. Garsales was so clever with his coffee and cigarettes, his cold drinks and fans. I was losing my immunity to prison life. One morning I was shocked to see that I'd forgotten to mark the passage of time on the wall, and I worried all day trying to remember when I'd made the last scratch mark. I looked around for someone to ask but their faces were vacant and devoid of expression. Even the brigand looked like an old mummified warrior.

Then, one day when I was at the end of

my tether, it was over. When I saw Garsales he was tense and distracted.

"We're leaving tonight."

"Not without Linda!" My heart was pounding like a steam engine.

"Of course not." He was irritated by the remark and instantly I could see that today was not the day to push him. He went to a cupboard and took out some clean jeans and a whitish tee shirt, then jerked his head in the direction of a shower cabinet in the corner of the room.

"Have a shower. You're not going back to the cell. You'll stay here until it's dark." He slammed out leaving me alone.

I scrubbed my skin raw under that blessed water—saying over and over, don't count on it, don't count on it!

When he came back I said, "What's the plan? Is the contract settled?" His pupils were enormous and he seemed to be having a job concentrating. And he was sweating—Garsales doesn't sweat, it would spoil the cut of his uniform. But he was today. Suddenly, I knew it was for real. If it went wrong he'd be shot too.

"A private plane will take us to Hong

Kong. Your father-in-law will be at Kai Tak with the contract. I leave first then, if everything is in order, you will be allowed off when I'm on the Cathay flight to London."

For a second he looked at me as if we were conspirators and it was so contagious that I smiled back. I turned away, disgusted with myself.

I wandered round that room as the hours limped by and gradually the place took on a different ambience. The sub-human who cowered in the wooden chair receded. At mid-day a goon brought in some decent food on a tray and a bottle of wine. I looked at it with longing but didn't touch it; alcohol might eat away the last vestige of mucous membrane in my so-called stomach and I'd have to say to Garsales, "Sorry old chum, can't go today —my ulcer's playing up."

Then I thought of McMahon and I wasn't hungry any more.

After a siesta they brought my passport, my wallet and my Walkman with new batteries in it.

At midnight the air was still hot and

Garsales and I stood in the shadows near the gate waiting. There were no guards. Two men who were always with Garsales came through the gate of the Women's wing. They were supporting Linda as if she had lost the use of her legs. I ran towards her but she still only looked at Garsales. I dragged her away from them and felt her bones through her tee shirt.

Then we were through those gates and in a large black limousine. The car lights shone on Garsales' resplendent leather jacket and I realised I had never seen him in civvies. In the back of that car his hair and moustache were trimmed and luxuriously clean. I could smell his after-shave. On my other side Linda trembled violently and I struggled with the Walkman and put it over her head. The disembodied strains of Gershwin's *Blue Skies* came and went as we rushed towards the airport and palm trees bowed as we passed. Then we were running across the tarmac towards a small white plane and when we were inside, it rose like a bird in the sky.

The plane landed at Kai Tak and taxied to a distant corner of the airfield. The Doc stood in the shadows clutching a sheaf of papers.

"Look, there's your father." But her eyes were still fixed on Garsales who was sitting on the other side of the aisle.

Without a word he stood up and walked off the plane. I watched him stride towards the Doc, snatch the papers, flick through them, then turn and disappear into the darkness.

We sat there for forty minutes.

When the car with the British Flag flying on the bonnet skidded to a halt beside the plane I could hardly stand. Several men in anonymous suits leapt on board, followed by a Hong Kong police officer. One announced he was the British Consul and I said, "You took your time!"

Then we were hustled out and the Doc grabbed his daughter and she stood there unresisting. He said something calming, but it was *his* face that was streaming with tears.

It was only when we got to Anna's I realised that she hadn't spoken.

8

IN Anna's flat an ordered emotional welcome, orchestrated by Mama, attended our arrival. A shriek of pleasure, a wail of pain, bitten off at source by a look from Mama. But she couldn't control the hands that crept out to touch us, and nearly faltered herself when her gaze stayed with Linda too long. With a frightening lack of response she allowed herself to be guided into the bedroom where the door was firmly shut.

I looked for my little girl and found her sitting shyly in a corner with an acquiescent cat on her lap. I held out my arms and for a moment nothing happened. Then she hurtled towards me and buried her face in my concave middle.

It was two weeks before the Doc let me near Linda. Two weeks of sleep and food. More sleep and more food, and gallons of milk with my tablets. The pains in my gut mellowed to endurance level and I went for short walks, but I couldn't stand crowds. The Doc drove up to the Peak —and to the New Territories, but there seemed to be no space without people and I became agitated when I was away from Linda.

After that I sat by her bed for hours. At the end of the third week the Doc reduced the dosage of her drugs. Her sleep was interspersed with moans and sudden shrieks and I begged him to return to the original strength.

"We must give it a chance Hugo. Her consitution will adjust."

Slowly the nightmares shifted from peaks to troughs and she didn't sleep so much. When I roused her to eat she answered me, but most of the time she lay there staring at nothing. The Doc decided to leave the bedroom door open so that she might relate to the daily activities in the flat. He encouraged the relations to visit but they had a poor control over their tears.

Sylvie loitered in the doorway asking plaintively, "When will Mama be better?"

When Linda didn't answer she drifted

disconsolately away and I was torn between the two of them.

One day, after a lunchtime nibbling at unwanted food I held her in my arms trying to stop her slipping back into sleep.

I said, "Please Linda, *please* get up for a little while, just for Sylvie."

Her empty eyes focused and looked surprised, and she said, "Of course."

She sat on the side of the bed and watched as I put on her slippers. Then I wrapped her dressing gown around her and we tottered into the dining room.

The family can't break the siesta habit, so only the Doc and Ma-in-law and an ancient aunt were sitting over the remains of a Chekhovian tumble of half-finished food. Linda sat down, her face reflecting the effort to concentrate on Sylvie, and there was fear that the idea might drift away.

Distractedly she looked at the half-finished lunch and said, "More quiche, Sylvie?"

It was uncanny, as if she was continuing a conversation started two years ago. We stared, our faces full of trepidation. Then she stood up and returned to the bedroom.

"I shall have to find a psychiatrist," the Doc said finally, "I don't know how to handle it."

"You always said there were no good consultants in Hong Kong."

"I'll find one."

He returned that evening with a man I disliked on sight. He ignored me and addressed himself solely to the Doc. He asked me to leave the room and I refused. Then he used long obscure words as if switching to a foreign language. He sat Linda up to do reflex tests.

She looked at me through her drugs and asked, "What's happening Hugo?"

"Nothing to worry about, kiddo."

I was full of fury at this man who treated symptoms instead of the patient. He took the Doc into the sitting room and Linda held my hand tightly. Through the open door I heard him pontificating.

". . . at the same time there are clearly some people who find contact with other human beings so threatening or so invasive that they feel the only safe thing to do is to prevent it happening. The particular reasons why a person wilfully decides to withdraw are unique and can only be understood in relation to that person's psychological development. If this recluse pattern isn't broken she will become clinically ill. Most of the time the world is just about a manageable place, but depression gives one a sense of being puny. One feels one carries the world's burdens on one's shoulders and it all becomes too painful to deal with."

The Doc said, "You are not describing my daughter. She's an extrovert, an outward going type of girl."

"Was she unstable before this—er—unfortunate period in her life?"

"Never!"

The consultant wasn't convinced. He continued with his monologue. "Overnight she lost the reassuring presence of others. When circumstances are threatening and coupled with isolation the individual suffers from a high degree of anxiety. In short, she feels abandoned."

"Why won't she talk about it?"

The simple question got to me. The Doc, with all his unstoppable kindliness, had more feeling for people than this man would ever understand.

"Recluses are rarely willing to explain their reasons." The authoritarian voice was fading as he moved to the front door. For a minute or two they stood talking but now I couldn't hear.

His voice was raised prior to departure and I heard him say, "I'll leave you to discuss it with your son-in-law." The door slammed.

The Doc was not happy when he returned to the sitting room.

"Discuss what?" I was already hostile.

"He wants her to go into his clinic, to observe her away from the family."

"That's not right. She needs the familiar around her. She won't be able to cope with another new environment."

"I know that. But the danger is that she might withdraw to a point where nothing reaches her. Sometimes a jolt stirs the perceptions."

"*Jolts!* Electro convulsive therapy?"

He started to walk around the room to avoid my accusing eyes. "Only if the drugs don't take effect."

"*Never!* What's the matter with you all?

Don't you realise the *jolts* have reduced her to this state! She's had enough electricity to last a lifetime!"

"I agree with you Hugo, but what's the alternative? Time is very important at this stage. Something must be done."

I hung on to my nervous system and tried to think.

"Pop—I've got to take her away. I—I know how she—she feels. We're too—too close to Manila here—everything here reminds—reminds us." My stutter was back—the stutter I'd left behind at school . . .

"Sit down Hugo, and let's talk about what you would like to do if Linda was well. Obviously you're not ready for work yet." His voice was mild, the tones of a good man.

I made an enormous effort to think constructively. "I can tell you what I don't want. No cities, no people. I want to walk in the country where there are very few people."

"Take her to England, go to Scotland. If she gets worse there are excellent medical facilities to hand."

England . . . Charles and the company

. . . decisions . . . telephone . . . Garsales . . .

"Not yet," I muttered. "I'm not up to it."

"What do you think then?"

And there it was, clear and fresh, and I was afraid because I hadn't thought of it sooner.

"We'll go to Kenya, to my mother's!" My first decision! Then I was fearful because I hadn't realised I couldn't make them.

The Doc was on his feet, hand on my shoulder, saying, "There—there, Hugo, it's still early days," and to my disgust, once again, a tear had let me down.

"Are you sure you can manage the journey with Linda? I could come with you." The Doc's face was grey. I thought of the angina tablets in his pocket.

"I had a friend once whose wife was paralysed in a car crash. He pushed her round the world in a wheelchair, with a little help from the airlines. I'll manage."

He patted my head. "Go and tell her then. Go and tell her about your Africa."

We lay on the bed all afternoon and I told her about the White Highlands and

Ngong Hills and the animals and the wonderful mornings. She seemed to be listening. Once she turned to me and ran her fingers under my eyes.

"You've been crying, Hugo," she said.

The lump in my throat returned and I replied gruffly, "All we need is tender loving care."

I stared at the filthy aluminium bowl in the toilet and the word Emergent took on a new meaning. I prayed that Linda wouldn't need to use those toilets during the flight. My gut had been playing up again so I sat there for ten minutes waiting for the tearing gripes to pass. Later I asked the coloured steward for a drink in the galley, then stared out of a porthole with the glass of water in my hand, bent forward in an oddly stooping position, and took some tablets.

Linda hadn't spoken at all during the flight from Hong Kong to Bombay, but I wasn't worried because the Doc had given her an injection before we left. When we were hanging round the transit lounge in Bombay waiting for the connection to Nairobi she watched me, her eyes fixed on my face. It was a prelude to speech. I looked round at the torn leather seats and felt the squalor that was India. Don't be ill here, Linda.

I jumped when she said, "Can I have a coke?" she was smiling.

I had stumbled to my feet, hurrying in that dirty heat-laden night, and shambled over to a grubby counter.

An Indian with a monumental chip on his shoulder slammed a can down and muttered. I turned my pockets out and put down Hong Kong dollars, US dollars, English pounds and Kenyan shillings.

He snatched the can back and returned it to a shelf.

"Only rupees!"

I stared and said, "But we can't change money . . ."

He didn't bother to reply. In desperation I looked around at the other passengers. Suddenly there was an agitated, high-pitched shouting and we were being urged to queue for boarding. I rushed back to Linda and draped the hand luggage on my person. Holding her firmly round the waist, we joined the anxious passengers, boarding cards at the ready.

Eight hours later the African heat was building up in the plane. People were stripping off top layers of clothing but Linda didn't seem aware of it. I looked at my new watch; only three more hours to Mombasa. I'd booked into a good hotel for four days to give us a rest before being swallowed up by the other family.

Finally we were out of that aluminium tube and into the humidity of the Indian Ocean. Speechless, we climbed into the hotel's mini-bus.

The hotel bedrooms were air-conditioned. Falling onto the bed we slept.

The monkeys woke us in the morning, staring in through the windows, their small anxious faces pleading for breakfast. I turned away still feeling monumentally tired, then glanced at Linda's side of the bed. It was empty. My nerves shrieked and I shot up. The room started to go round so I sat down abruptly. She came out of the bathroom with a towel round her head. Sitting beside me she stroked my face and ear and said, "Poor Hugo."

Stupefied I stared as she got up and walked towards the monkeys.

"You look better. Do you feel better?"

She looked round and answered, "I do believe I do. Do you?"

Later, we walked along the beach and she laughed out loud when an Arab tried to buy my shoes. That evening we had our dinner at a restaurant near the shore and marvelled at the food and the moon on the ocean and the crabs doing their fast sideways scuttle across the sand.

The next day we took a taxi to the port and wandered through the old town, watched by ancient Middle-Eastern eyes behind *chadors*. There was only one bad moment as we stood on the roof of the fort looking down at a large wooden dhow riding on the water below.

She said, "That's a Slaver. They packed the slaves into that."

I pulled her away. "Don't think about it."

But she was drawn back. "Thousands, year in, year out."

I put my hands on her cheeks, still white with prison pallor. "Don't. Put it behind you."

"I am trying."

She was too tired for dinner when we got back to the hotel. I went back to the

128

restaurant on my own, but it wasn't the same.

On the following day we got on a small plane for the last forty-five minute flight to Kenyatta airport. It was a long walk down the corridors and we were feeling the altitude, so we sat on the edge of the carousel waiting for the luggage to arrive.

"God, I'm exhausted." Her face was blanched. Her cheekbones seem to protrude, stretching the skin. Then she said, "Hugo—why are we here?"

I opened my mouth to reply, but her eyes had gone blank. I spotted our cases coming through the flapping leather opening and the old familiar knife twisted in my guts. I dragged them off as they came level . . . then rushed for the bog.

Part Two

1979

1

Sarah

I WENT to meet them at the airport today.

I am so nervous I disgust myself. I push my way through a jostling crowd of Kikuyu taxi drivers and porters, shouting at each other about their rights and for a moment they stop and stare, united against the interloper. I stare back. We are still wary of each other. Then, leaning against a pillar, my sights on the Exit, I light a cigarette and try to look nonchalant. A ludicrous picture of our last meeting two and a half years ago creeps into my mind.

Hugh had nodded at the current packet and said, "Untold dangers there, Ma. Chuck the weed."

"Just living dangerously, Hugh."

I thought of the hundreds of packets I'd sent to the Doc, hoping they might find their way to whichever prison Hugh was

133

in. I might know quite soon if he'd ever received them.

A goggle-eyed Masai youth, new to the city, unused to its ways, hovered near me hopefully with his home made cart. I could feel his unease—so far from his cattle. The city men avoid us white Kenyans because we are careful with our money and know their little ways, unlike the tourists who are full of foreign currency and bonhomie.

With a jolt I noticed that he had distracted me from the Arrivals who had started to drift through the exit. A self-important little Indian, who worked at the university, walked briskly past, shooting me a look. We'd met at a party some months before where he had been shrilly advocating the need for forcible vasectomies. A faint smell of curry wafted off his crumpled striped suit. He'd be in the government next year. Heaven help us!

Wealthy Kikuyu wives with Harrods luggage, erupted in a group calling importantly to their chauffeurs. Businessmen with briefcases and tired Heathrow faces followed. Their legs moved purposefully, unlike the VSO volunteers who loitered struggling with too much luggage and guitars. The porters ignored their friendly enquiries. They are used to the Do-Gooders. Would we have all these latter day missionaries if the climate wasn't so good, I ask myself?

After this, the pause when nobody comes through that space, the natural break allowed by the airlines when relatives may consider if their kin have got on the wrong plane, or are sitting in some distant Departure lounge.

Then I saw them and it was worse than I'd expected . . . worse than all the Doc's warnings.

They seemed to be holding each other up. So thin that the pair of them didn't make a whole. Linda had Hugh's Sony Walkman over her head, his old green overcoat over her shoulders. Her face—white and sunken like an old woman who'd lost her teeth. She's shivering. How can she be cold in this heat?

I vented my shock on the greatcoat. I'd been trying to get Hugh to throw it away ever since he became Managing Director. It was second hand when he was a student. But he never would. He called it the greatest all-purpose garment ever invented. Capacious, a boon in unreliable climatic conditions, better than a sleeping bag—and fell neatly into place after being stowed in an airport locker. Besides, hired car drivers recognise it.

Then I forced myself to look at my son . . . to look at the strain and the jail pallor . . .

They ambled over and Hugh fished in his pocket for a pair of steel rimmed spectacles. I had never seen him in spectacles.

Focusing vaguely he said, "There you are Ma. I recognised you at once . . ." He sounded pleased and shoved his cheek forward for a kiss.

"Well done," I replied encouragingly. I reached out for Linda.

She rested her head on my shoulder and whispered, "Hello Mom."

Arms round each other, we walked slowly out of Kenyatta airport towards the car park.

As people do, I asked, "How was the flight?"

"Sticky in Bombay." The glasses disappeared into his pocket now that the recognition formalities were over. "Is E-Woh with you?"

"No. She had to go to the hospital today. I dropped her off." E-Woh is my adopted daughter and Hugh's half sister. She is my former husband's child, born just before he died. She had polio when she was little.

"How is she?"

"Better. She calls herself Joanni at school now."

"Joanni—why's that?"

"They couldn't seem to manage her name, so they suggested she picked a European one."

"Joanni . . ." Hugh repeated the name as if he was learning it.

We clambered into the hot car and Linda curled up in the back seat. I wished she'd speak. She always used to chatter so.

We left the city suburbs and the golden countryside burst around us. The sun glinted on a lake in the distance with acacia trees round its edges. Coffee bushes in neat lines crept down to the road waiting to be picked. On the other side of the road were shambas with women tilling their sweet potatoes. Totos stared at us, their fingers in their mouths and some waved. Older boys jumped out of the dust in front of us as we passed and I didn't dare take my eyes off them to see how Linda was.

Further on seas of maize rippled in geometric curves blown by the winds from Arabia. And sailing at a great pace above —huge cotton wool clouds in a blue sky. In the distance the slopes of the Ngong Hills.

Twenty minutes later we turned onto the rough track that climbed and twisted towards our land, the land that had once been my father's farm. By dint of much financial manipulation I had managed to buy back part of the land when I returned from Malaysia. Then I'd sold some of it so that I could rebuild the house. The days of being wiped out by drought and coffee blight are over. Like most of the old settlers, I waited for my quarterly dividends from the company and spend a considerable amount of time wondering what I can sell next if the cost of living continues to rise.

The undergrowth stopped beating on the roof of the car and there was my circular lawn spreading towards the trees and E-Woh was running across it. The limp disappears when she is excited. People say we are alike; the truth is we both limp when we are nervous.

Running along beside the car she yelled at Hugh, "Hello, Rat-features."

He grinned and his face relaxed, "Hello Fink."

"Has she grown?" I looked at her brown limbs and pony tail through Hugh's eyes.

"I'll say . . . she's going to be taller than Shen San . . ."

"She seemed to grow when she was in plaster."

"When did she have the last lot off?" He was struggling with the hot handle on the car.

"Six months ago—but she still has physiotherapy twice a week."

When the hoo-ha had died down and they had picked at the lunch I'd prepared, they both went to bed and stayed there until the following morning. Nobody noticed the improvements I had made to the bungalow. I put my head round their open door before I went to bed. Linda was moaning in her sleep—tossing and turning as if trying to escape from something.

Hugh stirred from a bottomless well of tiredness and put his hand over her mouth. Silently I moved back into the passage away from that trauma-filled bedroom and wondered how long they'd need to distance themselves from the horror.

After a few days they emerged blinking in the sunlight like children recovering from some weakening disability. Hugh didn't talk much and Linda didn't talk at all. One day I made the mistake of asking him if he'd received the cigarettes. His face went rigid, then with an effort he shook his head and looked away. It was then I realised there weren't going to be any chats about the prison.

It was at the end of the first week I found him thumbing through my address book.

"What do you want?"

"Your dentist. Our teeth are loose."

"Oh, let's have a look." E-Woh peered into their mouths, adjusting their heads so that the sun didn't cast shadows, then confirmed, "Yes they are—their gums are rotting away—" She seized the phone and talked forcibly into it for some time. Then —"Tomorrow at eleven. I'll go with you."

Next morning they scrambled into the old pickup and I called, "Why don't you buy some new clothes in Nairobi?" I sounded like an old mother hen—trying to be a calm mother hen. When they'd gone I sat on the verandah and stared at the tyre marks in the dust through my tears.

Then the phone started ringing. I said no to neighbours and friends. I wasn't having them displayed like freaks; but to Charles and Peter Hennessy I had to say yes. How could I say anything else after all their efforts to get them out? In any case Hugh and Linda had to get used to facing the world sometime—and who better to start them off?

Charles and Peter arrived together early one morning ten days later. It was still dark when I woke—that inky dark that in Europe would make you turn over and go back to sleep—but by the time I'd drunk some coffee the sky had turned from lavender to pink. I strolled across the lawn towards the dip in the land where the acacia trees mass together, looking for some Thomson's gazelles that had been feeding there for some days. I love these miniscule fawn things and live in fear of predators. Although leopards are a thing of the past, with all the new buildings spreading out from Nairobi, I kept a wary eye on the tree trunks above my head.

Suddenly a car roared up the drive and backfired. A group of impala leapt out of the thicket and made off. One male jumped across me at an angle and I saw his horns only feet away. I started to run up the path and across the lawn, tying the cord of my white towelling dressing gown. Charles had his back to me as he paid the driver.

A tall man with a grey crewcut stepped onto the grass and came towards me. He seemed to bring the morning sun with him and the delicate dawn colours dissolved into the blaze of an African morning. I felt such gratitude to Peter for fighting to show that film, the film that had kept Hugh's plight from slipping off the front pages of the world's newspapers. When I flung my arms round him I couldn't speak.

"How are they, Sarah?"

Swallowing hard I said, "A bit better each day."

I was so glad to have them here—to have someone to share the strain. Charles was stripping off his jacket when we got to the verandah. His shirt had sweat marks on it and he looked very tired. The same old crumpled Charles. He hugged me tight and kissed my cheeks.

"One from me, one from Penny," he said, falling into one of the basket chairs.

"Breakfast?"

Charles is always hungry but he shook his head. "We had it on the plane. Perhaps some coffee and a brandy."

I looked at Peter and he nodded so I went into the kitchen and made a gallon of the stuff. They both stood up to take the tray when I returned but Charles sank back in his chair patently relieved to leave it to Peter.

I had seen a lot of Charles during the past two years because we both had Power of Attorney during Hugh's absence and he was always to-ing and fro-ing with papers to sign. The three of us looked older, especially Peter who had the additional trauma of that terrible business with Frances.

"How are the children?" I asked him as I poured the coffee.

"They're with their grandmother. I've fixed them up in schools in England."

"That sounds like a good idea."

It was a relief not to have to put a good face on things. This business is like a stone thrown into a pond; the ramifications, like the ripples, spreading, eroding our lives. A sentence with no time limit . . .

Half an hour later Hugh padded out of his bedroom with sleep filled eyes.

"Me thinks I hear humans." He grinned at them.

Furtively I watched their faces. An unnatural jollity crept into Peter's voice. "Well you're not looking so bad."

Hugh rubbed his eyes and replied, "No. We're quite brisk. Had a week up at Baringo staring at the birds."

His prison pallor was now covered with a mild tan that made him look jaundiced.

Charles snorted and said, "You look as if you need a few square meals!"

For a while they chatted and it was nice to hear Hugh laughing.

Then he asked "How's Frances?" There was an awkward pause.

"Frances was killed in a street accident three months ago, Hugh," I said to save Peter having to talk about it.

He didn't reply but got up to slide the glass doors open. When anything upsets him he always opens doors. Then he slumped in his chair again and stared into the garden.

"Why didn't you tell me?" He was looking at me in a way that was almost hostile. I didn't know what to say. "I don't need to be mollycoddled."

"No need to pile on the agony for a week or so, Hugh," Charles commented.

I got up and fiddled with the coffee tray, then picked it up to return it to the kitchen. I saw Linda's back disappearing into the bathroom. I stepped back on to the verandah and said, "Linda's coming." Hugh appeared to pull himself together and leant forward towards Peter and Charles.

"What ever you do don't mention

Garsales in front of Linda," he said, under his breath.

I don't sleep well. It really started when Garsales' scheme started to filter out of Manila. I'd fall asleep like the dead then wake with a start thinking I'd heard the phone ringing. Then the silence in the house got on my nerves and I'd wander round, drinking coffee and smoking until the wretched instrument drew me like a magnet and I'd phone the Doc. The times I must have wakened him.

Tonight it really did ring and I snatched it up before it woke the others.

"Sarah?"

It was the Doc. "Were you asleep? Mama has been plaguing me to find out how they are."

For a few moments I didn't know how to reply. I tried to concentrate on Linda. "I think she's a bit better. She sits with the others and listens to the conversation, but if they try to include her she gets up and comes into the kitchen with me."

"Is she sleeping so much? Does she stay in bed?"

"No she curls up in a chair on the

verandah and drops off, but she's looking healthier. They went up country for a few days. Charles and Peter are here now."

"Is she still taking the drugs?"

"I don't know. I have to be so careful, Doc. They don't like to be questioned."

I heard him sigh. "Patience, Sarah, we can't expect miracles."

"How's Sylvie? I was quite shocked when she didn't come with them, but of course I understand now why you decided . . ."

"She was getting very distressed, Sarah. She couldn't understand. She's still so young."

"I know." I wasn't giving him a good enough picture of his daughter. "Charles is so good with Linda. He's always telling her how much better she's looking, trying to interest her in things; he's got such a practical way with women. But if he touches her, just to put his arm round her shoulders, she pulls away and slips out of the room."

"Is she like that with Hugo?"

"No." I thought for a moment then added, "No. It's as though she's still in

147

prison and he's the only one who understands that."

The night reverberated with our low voiced anxieties and finally we hung up, promising to ring again soon.

Charles was up early next morning. He had papers spread over the table on the verandah.

"Come and sit down, duck, I want to talk to you before the others get up." He had two deep vertical lines in between his eyebrows. Sometimes he reminds me of those pictures of Atlas carrying the world on his shoulders.

"I've had to take on a new chap. His name's Michael Turnbull. He's a whizz kid with the old stocks and shares, the proverbial expert on Who Owns What. I was getting nowhere with this market movement and the longer Hugh was away the more the work mounted up. I decided some time ago we needed a Trouble Shooter, so when I heard he was available I put out some feelers. He's got more contacts at the end of the phone than anyone I know."

"Are things levelling out?"

It seemed strange to be discussing the company with Hugh sleeping in the back of the house. Everything seemed strange.

"Up to a point. But things move at such a pace. Suppliers go bust, one doesn't know who one's dealing with half the time. Michael is going on a grand tour to check up on them, but he's got to meet Hugh first." He shot me a look to see if I disapproved. "After all, it would have been Hugh's job if it hadn't been for this business. He's still got a lot of information locked away in his head, even if it is two years out of date."

Charles was trying to break something to me. "So you've asked this Michael to come out here?"

Charles stared into the garden, and said, "I feel rotten about this, Sarah. I won't put any strain on him. Michael can stay in Nairobi."

"No, he must stay here, it will be more relaxed. When's he coming?"

"He's on his way now."

"OK."

Charles leaned across and patted my hand. He said, "Hugh spoke to me about prison yesterday for the first time."

"He did? What did he say?"

"He said, 'When I was in that cell I swore that if I ever got out I'd trek through the Sudan and show Linda that house by the Nile where I was born,' then he continued as if he was talking to himself, 'Of course Mum will never go back because of Sophie. Sophie was my sister. She was kidnapped.' I was shattered. He'd forgotten I knew all about it. I think he'd forgotten about our boy dying in Singapore. There's gaps in his memory. I'm only telling you to show that I won't put any strain on him, Sarah."

2

Michael

I MADE a small mistake, in my favour, about my arrival date when I was discussing the subject with Charles on the phone. In fact, I arrived a day earlier than arranged with the intention of giving Nairobi the once over before being swept into the bosom of the Aitkin household. I'd heard from various sources that Nairobi was the most go ahead city in Africa and potentially prosperous from a trade point of view. I booked into the Norfolk and during my twenty-four hours of freedom, cultivated some likely looking business contacts. I weighed up the position with care and can now categorically state that the town is about as forward looking as a shitty Milton Keynes.

Take currency as an example. One is advised to obtain the readies at the hotel. One queues at the appropriate desk in the lobby only to have the grill slammed in one's face. Other queuers warn *sotto voce* that, "They do a fiddle with one's Visa carbons and to insist on their destruction."

New times are displayed but on returning, there is no one there. Managers insist that it is not their responsibility. Deputies talk of borrowing cash from other hotels. Staff flee from enquiries. One wanders into the streets searching for banks. They are all closed *all* the time. It dawns on me that the country functions economically on a daily basis.

So it was without regret I phoned to inform them of my arrival. A woman with a cool, withdrawn voice answered the phone and I listened to her double vowels with disbelief.

I considered the voice whilst eating my dinner and admitted, with the self-knowledge and clarity I pride myself on, that that particular English tone which reeks of position and lineage always has me at a disadvantage. So, fortified by a bottle of imported claret, which Charles will find painful when he spies it on my expense account, I sallied forth to sample the local night life.

An astonishing assortment of the

populace, both male and female, accosted me before I settled on a night club in the bowels of the earth under a shopping mall. It was noisy and full of blacks in expensive suits, aping their European brothers who couldn't control their sweat glands. In no time, so to speak, an olive skinned girl, her head covered in tiny plaits, stood by my table drooping tiredly in the rotating coloured lights. After a couple of sticky drinks we got up and left and made for her place down an unsalubrious alley. It's curiosity really. But I had to find out if it was different in the jungle, and I must say she had a novel repertoire.

So that was why I didn't arrive at the Aitkin ménage until tea time. Not to put too fine a point on it—the drinks hadn't gone down too well with the claret and brandy and I'd been as sick as a dog.

They were gathered on the verandah drinking their tea out of fine china looking like the last days of the Raj. But I was distracted by the house, which I'd expected to be grand and rather palatial. It was, in fact, more like a mock Tudor bungalow in Surrey.

Charles came across the lawn and made

welcoming noises. He escorted me up the steps and introduced me to the assembly. The Voice first, who turned out to be the prodigal's mother and was quite an eyeful. Then a shrinking violet who looked about to have a major breakdown. But this was no time to assess the feminine situation, so I gave my full attention to the two men who had dragged themselves out of their chairs at my approach.

"Michael, this is Peter Hennessy, an old friend of the family."

The old friend of the family reached out to shake my hand. Pleasant, about the same age as the dowager duchess—wouldn't feature a great deal in my career. Then I gave my full attention to the one that mattered. My boss who, with such poor timing, had got himself out of prison just when I had Charles depending on me.

Hubert Aitkin hadn't risen more than an inch or so from his chair and seemed relieved to sink back into it when he'd touched hands. I was pleased to see he looked distinctly unwell. During the kerfuffle of getting seated I could feel him watching me. Being a firm believer in the lasting effects of first impressions I winged him a sincere smile but his eyes were on my Rolex watch. He wasn't impressed. To counteract this I whipped a couple of bottles of champagne out of my briefcase, put them on the table and let them speak for themselves. They made civil sounds and the mother, whose name is Sarah, got up to put them in the fridge. Then the boss-man spoke.

"How are you settling in with the company, Michael?"

His voice was totally unlike his mother's. It had the unassuming cordial tone of someone who had never considered his assets. But it was all there—the right schools, university, father in prestigious employment, Christian name terms with people who count.

"Extremely well. I find it very rewarding."

I wondered what to call him. Mr. Aitkin seemed wrong, he was younger than me. I couldn't rush the gun with Christian names, and Sir was ludicrous.

It sorted itself out when he added, "Turnbull. That's a good old colonial name. Used to be Turnbulls all over the so-called Empire."

Now I'd come prepared for this and answered easily, "Yes, that's why my father chose it." Well, people can find out anything these days.

That caught their attention.

"Chose it?" The older man leaned forward as if he was on the track of something interesting.

"My father was Latvian. We came to England in 1939. He was a complete anglophile—read Conrad and Forster, and the history of the country—so when it was time for naturalisation he picked the name Turnbull."

Now the English are funny. They become self-conscious with strangers who have had it tough . . . who call themselves British rather than English. When this thought has flickered across their minds they bend over backwards to be cordial and terribly equal and they have no idea that all this shows on their faces.

"Have you any relatives in Latvia?" This Hennessy character seemed genuinely interested.

I shrugged. "Who knows? We've never been able to communicate."

"But your parents are here?"

"They are both dead now, unfortunately." My father was probably still tailoring away in the East End and struggling with the language.

Just then an extraordinary thing happened. The most gorgeous Eurasian girl strolled on to the verandah. Her skin was like porcelain tinted with delicate pastel colours. Slowly she raised a rifle and pointed it at my foot. Her wrist bones were so fragile I could only wonder how she could lift the heavy gun.

There was an explosion that blew my mind and a terracotta pot full of hibiscus smashed into a thousand pieces. Nobody moved except me. Then the duchess came to the window and asked with sickening calm, "What was it?"

The beauty replied, "A scorpion. It was just about to climb up the visitor's leg."

She sat on the verandah wall and smiled at me sweetly, then started to clean the gun.

The duchess said, "Oh" and walked away and the rest of them laughed at me. Overcoming an urge to hiss, I smiled too at the hilarity. But Charles had had enough of this local sport.

"Hugh, I've laid out Michael's itinerary in the dining room. Shall we take a look at it?"

The three of us sat round the table handing documents to each other and commenting on the agents. This was my first overseas trip to check on the suppliers so I had done my homework pretty thoroughly. It wasn't long before I noted that Aitkin's knowledge was out of date. For instance, the man he mentioned who was supposedly in charge in Jakata had been arrested for Communist activities eighteen months ago. His son was now running the show, but I didn't mention this, as there might be something in it for me when I'd seen the local layout. Charles knew nothing in detail because his side of the business was sales.

The discussions waffled on for some time, sidetracked by Charles' efforts to put Aitkin in the picture and bring him up to date. Soon he was turning more frequently to me with instructions.

"Be sure to check out the opposition, Michael. Telex if you contact companies that offer a better deal. Then I can arrange water-tight contracts."

I sat there making copious notes long after Aitkin had wandered off to find his wife.

They didn't surface for dinner. Charles took Mrs. Aitkin senior off to read and sign documents. Peter Hennessy and I chatted over a few drinks, before he retired to his room. This gave me the opportunity I had been searching for; ipso facto to have a chat with the Oriental beauty. We sat on the verandah—or rather I did—and I watched her roam around with the restlessness of youth.

"What does E-Woh mean?" I asked.

"Happy Harmony," she replied in a tone that said, I've been asked that a thousand times.

"Where did you get that name?"

"My mother was Chinese."

"So we're both foreigners," I commented trying to cement a bond.

She shot me a look. "I'm not foreign, or at least I don't feel it. My father was English."

"So you and Hubert are half brother and sister?"

"Yes—except—I'm the bastard."

I grinned. "That sounds a bit extreme!"

"No." She didn't sound perturbed by this ancient problem. "My mother died before they could get married."

"I'm sorry. Do you remember her?"

"Not at all, but I remember my father." Then, looking a bit down in the mouth, she added, "Or perhaps I only think I do."

"So where were you born?"

"In China—but I don't remember that. I only remember this country."

I watched her for a while, then said, "Why don't you come to England?"

She looked surprised. "What for?"

"Well, it's a bit limited here, isn't it? It's all going on in Europe."

She mulled this over for a bit, before saying, "I'll take you out tomorrow if you like. You haven't seen much yet, have you?"

Without waiting for a reply, she drifted off.

A jeep was standing in the drive when I surfaced next morning and E-Woh was packing things into it. She looked slight and delectable in khaki battledress. As she scrambled into the back with plastic bottles the jacket rode up showing an expanse of tanned back.

"Shall I drive?" I asked eyeing the monstrous four wheel thing uneasily.

"Better not. It needs a firm hand." Her tilted eyes watched me mockingly as she adjusted the black hair that had escaped from its pony tail.

We swung on to the highway where the sun was at its fiercest and frequently encountered most of the white population, all of whom seemed to be close friends of E-Woh. These fellow travellers consisted of mahogany tanned young men in slouched hats. Brakes were applied indiscriminately and conversations exchanged in confident shouts. I began to feel very pale and a bit of a Charlie in the passenger seat. It was better when we crossed a river, when undulating land opened up around us and there wasn't a fence or a ditch in sight. Giraffe nibbled at leaves delicately and gazelles leapt prettily whilst the sky touched the horizon in the distance. It was all very idyllic and reminded me of Whipsnade, except the weather was better. Two young lions gambolled in a dried up river bed but I couldn't take them seriously. Large birds nested on top of thorn bushes. I asked E-Woh what they were.

"Vultures," she answered shortly.

I took the opportunity to see if her gun was in the back of the jeep. It was there nestling among some blankets.

Then we turned on to a wide red sand track and mountains were suddenly close. A group of zebra were feeding nearby. We stopped to watch them and drink some coffee. The silence when the engine was off was like the world before man became acquisitive. The zebra drifted closer and closer with such trust. I turned to E-Woh to communicate my thoughts on Camelot when I became aware of an audience. Seven small boys in ragged tee shirts had appeared out of nowhere and were watching us intently. Their eyes never left our faces.

"Bugger off!" I waved a hand at them in case they hadn't understood.

"Don't speak to them like that," E-Woh said.

"They were staring."

She turned to the boys and said something to them in their lingo. They laughed and wandered off.

"What did you say?"

"I said you were a city man." She turned on the engine, then, in mock reproof, "Don't let me catch you staring at the zebra!"

Later, after we'd watched a family of elephants moving majestically in the distance she drove some way towards a thickly wooded area talking about some buffalo or rhinoceros that bathed in a river. It was very hot now and personally I was ready for lunch. After a lot of effort we found the place but a big black chap dressed up as a warden tried to stop us. He kept saying "Jambo" then there was a lot of jabbering, but when he saw E-Woh's gun he allowed us to pass on foot. We walked for about half a mile along the jungle-like bank, staring into the murky waters.

Finally she said, "They must be sleeping on the river bed. We'd better go back."

I looked at a nice little glade by the bank and said, "Why don't we have our lunch here?"

She looked doubtful, but agreed. There followed a short altercation about who was going back for the food. She said she would be quicker, and she was right, so I let her. Whilst she was gone I got out my hip flask and had a good pull at the hard stuff. Then I looked around. It was really very pleasant with the thorn trees and brilliantly green grass and the water slipping by.

Then she returned with the plastic boxes and a bottle of wine. She kept popping food into my hand. I didn't notice what I was eating because I was engrossed with visions of loose limbed youth.

When the bottle was empty I ventured, "How old are you, E-Woh?"

"Sixteen, nearly seventeen." She brushed ants off the boxes. I leaned forward to help her.

"And you're still at school?"

She nodded. "I got behind because I've been ill."

I took her hand in mine and smoothed away an intrusive ant.

She looked me straight in the eye and said, "Stop groping!"

"Oh, come on, you don't want to be

behind in everything!" She giggled and I saw that the wine was relaxing her so I returned to the theme of Europe which appeared to have caused a certain pause for thought on the previous night. We started on a verbal journey around the Mediterranean. Her eyes grew dreamy. At Cap Ferrat she hadn't noticed I was holding her hand. As we crossed the border into Italy I manoeuvred her head into such a position that would have made it difficult for her to wriggle away.

Suddenly to my intense surprise, she hurled herself at me and our clenched bodies rolled over several times. Through sweaty eyelashes I noted shock, not abandonment, on her face. A small outcrop brought us to a halt and she pointed speechlessly in the direction of the river. A snake as thick as my thigh was hurling itself through the grass on the bank— intent on its muscular progress towards the water. There was a sinister plop as it reached its destination.

The minute she heard that sound she was on her feet with rugs and boxes and all the paraphernalia and we were back in the jeep at a rate of knots. Foiled by a serpent in the Garden of Eden!

When we got back to the house I could tell something had happened during our absence. The first item to surface was a theft in Charles' home in London. His wife had telephoned to say that the house had been burgled, but the strange thing was that nothing had been stolen except papers from the safe.

Charles couldn't have been more alarmed if they'd cleared the place. They all kept talking about a chap called Garsales, but not, I noticed, in front of Aitkin's visibly fading wife. I tried to enquire who Garsales was but these people have a way of not hearing you if they don't want to.

By dinner time the subject was no longer on the agenda. Conversation was of this and that but nothing was said to assuage my curiosity. Later Charles went over the rest of my itinerary and gave me detailed instructions about phoning London. As I was leaving early next morning I packed and went to bed. I didn't see E-Woh again.

3

Linda

IT'S so quiet since Hugo left. Three days and nights without him . . . a ship with no sails . . .

The others worry because I don't talk, but Hugo knows that it is best to be silent, that talking inflames them. Behaviour patterns are hard to break.

Charles and Peter were here and I was learning to relax to the sound of Anglo-Saxon laughter. And now they are gone, taking Hugo with them. No laughter now. The trouble was they didn't come alone, but brought the company with them; plus the man Michael, and he has gone too and that is good news. He has no goodness in his heart, and I am an authority on his kind.

Yesterday Sarah said, "Let's send for Sylvie," and I stared and my eyes opened very wide and I couldn't speak.

She wrapped her arms round me,

167

saying, "When you're ready, darling . . . when you're ready."

I love that woman but how can I tell her about this atrocity that's always with me? Why I don't like to be touched, daren't touch others, can't have Sylvie here.

The night before he left Hugo said, "Let's laugh and play that silly game that solves all problems." But I couldn't—and couldn't tell him why.

Just a little help, God . . . just a little help . . . I'll give it one more month—then I'll solve it because I'm not fit to be amongst them.

The strangest thing is E-Woh. She's always with me as if we had made prior arrangements, but she doesn't talk—just looks at me with those far seeing Oriental eyes, and we communicate. I'm grateful, and wanted to tell her so but I'd forgotten how old she is, thinking she was still fourteen.

As if she could read my mind, she said, "I'm almost seventeen."

This morning I stood watching a mother hog—tail in the air—trotting along the path at the side of the house with her two babies, wondering how anyone could be so busy. Then E-Woh's hand was in mine and I instinctively pulled away saying, "Sarah wants me!"

"She's gone to Nairobi."

Instant alarm. "She didn't tell me she was going."

Wise young eyes watch me. "Don't replace one crutch with another."

I stand there irresolute.

She says, "I'll play one record, then we're going to see a herd of antelope."

She turned and pointed, "Look—down there on the plains."

The old-fashioned turntable clicks and the needle comes down on the rotating disc and the music floods out into the sunny morning.

"Blue skies . . . where have they gone? Blue skies . . . from now on . . ." and the tears are pouring down my face and I'm back in the cells and the gates are clanging . . .

She is on her knees, both my hands clasped in hers, saying, "Let it out. There's no one here. Get rid of it." Her eyes are willing me to eject the last two years. I listened to myself sobbing and thought, that's for my lost youth, for my shop-soiled self, for my lost innocence, for the pit I fell in.

"My mother used to say, 'Every banquet has to end.'"

My tears ground to a gurgling halt because I was so surprised.

"I didn't know you knew your mother."

"Hugo did."

"And he talks about her?"

She rolled onto the grass, lying on her back and replied, "All the time, but that was before he met you."

This shade from the past brought me up short and I said again, "I didn't know."

In a practical tone she said, "He wasn't much older than I am, then."

She got to her feet, pulling me up. "She taught him to do these exercises. The Chinese do them every morning before breakfast—they are called *Tai Chi Chuan*."

Slowly she raised one arm to the sky then stretched the opposite leg behind her and held the position like a bird in flight. I copied her and in ten minutes the tension flowed away.

When we were relaxing on the lawn I asked, "Do you ever think of going to

China?" E-Woh's mother died in China. She shook her head. "Why not?"

"It could happen again."

"What could . . . ?"

"Some cadre would get me for being different."

Carefully I looked at her. She was different with her father's height and her mother's fluid bones.

"Yes, they probably would. I'm not going back either. It's a mistake to go back . . ." and I thought of the madness that gets into men.

Sitting up she pointed to a hillock overlooking the plains. "Come on, we'll go and sit there and watch the herd go by."

I followed her down the path towards the wooded knoll which seemed to overlook the whole of Kenya and it occurred to me that I hadn't thought of myself for twenty minutes.

As far as I could see there was fresh grass interspersed with crystal-clear springs running into swamps and thorn scrub. The sun glinted on the water and there was no sign of life except zebra grazing in the distance. Suddenly antelope appeared on the horizon and hurtled through a fissure in the rocks and followed a dry watercourse.

"Those are the Bongos," E-Woh said.

It was so silent that we could hear the insects humming and the birds chirruping with that freedom that only happens when no people are there to destroy it.

"Why is the grass so green? I thought the land would be dried up."

"We had the rains a few weeks ago."

In the distance the snow covered peaks of Mount Kenya merged with white clouds and there was stillness everywhere. The sun shone and everything looked new.

E-Woh stood up, walked towards the edge of the knoll and started to slide down the bank. She pointed at something but her words were lost because her head was turned away.

"What?"

She pointed again towards a sand dune and my eyes adjusted and I saw two lions rolling and playing, their fur the same colour as the sand.

"I said, do you feel right here? I mean, does this place give off the right vibes?"

I stared at some gazelle too near the lions, trying to think. "I'm not sure. I would have loved it—but now—I'm confusing it with being with you and Sarah."

"And that's good?"

"Yes."

A green and brown lizard shot out from under a rock and E-Woh turned the rock over to see if there were any more. She pushed her hair back and there was a long streak of dust on her cheek.

"Would you rather be in Hong Kong with Anna?"

I shook my head. "No—that wouldn't be right."

"Why not?"

"Too many relations all talking about Manila and looking sad."

"What would make things better?"

I shook my head again. It was so hard to answer. "I can't tell you. There's a lack of substance to everything. But in a little while I think I'd like to be somewhere where nobody knows about it."

A hand bell started to clang from the direction of the house.

"Someone wants us. I expect it's the phone," she explained.

As we returned through the woods she

173

asked, "Are you sleeping well?" and an opportunity clicked in my head.

"Not so good. Do you know a good doctor in Nairobi?"

"Sure. I'll phone when we get back."

But Sarah was on the phone when we got home and I instantly caught her tension.

"Is it Sylvie?" and I was shaking and had to sit down.

"No—no. That was Charles."

She walked to and fro, then said carefully, "Hugo's not well. He has to go into hospital." She said it too carefully.

There was a humming in my head and my voice didn't belong to me as I asked, "Is he going to die?"

She was beside me with a look in her eyes that made me feel I was pushing her too far. My head dropped on her shoulder and I muttered, "I'm sorry . . ."

A kiss on the forehead. "Nothing to be sorry for. Try not to think the worst."

E-Woh's practicality punctured the doom-laden atmosphere. "Come on Ma, tell us."

I stared at a bowl of flowers on the

dining room table as I waited for Sarah to answer.

"His ulcer's burst. They're going to operate . . ."

Then we were all moving around the room in an aimless way trying to absorb this information. We had coffee and brandy, and Sarah and E-Woh talked quietly but I didn't seem able to concentrate. One of Sarah's Kikuyu hovered outside the window as if he was tuned in to the dramas of life, then drifted off to tell the gardener.

Later, Sarah said, "I think I should go to London. We can't leave everything to Charles." She was looking at me. "You'll be alright with E-Woh?"

My useless voice said, "I'd like to come too."

"I'm not staying on my own." E-Woh stared at her mother.

There was a vacuum as we waited for her reply.

"All right—we'll all go."

The tension lessened. E-Woh was on the phone to the airport and I tried to think of something to comfort Sarah. I stood by her chair and said, "He'll probably find it quite restful in hospital, after the past two years . . ." and Sarah hugged me.

Then we were on the plane again and after twelve hours we got off at Heathrow and Charles was waiting. I was so pleased to see his reliable face that I flung my arms round his neck and buried my head in his overcoat. We climbed into the big company car and moved away from that huge airport.

The driver kept glancing in the mirror and I turned round to see what he was looking at and saw a man running and waving, trying to catch his attention. An ordinary nondescript businessman in a Burberry raincoat.

The driver braked. The man is struggling to open the door and get in out of the rain and the light is too bad for me to see his face. It all happens very quickly. But when he is sitting with us and we are driving through a tunnel, the car is full of sickly smells of brilliantine and after-shave, and I think that I am going to die.

I have never seen Charles in such a rage. His voice slashes at Garsales and the words are distorted by the acoustics and the

176

draught and the other cars tearing by. On the other side of the tunnel the car stops at the side of the road and Charles drags him out onto the pavement.

The rain turns to hail and I can't hear what they are saying.

The two of them are getting soaking wet. Charles looks around at the suburban no-man's land and I can tell he is wondering whether to leave him. Finally he shoves him into the seat next to the driver and returns to the tip-up seat opposite me, shutting the glass partition.

E-Woh and Sarah are on either side of me, holding my hands. Sarah questions Charles in a low voice but I don't listen— just watch the cars rushing by, splashing up water on the black, glittering by-pass in the dark and think that this is a new kind of hell.

Garsales scrambles out in the Cromwell Road and for a moment his eyes linger on me through the glass like a reptile. I know he could have taken a taxi and has only done this to frighten me. Like a snake he slithers off into the crowds.

Soon, we are at a small hotel in Kensington and I am standing on the pavement waiting to be told what to do. In my room Sarah gives me pills and gets me into bed. As I drift off to sleep I remember that I haven't asked about Hugo.

In the morning the sun shines through my window, surprising me because I thought it always rained in England. Someone is knocking on my door, and opens it an inch and is speaking Tagalog to someone in the corridor and I think I'm dreaming. Then there is a big tray with coffee and rolls and I thank her automatically in the same language. We stare at each other in astonishment.

"Where are you from?" I ask and her hand rushes up to her mouth and she backs towards the door.

"Mindano." She is in her thirties and reminds me of Francesca's daughter.

"Come back. You can't be afraid of me!"

Her eyes fill with tears and her troubles come tumbling out. She has no work permit. Her voice is almost a whisper as if someone is listening. Her family had collected money from all the relations to send her to England because there is work. They wait for half of her earnings because they have been evicted from their farm by the landlord who wishes to expand his plantations.

"Do you want to stay in England?"

She nods violently.

"Is it safe?"

Vehemently, she nods again.

"If your papers are good, very, very safe."

She pours my coffee, anxious to do something for me.

"What's your name?"

"Elaina, Madame."

Then she creeps out of the room leaving me to finish my breakfast.

Later, hesitantly, as if to confirm that I really exist, she returns.

"You will be staying in England, Madame?"

"I think so. My husband's in hospital here."

Her face has the awful humility of oppressed people and suddenly I am raging again at dictators who ascend on the backs of these people.

"You go see him today?"

"Yes."

"Then I wash your hair." Her face is transfixed with eagerness to please and I can't refuse. She picks up the uneven ends.

"I cut it a bit, Madame?"

Why not? It can't look worse than it already does.

"OK, but don't call me Madame, my name's Linda."

In fact it looked very nice, short and curly, and, in the mirror I thought I looked more controlled and less like a refugee. I watched Elaina's face behind me and resolved to fight this terror of Garsales, not because of my improved reflection, but because of the fear on her face which had taken root so permanently.

"That's lovely. Now go and get me your papers."

She returned with her life in a stiff plastic envelope and waited, hands twisting.

"Are there any more of you?"

"Oh yes Madame Linda. Three in this hotel, but many more in Ken-sing-ton."

"I think I know someone who could help you. Same time tomorrow?"

Her face was radiant.

"Same time tomorrow, OK."

"OK".

The door closed quietly behind her and I knew that she was on her way to urge help from her Madonna. Filipinos pray a lot to their Madonna, but she doesn't often hear.

In the car on the way to the clinic Charles says, "You look better this morning Linda. Wonderful what a good night's sleep can do," and I'm appalled at how awful I have been looking.

"How's Hugo? Have you phoned?"

"I phoned," Sarah said. "He's stable—but not to expect too much."

"That doesn't sound too good." E-Woh is nervy, but excited to be in London, her nose pressed to the window—pointing out shops and boutiques. Then we are silent as the car whizzes through the city traffic and the hospital gets nearer.

The sister is waiting as we get out of the lift on the sixth floor. She hands me over to another nurse then takes Sarah into her office. Charles and E-Woh sit on chairs in the corridor. The nurse pushes open a green door and I creep in. The tubes alarm me, the silence frightens me. The room is brimming with silence.

"Speak to him, Mrs. Aitkin. He can hear you." She bustles, then leaves us.

"Hugo," I whisper.

Slowly his eyelids flicker and they seem very heavy. He feels my hand on his and he turns his head. The tubes make a bubbling sound and I bend to hear.

"Fantastical!"

The relief was so great that I slip on to my knees by the bed and put my cheek on his hand. Slowly his hand comes up and strokes my hair. Then the stroking stops and I look up. His eyes are closed and he has drifted off to sleep and his mouth is curled in a smile. I watch his face for a long time, then, when nobody comes, I climb on to the bed with great stealth and curl up beside him.

After that day I visited the hospital every afternoon and evening and very gradually Hugo improved. It was during those months that I got to know London. I drank many cups of coffee while Hugo slept or drank his liquid meals, and stared at the English who were so different from the English in Asia, and they stared back at me from behind their newspapers. It was very restful.

The nurses from the hospital dropped into the coffee bars during their split duty periods, and at first avoided me. It was when they started chatting that I knew Hugo wasn't going to die. Sarah went to the company offices every day and gradually I came to realise that I was not so dependant on her.

One nurse on Hugo's level talked to me a lot when she found out that I was a doctor's daughter. In passing, she mentioned that his Wassermann's test was OK. I'd forgotten what that was so I went to the library and looked it up. It is a blood test that confirms if one has sexually transmitted diseases.

After that I wandered round the streets near the hospital looking for medical practitioners' plates and when I found one, of course he thought I'd come for an abortion. I told him I wanted a Wassermann's test and put fifty pounds on his desk. He had a struggle with his

183

conscience, then decided it would be alright to take it as I was foreign.

When I returned five days later for the results he looked cross.

"How have you let yourself get in this state?" he asked in a voice that didn't expect an answer. He talked for a long time about a condition called Trichomonis that was derived from a neglected urinary condition and was in no way related to sexually transmitted diseases. He talked about a drug called Metronidazle or Flagyl which would cure it. Then he talked about my fallopian tubes, but I was so relieved that I didn't take it in.

By the time I got back to the hotel that evening I was on cloud nine. I wasn't surprised to find Elaina waiting for me because Charles had fixed her permit and I had left it on my pillow that morning. She insisted that I went to the flat where her friends lived to celebrate.

A noise like a fiesta greeted us from the street and I felt rather overwhelmed. As we climbed the stairs I could hear them calling, "She's coming, she's coming!" and it dawned on me that the party was in my honour.

Once inside it was hugs and kisses and all those tactile gestures we're so good at in the Philippines. Faces alight with laughter, every one a friend, brandy in my hand and home cooked goodies I hadn't seen since I lived a normal life.

Across the room I saw an old boyfriend of Anna's who had haunted our house in another age. He swept me up in his arms, saying, "I thought you were dead, Linda," and burst into tears and had to be led away.

When he recovered he made me sit on the stairs and asked me about all the people we knew and what had happened to them. When we became maudlin he said, "I'm not usually like this . . . it's seeing you again . . ." and made a super human effort to throw off the past.

"Have you got anywhere to live?"

I shook my head and told him about Hugo.

"You'll be alright, your In-laws are rich."

I shook my head. "I don't know about that. The Company's gone down while Hugo's been away. How are you earning your living?"

"I started a property business. One room flats for refugees like us. I can't go wrong."

"Has your brother gone in with you?"

His face dropped. "He didn't get out. He died in prison."

I was so shattered. All these good young people dying whilst that awful old man lives. I felt him vigorously shaking my shoulder. "But we didn't die Linda. Death only jostled us, then changed his mind."

He went to fetch more drinks, got side tracked, and I got caught up with Elaina's friends. But when we were leaving, he returned flushed with enthusiasm, full of a proposition. An old Filipino recluse had recently died leaving a house in Chelsea. All his life he had been an absentee land-lord with a vengeance, his whole lifestyle supported by workers on the other side of the world. As death crept closer, so did his conscience. His solicitors were informed that all his assets, including the house, were to be formed into a charitable trust and used for accommodation for his fellow countrymen. The only stipulation being that a Filipino approved by the lawyers should live on the property and administer the trust. Tomorrow, I must go with him to see them.

I backed away. I prevaricated. I procrastinated. Then I saw Elaina's face, longing for a home, even if it was only one room. And I thought of my luck today and how someone up there had helped me when I'd asked for it, and given me another chance.

4

Charles

I BLAME myself totally for Hugh's collapse. Share quotations have been all over the place during the past months and when I left London confidence in the company was at zero. The press we've been getting in the financial papers shouldn't happen to a crook.

I talked it over with Peter on the flight out.

"You see, it's not just the market. The accountants have found discrepancies. We're forced to believe that unknown persons are helping themselves to a considerable rake off. There's a limit to how much can be written off. If the bank forces an audit we will be at the mercy of the next Asset Stripper out for a swift buck."

We tossed the subject to and fro for most of the trip. Peter asked questions that got to the nitty-gritty and, I can tell you, it was a relief to share the bad news.

Finally he said, "What you need is a shot in the arm for the whole group. And that means good Media coverage. If Hubert goes on the TV, preferably one of the money programmes, looking as ill as possible, you'll have every businessman in Europe and the States identifying with him. The banks won't want to make an unpopular move and the papers won't want to seem to be knocking a hero."

With blinding clarity I knew he was right. But it didn't stop me feeling split down the middle at inflicting such an ordeal on Hugh. That reaction lasted for three days and was reinforced every time I looked at him. I struggled to be natural when I talked to this walking skeleton who was my best friend. I think the worst thing was watching him trying to cope with the business, struggling to concentrate, then mocking himself with his old sense of humour. When he laughed his cheek bones protruded like a Belsen victim and I had to look away.

At night I tossed and turned and thought of how long it had taken me to pass sixteen exams to become a lawyer, and how ineffectual the law is, and what a fine line civilisation is, and what I would do to that other lawyer in Manila if I could ever get him in the dock.

All that dissolved and was as nothing after I heard about the burglary.

We flew back First Class so that he could rest, but we talked to him too much.

I heard Peter say, "If they see an Aitkin in the city again, it will do the trick, Hugh . . . It's mainly a question of loss of confidence with you out of the picture . . . nothing but mergers and takeovers . . . everyone listening to rumours instead of putting effort into increased growth . . ."

He ate nothing on the plane. We had to wake him when we circled over Heathrow. He looked like a bag of bones in his old green overcoat.

Mercifully it was the dead period and customs were disinterested so we were soon on our way to my house in Chiswick, but it was still two o'clock before we got him to bed. Penny had gone as white as a sheet when she saw him. She kept getting up in the night to watch him tossing and turning. Once I shot up myself thinking one of the girls was ill. The truth is, we are all on the point of exhaustion . . . too much worry . . . too much flying.

Peter had the least sleep. He phoned the TV News Desk as soon as we got home and after that the phone rang intermittently during the night as his contacts put the programme together.

We got Hugh to the Company office by ten the next morning. The Board had insisted on gathering to welcome him back and I could have wished they'd delayed it until after the interview. Newsmen hung around on the steps when we arrived and one of them yelled, "Is there any connection between your arrest in Manila and the company's troubles, Mr. Aitkin?"

"Are you selling up, Mr. Aitkin?"

Hugh hesitated and looked confused but we hustled him through the doors and Peter stayed to placate the press.

The Board were genuinely pleased to see him. They slapped him on the back and said how well he looked, which was a downright lie. But I knew that there was more than a touch of "there but for the grace of God go I" in their welcome. The Mile was seething with rumours about arrests of executives on trumped up charges in distant parts. With top men absent at crucial times deals are lost and confusion reigns. There's a sick joke going around that firms are only sanctioning the purchase of single tickets on long hauls in case the return half is wasted. But Hugh knows nothing of this deteriorating situation. It's too soon.

When we were all gathered the security man came round with his detector and ran it over our briefcases before he started on the fixtures and light fittings. Hugh looked stunned and I had to tell him about the buggings. Old Lord LeRoy Bannerman started waffling about an upsurge of confidence now that Hugh was back. Then he broached the Headhunter Ploy and we voted to employ a top Industrial Enquiry Agency.

"Staff are being wooed away by competitors. Fees offered are so enormous that applicants divulge marketing plans. Half the time the job never materialises," I explained to Hugh.

A young chap, sinister in his keenness, suggested we place trusted Librarians in the employ of opponents to ferret out details of new products, patents and technical data. Mentally I put him on my *caveat emptor* list. These new fellas fill me with horror. They know nothing but ruthlessness.

All this took us up to lunchtime. I glanced at Hugh and was startled at his pallor. I rushed out to get him a glass of milk.

A secretary came in with a message from the TV studios to say that the recording had been brought forward and would we head for the studio at once. Amongst a shower of good wishes, we departed.

Peter was with the producer when we arrived and we spent an hour going over the questions and procedures. Gallons of coffee was passed round and I worried because Hugh had had nothing to eat. I managed to get some sandwiches sent up whilst the girl did the make-up.

Then we were in a vast studio with cameras zooming in on Hugh and the interviewer. He had a drink just before they started and it went better than I'd dared to hope. The presenter took him through it all very gently and there was a wave of sympathy and good feeling from the crew and staff who had come to watch. As the recording came to a close Peter gave me the thumbs up sign and I sighed with relief.

When it was all over I was determined to get him to a restaurant for a late lunch. Peter went off to the cutting room to check on the finished product before it was shown on the early evening news. We got a taxi to the Brompton Road because the company car had returned to take old Bannerman home.

The Patron knows me and is very civil but that didn't stop him seating us in the back section of the restaurant near the bog. Hugh looked up at the sign and said, "How considerate!"

I ordered for him and after he'd shovelled in the poached scallops he started to look better.

When he put his fork down he said, "Lot of changes."

"Don't worry about it. You've done your bit now."

He was distracted by the arrival of the Sole Meuniere and attacked it with enthusiasm.

Half way through he paused to take a

sip of white wine and asked, "What's a Chinese Wall?"

"A conspiracy of silence . . . hiding information that should legally be made public. For instance when a company . . ."

I looked up and he had gone as grey as an old blanket. He went to return the glass to the table but it dropped from his fingers and spilled onto the cloth. He pushed his chair back and lurched towards the gents. When I got there he was throwing his guts up in the wash basin and I was horrified to see a lot of blood in the vomit. Finally the dreadful heaving stopped and he turned on the cold tap and stared vaguely at himself in the mirror. Then, slowly his legs buckled and he slid to the floor.

The management had a doctor there in no time. Together we carried him back into the restaurant and laid him on the carpet. He was unconscious now and I thought he was dying. The doctor gave him an injection and covered him up. He started asking me questions. I remember saying we had an arrangement with the

Wellington and he went into the boss' office and phoned.

When he returned he said, "It's Hubert Aitkin, isn't it?"

I nodded but I had to keep my eyes on Hugh.

"He's only been out of prison a month."

I nodded again.

He shook his head. "He shouldn't be working, but I suppose money comes first with you chaps."

I looked at him without enthusiasm. "How bad is he?"

"Very bad. If he gets over this you keep your corporate concerns to yourself. Understand?"

They got him to bed and fixed up a drip. Then they gathered in the sister's office and told me to sit outside. I could hear their voices chuntering to and fro and I could tell they were not in agreement.

"He won't tolerate the operation. He must have at least four pints . . ."

Another voice said, "I'm doubtful about the anaesthetic."

They sent for tea.

They discussed the merits of working

under the National Health against the advantages of Private Practice.

I walked in without knocking and the sister tried to block my way with her blue uniformed bosom but I held my ground.

The consultant was sitting in the one armchair and his side kick was perched on the edge of the desk, swinging a leg. Another man of medicine stood at the window, staring out.

"What will happen if you operate?" I asked.

They stared and didn't answer. The man by the window turned. "He could die," he said.

"And if you don't?"

"He could still die."

I ignored the others. All professions have them—these men who take refuge in inaction, but they are very prevalent in hospitals.

"Then get on with it."

He smiled and commented, "You're not the next of kin Mr. Ah . . ."

"No—but the law allows a friend in court."

He liked that and proceeded to meet me halfway.

"Can we get the wife's permission?"

"She's not fit enough to reach decisions."

They mulled this over and I added, "There will be bad publicity for the hospital if he dies."

"Parents?"

"Father dead. Mother lives in Nairobi. Will you speak to her if I can get through?"

He nodded. The others looked annoyed.

I knew we were making progress when Sarah spoke to the surgeon. She asked all the right questions and an hour later Hugh was taken down to the theatre. Then I sat through the worst night since my boy died in Singapore.

Hospitals are strange places. One sits in a brilliantly lit No Man's land and people keep a distance from each other. The outside world is suspended, but we note the dying hours. Major incidents long past hover in the mind like yesterday. A woman in furs sitting obliquely opposite shivers at her imageries and has to light a cigarette to shift the projection. An Arab with desolate eyes, locked in thought, has to keep moving.

The Aitkins—my family, except for Penny and the girls—David, Hubert's father, a giant, who had scooped me out of a no-hope job and made me a partner in this conglomerate, which, for all its anxieties, has brought me self respect. And Sarah who had made only one mistake and that was to marry him. And Shen San, his mistress, mother of E-Woh. Both dead in that horror called the Cultural Revolution. And Hugh, who had also loved Shen San. Hugh, like a younger brother, suffering from imagined inadequacies, never attaining his father's pinnacle, but liked where David was not.

The woman in the furs was wearing a scarf with our logo on it. The multicoloured butterfly pitchforked my mind back to the Silk Farm and those heady days of early success; David handing round those first cheques in 1960 when all the world started to notice our silk with the Mandarin design.

After my tenth cup of coffee I must have dropped off because the surgeon was standing beside me.

"All over Mr. Winthrope. Mr. Aitkin is back in his room."

"How is he?" My mouth is very dry.

"Too early to say . . . as well as can be expected. We must be patient."

Non committal . . . non committal . . . "Can I see him?"

His face relaxed into sophisticated understanding. "Just a peep." Like a pair of robots we rode up in the lift together and he stood by me as I stared through the glass in the door. I didn't like what I saw. Hugh immobilised . . . tubes from nose and mouth . . . drips to left and right . . . a nurse flicking the rubber with the back of her nail. And the screen limping along with miniscule movement.

Oh God . . . get us over the next few days . . .

After I'd phoned Penny I went back to the office. Whilst I was in the shower my secretary brought in the feasibility study on the three companies in Lancashire and left it on my desk.

The file stared at me reproachfully. I knew what I had to do, but I didn't like it. Their order books were nonexistent and there was nothing coming in to cover expenses and wage bills. Besides, work was duplicated and rents astronomical. I rang for Jim, the joyless head of accounts. Five minutes later his stooping figure stood in the doorway. He looked like a man who was grimly welcoming retirement.

"These Lancashire accounts . . ."

He nodded. He knew what was coming.

"They're nothing but a liability."

"Yes."

"Got any ideas?"

"They should be closed down, but it will throw seven hundred out of work."

It was my turn to nod. "Can we convert to warehouses?"

Moodily he shook his head. "The railway's closed. They're damp and decrepit. No money's been spent on maintenance. The cost of renovation's too high . . . good money after bad . . ."

We sat there, each waiting for the other to give the thumbs down. Then I remembered I was the boss, "Close them down this Friday, Jim. But keep the companies on hold until after the next tax year. We can't have a mammoth bill from the Revenue. With a bit of luck the figures will get lost."

He nodded and sloped off. It wasn't really legal but he wouldn't be here to answer awkward questions from the Tax Inspector next year, and he'd get a Golden Goodbye which was well deserved. Also his wife is sick.

I looked through the telexes but there was nothing from Michael. I hadn't really expected anything yet.

I phoned the clinic but there was no change. So I went across the road for a beer and a beef sandwich. As soon as I was settled I wished I'd gone further afield. The place was stiff with city competitors and their voices battered on my ears.

"Basic salaries are up 75 to 100%."

"One of our young chaps left last week, earning £35,000. Hear he's getting £130,000 from an American set-up. He's twenty-eight."

"It's not helpful when the rest of the country's pulling in its belt . . ."

"I'm getting out before there's blood on the streets."

I turned away and was bombarded by three ex-Public School boys on my left.

"I don't think I'm a shit—per sé," one

of them said, "but the dealers are making a quarter of a million."

I left the beef sandwich and returned to the office.

When I got back there were several messages on my desk. One from the bank asking me to call in at my convenience. Well it wasn't bloody convenient, I thought, as I chucked it in a tray. Murmurings of a strike in Bradford. Endless bumf on Pension Funds. Queries on staff expenses and a message from Sarah to say that she and Linda and E-Woh were catching the next flight to Heathrow.

Nestling amongst this lot like a tarantula hiding in a bunch of bananas was a message from the Chicago office. Garsales had walked out. No warning. No explanation.

I sat there for the next hour wondering how I was going to keep control over that bastard.

5

Michael

I PARKED the BMW in an underground car park and started to walk towards the house in Chelsea. Tonight was the night when we all celebrated Hugo's homecoming and Garsales had told me to be sure not to miss it. As I walked I stared at the plane trees surrounding the private parks, locked and padlocked against the hoi polloi until their privileged tenants were moved to use them. As Garsales' man I might soon have one of those keys in my hot little hand.

Jakata was the perfect background for Garsales. There, his rather over the top type of good looks were an advantage giving him an air of authority like an old fashioned satrap or generalissimo. Whereas in Europe, with all its egality, he was diminished, lost in the crowd of transient foreigners. In London I could feel we were equals, but in Indonesia I'd met my match.

I'd been flattered four months ago, when he'd come all the way from Chicago to seek me out, and soothed that my potential was recognised after that time-warp of an experience in Nairobi. And he had been straight, right from the start, spelling it out that I had openings in the Aitkin Group that he could never hope to attain. It was a struggle not to react when he mentioned remuneration. It would change my whole lifestyle. But it would have been downright rude not to enthuse at the bonus when the deal was completed. What a stroke of luck!

I'd made a point of visiting Hugo in the clinic. Without that family of his around I found him easy to deal with. He had an other-worldly look about him as his health improved like someone who's been given a second chance. He always sat by the window these days reading the Financial Times and greeted me like a long lost friend.

"Oh Michael, just the person. Tell me, how is it the foreign boys have moved in in force since I've been away? All the big battalions are backed, not to say owned by them."

"You chose a bad time to fade, old chap. It's the abolition of Exchange Controls that's done it. Eurobonds. The whole world's a market place. The foreign players are walking all over us."

He'd picked up a list.

"Why have these stockbrokers sold out? They were some of the most respected in the city."

"They were under capitalised."

"I don't follow."

"It was the disappearance of restrictions. One morning they woke up to find themselves without the readies to climb on the band wagon. They looked in the mirror and saw they weren't as young as they used to be and it dawned on them that they needed one last killing. And there it was in the form of Golden Handcuffs, held out to them by our cousins across the Pond."

"But they don't give nothing for nothing."

"No, the Americans needed trained expertise until they got the hang of things."

He looked glum. "It's a jungle."

"That's the world we're living in."

I decided that enough was enough. If I went on at this rate he'd know as much as I did.

"When are you leaving here?"

"Next week, as soon as the women have got the flat ready."

"Look," I said carefully, "I've got a place in Spain. Why don't you and Linda, and Sylvie, of course," they'd got the brat over, "go there for a month—longer if you like. It's standing empty." I would prefer him out of the way.

He was really grateful.

"That's jolly decent Michael. I'd love a bit of sun. But . . ." then he frowned.

"But it might not be a good time for Linda. She runs this hospice place where we have our flat. You've probably heard, she's in charge of a group of expat Filipinos."

All that was last week. But the word Filipinos had linked in my head with Nominees and I tucked it away in my mind for Garsales.

Turning the corner into the Aitkin's street

I recalled another occasion when Hugo was wringing his hands about the closing down of three factories in Lancashire. One would have thought that the laid off men were close family friends. This paternalistic attitude makes me want to throw-up. He had actually calculated that one worker earned in a week what a dealer gets in an hour. What can you do with this maudlin attitude? But he's so popular in the city— one can't ignore that.

The house was old and stood back from the pavement. Bushes and trees encroached up to the sash windows. It had taken on the air of the recluse who had sheltered there for years. But, although neglected it still had style and I started to calculate the price of the plot if it was pulled down and used for development. The front door was open. On the left was a battery of new bells and a grill to speak into. As I stepped into the hall a posse of Filipino girls rushed passed me in a high old state of excitement.

The unmistakable sounds of a social gathering greeted me as I climbed the stairs to the first floor. Double doors stood open and the lights from the street shone into a spacious elegant room. Knots of people stood around chatting or loitered on the small wrought iron balconies. High ceilings gave it all a graceful symmetry and I was glad I'd changed into a decent suit.

A small girl rushed across the carpet like a whirlwind and crashed into a table with glasses on it. Several fell onto the floor and one broke. The child subsided on to some spilt wine and said, "Oh f—."

Linda, looking unnecessarily fit, followed her offspring and said, "Don't say that," then to me, "she's just started school."

She looked at me without smiling and followed it up with a conventional, "I'm glad you could come." Her manner cemented my suspicion that she didn't like me.

The exhibitionist on the floor wasn't going to lose out on her moment of glory.

"I know a really bad word," she announced.

"What's that?" her mother asked with commendable disinterest.

"Kick up the bum."

We both stared at her for a moment

then Linda turned to a drab and said, "Fetch a cloth Elaina."

I made an effort and asked, "How do you like living in London?"

"Very much."

This didn't get us far so I looked around for someone else to talk to. Hugo was standing with his back to me bending over a new music centre. His arm was draped over the shoulders of a girl. They both turned towards me and I saw again the stunning beauty of E-Woh who had emerged from her khaki chrysalis and was now a fully formed London butterfly.

"Hello Michael." She turned back to the music centre and said, "Look what we've bought old Stumblebum."

The words seemed incongruous emerging from those delicate lips. The Duchess came over with some champagne and I made the usual expected comments about the conversion.

"How many flatlettes are there?" I asked.

"About nine or ten," she replied. Her hair was piled at the back of her head in a chignon and I had to admit there was an improvement if you like the sophisticated type.

"The girls like to share . . . three to a room." She drifted off.

I turned back to E-Woh.

"Well, you all seem very settled. What are you going to do with yourself?"

"I'm going to university."

I tried to hold her gaze which has proved effective in past manoeuvres but she didn't seem put out and stared back tranquilly.

"What are you taking?"

"Economics, maths, that sort of thing."

"So you're clever too."

She tossed her ponytail. "Oh, I wouldn't say that, but it'll keep me off the streets."

"I should think so, exquisite child."

The blue-black eyes were on me again, and she replied, "Oh—I'm not a child."

"What are you then?"

"I'm an exotic oriental succulent."

I was mildly astonished, which seemed to amuse her.

A couple of hours later I made my way to Garsales' flat. Now here was the other side of the coin. It's off the Cromwell Road in a nondescript block, one of hundreds rented out to businessmen. He had made no mark on it during his tenancy. If he left tomorrow there would be nothing of Garsales left behind.

He poured me a brandy as I entered the sitting room and indicated a chair. There was never anything but brandy, and today there was no welcome in his manner.

"Who was there?"

I listed several members of the board and their wives.

"No outsiders?"

I racked my brains to find someone that might interest him but, really it was just Hugo's Welcome Home Party, nothing more.

"Was Charles there?"

"Of course."

"You didn't mention him."

"Well of course he was there, what did you expect?"

An irrational look of frustration tightened his facial muscles and for a moment I felt alarmed. But I was getting used to his unpredictability and normally I could talk him out of it. I tried to think of something to say about the boring job Charles had shoved him into, secretary and treasurer to a group of inter-related small companies, but there seemed little to comment on. I wondered if he remembered telling me he was creaming off Handling Charges by manipulating the accounts whilst comfortable sums mounted up in his Liechtenstein bank account. On second thoughts another subject might be preferable.

"They've got a lot of your people living in the house."

I'd caught his interest. He wanted to know about them. I'd already given him details of the deceased landowner's will.

"How many live in the place?"

"At least thirty, but grants are paid from the interest to other Filipinos who are in private accommodation."

A glimmer of something started to edge the antagonism from his eyes.

"We could use them."

"That's what I thought. In fact I had an idea this evening."

He just watched me. I don't know why he makes me uneasy, but I knew I had to come up with something good.

"My notion was to use them as Nominees to buy up shares, but the how to do it will require some thought."

I watched him considering this and wondered why he bothered. Sitting in this flat in London, he was like a spider in the centre of his web. A lot of the errands I did for him involved meeting incoming businessmen at Heathrow, handing them documents, and seeing them onto their forward flights, mostly to the USA. Amongst the documents were always currency transactions involving huge sums, but he never gave me these papers until the last minute, consequently there was little time to read them. Legally, they were complicated, and the Gents is no place to concentrate on the fine print. But one thing hit me. This piddling about with the Aitkin Group was peanuts; I could only think it was a front because, say what you like about them, the Aitkins are kosher.

"Get a list of them, names and place of origin. Now, it's time you were off."

I stood up and took the briefcase from him. Separately he handed me details of the passengers' flight, but this time there were two arrivals; the man to be brought back to the flat and the woman to be handed the briefcase and put on the flight to New York. For a moment I was surprised because women don't feature much in Garsales' life.

"Will she be met at the other end?"

"She knows her way around. It's my sister." He stopped and I knew he'd made a mistake. "But that doesn't concern you. Get the man here as soon as possible. He'll be staying for two days—then you transfer him back to Heathrow. The only thing to watch out for is that he doesn't cross Mrs. Aitkin Junior's path. She would recognise him."

A couple of hours later I had the man back at the flat. They instantly picked up the threads of some previous conversation. It had to do with funds for property purchases in New York. He was tired. He said, "I've arranged for my cousin to supervise the construction and act as agent and treasurer. The Lady insists on it."

His eyes slid towards me and back to Garsales with an imperceptible question.

I picked it up before Garsales and said,

"I expect you'd like some coffee," and walked into the kitchen, shutting the door. It was a flimsy door and I could take notes while I listened. I couldn't get down all the details because they would keep breaking into that language of theirs. But it was enough to confirm my opinion that Garsales was only feeding me titbits, the tip of the iceberg. American Holdings, property on both coasts, microchip companies in California, even banks—and everything registered in lucrative spots like the Caymans or the Virgin Islands.

When the man had gone to bed Garsales and I worked through the night.

The first item was for steel to be exported to a small African State. At the same time there was a plethora of buying and selling of shares in the company which had a listed capital of £35,000,000. It didn't take a great brain to see something was wrong because the country was bankrupt. What a tiring transaction for the accountants!

But the name of the game that night was arms. A warehouse in an obscure region of the Costa del Sol. A bent captain and a transfer at sea. False insurance claims etc

etc . . . And where had Garsales been two weeks ago? Libya. I know because I bought his ticket.

A certain look comes over Garsales' face when he reaches a high spot in his wheeler dealing; he gets a buzz when he's going to bring something off. And I had come to notice that he concealed important things in a cloud of unimportant ones. I could just imagine him with Gadaffi—both asking for grenades for their birthdays as boys, Garsales selling his at a profit.

I'd arranged for a search on Gadaffi whilst Garsales was in Libya. The Arab has connections with merchant banks in Frankfurt, Madrid and Chinese banks in Hong Kong. His commercial investments are channelled through the Libyan Arab Foreign Investment Company which has offices in Rome, Athens and Malta. He has private investments in ninety-four companies in Africa, Europe, the Middle East, Asia and Latin America. But in Italy he is particularly active—he's come a long way since '74 when he didn't know what to do with his new found oil revenues.

It was a quarter to four and Garsales' pupils were receding from their high to more normal tiredness. He stuffed papers into a file, then walked into his bedroom where there was a wall safe. A sheet of paper had dropped under his chair so I picked it up and glanced at it from force of habit. It was in Spanish. There were lists of cargos all awaiting transportation in every obscure region in Andalusia. There were sailing times and destinations. There were routes by land into Europe and times for border crossings. But most of the traffic was by sea to Africa and the Middle East.

I dropped the typed sheet back on the floor beneath Garsales' chair and a hazy vision of wellbeing engulfed me. My bonus was fleshing out nicely—and no one was going to diminish it in any shape or form.

Part Three

1980

1

IT'S three months since I was discharged from the hospital. I have a brand new stomach but the same old fraught mind. At the slightest opportunity I join Charles for food, glorious food, which helps considerably when trying to cope with this can of worms called *The Company*. But somewhere along the way I've lost the habit of sleeping and the minute my head touches the pillow I know I'm in for a rough time.

Take last night. Marcos visited me with a plausible scheme. His quiet, reasonable voice went on and on and, concentrate as I might, I couldn't put his words together to form any sense. I kept getting distracted by the medals on his chest and was driven by a compunction to count them. When I got to twenty-seven the lawyer's jargon started to fall into place and I realised he was telling me to sell the company to finance back-pay for his *Mahalika* guerillas who fought the Japs during the war.

221

Struggling to get the words out of my mouth, as one does in dreams, I protested.

"But you were busy with the Black Market . . . selling munitions to the Japanese . . ."

But I'd lost his attention because he was watching Imelda who was slowly dancing round my bed singing "What Imelda wants—Imelda gets" and her diamond necklace lit up the room like a discotheque. I was shouting to attract their attention.

"Make her sell the necklace to pay the men."

They both stopped and stared at me reproachfully. Then Marcos said, "She needs it to buy shoes." Arm in arm, they turned away and walked through the wall.

Later, when I had been tossing and turning for hours, wrestling with schemes to pay Marcos off, I found that McMahon was standing by the bed. He stared sightlessly over my head, because he had coins for eyes.

"Hugo . . . don't forget . . . don't ever forget . . ."

Linda brought my breakfast in and I felt

churlish because she'd slept in the spare room. She stood in the doorway staring at the room which looked as if a hurricane had hit it.

"Had another energetic night?" she asked.

I raised myself an inch on the pillows and groped for the electric fire switch.

"You're shoving your nightmares onto me."

She found a place for the tray, then came and sat on the bed beside me, ruffling my hair.

"Poor old man. It's the pills that make you dream."

Mollified, I put my arms round her and attempted to lure her under the bed-clothes.

"The eggs will get cold. Come and eat them in the sitting room."

Ungraciously I draped the duvet round my shoulders and followed her.

Snow had fallen overnight and the room was full of a blinding light. I stood at the window blinking like an owl, then sloped off to the bathroom. On my return the sunshine drew me back and I stood staring at the park across the street. Hoar frost had woven delicate patterns in the trees, meshing the branches together as they drooped towards the carpet of white grass. Picking up the plate of scrambled eggs, I watched the robins cavorting about and the eggs slid down like a panacea. Linda held out a cup of coffee.

"Sylvie get off alright?" I asked rather hoping it was half-term or something. She's a great one for getting the day under way.

"I've taken her round to Sarah's. I've got the accounts to do today."

My mother has a flat a few streets away because she has to be on hand for voting. She's always to-ing and fro-ing to Nairobi but I have to say she never lets us down when it comes to board disputes. They've all found themselves a niche since I've been ill; Linda with the hospice administration, E-Woh at college, Sylvie with her fickle attachment to the novelties of school, and my mother, whose mind is constantly with Klaus. As my health improves the thread of her attention slackens and distances itself. I love my mother but there are times when I can't stand her.

A ray of sunlight shone through the glass and landed on Linda's head, turning a streak of hair chestnut. She was bent over the newspaper she picks up from a shop near the school each morning. The bouncy curls fall forward over her face, hiding the suspended distant look that is so often there. She is much better these days but we are too careful with each other and avoid too many subjects. It started when I censored my conversation in an effort not to mention Garsales. She, in turn avoids talking about the company because I come home in this state of exhaustion. We are both too concerned with mutual consideration, but sometimes I feel that our individual conditions gyrate and jostle for pride of place.

I turned back from the window feeling there might be a small space free in my mind for work considerations, when I felt a vibration coming from Linda. My sleeping-pilled mind watched as her hand tried to connect with a table beside her but her eyes were still on the newspaper. In slow motion the cup crashed to the floor and brown liquid trickled across the carpet.

Sluggishly I thought that carpet's damned. I leaned forward to pick up the cup.

"Hugo, Marcos has let Ninoy out of prison!" she shrieked.

"*What* did you say?"

But she was across the room with the page in her hand and the rest of the paper slid silently into the coffee. I snatched it from her and there in a small column reserved for foreign news was a few lines from Reuters.

"I can't believe it!" Together we read and re-read it.

"He's going to America for heart surgery!"

"Are you sure? Or is it all empty promises?"

Somehow we couldn't take it in, were afraid to take it in. I stopped my eyes racing over the print and started to read again carefully.

"It says he left three days ago."

Linda's eyes were full of tears, as she said, "He must be very bad. Marcos doesn't want him dying in jail. He would be a martyr." I paced up and down.

"There must be somewhere we can get

more information." In the mirror my hair stood on end and I looked like a wild man.

"The newspaper!"

"Of course!"

With a speed that was abnormal for me in the mornings I pounced on the phone and was through to the newsdesk in a flash. Then I hung on for an age while they checked files. Linda was at my elbow, rattling on about the Aquinos making Marcos an offer he couldn't refuse. All I could think was seven years, seven years and eight months. Please God, let him be out of the country. Suddenly, the voice was back.

"Mr. Aitkin? We've been checking with Universal Press and the Reuters entry is correct. Mr. Aquino arrived in Boston last night and was admitted to a private clinic."

I thanked the newsman so profoundly and at such length that finally he laughed and said, "Not my doing, Mr. Aitkin. But it's nice to be able to please."

"It's true!"

Linda rushed into my arms. I switched on Ravel's Bolero and we whirled round the room like things possessed. By the time the music reached its crescendo we were so overcome with excitement that I felt like hurling a few glasses into the fireplace. The thought of glasses cleared my mind wonderfully. I let go of Linda and she nearly fell over, but I was in the kitchen by then, struggling to open a bottle of champagne. The cork flew up to the ceiling and it spilled all over the table but we'd drunk it before the cork came to rest. We stood staring at each other.

"Who shall we tell?" asked Linda.

"Elaina." We both spoke at once.

We were out of the front door, in the corridor, yelling up the stairs; waiting for those feet to come tripping down. Chattering, interspersed with more shouts which started to die away.

"Where is she? She can't be out."

Filled with impatience I bounded up the stairs and hammered on her door. No answer. So I opened it and stared at the tidy room—the unslept in bed.

"She's not here."

I leant over the banisters and Linda looked up at me.

"How very odd."

Elaina is a paragon of quiet efficiency.

She leaves little notes when she goes out. She says unobtrusive goodbyes and goodnights at the same time each day. You can set your watch by Elaina.

"See if she's left a note in the kitchen."

Linda's head disappeared and I returned to the bedroom and looked around. Clothes in the cupboard, plant watered on the window sill.

I heard the morning stampede on the stairs as the girls rushed off to work.

"Have you seen Elaina?"

They shook their heads and edged round me, their minds not to be diverted. Linda shook her head, and intercepted them on the ground floor. I watched her pour out the story of Ninoy's release in Filipino and a strange thing happened. Those happy faces suddenly became guarded and they edged away avoiding her eyes. One or two moved towards the front door and the rest hastened to follow. They erupted onto the street and their relief was almost tangible.

Back in the sitting room Linda looked crestfallen.

"Perhaps they're not sure who it is."

229

Her face made me sad. "Of course they are. Everyone in Manila knows Ninoy."

I sighed with the weight of knowledge of human nature, not shared by Filipinos.

"Linda, people forget. He's been out of circulation for so long. Besides, the girls aren't all from Manila."

Every so often there is a peep of the old Linda, and now was one of them. Exasperated she replied, "Hugo, those girls spend their days gossiping, they all know the Aquinos."

Then she was off.

"I'm going upstairs to look for the ones on shift work."

When she'd gone, dressing-gown flying, the thought crossed my mind that too much was happening too early.

I was having lunch with Charles today but before that there were papers to go through, so I sat at the desk shuffling through them. A quarter of an hour later, she returned.

"Something's up," she said: "Now don't start rationalising Hugo—they are all agitated—they're so transparent." She rushed into the bathroom, emerging ten minutes later in her outdoor clothes.

"Linda are you going to see thingee?" I asked.

Linda gravitates to the property fella when she's got problems.

She nodded, and started searching for her handbag.

When she'd gone, and I was left staring at my papers, for some odd reason Francesca's face kept jumping off the pages.

About an hour later when some sense was emerging from my homework a key grated in the lock and E-Woh walked in.

"What are you doing here? Haven't you any lectures?"

She stood there scruffy in her student gear; legs in flimsy jeans that couldn't possibly keep out the cold, layers of wool mounting thickly towards her ears.

"Exams tomorrow. I'm staying at home to study."

Today her black hair was woven into one thick plait which hung over her shoulder. She slumped into the chair on the other side of my desk and carelessly flicked the papers round to read.

"Don't do that."

She pushed them back untidily, then

took a large apple out of the dish and stood by the window eating it.

"Why don't you go upstairs if you're going to revise?" She has a small flat in the attics.

"I thought I'd come and see how Old Stumblebum was."

My eye caught a date in my diary. "Don't forget the board meeting on Tuesday, I'll need your vote."

She had been voted onto the board when I was in hospital and the arrangement had continued. I have to admit she has a sharp mind and the fuddy-duddies like her. She has a knack of bringing up ideas that they think have emanated from them.

"I've jotted it down."

The apple was disappearing at an alarming speed, and she showed no signs of leaving.

"Seen Michael lately?"

He was always phoning or taking her somewhere since the party.

She nodded. "We went for a drink last night."

"Do you like him?"

"He's alright," she replied, with the terrible disinterest of a teenager.

"Do you trust him?"

I don't know why I asked. It just came into my mind.

"Oh no."

Her look was pitying as if I was getting past it.

"Why not?"

"Well, he's so obvious about covering his tracks," she said, as if it was common knowledge. "He never gives a straight answer."

She flopped back in the chair.

"Funny thing happened the other night." One leg swung over the arm of the chair. "We went to that spaghetti place near Harrods. We were sitting at a table behind one of those wrought iron screen things. Half way through the nosh Michael looked up at someone standing behind my chair. I couldn't see who it was because I had my back to him and the lights are dim anyway, only candles on the tables."

There was a noise as something banged on the window and she got up saying, "Look—that bird's bashing its brains out on the glass."

Side-tracked I watched the silly thing.

"Get on with it."

Absorbed, she stared at the fluttering bird. "It's lost its sense of direction."

She opened the window and a cruel gust blew in.

"That way birdie."

She stood on the balcony waving in the direction of the park.

"E-Woh, you are taxing me beyond endurance! Return and complete your little story."

"I'll just get it some bread."

She flitted towards the kitchen. The window was wide open and all the horrors of winter were blowing in so I shut it and told the bird to buzz off. Then I followed her into the kitchen and grabbed the plait, using it as a leading rein to return her to her seat.

"You shit!"

The Oriental eyes were several shades darker.

"Finish!"

"F--- off!"

"Who was standing behind your chair?"

She didn't answer, just sat there smouldering.

"E-Woh, I do not believe in the superior

234

forces of violence, but you are not leaving this room until you've told me!"

"Bully!"

There followed a silent tussle of wills. Finally she continued, basically because she wanted to tell me.

"The man started shouting at Michael. Michael looked stunned and glanced at me warningly. He stopped for a second, then continued as if his rage was out of control. By this time I'd managed to swivel round. Guess who it was?"

Carefully I replied, "I don't know who it was."

"It was Garsales."

Well, I hadn't expected that.

"How can you be sure? You've only seen him once, that night in the car coming from Heathrow."

"You'll have to take my word for it."

"But how does Michael know Garsales? Charles put him in that crummy office down at the docks to keep him away from the staff."

"I dunno."

E-Woh got up and stared at herself critically in the mirror.

The anger was receding so I ventured,

"Can you find out how well Michael knows him. If they meet often? No, perhaps not, it would be difficult."

"Of course I can." Witheringly she looked at my reflection in the glass.

"I can lead him by the nose. I don't know what gets into men of his age. He's under the impression that he's in his prime. But he's really old."

Severely I replied, "He's not much older than I am."

"That's what I mean—Fink!"

After she'd flounced out I stood under the shower, then got dressed. Outside the front door the full horror of an English winter hit me and I leapt niftily into the car. Once the engine had agreed to start we roller-coasted along the back streets over pack ice and mounds of snow left by crazy neighbours. In the High Street grey people inched along grey streets, and buses lurched by soaking feet. When I reached the city the snow had disappeared and the gutters were awash with filthy water. Scowling businessmen flicked at splashed trousers and broke into speedy two-steps to avoid a further onslaught from the traffic.

When I arrived at the office I left the engine running, dashed in to tell the porter I was here, and returned to the car, my eyes on stalks for wardens. Which was why I didn't notice a weasel-faced individual with press written all over him until he stuck his head through the car window.

"Is it true that you're living in charity property Mr. Aitkin?"

I resisted the impulse to wind the window up, catching his none too clean mush in it.

"What can you mean?" I snapped.

"Does your wife work for a Filipino charity?"

"Indeed she does."

"And you're cashing in on her nationality to get free accommodation?"

I could have smashed his head in!

At that moment Charles pushed his way through the swing doors and started down the steps. When he saw the reporter he broke into a trot and slammed the passenger door just as the bloke started to yank his pad out of his pocket.

"The rent for our flat is paid directly into the accounts of the trust."

I spoke with great clarity and revved the

engine to drown his voice. I backed the car away from a pile of grit.

"What a little shit!"

The reporter stepped forward, his hand raised like a symbol of the free democratic world. I stamped on the accelerator and witnessed a satisfying shower of muck drench his raincoat.

"You shouldn't have done that. He'll get his own back."

Charles shook his overcoat and handed it to the girl in the cloakroom. Underneath he was wearing a new, neat suit which surprised me because he usually looks as if he's not bothered to undress the previous night.

"How can you stand a waistcoat?" I asked.

Self-consciously he replied, "Penny says it detracts from my stomach."

He gave his full attention to the menu and undid the top button of his shirt.

Later we laid down our implements and I gazed round the restaurant. I thought, not for the first time, that this was the most satisfactory part of the day. Other lunchers had similar expressions and it crossed my mind that these feeding places were the bolt-holes without which the city of London would cease to function.

We were drinking our coffee, relaxed in the knowledge that nobody could get at us.

"What's the company worth, Charles?" I asked.

He picked up his napkin and muttered the confidential figure into it. I stared at the flock wallpaper and wondered why it didn't bring me greater comfort.

"Debits?"

"Five and a half million. If it was all called in we couldn't cover it. There'd be a run on the shares. We'd be finished in a month." There was a fine sheen of sweat on his forehead. The responsibility was taking it's toll.

"What about bad debts?"

He sighed and the spoon in his cup looked as if he was moving mud.

"There's the rub, Hugh. Paying up is going out of fashion."

"Give us a for instance, Old Sport."

He put the spoon in his saucer as if the effort wasn't worth the candle and sighed.

"The Houston account is a good for instance. They haven't settled for nearly two years. When I get on to them the Chairman is permanently on his hols in Bermuda. His Deputy is always at meetings and will phone back and never does. Finally he left a message saying that cheques are signed on the first of the month. Funny lot, the Americans. I can never work out their point of reference when they come up with remarks like that."

"Is that it?"

"That is not it, by any means."

Charles was simmering with controlled wrath. "I had a search done on the company."

"Are they solvent?"

"Oh very!"

"Charles, please get to the nitty gritty!"

He leaned back in his chair looking at me. "I can see you are wondering how I allowed it to linger on. It's become a way of life whilst you've been away; to pay up at the latest possible date thereby maintaining the company's gross at the highest level thus reaping maximum interest. When the big boys are slow to pay there's a general drying up of finance and the smaller companies have a cash flow crisis and go to the wall."

I watched businessmen collecting coats and spilling onto the pavement and wondered if they too were affected by this dismal news.

"I kept the results of the search in a safe at home. You know we were burgled when I was in Kenya? Nothing was taken except the files."

This *did* bring me up short.

"Why didn't you tell me?"

"You were ill."

"What's behind all this? Are they trying to wriggle out of their contract?"

"No."

"Then why don't we stop supplying them?"

"And leave ourselves open to breach of contract and God knows what?"

I tried to think what I would have done in the circumstances.

"We've got to have a complete shake-up."

"There's more!"

Charles had left the best bit until the end.

"While you were in hospital the Deputy-Chairman finally made contact. Said he was coming to London and would I have dinner with him at the Connaught? Later it crossed my mind that he picked it because the tables are so well spaced, well away from listening ears. His proposal was this. The discount for bulk purchase stands at thirteen per cent. Reduce it to eight; he would see that there was no trouble with his board. The remaining five per cent to be paid directly into his Swiss account. In return our accounts would be settled monthly, on the dot."

Speechlessly I ground my cigarette out in a saucer and watched as a reproachful waiter removed it and returned with a spotless glass ashtray.

"What did you say?"

"I pretended I hadn't heard, and I've gone on pretending ever since."

There were two free hours before the meeting started so I decided to go for a walk to think. I mosied around in the cold, searching for the unknown factor. Something had to change or the company was going to slide into oblivion. The afternoon was freezing and the few people about looked bleached with the February weather. Finally the sub-zero temperature drove me into the Victoria and Albert Museum and I walked from room to dim-lit room blind to the marvels. Gradually I thawed, and by some fluke found myself in the Chinese room. I stood staring at terracotta Mandarins in heavy silk raiment. I stood there thinking about the tales my father used to tell me; tales of power struggles, poisonings, and Machiavellian schemings.

Should I go to the bank and make a clean breast of it? "They're all over you when you don't need them, and call everything in when you do." How often I had heard him say that.

"It's all very well for you. You knew your enemy."

A middle-aged woman, up in the capital for the day, looked at me strangely and I realised I'd spoken aloud. She suddenly remembered an urgent appointment and the room was empty.

"Get out in the field . . . stop hanging about here."

"Of course!"

"Go and sus out the troops?"

"I will!"

At the end of the meeting I told Charles I intended making a swift tour of the works.

He looked worried. "Are you sure you're up to it? It's not the best time of the year to traipse up north."

"I can't wait for the weather to improve. Now, on no account let them know I'm coming. If anyone's got their trousers down I want to catch them at it."

"When are you going?"

"I'll leave on Sunday. Then I'll be in Nottingham by the evening and ready for Monday morning."

I spent the rest of the day going over the accounts of the factories I intended visiting, engraving their figures on my heart. E-Woh was sitting talking to Linda when I got back.

"His bank accounts are all in the Channel Isles," I heard her say.

Linda replied, "I never trusted him an inch. How did you find out?"

"He was talking about credit cards and how you could make them work for you, paying on the right dates to avoid interest.

He's so conceited. You'd think he was a financial expert."

She looked up and saw me standing in the doorway.

"Listening at keyholes, Stumblebum?"

"Whose bank account's in Jersey?"

"Michael's. It's Guernsey."

"Are you hungry?" Linda asked.

"If Elaina's cooking, yes."

She glanced away.

"She's not back!"

"Not back!" With all the day's angst I'd forgotten about Elaina. Linda looked drawn.

"She'll turn up, people always do in England. Do your trick with an egg."

When Linda had left the room I said to E-Woh, "What do you think has happened to her?"

She shrugged. "I don't know. I didn't know her very well. It was Linda she was close to."

We sat staring into the flames and I wondered what I should do. Because I couldn't think precisely what, I asked, "How did you find out about his bank accounts?"

"It happened last week. I didn't know

you were interested then. I was arguing that the finance houses and their experts are lined up against the little man. Michael said that kind of thinking was for the plebs, so I said I was one of the plebs and to give me a demonstration. He got out his wallet and spread a whole heap of credit cards on the table. Then he showed me how he borrowed from A and B to buy foreign currency. The following month he borrowed from C and D to pay back A and B. It was at this point I accidentally knocked his wallet on the floor and there, as I was replacing the stuff, was his pretty pink cheque book."

"Hmm. It takes a lot of capital to play the currency markets."

Linda came back with a tray. She had forgotten I'd had scrambled eggs for breakfast. Just as I picked up my fork the telephone rang and she walked across the room to answer it. There was much prevarication but the caller was insistent on speaking to me. Stuffing my mouth full of eggs I picked up the phone. A deep authoritative voice went to a lot of trouble to verify my identity.

Finally he said, "My name is Chief

Superintendent Foster. I must ask you to come to the police station, Mr. Aitkin, or if it is more convenient, the local hospital."

"What's it about?"

"It's your Filipino maid, Elaina." He stumbled over the foreign name.

"Is she hurt?" The eggs were suddenly a solid lump.

"She was picked up near the river, on the steps of the Embankment, to be precise. Some of her friends found her."

There was a humming in my head and I waited for the familiar symptoms of shock to subside.

"I'll come to the hospital. Where shall I meet you?"

"At the mortuary, Sir."

I sat down rather hurriedly and E-Woh put the phone back on the hook. All I could think was, sod it, and on Ninoy's day.

2

IN the winter the provinces have a life all their own. Or perhaps it's the lack of life—the feeling of hibernation—the turning in on itself, till Spring. The soul of the Industrial Revolution clings to the streets and buildings, whether they be modern glass or ancient factories cheek by jowl, that have stuck it out from the turn of the century.

During the following two weeks it was a case of, if it's Tuesday it's Loughborough, and I drove between the various works anaesthetised by the cold and rain and sleet, which could turn to snow in a flash if I did anything silly like crossing the Pennines because it looked quicker on the map.

Towns had extended and there were complicated one way systems that hadn't been there three years ago. Consequently I didn't arrive at my various ports of call in the best of moods. Take Nottingham, it had taken me half an hour to get inside the place.

"Y'r can't park there y'r daft bugger. Can't you see we're unloading? Reps round the back."

Finally I'd parked in a street twenty minutes away and the idea of travelling incognito had lost its charm. When I did get inside the place the manager was away and the office staff looked shifty. After numerous phone calls they allowed me to look at the order books and I was horrified to find that they had only three months work booked. To say they were unhelpful is tantamount to comparing Filipino jails to seats of humanitarianism.

Information had to be chiselled out of them as if they'd signed the Official Secrets Act. When it was obvious I was getting nowhere I moseyed down to the factory floor on my own and started looking for familiar faces. One or two of the older men looked at me twice then looked away again—most stared blankly. I scrutinised the equipment. Nothing much had changed but it was going to take more than new machinery to alter the look on the men's faces.

By the door was a chap about my age who I remembered being famous for his union activities. I couldn't tell if he remembered me, but I indicated I wanted to talk to him. He gestured to another chap to watch his loom and came over. Perhaps he thought I was from the Safety Standards. As usual the relief from the noise was great when we were outside that door.

"Do you remember me? I'm Hubert Aitkin."

He fished out a cigarette and muttered over the flame, "I remember."

"Why is the work falling off?"

Furtive eyes watched us through the glass partition. Grudgingly he answered, "We're not told."

"Who comes up to supervise?"

"Mr. Turnbull, and he only comes to lay us off."

I looked at my watch and saw it was nearly knocking off time.

"Come on, we're going for a drink!"

He looked surprised as if drinking with the London lot was not the done thing and would prompt questions at the next union meeting. Ten minutes later we met at the bar of the pub next to the works. He had combed his hair when he'd got rid of his overalls and had on a leather jacket, the kind they sold in the market.

The publican had made a concession to the times by placing coasters on the grubby oak tables. I put down his pint in front of him. He had a face that had started to line and furrow as soon as he left his teens, but he started to relax when he'd swallowed three quarters of the beer.

"You'll be closing for Wakes week this year?" I wanted to give him time to get that stuff inside him.

"Depends."

"On what?"

"Mr. Turnbull says we work if the work's there this year, otherwise its time off without pay."

I made an effort to hide my surprise. The work force always have two weeks paid leave plus Bank Holidays. In fact, three years ago we were negotiating for three. I got up and went across to the bar for refills and noticed some stragglers from the works come in and place themselves in a position where they could watch us. I decided to push him. He'd be the butt of the other men's ridicule if he didn't have some information to pass on.

I sat down again and said, "Look here, Powell, I've got a lot of ground to cover. I shan't be coming back here for several months. It's obvious this place isn't a bundle of fun. What's gone wrong since I've been away? Are you going to tell me or are things to go on as they are?"

His face had that defensive, truculent look that our class system breeds.

"I'm on the floor Mr. Aitkin, I don't know what goes on upstairs."

"Well, let's hear an educated guess."

He didn't answer so I jogged him.

"When did the orders start dropping off?"

"When Turnbull started doing the inspections."

That came out fast enough.

"How do you account for that?"

He shook his head and stared into his glass. "I'll get the shove if he hears I've been talking."

I sighed, and fished out my wallet. I gave him one of my private cards.

"If anything like that happens, phone me."

He stared at the card then carefully put it away in his pocket. With dignity he got up to buy his round and when he returned I could see he'd decided to talk.

He took another long swig—Adams apple working like a piston, and the glass was back on the table before he began.

"I've got a cousin who works in the office of—". He mentioned a competitor of ours on the other side of the city.

"When the orders started to slow down I asked her if her place was in the same boat. No, she says, their order books were full. I was surprised. I thought, they're undercutting. But no, her best friend is in accounts and she found out there had been no price changes. So I asked my cousin to keep her eyes open and to tell me what she heard."

Now by nature Powell is not one of the world's great conversationalists. This must have been one of the longest spurts he had for a long time. I paced myself, trying not to hurry him.

"And did she find out anything else?"

"Yes. She told me that every time Turnbull paid us a visit he had lunch with their director."

He watched me, waiting for me to align myself with my own kind.

"Does he!"

I fished out my fags and offered them to Powell, trying hard not to jump to conclusions. There could be a simple explanation and I'm sure Michael would come up with one if asked, but Michael is not a simple man.

We chatted for a while. A lot of the older men had taken early retirements and been replaced by unskilled youngsters. A few things he said about the manager would need looking into. Then we went our separate ways.

With Nottingham and Loughborough behind me I drove on to Leicester to our prestigious shirt factory, in weather that couldn't decide between rain or snow and finally settled for the latter. And my luck turned. The manager was one of the old school and I'd forgotten to check if he'd retired. I should have known better. He wouldn't leave until they carried him out. He'd been with us for twenty years and, like Lloyd George, had known my father.

"I was coming to London to see you

Mr. Aitkin. Just giving you time to get over your sickly spell."

God,—I was pleased to see him.

"Well, I won't have to drag you round to the pub to make you talk," I said as he wrung my hand. I told him word for word what had happened at the other works.

"He's a crook, that Turnbull."

He stuffed his pipe vigorously.

"And your orders are running down?"

"Not a bit of it, orders is fine. He only wanted me to pass off cheap Japanese stuff as ours! To get the orders moving faster, you understand Mr. Aitkin."

"But he would have been caught. You would have told me."

"You weren't here to tell, Mr. Aitkin. He tried to cover it up when you were released."

We did go to the pub, but this time lunch in a nice Tudor dining room.

"When did he start this lark?" I asked over the steak.

"About eighteen months ago."

"How did you fob him off?"

"Threatened to report him to Mr. Winthrope. In fact I did pick up the phone one day but the poor gentleman was not

255

himself, what with all the extra work while you were away."

"What do you mean exactly?"

I didn't like talking about Charles behind his back, but this was too vague.

"It was the time everyone was running around in circles trying to get you out, Mr. Aitkin. I got the feeling that Mr. Winthrope didn't want to hear anything against that Turnbull. Not that I'm blaming him, you understand. It's not been easy running a big company like this on his own. Those buggers on the board don't work . . . they're just a lot of pretty names."

I don't know if I was shocked or relieved, but I knew one thing. I was exhilarated to have it out in the open.

The dining room had that half used lunchtime look when it nears two o'clock and staff were clearing up. But Ramsbottom hadn't finished yet.

"As it happened, I could tell Turnbull I'd had a word with his boss, and it worked. He kept out of my way when he was next in these parts. I knew I was on safe ground because, from what I hear, ours is the only plant making a healthy profit."

He shot me an astute look over his bifocals. "Are you going to be fit enough to take things on your shoulders Mr. Aitkin? We'd all be sorry if you sold up."

I took another baked potato and thought of all the redundancies if Charles and I did such a thing. I put my fork down and filled up his glass with dark red claret. They don't shilly-shally around with dry whites up here.

"Joe, do you think I'm going to let a little local fiddling defeat me when them foreigners didn't?"

He spluttered with laughter, making some corn filled statement on behalf of the men about the merits of me and Dad. The emotion of the moment put him off his cheese and I led him firmly back to the bar for a brandy.

The pattern repeated itself and was most pronounced in Manchester. In the mills the women cheered lewdly, comparing me with "that bugger Turnbull". I was pressed to overall-clad bosoms and kissed and I answered their "Are you better love's like a gent. Behind all the laughter I was very touched.

But there were small works where unemployment was bad, and here the bully reigned supreme. I came to recognise them as I walked in the door—before I looked at the books, before I started asking questions. Upstairs in the offices, eyes looked up sharply from typewriters, then quickly looked away.

Every night after my solitary dinner I phoned Linda, and then Charles.

"When will you be back Hugo? Sylvie isn't herself when you're away."

"And what about you, Honeychild?"

"I'm not myself either."

"The bugger! I promise you Hugh, no matter what the cost, I'll get him!" was Charles' usual reaction.

But tonight he said, "I think you'd better cut it short, things are happening."

"But I've just spoken to Linda."

Anxiety is a hard emotion to block.

"It's nothing like that. I put an enquiry agent on to Michael and he's come up with quite a mouthful."

"I thought we did that before?"

"You're thinking of the Americans."

"Can you talk about it?"

He paused, considering, "There's a lot of stuff to read, difficult to absorb over the phone."

"Give us a clue."

"Michael is involved with Garsales."

I didn't reply.

"Did you hear?"

"I heard. E-Woh's seen them together."

"There's more to this than casual meetings. There's another thing. That girl of yours, Elaina. The police say she was murdered."

"Murdered! I thought she drowned!"

I leant against the phone box feeling sick.

"The Path report says there was pressure on her neck before the drowning."

"Oh God! I'll come straight back. I wonder why Linda didn't say anything?"

"She's alright. Penny's been with her all day."

"Phone her for me Charles, say I'll be back about two."

Everyone should go away more so that

they can appreciate coming home. I don't mean to carry that logic to extremes as Linda and I did, but after those soulless hotels, the flat glowed. I hadn't thought of the place as home before, but tonight with daytime things scattered round the sitting room and the fire burnt low in the hearth I realised how lucky we had been to get it.

I crept into my daughter's room and watched her sleeping with a woollen teddy tight in her arms. Her eyes opened and she stared at me with sleep filled eyes.

"Dad," she said and flung herself over on her other side. I shut the door and started to peel off my clothes before going into our bedroom.

The bed was warm with Linda. She held out her arms.

"Hugo, Elaina."

When I'd finished kissing her, I said, "Tomorrow . . ."

"He doesn't own the Spanish villa."

It was the following evening and Charles had come back with me for a drink or two before toddling back to Chiswick. He pulled stacks of papers out of his briefcase and spread them over the dining room table, anchoring them in place with his gin and tonic.

"He doesn't own it," I reiterated.

I wasn't surprised. Somehow I couldn't see Michael tying up his capital in property. But it was in character to pretend to own it.

"Who does?"

Charles consulted a wad of papers stapled together.

"The *Escritura* is in the name of an Italian publishing company."

"I suppose he rents it."

"Perhaps, but it's not of great consequence because the subject now shifts to the publishing house. It was routine to put the company through the agency's computers and what came out was highly suspect. They own all sorts of holdings not related to publishing at all. That wouldn't have been unusual except that they were registered in the usual unsavoury places—Liechtenstein, Panama etc. And all these holdings had one thing in common. They lend money to private banks in peculiar places."

He thumbed through the papers.

"Here's a for instance."

He started to read: "*A private bank has been recently acquired in Buenos Aires, capital ten thousand dollars.*"

I took a swig of my gin. "The last of the big spenders!"

But Charles didn't laugh and continued reading from the enquiry agent's report:

"Our man on site has seen no clients enter the bank. Enquiries show that the sole purpose of this bank is to channel funds to an Italian company that makes Exocet missiles which are then sold back to the Argentinians. The bank's other clients are arms dealers functioning within the South American countries. These transactions are minor compared with the above currency movements and not relevant to the enquiry."

Charles leant forward, his thumb above a figure, "That's the gross sum that has passed through the bank's books during the past five months."

I stared at the sum, taking the papers from him to make sure I'd got the noughts in the right sequence.

"My God, could this be a mistake?"

Charles shook his head.

"Not this chap. He's a specialist in Continental finance."

Here a natural pause occurred when Sylvie decided to join us. She had changed out of her school uniform and was wearing one of last year's frocks which was too short. Spindly legs in socks were disproportionally long and, when she bent over, her knickers showed.

"Uncle Charles."

"Yes Petal."

"When can I come to your house?"

"Whenever you like."

"Yes, but when?"

Charles sorted papers and arranged them into new piles.

"What about Saturday? Why don't you phone Penny and ask her?"

Boredom lifted marginally and Sylvie's face brightened. She likes to have a project in hand. She hurried to the phone. I intercepted her.

"Use the kitchen phone, duck."

She shot across to the door. Before it banged I cautioned, "And when you've

263

finished find something incredibly useful to do."

I turned back to Charles.

"And Michael's connected with this lot? He'll have to go."

Charles shook his head. "He's only small fry. Better to watch him. There's more. I haven't come to the big stuff yet."

He accepted replenishments and leaned back in his chair.

"The company my chap works for has been engaged in long-term enquiries for firms that have had inexplicable goings on with their foreign branches. So far all their findings have led back to an Italian society called P2. When he put this Italian Publisher through the computers he found that they are on the list of members."

"What's P2?"

"It's an illegal Masonic Lodge called 'Propaganda Due', very powerful in Italy. I'd call it Fascist except the structure is more for personal power than politics. They have members in every walk of life —newspapers, television, the police, the courts, government, industry. Some even say the Vatican is involved. All people at the top. Their influence isn't confined to

Italy. It spreads to the USA and South America, hence the Buenos Aires connection. It's even rumoured they backed Gadaffi, Pinochet in Chile, and whatever passes for government in Peru. There's an archbishop in Chicago who's tainted with banking irregularities, suspect private banks in Bermuda. Oh, I could go on and on. Here." He pushed the thick file towards me. "You'll have to read it yourself. It's quite indescribable. He lit a cigarette, but immediately put it in the ashtray and hit himself on the forehead with the palm of his hand.

"Christ, I'm slipping. I've missed the most important thing. Whilst checking through the list of members of P2, who do you think he found? Garsales!"

"Garsales!"

". . .is a member of P2 . . ."

We stared at each other and I swear we were thinking the same thing. All this incestuous concern for the Group was only a small cog in a much greater plan. Garsales could have bought shares in the company through nominees to strengthen his hand when employed by us. But all this was only the tip of the iceberg.

"Hugh, I think I've been going up the wrong creek with these fears of a takeover. Something much bigger's going on."

"The thing is," I was struggling to think clearly, "have we got one problem or two separate ones?"

"You mean Michael as general fraudster and Garsales up to some devious business unconnected with us?"

I shook my head in bewilderment.

"I did mean that, but now you say it, it can't be right. I've got this gut feeling the two are connected!"

"Mmm."

"Look at it like this. Michael has had a completely free hand. No one's been checking on his movements."

"He seemed reliable. He's very competent."

"I'm not criticising. You've been too close to things. I've come back with a new eye, as it were, and the onlooker sees more of the game."

Charles took out some Panadol and swallowed them with the rest of his tonic. The truth is that Charles is a great number two and did brilliant work when my father was alive. It didn't stop there. He'd constructed the group from a legal stand-point as it had grown, but he is a man who needs partners. Perhaps I'm the same, perhaps we're all the same.

"Have you had a holiday whilst we've been away?"

He shook his head.

"Well, take one. Do it now."

"With all this on our plate? I can't Hugh!"

Exasperated I said, "Look mate, I'm back, in case you haven't noticed. Besides, I feel better and we've both taken a step forward. The factories need closer super-vision and I'm here to do it, and this stuff on Garsales clears the mists and points us in a direction we didn't even know existed."

But he's stubborn. "I'll take a holiday when you've had one."

I knew from his tone I wasn't going to budge him.

"I don't need one."

"You may not, but Linda does."

That jolted me. "I thought she was better."

He smiled. "Of course she's better. But

can't you see, she needs your undivided attention for a bit."

That brought me up short. I sat there struggling with a guilty conscience. That lovely hair hid a face that was still too thin. And she was quiet. Too often she sat sunk in her own thoughts. And I was too full of the company.

There was a sudden clamour on the stairs and the key rattled in the front door then a confusion of voices sounded in the lobby. Filipino chattering erupted into the sitting room as Linda and her cousin Roilo came in. The incident was a confirmation of Charles recent remarks. I'd forgotten all about Roilo's arrival, forgotten that Linda had gone to Heathrow to meet him.

"Roilo, how marvellous to see you, after all this time!"

I stood up and took the full force of his weight as he flung his arms around my shoulders.

"Hugo, how splendid, how splendid." He kept on repeating it. I felt myself drying up and somehow the words wouldn't come. I was so pleased to see him. His presence brought back the good years like a time warp. In an effort to dent the emotion-charged atmosphere I turned him in the direction of Charles and introduced them.

"Roilo, this is my partner, Charles Winthrope. Charles, this is Linda's cousin from Manila."

My friend was Roilo's friend and he pumped Charles' hand like mad. Then Linda came out of the bedroom and behind the excitement and stimulation I saw fear. She walked across to me and wrapped her arms around my waist and I could feel a slight tremor where her body touched mine.

I held her at arms' length and asked "What is it?"

"Who do you think we saw at Arrivals?"

"Who?"

"Garsales."

As she said the word her arms tightened in a mini convulsion.

"On his own?"

"Yes, waiting."

"For the same flight as Roilo?"

"Yes. Of course I didn't know that at the time. He kept checking the indicators. Then he started waving and I caught sight of the flight number on a passenger's case

269

and knew it was the same. I turned to look at the crowd coming towards us. I had to know who he was meeting. Two people, a man and a woman raised their hands and I recognised the man. It was Herrera, my boss in Manila."

"Herrera!"

The last time I'd seen Edgardo Herrera —Professor of English at the Ateneo de Manila University rushed into my mind. With Garsales. Talking to me so blandly when Linda was probably already in jail. I was more than ready to think the worst of Herrera.

"And the woman? Did you recognise her?"

"She kept on turning away. She was wearing a fur coat and hat. It was pulled down over her face. I can't be sure, but it could have been his sister."

Linda's face had gone grey.

"Herrera's sister? I didn't know he had one."

"No, Garsales' sister."

Why should this sound so ominous? Had E-Woh mentioned a sister? I couldn't remember.

"How did you know Garsales had a sister?"

Linda opened her mouth to answer but she had to stop.

"He used to bring her into the prison to watch the proceedings."

A bubble of horror burst and drifted around the room, bits catching and clinging to each one of us. Over Linda's shoulder I watched Charles' face become transfixed. Roilo rushed across the room and seized her in his arms and rocked and crooned.

"When they thought I was unconscious they talked about a plan to get her to America." Her face was quite blank now. A wave of desolation caught me as I thought of all the conversations each of us had had with Garsales. Conversations that we couldn't bring ourselves to tell the other.

We talked into the night—not watching the clock. Once I was in the kitchen cooking spaghetti. Roilo was beside me levering off the lids of sauce Milanaise. He talked all the time, possibly because we'd had a lot to drink, each trying to blot out the picture Linda's words had evoked.

271

"When I was hiding out in Mindanao I heard his name mentioned a lot. It was linked with a certain General who has aspirations to replace our beloved leader. Hugo, I can't budge this top, do it for me." He handed over the jar.

Leaning on the sink, he said, "Do you know what the going rate is to be a Marcos goon these days?"

I bent down to get a dish for the spaghetti out of the cupboard and shook my head.

"Eight hundred pounds!"

"Many takers?"

"Many many takers! They get tee shirts with a picture of Marcos fighting off Japanese guerillas *and* a comic book with all his exploits!"

"Roilo, get back to Garsales."

I tipped the spaghetti into a collander and the steam rose to the ceiling enveloping our faces in a damp cloud.

"He's the General's treasurer and fund raiser."

"How can he do that from England?"

"I don't know how he does it, Hugo. There must be many different ways, but I did hear of a blackmail system he's got going amongst expatriate Filipinos. He has agents who spread alarmist tales amongst these people. You know the sort of thing, money needed or the goons will burn down their crops, . . . money to get a relative out of prison, money for food, money for illness. The poor things have no way to check these stories. They press their savings into the hands of these evil ones. Leave it to us, we will see your people are OK. Just sign this little bit of paper to say I can act for you. It's a tax form so that we can claim back the tax for our charity. Charity they understand. Papers they respect!"

He went to a drawer and collected forks. "Then there's the Nominee Shareholders fraud which is similar but the signature on the papers is more important than the money."

He followed me into the dining room with the plates whilst I thought about the Filipino faces on the stairs the day that Elaina died.

After we had finished our cordon bleu food Charles cornered Roilo. They sat very close to the fire, because Roilo was feeling the cold, and talked and talked. I half listened as Linda made the coffee.

"You think it was a put up job?" Charles asked.

Roilo shrugged. "Who knows? Perhaps he saw an opportunity to become legitimate when he found they were in his jail. But that could be an over simplification and I, personally, don't believe it. In my view they were picked out, put on ice, as it were."

He flicked his ash in the flames. "If his sister was involved, as Linda said, then I favour the latter idea."

There it was again. I sat forward on the edge of my chair.

"Tell me about this sister. What's her name?"

"Rosana Garsales. She lives in New York now."

Roilo's expression was a picture. He was trying hard to behave like the lawyer he nearly was—objective and factual—but he wasn't succeeding.

"She influences Imelda, who's always visiting the States. She's behind the freeing of Ninoy for the heart surgery."

I felt a bit bewildered.

"Well, that's something in her favour, I suppose."

I jumped at the snort-come-roar that exploded from Roilo.

"Hugo, stop thinking like an Englishman! Whoever wins in the next few years, whatever changes take place, Garsales and his sister are going to be on the winning side. If Marcos hangs on he will remember those who have supported him. If the Generals oust him they will reward their own. And if Ninoy shoves them all out he will think like you because he's a decent man. He will always remember that the name Garsales gave him another chance."

I opened my mouth to say something but Roilo hadn't finished.

"Do me a favour Hugo! If you are ever tempted to think anything good of those two, don't. Keep your mind on the very worst always and you will still be nowhere near comprehending them."

He started to recount endless stories of deaths relating to land deals . . . whole villages laid to waste . . . children massacred . . . and Garsales' name featured in all of them.

When Linda came in with the coffee he made a super effort to talk of other things and Charles helped him with vague advice about law courses. He got up as soon as he had finished, complaining of jet-lag. He certainly looked exhausted. But he turned, his hand on the door knob of his room.

"In case I forget, there's something you should know. Did you know they are twins?"

"Do they look alike?"

"Not particularly."

"What then?"

"They have identical handwriting."

"You mean there's no difference at all?"

"That's it exactly. They can forge each other's signature."

3

I WAS awake early next morning and my brain was goading me to get up and make a start—to pick up the threads where we left off last night. Linda's face was tender and untroubled in sleep so I eased myself stealthily out of the bed. Without opening her eyes she stretched and spread her limbs luxuriously over my space.

While the coffee was bubbling and dripping from one glass bowl to the other I went through the papers Charles had left me to read. I put the papers on P2 to one side to read later, and read the agent's earlier reports, then scribbled Garsales' address on a pad. On the same page was the branch of his bank and I made a note to see the manager.

Today I had to take refuge in action or I'd lose my marbles. Today had to be spent away from this flat; away from last night's faces and last night's memories. Today I was going to catch up with

Garsales and stop this manipulation by other countries' shitty politics. Today I was going to make it *go away!*

She'll be alright, I thought, as I put on my jacket. She's got Roilo and Sylvie.

It was still very early and the air was full of a false spring, all signs of snow vanished. A milk float bumbled along the road and bottles clinked in doorways. I crossed the bridge and found myself in Cheyne Walk where pale-faced au pairs peeped out of doorways as if to orientate themselves in this foreign city. One girl stared at me, trying to relate me with her new employer, then realising her mistake, siezed the milk and rushed indoors.

Then I was in back streets . . . passed a hospital . . . Beaufort Street . . . Drayton Gardens . . . then Gloucester Road tube station at the end of the road. Cromwell Road's broad expanse presented itself and double decker buses slid out of the Air Terminal buildings and turned south. A member of London Transport was smoking an early morning fag so I shoved Garsales' address under his nose. He shook his head. I suggested he might have a map but couldn't gain his interest. Finally, I caught a taxi which drove me round in circles and we ended suspiciously near our starting point.

What can I say about that neutral block of flats? Faceless in it's dateless beige and brown paint. I stood staring at the dusty cards over the bells; they were very old and tattered and I had the feeling that the occupants didn't take the question of identity too seriously. There was no card over Garsales' number so I pressed the porter's bell. A long way off there was a grinding sound and the door moved imperceptibly on its hinges.

Lies filled my head as I walked towards the uniformed figure drinking tea and doing his pools. A friend, I expounded, wanted to sublet his flat due to the fact that his company had to pay a year's rent in advance and why should these property boys have it all their own way? I leant over and pointed to a likely draw, leaving a five pound note on his coupon. The porter seemed weighed down with a terrible boredom but he got to his feet and led me to an iron cage. Silently and slowly we rose to the sixth floor. Numbly I followed him along the deserted strip of beige carpet and watched as, with old world charm, he shifted his fag and dragged out a huge bunch of keys. He flung the door back and I was just in time to see the room was in darkness before it rebounded on an inside wall and slammed shut again. We had more luck on the second attempt and he pushed passed me and jerked up a blind.

More beigeness covered the floors and a coffee table that had once been teak stood in the middle of the room. The carpet round it was splattered with old stains. A sofa and chairs, again beige, were grouped around the table and a gate-legged table was pushed against a wall. I looked into the kitchenette, where mildew was pervasive, then headed for the bedroom.

Thin folded blankets and two stained pillows graced the divan; but there were cupboards and a chest of drawers. The porter was still occupied with the view so I opened the doors of the cupboard, looking under the shelves as well as on them, and found nothing. When I jerked the thing away from the wall, the result again was a big 0.

Exasperated I turned to the chest of

drawers and started wrenching at the drawers. The whole flat was permeated with staleness and damp-cloth cleaning of an elementary kind. But here in the bedroom the smells were overlaid with Garsales' aftershave, a fact that made me nervy and exhilarated at the same time. The drawers were warped with damp but I persevered, convinced that everyone left something behind in their travels. The bottom drawer was empty except for grubby lining paper with nothing beneath it and so was the middle drawer. I was nearly defeated by the top drawer when a card that had been used as a wedge between the drawers and the base fell onto the lining of the middle one. I picked it up and palmed it into my pocket as the porter was dropping matches into the ashtray en route for the bedroom. I muttered something about bringing my things round that evening and we returned to the lift.

Once on the pavement I looked round for a call box and phoned the bank manager. He had half an hour free in forty-five minutes.

Now ideally Charles should have been

participating in this part of the manoeuvre because he was the one who had introduced Garsales to Spalding, the manager. But Charles had nobbled me in the kitchen at about two o'clock this morning in an over-excited state with other fish to fry. His computers had come up with the fact that Michael had built up more than a five per cent interest in the stock in the company accounting period. Under the Company Securities Act this fact should have been declared, and hadn't. The Act was very hot on staff fiddles for personal gain, so Charles was going to get the pot simmering because Michael's days were numbered.

So that was why I was sitting in the anonymous plushness of the manager's waiting room considering what line I should take. The enquiry agent's findings had come to a halt when the bank put the mockers on information about Garsales' account, saying it was a breach of confidentiality. The only information the agent had obtained was that the account was closed and had been cleared two weeks ago; at approximately the same time as I was on my grand tour. It also coincided with the fact that Garsales hadn't been near his dockland office during this period.

It was essential that I unblocked this stoppage in this mad game of snakes and ladders, because money was one of the chief ingredients.

"Good morning, Mr. Aitkin."

The hand was out, the guileless smile in place.

"Mr. Spalding." I wrung his hand with true sincerity.

We eyed each other across his desk and he expounded on the subject that the fact that we had not previously met had left a vacuum in his life. He enquired about Charles and all the little Winthropes, then, with infinite patience turned his enquiries closer to home. How was my health? How were my family? Was I settling to work again after my misfortune? It was at this point, from the slightly fixed look in his eyes, the almost concealed curiosity, that I realised he was identifying with me; that awful word "hostage" was uppermost in his mind.

Bracing myself, I socked it to him from beginning to end. I told him things about Garsales that should have been locked away for ever. I told him about the jail, about McMahon, about the effect of unspecified time, and I tried to tell him about Linda . . . but had to stop . . .

"Can you imagine what it's like to have that creature working in my company?" The room was full of the unspeakable. Speaking for myself, I could have done with a drink. To keep a grip on things I brought the subject back to our anxieties about the Group. He seemed relieved to return to the things he had been trained to deal with.

"We're not living in chivalrous times, Mr. Aitkin. Competitors take advantage of any situation. It's a jungle out there. My advice to you and Mr. Winthrope is to come down hard on them. Sue non-payers left and right, get yourself a name for being hard men. Make them aware that you are back and things are changing. At the same time appreciate the fact that you are both probably over-reacting, seeing the situation as one great enormity—it would be surprising if you saw it any other way. From a practical viewpoint, the ideal thing would be to find someone you can trust and have him buy up all the small lots.

Then you will have more control. The company troubles stem from the fact that you have both lost control. And that's a bad thing."

Of course he was right, but he didn't know about our dearth of capital.

"Perhaps you might consider selling some less profitable concerns. It would maximise your capital. What about an independent assessment? The bank could fix that."

"I've been thinking along those lines, but quite honestly I don't trust my own judgement at the moment. Too much is happening too fast and with Garsales on the loose I'm for ever looking over my shoulder. He's not your average client Mr. Spalding. If I could get something concrete on him I'd make a report to the Home Office. He's not a British citizen and he's only here on a temporary permit!"

I watched the man struggling with the bank employee, finally Spalding got up and went over to the door with its double locking device. He fiddled with keys attached to his person, locks clicked and he went out. I sat there trying not to think claustrophobic thoughts until he returned with a file in his hand. The file had a section for correspondence, he removed the contents and spread letters on the desk, comparing dates with those in a ledger.

"You know the account was closed three weeks ago?"

"Yes."

"It has only been active for a matter of months."

"Quite."

"Normal household accounts, nothing out of the way."

Then why did you bother to get his file, I thought, if it was all so normal?

"I'll come to the point Mr. Aitkin. The only unusual transaction was the purchase of a yacht."

"A yacht!"

"A very expensive sea-going yacht. I remember being surprised that a relatively new client should embark on such an enormous outlay."

A yacht! I hadn't somehow connected Garsales with nautical activities.

"How big was it?"

286

Spalding consulted a document. "Fifty metres. Turbo Charged Diesel," he read.

"Impressive. He won't be sailing that on the Serpentine! How was it paid for?"

"A draft on a New York account."

"Whose signature was on it?"

"His own. It was his account. The money was transferred."

"Which was checked, of course?"

"Naturally." Spalding looked slightly defensive. "I'm sorry, I haven't made it clear. He said he was buying for a syndicate; he paid one quarter of the total and asked the bank to cover him for ten days until the other three cheques arrived."

"And did you?"

"As it so happens we did. The Southampton shipping brokers gave a good report and Garsales took out insurance to cover the period. I can't say I would have done it if Mr. Winthrope hadn't introduced him to the bank. Anyway, there was no delay. The drafts arrived on the day he promised." He was frowning now, and I thought even bankers have near misses.

"And the monies came from . . . . ?"

"Italy. All three came from Italy."

And that was all he was going to tell me. No dice when I tried to find out which Italian banks, or which town they had been issued from. Talk of the cheques had brought about a return of banking caution.

It was nearly midday and I had time for a sandwich before returning to my office. Then, because I was near, I popped into my tailors. When I say my tailors, I really mean my father's. Linda had been hounding me to get a new suit, aided and abetted by my mother who had been encouraging her to burn my entire wardrobe as Oxfam would refuse them on the grounds of hygiene.

Chatting to Maurice is pure pleasure. He is one of the old school and talks about my father as if he was a founder member of his emporium. In fact Maurice had underwritten my father's purchases for years. Every year when Dad took his leave he allowed Maurice to talk him into being measured for a new suit on the understanding that he didn't send in the account for six months. When the statement arrived on dense white vellum, glorious in it's embossed perfection—Gentleman's

Outfitters and Tailors, Saville Row—David Aitkin Esq was in some other remote corner of the world. The bill was chucked in a drawer with others and forgotten. Six months later, if he remembered, he sent off a cheque for half the cost. But my father recommended him to other expatriates and Maurice, who had never left these safe shores, had a continuous trail of overseas clients, and lived the life of a surrogate traveller. When I was winding up Dad's affairs after his death I found that he was three suits in arrears.

Maurice was dealing with an Arab gentleman when I made my way through those discreet portals. His face lit up when he saw me, but composed itself as I examined ties. He indicated a changing room and the Arab disappeared in a rustle of starched sheets.

"Mr. Hugh Sir, your fitting's just ready."

He always called me Mr. Hugh Sir and made me feel as if I was still being kitted out for boarding school. Maurice has a way of raising a hand and little Maurice comes running. This happened today and I was

helped into an intimidatingly smart charcoal grey suit. He slashed it freely with
white chalk.

"The family's well?" he asked but his
mind was on the suit. He focused on my
reflection in the mirror and asked, "Now
how do you like that Mr. Hugh Sir? Very
smart if I may say so."

I, in my turn, was waved to the
changing rooms and the Arab left discon-
certingly in jeans.

Back in the body of the shop Maurice
had his pencil poised over his appointment
book and asked, "Next Wednesday?"

I nodded and he replaced the pencil in
the back of the stiff exercise book and shut
it firmly. Then he leant on the glass counter
. . . Maurice was now ready for the
important things.

"You've put on a bit of weight since
your last fitting Mr. Hugh, I'm glad to say
—too thin you were. Now tell me about
Mrs. Aitkin Snr. Is she still in London or
has she returned to Kenya?"

I was happy to be able to tell him that
my mother was again taking charge in the
Colonies. He reminisced about a geranium

coloured suit he had made for her once for Founder's Day.

"And how is young Mrs. Aitkin? Getting over that nasty business, is she?"

I assured him that the "nasty business" was quite behind us. Then he surprised me by thanking me for sending him a new client, a Filipino gentleman. I couldn't think who it was, unless it was Linda's property chap, because our people couldn't afford Maurice's prices.

"Very charming gentleman. Said he knew you when you were both living in Manila. Very superior type of person I thought, Mr. Hugh Sir."

A horrible premonition started to creep over me and I stared at Maurice as though he had admitted keeping snakes for a hobby.

"What's his name?"

"Mr. Jamie Garsales."

"Oh yes." I assumed a degree of normality but all those weird coversations about London came rushing back. "How far is it from the Strand to the City, Hugo? Can you walk? Do the buses run from the City to Buckingham Palace and why is

London University in so many different buildings?"

"Are you feeling unwell Mr. Hugh Sir?"

"Fit as a flea Maurice. Did he leave an address?"

The address Maurice gave me was off the Cromwell Road.

"When is his next appointment?"

"The gentleman isn't coming in again. He arranged to have the suit forwarded to his new address in Weybridge."

"I'd quite like to look him up. Can you give me the Weybridge address?"

"He's phoning me about that, Mr. Hugh. Something about completion and not wanting to risk the suit being lost in the post."

"Ahh, well as long as he doesn't pull my father's trick." Maurice's face broke into a grin which I can only describe as artful.

"Paid in full at the first fitting." He seemed regretful. "They don't make them like Mr. David any more."

I got back home at about seven. Charles had been deep in conference with the accountant so I'd decided to phone him with the day's findings later in the evening. The phone was ringing dolefully as I walked in, as phones do in an empty house. I had a premonition that it was long distance as I walked across the sitting room to answer it.

"Hello."

The sound of the ether drifted down the wires and a woman's voice reverberated with that playback effect. "Hello-llo-llo."

"Is that my mother speaking."

"Hugh? Where have you been? I've been ringing all day."

"I have been working Ma." She has difficulties with time-change. "And I'm very well. How are you?"

She ignored this. "Hugh, I have a favour to ask."

"Oh yes." My voice was wary.

"Klaus is ill. He's coming to London to see a consultant."

"I'm sorry to hear that." This wasn't strictly true as I had little room for my father's ex-partner. The reason escapes me why Sarah remained on good terms with him. But she knows I don't approve. Mothers are hard to control.

"When is he coming?"

"He's on the plane now. He'll be in London tomorrow morning."

When I didn't answer her voice became more urgent. "Hugh, I want him to stay with you. He's too ill to go to a hotel."

But I didn't want Klaus in my flat for an indefinite period.

"That wouldn't be awfully convenient. Why can't he stay in your flat?"

"Because I no longer have a flat. If you remember it was on a six monthly lease. He won't be under your feet, because he's going to Guy's for tests."

"Doesn't he know anyone else in London?"

"You know he doesn't!"

I dropped the pretence of being civil. "Then why doesn't he go back to Germany?"

"Hugh! Don't be so vile!"

"Does he hear from Liang these days?"

There was a fraught pause. "Is Linda there?"

"No. My wife is out." The silence was nasty.

Her voice was distant when she spoke again. "Hubert, if you don't do this for me—I'm sorry to say this—but if you don't take Klaus in when he is too ill to look after himself, I shall not be available to vote in your favour at the next board meeting."

A wave of rage surged through me and I don't know how I resisted the temptation to slam down the phone.

A key rattled in the door and I snapped, "Flight number?"

"K/347," and the line went dead.

When Linda came in with Sylvie I was sitting in a chair with a large whisky. I glowered at them.

"Prepare yourselves for a holiday," I snapped.

Later, after Sylvie's reluctant departure to bed Linda asked, "Why do you dislike him?"

"He did the dirt on my father when he was in China looking for E-Woh's mother. He threw in his lot with Liang, a Chinese who tried to ruin us in 1963. They went to prison and I've always half blamed Klaus for Dad's death."

"Then why is Sarah still friendly with him?"

A good question, one I'd often asked

myself. "The parents had been separated for a long time. Mum was keen on him."

"Then there must be more to it than you knew. Sarah's no fool."

This I didn't want to hear. Wives should keep over-simplifications to themselves.

"I'll make up a bed for him. What time is he coming?"

At the door she turned and asked, "Are we really going on holiday? Where are we going?"

I took the card out of my jacket that I had found in Garsales' flat. It wasn't a visiting card. It was a mooring card for a marina in Andalucia.

"Spain."

Klaus arrived after lunch on the following day. In spite of everything, I was shocked to see how he had changed. He was wearing that faded expat's suit which hung in my mother's wardrobe and only surfaced on the rare occasions he left Africa. But today it hung on him as if it belonged to someone else and his leanness had turned to stooping thinness. His blond hair had lost its life and drooped lankly away from his forehead.

After he came out of jail he could never work inside. In the club once in Nairobi a man I knew slightly had said he was working for the rebel forces in the Southern Sudan. It sounded feasible . . . Klaus as a mercenary . . . but I could never bring myself to ask my mother about it. Some years ago I'd heard about a German organising the tribes in the Equitorial South against the Muslim North. Once I came home unexpectedly and he came striding in as the sun was setting— mahogany brown, in khaki, blue eyes glinting with health. The thing I remember most clearly was how pleased he was to see me . . . but then it wasn't Klaus' nature to hang his head about the past. It was me that was ashamed that, in his presence, I couldn't maintain my grudge. Also I was peeved that he didn't see me as myself—a person in my own right, as the rest of the world saw me. He saw me only as Sarah's son . . .

But time passes and today was different. The colour had faded from those blue eyes. Very correctly he acknowledged each one of us, lingering over Linda— observing her with care. Then he asked if he might lie down for a short while. I saw him swallowing pills in the bathroom.

He had an appointment in Harley Street the following day and in the evening I asked him how he had got on.

"It was as I had expected," he said and went on to talk of other things.

After that he went to Guy's Hospital each morning. In the afternoon, after a rest, he walked in the park with Linda and Sylvie. They seemed to get on very well.

"He's a lovely man, Hugo." Linda had found a friend.

"He's got a way with women," I grunted.

"Yes. I can see that." She seemed pleased that I could see his good points. Filipinos are obsessed with good points.

One evening after he had started to look better, he shot up from the dinner table and rushed into the bathroom. We could hear him being very sick.

When he returned he sat in an armchair saying, "I'm sorry. I'm so sorry . . ."

Linda rushed across to him. "You mustn't be sorry, don't be sorry," she soothed.

Awkwardly I handed him some Perrier water.

He caught my arm and said, "Hubert, I must talk to you."

I sat down and waited. He sipped the water with care, waiting to see how it was going to affect him. Gradually he started to look better and his colour improved.

"Hubert, when you were in prison I helped Sarah with a number of things." He paused and I wondered what they could have been. Other people's lives were a blank during that period.

"I got to know Linda's father. We talked a lot on the telephone. At first it was about people we should contact. He felt isolated in Hong Kong. Then, when there was hope that you both might be released, there were the authorities to deal with. Of course, Peter Hennessy did far more than I did by keeping you both in the news, but that is another story. The long and the short of it is, it became a habit. We phone each other once a week."

I could imagine them pontificating over the airways.

"To get to the point of my story, when Linda's cousin Roilo arrived in Hong

Kong with up to date news of the Philippines the subject of blackmailing expatriate Filipinos came up. The Doc talked to people he knew, people who went back to see their families regularly. He questioned them and they brought back information. They also brought back papers and gradually a picture formed. Amongst those papers were indications that unsavoury people were buying into Western companies, using unlettered peasants as Nominees."

How it took me back to hear Klaus talking of "Unlettered peasants".

The epithet peasant, hurled at someone with a flash of icy contempt, was the intrinsic essence of his character. People were categorised by intellect in his order of importance.

"The Doc rented a room, and sorted and filed those papers. The Filipino maids in Hong Kong gossipped to each other and vied to return with a paper in their hands. Some, of course, were useless, but *some* had the name of your company on them."

He had paused for effect in his Teutonic way and I watched, astonished as the old Klaus emerged, dominating his frail body.

"Anna has been helping the Doc for the past three weeks. She shows the girls one of your papers and offers them some pesos if they can find any more like it. Gradually the area where the men had been canvassing clarified. The Doc started paying for the girls' flights and they were swamped with documents. Now . . . this is our plan, the Doc and I will buy back those shares and your company will be safe again."

I felt bowled over by this saga. "You are talking about a great deal of money, Klaus."

"That is no problem. The Doc and I have raised the money."

A terrible doubt crept into my mind. He's trying to get back into the company, and I was never going to have that.

"We are going to offer them a small profit on their shares. The Doc will be the treasurer and co-ordinator—"

"And who will own these shares that you are about to purchase?"

He looked surprised. "They will be divided equally between all the Aitkins on the Board. How else are we to negate the hold Garsales has over you?"

"And you Klaus, you and the Doc, surely you both want something in return for your capital?"

He smiled then. "Allow us to do this for you, Hubert. The Doc wants only your and Linda's happiness, and a few basic changes in his country, of course. As for myself, I shan't be needing anything."

Suddenly he looked shrunken and exhausted again, and excusing himself, went to bed.

During the following weeks our share prices rose and Charles was over the moon. I read the financial papers from cover to cover each day and was lulled into a false sense of security. By chance, when I was about to chuck some out, I turned to the back page of a prominent paper. They ran a light gossip column read by commuters which had become more and more deadly of late. The columnist was intent on sowing mayhem and had recently announced his intention of "boring into" insider trading. He had also coined the phrase "junk bond" which was a high yielding and risky form of borrowing used by companies in trouble. I read the devastating entry with horror.

"Is it possible that Insider Buying could account for the brisk movement in the Aiktin Group during the past month?

"Could the use of junk bonds have improved the health of the company along with the health of the chairman— Hubert Aitkin?

"This company could stand watching."

Underneath, in small print, were two lines saying that the Group would be the subject of a feature in the Business News on Sunday.

Four days later there it was, spread all over the front page. It was headed "Disappearance of a Filipino Business Man". First there was a resumé of my incarceration in a notorious Manila prison. Then, on page seventeen, they had really gone to town. They talked at length about a brave Filipino army officer, who, at enormous personal risk had been responsible for my escape. How, in the first flush of exhilaration at my new found freedom I had

303

offered him a job. But, when every day normality returned I had regretted my action and delegated him to work that was an insult to his intelligence. There followed hints and innuendos that pointed to illegal trading practices. The writer continued with financial details of the Group, the Silk Farm, and our private trust fund. The final paragraph explored the details of Garsales' disappearance, implying that we had driven him out. He ended by urging Garsales to sue for wrongful dismissal.

I chucked the bloody thing on the floor and picked up the phone to speak to Charles, before remembering that Penny had forced him away for the weekend. Klaus, Linda and Sylvie were in the park. I walked out onto the balcony wondering how I was going to get through the rest of the weekend without talking to someone.

The street was empty as people digested their Sunday lunch. Two people and a child turned the corner. Even at that distance I could see that they were distressed. The child was Sylvie and she was calling out to the others and running and waving at me.

I tore down the stairs and into the street just before Linda collapsed. I caught her in my arms. "What's happened? What's happened?"

"Just shock, only shock!" Klaus explained.

"Tell me! For Christ sake, tell me!"

I watched Klaus' hand come up to his face . . . watched the tremor.

"We were by the swings. I had my back to Linda because I was pushing Sylvie. She was near some trees on the edge of the recreation ground. Suddenly I heard her shriek as if she had been trying to contain it, but the scream had been forced out of her. A man was standing near her, very near her. His hands were inside her clothes, all over her. She was petrified, unable to move."

For a second I thought I was going mad, then Klaus continued.

"I ran. Sylvie was good, staying where I told her to stay. When the man saw me coming he stepped back into the trees and disappeared. I could hear him laughing." The memory of that laughter brought Klaus' account to a halt.

"When I came back to Linda she was

shaking terribly and fighting to control herself because of Sylvie. She was breathing so fast and in between those breaths she kept saying Garsales, Garsales."

I thought my head would burst with tension. I struggled to get her on her feet, up the steps, through the front door. On the stairs she put her feet on each step, but her legs gave way. By the time we reached the sitting room she was a dead weight. Klaus helped support her and Sylvie flitted around, half frightened, half excited.

We put her on the sofa and Klaus tried to give her brandy.

"You've got to get her away," he kept saying. "Nothing else matters . . . right away . . . right away . . ." He dabbed her blouse, where the brandy had spilled, with his handkerchief. Looking up at me he asked, "Hasn't she told you about it?"

I shook my head. "Has she talked to you?"

Slowly he nodded, as if the weight of the unbearable was upon him.

4

"**K**LAUS, nip up stairs and ask E-Woh to come down. I'm not leaving Linda alone, not for a minute. When you're out she must stay with her."

Linda was in the bedroom, drinking lots of sweet tea and making a good show of having got over it. But she was wearing three sweaters, and still shaking.

"How could I have made such a display? Why didn't I kick him in the groin? It was such a shock. I hadn't thought about him at all today."

"Thank God you weren't alone. Klaus is right. We've got to get away."

I felt suspended with shock and total disbelief. Why can't I take it in that Garsales is the sort of man that goes around touching up women in parks? It's not surprising when you think of his past. I'm not being any comfort to Linda because that bugger's getting too close, forcing me to think of things I've shut away, concealed from myself.

"Will you be alright? I'm just going to make a phone call."

I picked up the phone and dialled the number of the detective I'd met in connection with Elaina's death. The ringing went on for a long time, because it was Sunday, I suppose, and I was beginning to think that calls were transferred to other police stations. Then a hoarse voice spoke and I asked for Chief Superintendent Foster. The voice demurred but didn't actually say the chief wasn't there, so I persisted and was very relieved when finally that quiet unflappable personage was on the line.

I launched into the subject of my identification but he remembered me at once so there was no delaying the details of what must be a very common occurence to a policeman.

"There's no doubt about the identification of the attacker, Sir?"

"No possible doubt. My wife's had too much to do with him to make a mistake."

He asked questions about place and time, before remarking, "From the newspapers it appears that this Garsales doesn't work for you any more. Could this incident be in the nature of a grudge attack, Mr. Aitkin?"

This was difficult to answer. "It could be. Perhaps he thought it might deter my partner and I from taking steps to have him deported. But it's a strange way to go about it."

"The circumstances are strange."

He talked about coming round to take a statement but I dissuaded him, saying it would upset Linda and that we were going away at the first opportunity. Finally, he agreed to start a search for Garsales and possibly induce him to leave the country voluntarily. I gave him the address of the empty flat and mentioned the house in Weybridge, along with the name of Spalding's bank and the secretary who worked for him at the docks office.

I was replacing the receiver, feeling comforted that Garsales' name was on police files at last, when Klaus came into the sitting room, holding a letter in his hand.

"She doesn't appear to be here, and her clothes are missing."

I opened the note and recalled that I

hadn't seen E-Woh for several days. It said:

Stumblebum, I'm on to something. I have allowed the ghastly Michael to lure me to Amsterdam for the weekend. We may go on to Spain but, never fear, I'll phone before he has me on the streets. DON'T tell Mum. Love to Linda,
                    Your obedient sister, E-Woh

I stared at the scrawl sloping across the page and didn't like it at all. The situation had taken a nasty turn since our conversation and the thought of E-Woh drifting around Europe with Michael did nothing to improve my day. I handed it back to Klaus.

"Does she often go off like this?" he asked.

"No she doesn't, but she's had more freedom since we've lived in London. I suppose she thinks she's helping."

I was irritated. Irritated with the inconsequential behaviour of youth, and not a little alarmed. I sat down with a whisky and tried to sort out the convoluted parcel of thoughts jostling my mind. A tantalising smell of garlic emanated from the kitchen, reminding me that Klaus was doing his thing with goulash tonight. The smells lured Linda out of the bedroom and she sat on the rug by the fire.

"Are we really going tomorrow?"

"We are really going tomorrow."

"Would it be better to leave a message for Charles? He might want to put it off."

"Don't worry! I'm putting you first this time."

She seemed satisfied and went into the kitchen. Through the open door I watched her roll out Klaus' semolina dumplings and listened to them talking about Dutch veal and trout. Food is morphia in this household.

"Will you be alright on your own?" Linda asked. There was a pause then Klaus was in the doorway.

"I can move to a hotel, it's no trouble," he said.

Linda answered him before me. "Certainly not! I'm not hearing of that. You're in charge whilst we are away." Turning to me she asked, "What about flights?"

"Flights be damned! We're going to

potter down to Dover and get the ferry and drive through France."

Klaus walked in with a steaming dish and Sylvie followed like a Bisto kid. Sternly I said to my daughter, "Go and pack, we're going on holiday tomorrow."

"Shan't! I'm busy with Uncle Klaus' supper!"

"OK, but we *could* go without you!"

We were still fraught on the ferry. My own particular difficulty was keeping an eye on Linda and Sylvie at the same time. Sylvie had never been on a ship before and was determined to check all systems. She disappeared for long spells. We consulted our watches, and concentrated on the approaching shores of France. White limbed tourists in improbable summer gear milled about with children strapped to their backs. When Boulogne was almost on the deck I could stand it no longer and leapt up, spilling coffee. At the same moment a naval type loomed in a doorway with Sylvie attached to his hand. I shall never understand why, amongst those milling hordes, he made straight for me.

Three hours later we approached a small

town and it's market and dredged up sufficient impaired French to buy some comestibles for lunch. Sylvie consumed bread and paté without throwing up and we all stared at the flat fields of northern France.

At seven o'clock, our hip bones set in their socket, we stepped out onto foreign pavements and made for an auberge. In the restaurant I hissed at Sylvie, "Choose from the table d'hote."

"Why?" she queried, in a voice that sensed treachery.

"Because I say so."

"I want that." She stabbed her finger at a shell fish dish with a price that made my hair stand on end. Sylvie is precociously adept at reading menus.

I guided her finger towards the dish of the day and her suspicions increased.

"What's that? I don't like it!"

"Tripe."

Heads turned as her sobs filled the room. Centuries of prejudice permeated that French restaurant.

"Let her have what she likes," Linda muttered.

The waiter sniffed at my accent. Food

arrived on the native's table before ours. But when it finally came the expenditure per capita on food in this country justified itself. I poured vin ordinaire into Sylvie's glass and didn't care. Three hours later we fell into bed and slept the sleep of the dead.

In Lyons we had our dejeuner on the balcony in unaccustomed sunlight. At Saint Maximim we ate poulet Provençal in a courtyard with French families and the warm southern breeze laid a balmy hand on our souls. Sylvie stared thoughtfully at the well-behaved young people called children at the next table and smiling became a habit.

However, the most amazing metamorphosis took place in Spain. Four centuries of Spanish influence in the Philippines surfaced in Linda, and she started to look Spanish. The language bubbled off her tongue like a star Linguaphone pupil.

"You're looking better," I said when we were in Burgos.

"That remark fills me with horror," she replied. "I ask myself, what could I have looked like before?"

We looked at each other remembering.
"Klaus says, never look back. It's one day wasted of the rest of your life,"—and I didn't inwardly snort at "Klaus says"—"But I can't always put it into practice."

On the road to Salamanca she asked me, "Hugo, what stays with you? What do you dread?"

I thought for a while, surprised that she had brought the subject up.

"Locked doors, I always leave them open. Haven't you noticed? and blood." Why was I getting into this? "Certain smells. What about you?"

"Being touched. Not you and Sylvie and people I'm familiar with. Being touched unexpectedly. That's why I was so irrational over Garsales. I can't move."

I stared at her, "What started it?" But I didn't know whether I really wanted to know.

"The goons. If they got bored they would come up behind me and start touching me before they raped me."

My foot came down sharply on the brake and I looked round in horror at Sylvie but she had my Walkman on and was swaying in time to the music.

"Raped you!" My mind was saying, the others yes . . . even Lyla . . . but not Linda . . .

Tolerantly she said, "Of course Hugo. Did you think if you didn't talk about it, it would go away?"

"You mean, Garsales?"

"Garsales was an organisation man. He was more of a spectator. His thing was pain . . ." then in a flat voice ". . . pain in the afternoon . . . they got bored in the afternoon . . ."

"Linda, why are you talking about it now?"

"Klaus says I must talk about it or it won't go away."

"Klaus—Klaus! You talk to him, but you don't talk to me!" I felt savage with jealousy.

"I have to make an appointment to talk to you."

There was a braid edging on the waistcoat she was wearing; one corner was loose and as she started plucking at it the stitches gave and the whole thing fell away.

"Besides, I can't talk to you."

"Why not?"

"You shut me up or jolly me out of it."

"I do *not!* I didn't know you wanted to dwell on it."

"Dwell on it! *Dwell* on it! Go and get yourself gang banged, then see if you can help *dwelling* on it!" Her face was tight with hostility.

She was shouting and Linda didn't shout. I stopped the car in the middle of nowhere. I hate rows on continental roads —one can't go home. But this wasn't an ordinary row. If I said the wrong word, or didn't say the right one, Linda would be off back to the Doc with Sylvie in tow.

"I don't intentionally shut you up," I started carefully. "It's the company, it takes up so much time."

"The company!" The word was almost spat out. "You're married to the company!"

"*You* would all go without life's little luxuries without it!" God—how predictable can you get? How *could* I have said that? She swung round to face me.

"*Hugo*, you have no self-knowledge. You *use* the company to shut me up!"

317

Sylvie took off the Walkman. "Are you two having a row?"

"*No!*" I replied tersely. "We are going for a walk." I strode round the car and yanked Linda out. "Aren't we?"

It is not true that the sun always shines in Spain. All that heat and dust and bull fights and Hemingway is all tourist-board clap trap. The sun can go in and hope can fade just the same as it does in northern countries.

I had picked an area of desolation for our walk that rivalled underdeveloped areas of the Third World. Because one looks at one's feet when one walks unhappily, I noticed that, under the dry lifeless grass was a cobbled road. In the distance —nothing. A large chunk of central Spain with a road leading nowhere. How apt!

Sylvie was skipping ahead, thankfully with the Walkman in place again when Linda stopped.

"Hugo, Garsales is going to beat us." She was despairing.

"Don't say that!"

She didn't reply. I caught her shoulders and shook her. "*Why* do you say that?"

"He's driving us apart."

I pushed her down on the grass, and sat facing her.

"Explain."

She stared at me, "Perhaps I should have said that it's you that is driving a wedge between us."

My mouth was dry. I didn't know what to say.

"You can't bear to think about it, can you? I suppose I'm a constant reminder. Another person would help you start a new life."

"I don't want another person."

"Perhaps I do. Someone with more humility. Someone I could talk to when I have a day when I can't keep it locked up inside me, festering and eating me away."

A cold wind blew off the mountains in the distance and Linda started to shiver. I took off my jacket and wrapped it round her shoulders.

Blankly she stared, then, "Do I repulse you?"

Her skirt fluttered bleakly in the breeze. The lump was back in my throat. I hugged her tightly.

"I wouldn't blame you. I wouldn't fancy

319

me." She went on. "Garsales used to send for me after your interrogations. He used to say, 'I've got something for you from Hugo'. Then he'd tear off my clothes and do it in front of the goons. But he couldn't manage it without beating me up first; sometimes he couldn't manage at all. On those days he'd chuck me to the goons, like—like meat to the pack."

The shivering had passed. Her body was limp. But I had caught the shivering. I felt raw, and it was never going to go away.

"There has been *No one* to talk to. When you were in hospital I went to the doctor because I thought I had caught syphilis. I had to go back for tests. I got used to him and I thought he will talk to me, but he didn't. He kept me at arm's length. His work had blunted him; he wasn't like Papa."

A sort of groan escaped from my throat, dislodging the lump. "Once—" a tiny mirthless sound, "I nearly talked to Charles. He just happened to be there. A look passed between us. He knew what I was going to say. Fear, stark fear on his face, stopped me. The English can't stand too much reality."

"Didn't you ever talk to anyone?"

"Only Elaina."

"Penny?"

"Yes, I thought of Penny. But I couldn't do it. Life hasn't equipped her for that sort of confidence. She would never be able to look at me without remembering. We're rejects, women like me. People are sorry for us, but they don't want to know the details."

I thought of the look on the bank manager's face. A kind of curiosity, mingled with fear of knowing. I thought of the look on the faces of the newsmen . . . sometimes on Maurice's face. I thought of McMahon. What can I do, Jon? Tell me what to do.

"I'll kill him—that's what I'll do. Will it go away if he's dead?"

Her face crumpled then and her hand came up to my face.

"I've thought of that . . . but there's Sylvie. It's not the best start in life to have a murderer for a parent."

"She'd understand when she's older."

"Oh yes, I don't doubt it. But think of the inbetween years. Think of the other girls whispering at school. Think of the other *mothers!* If there was some way to keep the world away from her I'd say do it, but there isn't so the answer is no."

Suddenly a little voice behind us said "Are you still sad?"

I swallowed—then said fiercely, "Who's sad? Are you sad? How dare you be sad on holiday!" I grabbed Sylvie and rolled her over on the ground between us. But her laughter soon stopped. She looked at Linda.

"Mama's sad. She's got tears that you can't see, Papa."

We arrived at Salamanca in time for the five o'clock promenade and joined the inhabitants in their nightly discovery of this ancient university town. I ducked into a shop tucked away under the medieval arches and bought Linda a black lace mantilla. When my change was handed to me a small person badgered me for her pocket money. I was thinking about the shawl over Linda's hair so, unthinkingly I stuffed a wad of pesetas into Sylvie's hand.

Linda wore the shawl over her shoulders for dinner that evening. The waiter thought she was Spanish or Cuban. Whilst she was correcting his mistake our daughter rushed in with a parcel and put it on her mother's plate.

"It's for your birthday." Sylvie's eyes shone and she hovered from foot to foot as little girls do when excited. She had the beginnings of a tan and I thought she looked quite Spanish too.

"But, darling, it's not my birthday."

Linda picked up the parcel, delaying the opening. The suspense was killing Sylvie. The waiter returned with a huge *ensalada* which he placed in the middle of the table and showered goodwill over this nice family. Slowly the box was divested of wrapping paper and Linda removed the lid. Under the tightly packed tissue paper was a German tape recorder with ear phones and a selection of tapes stuffed down the sides.

"Ohhh!"

But Sylvie had a message. "It's so that you can put it on and listen to the music when you're sad, like Papa does," she added. Then confidently, "But you won't be sad any more now you've got your own Walkman."

That night I asked, "What can I buy you so that you won't be sad?"

She was standing by the window in a long white dressing gown and the moon was shining across the tiled floor.

"Some new fallopian tubes."

"What?"

"This urinary infection. It's left me with blocked fallopian tubes."

"Oh, baby." My arms were round her and I tried to kiss away those tears.

"I did want another baby, Hugo."

Desolation, helplessness, as the sobs shook her, as I held her tightly in my arms.

"We'll go to see a consultant."

"I've been."

"What, on your own?" That really got to me. Linda on her own in a waiting room . . . waiting to know . . .

"What did he say?"

"It would be too dangerous . . . even if I could . . . which I can't. My kidneys are third rate."

What do people say to each other on these occasions? Why do they go through those emotions of not believing—not accepting—of being certain that some-where there is a key; knowing inside them-

selves that it is only words . . . a kind of
ritual dance . . . before closing a certain
door for ever. When I think about it
now the words we said to each other
have faded, only the pain lingers, as we
acted out that drama in a Spanish bedroom.

In restrospect I watch us lie on the bed,
exhausted with words, moonlight picking
up colours on old tapestries, Linda like a
princess under a canopy. She switches on
Sylvie's present and sweet mournful music
rises and falls tearing at us.

> How many times a day do I think of
>   you?
> How many roses are sprinkled with
>   dew.

"I used to sing that to the prisoners when
I was mopping floors."
"Sing it to me."

> How far would I travel to be where
>   you are?
> How far is the journey from here to a
>   star

—and if I lost you . . . how much
would I cry
How deep is the ocean—how high is
the sky?

I sang it over and over again as she drifted
towards sleep.

Once, she roused herself and asked,
"Do you want to trade me in?"

"I'm used to the old model," I replied
watching her long eyelashes flickering on
her cheek.

Once she said, "Stop watching me," and
threw her arms round my neck so that I
couldn't.

If I have a fault at all, it's doubting the
veracity of maps. The long term plan was
to rent a *finca* near Ronda in Andalucia,
but in so doing to proceed in a swooping
movement taking in Seville and Cadiz.
Linda pointed to a river which seemed to
be in the way and, in retrospect, there was
a lot of green round it. The road from
Salamanca to Badajoz, near the Portugese
border was one of life's little experiences.
The potholes looked as though Hannibal
and his kin had been this way and I

couldn't take my eyes off the road for a second. But we didn't care. We were all being good and Sylvie promised us a song when we next stopped.

By twelve o'clock we were very hot, thirsty and hungry, in that order, and the sun had become spiteful. An ancient townlet, famous for its dust, where they hadn't quite got the hang of sewage disposal, presented itself. We didn't so much park the car as leave it to fend for itself under a plane tree. We settled ourselves at a tin table and viewed the square. Old men puffing pipes watched us. Old ladies in black took a look, then scuttled into tiny shops.

When it came to hunger time they outnumbered me so I allowed them old bull and chips and we spent a happy half-hour chasing it round the plates. Fortified, Sylvie announced that she was going to sing her song. She stood up, arranged her skirt and let rip:

S'wonderful . . . s'marvellous . . .
that you should care for me.
S'awful nice . . . it's paradise . . .
that you should care for me.

Fixing her eyes on her mother—her voice rose to a wobbly quaver.

You've made my life so glamorous . . .
you can't blame me for feeling
amorous.

"What's amorous, Papa?"

When she didn't get an answer, just grins, she said, "I learned that for you to cheer you up."

When I returned after settling the bill she was asking Linda earnestly, "Did you really like my song?"

Linda bent down and cupped her face with her hands—then looked into her eyes and said, "You made my day, Poppet . . . you made my day!" and I thought, this is what it's all about . . . my last duchess.

During that afternoon we drove across parts of Spain ignored by the Spanish Tourist Board and, at dusk, arrived at a town called Merida. Sylvie had been asleep so she missed the swarms of birds, black and shrill that swooped in thousands over medieval roofs. Haughty young women with their *duenas* strolled the streets and angular faced men in black drank aperitifs.

The deafening ring of church bells was drowning everything and like a time-warp, we had lost a century. Dinner that night was in a massive hostelry with blue tiled floors and ceilings up to the skies and crowds of noisy Spaniards at plank tables.

All unawares, Easter had caught up with us and the next day was a fiesta. In the square men and young women in velvet jackets buttoned over flaring skirts and tight trousers; frisky horses—their hooves clattering on cobbles. And above it all the deafening, insistent clanging of cathedral bells demanding undivided attention to religiosity.

Swept along by the crowds, their faces fascinated me. A fierce hunger for their God must stand them in good stead when life became nasty. In the shadow of the cathedral I turned to Linda.

"Why don't you go in and say one for us? Lord knows we need it! Give him a completely free hand."

She was jostled and swept forward.

"You come too," she called.

"I don't know the form."

As she hesitated, I raised my voice and called back, "Go on, or you won't get a seat," and she disappeared into the vastness.

I loitered under those dwarfing walls and stared up at gargoyles. Then a torrent of noise rose from the avenue adjacent to the square and the Klu Klux Clan surged up the street beating the daylight out of the drums. Henchmen with whips belaboured small boys running beside them and it all seemed distinctly unchristian. Behind them men staggered under the weight of an enormous effigy of the Virgin Mary and women in the crowd fought to touch the painted wood. Slowly the assembly moved towards the south door of the house of God, poised, waiting for the first hallelujah. The stunning crash of church music drew me back to the cathedral and I joined the standing congregation at the back of the church. It was dark and massive, lit only by thousands of white candles. In the distance men and boys in medieval gowns, tiered in ranks, poured forth joyous masculine chants in a crescendo of triumph.

Under the mantilla, Linda's face had a quality new to me as she followed the procession out of the cathedral. She shone with an inner resource and flippant words died on my breath.

Horsemen with girls riding pillion—flounced petticoats bouncing and fluttering over the horses' haunches—rode past us as we meandered back to the hotel. Groups of Spaniards stood chatting in the sun invigorated by this ancient renewal.

Finally I asked, "What did you pray for?"

She watched me, weighing me up, considering if I was up to understanding.

"Strength."

The rough road up to our house was only used by farmers and other *finca* owners; the former in the morning before we were up, the latter at weekends, or not at all. A *finca* is often nothing more than a converted barn, normally used for cattle which has had extra rooms added as the spirit moves the owner. Our man had spent his money on a swimming pool. It was rough and homemade and the sewage emptied onto the flower beds, but we had a pool.

During the first week we saw a film star pass on his motorbike making for another house in the next valley and the subject kept our conversation going for several days. The silence that wasn't silence was the most beautiful thing about that place. I lay on my back in the pool, brilliant sunlight in my eyes, listening to the birds and the distant tinkle of goats' bells. Sylvie found a mother cat and her litter among the rocks beside our lane. Her days were busily occupied preparing flavoursome snacks and enticing them to take up residence in the more tasteful comfort of the house.

After a siesta we drifted towards the village as the light was going, wandering from shop to shop buying fresh fish brought up from the coast, hot bread, mineral water, oranges and strange things in tins. Then we slumped on pavement chairs and consumed many drinks. Every evening the same patron in the same restaurant waited by his bead curtain for us, stuffed our comestibles into his huge 'fridge, then led us to the same table by the open window. Red wine flowed to ease our way into the decision of the day . . . what to order.

Across the table Linda's face was shiny and tanned.

"I could live here," she said.

Sylvie echoed, "So could I." They were relaxed as two rubber dolls.

It was then that I made a tiny mistake.

"We couldn't *live* here," I said.

"Why not?"

"There aren't any phones."

Exasperation pulsated across the cloth. My wife said tartly, "Phones are not among the first essentials."

With great attention, we all studied the menu.

"It's the same as yesterday," Sylvie said tentatively.

Linda smiled, I smiled and the naughtiness passed. The patron bustled up, insisting that we had the veal his brother had supplied that morning. Relieved that this major hurdle had been surmounted we returned the menus and topped up our glasses.

I left it until we were fairly replete.

"I have to phone Klaus tomorrow, and before you say why tomorrow, it's because I've got E-Woh on my conscience."

I fished her note out of my wallet and handed it to Linda.

"Where's this come from?" she asked as she read it.

"I didn't want to bother you, it was that Sunday."

She read it again. "In future, bother me. Of course we must phone."

The following morning, as the car twisted and braked on the serpentine route to the coast, she said, "I have sent him a couple of cards."

"That's alright then." It got hotter and hotter. We stopped at the first hotel and I left them on the terrace with cold drinks whilst I went in search of the telephones.

Klaus must have been sitting by the phone because he answered immediately.

"She phoned yesterday."

"Where is she?"

"Morocco."

"Morocco!"

"She's on that yacht with Michael."

"Is she alright?"

"I couldn't tell. She was in such a hurry. She said she hadn't been able to get off the boat, but Michael had gone to meet

334

someone in Tangier so she had made him take her so that she could do some shopping."

"When's she coming back to London?"

"I don't know that either. They are returning to Spain today and she was just about to tell me where the yacht was making for when the line went dead."

"I don't like the sound of this," I said, trying to control a sudden feeling of panic.

There was a pause, before Klaus continued, "There's a message from Charles. The enquiry agent has found Gonsales' house in Weybridge. It's large, in its own grounds and container lorries arrive each day from the continent. A woman's supervising, but there's no sign of him."

"Does Charles want me back?"

"He didn't say. The agent's men are keeping watch on the house."

"Look, I'll phone every few days without fail. But if it's urgent phone this number. I'll drop in each day to enquire."

"How's Linda?" Klaus asked after taking down the hotel's number.

"Much better, but she needs a bit longer."

I put the phone down and stood thinking of a hundred other things I should have asked Klaus.

When I returned to the terrace Linda was relaxing in her canvas chair, her face turned up to the sun, strain lines ironed out, and I was glad we needn't return just yet. When she heard my footsteps she took off her sun glasses.

"Is she back?"

"No."

She sat up looking instantly concerned. "Where *is* she?"

I stared over the terrace rails at Sylvie who was wandering around the swimming pool on a lower level.

I turned back to Linda. "I've got to talk to you."

I told her everything that had happened since Roilo's arrival. I told her all the things I had held back, including the police findings, about Elaina's death. I told her everything the enquiry agent had found out, about the bank manager and the yacht, about the connection between Michael and Garsales. I even told her about Garsales' visit to Maurice. Finally I told her what Klaus had said about E-Woh.

When I'd finished she sighed and said, "Thank God."

"What do you mean?" I was mystified.

"For weeks before that Sunday I'd felt he was somewhere around—I knew it!"

"Why didn't you tell me?"

She looked at me for a minute without speaking.

"What would you have said if I'd said I *felt* he was around when I came out of shops—walked in the street—went to the park? You would have said—Did you see him?"

I frowned because it was true.

"We've got to find that yacht," she said. "Haven't you the slightest clue where it could be? We must find E-Woh."

I fished out the mooring ticket and handed it to her, watching as she turned it this way and that, trying to make sense out of the sequence of punched holes.

"If they're coming from Tangier today, they must be putting in somewhere along this coast. They wouldn't have time to get any further." She looked at the digits again. "This must mean something to a port authority, so let's search the ports."

The difficulties started when we could not buy a large scale map of the coast line. Shop owners shook their heads when we showed them the mooring ticket and it became obvious that each marina made their own arrangements and had no connection with each other. So there was no other alternative than to start at Michael's villa. The villa itself was well boarded up and the gardener spoke a gruff Andalucian dialect that sounded like an ancient muck spreader in action. Linda shrugged hopelessly and we retreated to the beach with our own map of Southern Spain. We circled places from Marbella to Gibraltar, that were obviously ports, after making rough calculations about the distance from Tangier.

Linda said, "They'll have to take on water and fuel and provisions with a boat of that size, so there's no point in fiddling about in the smaller quays."

For some reason that now escapes me we decided to go to the farthest point and work backwards. This meant going to Algeciras, which was folly because it was teeming with police and customs, all intent on catching smugglers and definitely not Garsales' scene. Cadiz, was a long way to the west and would be taking Garsales away from his P2 interests in Italy and his North African buddies.

On the return journey a large board of the type erected by property developers caught our eye, directing us to a marina down an unmade road. We stood on the cliff and looked down at smart new boats with blue canvas covers bobbing pleasantly on the waves, smacking the walls of a new jetty. It was midday by the time we had driven down to the water level and the sun flashed fiercely off the water. We strolled along the two sides of the quay and stared at the pristine shops and cafés facing us. There was one thing missing, people.

Sylvie put it into words quite succinctly. "There's nobody here."

"Rubbish," I said tersely. "There are shops over there," and I pointed towards the elegant arcade of arched doorways.

It was past our lunch time—a fact we were all aware of—as our footsteps hastened in the direction of the facilities. I pushed open the first glass door and took in the tasteful fittings, the advertising literature, and the total lack of stock. On the opposite wall was another door which I opened. I stepped out into a builders' yard which one day would be a car park.

Sylvie laughed and said, "I told you so," then ran round kicking up sand.

Linda caught up and said "Oh shit!"

"Look, there are cars over there." I wouldn't give up. "There's got to be someone to ask!"

It was a long walk across bricks and pipes and rolls of wire. When we arrived at the empty cars. Linda suggested that perhaps they had gone for their siesta.

Sylvie lolled against my legs in the midday heat and said. "Can I have a cornet?"

"Don't let's be silly," I replied unkindly.

We continued to drive round that vacant coastline until three o'clock, when a joint decision was reached to go home and start again when the day was cooler.

Whilst I cooled my over-heated body in the pool Linda pored over the map with a magnifying glass. When I returned to the sittingroom an hour later, leaving large wet footprints on the tiles, I looked over her shoulder and saw that she had drawn a red circle round a port near Marbella.

"Why that snotty dump?"

"It's just the place Garsales would make for. Good mooring, no dangerous rocks or under currents, and all the facilities."

"I can't stand those jet-setting places." I extracted a couple of beers from the 'fridge.

"You may not like it Hugo, but Garsales would. He'd love that false international atmosphere."

I watched Linda as I drank the beer and thought this "strength" thing's working. The look of being on the periphery of things had faded and her mind was ticking over as it did in the old days.

"Would you like to live in a place like that?" I asked curiously.

"You know I wouldn't."

"I don't know. We've both changed. Once you said you'd never leave Manila. Do you miss it?"

Sharply she shook her head. "I'll never go back. That's the past, it's over."

"Where would you like to be?"

"If it wasn't for the company, I'd like to go back to Kenya."

"Well I'm damned! You'd really like to do that?"

She nodded. "I'd really like to do that."

I was the one that didn't want to leave the *finca* that evening. The coastal resorts were not my scene and jet-setting leaves me cold, but we had a compunction to continue our search so Linda put a drowsing Sylvie in a sleeping bag on the back seat and we set off. A quick in and out, I thought, then back to Camelot. But when we arrived at the port nose-to-bumper hedonists blocked the road to the marina and bored police turned their backs. Horns blared and abuse in all languages filled the night air. Helplessly we inched into the town, our eyes on the sea-going yachts flying the flags of the world. They rocked on the water with the insouciance of the very wealthy.

I took my eye off the car in front for a second and gently grazed a bumper. A Gucci kitted Frenchman leapt out of the car and banged on the window with a gold signet ring. When I wound it up he pounded on the roof and attempted to engage the interest of pedestrians sitting at pavement cafés. I participated in a showy manoeuvre around his car and drove on to a tiny pier at the end of the jetty. The lighting was poor. We watched with pleasure as the frustrated Gaul searched for us in the inferno of traffic.

Linda slipped under some wooden rails on to the sand, and climbed up on to the first jetty which formed a walk-way between the boats. She stared at plaques near the water level by each boat and compared each one with the mooring card in her hand.

Then by some quirk of mathematical genius she announced, "We're in the wrong section, but the numbers have the same sequence."

We strolled out towards the sea five times along those unpeopled jetties; each time returning to the noise of the promenade. Five times the light and the noise faded as we reached the end of the walkway and the sea slapped against the harbour wall. The majority of the boats were empty, with wicker chairs on sundecks whilst owners lived it up elsewhere, or stayed on the other side of the world. A lantern was swinging on a hook near the gangway of the last boat near the Port Authority's office and in it's shadow stood Michael apparently watching our leisurely approach, his arm round E-Woh's shoulders. I couldn't decide if he was detaining her.

"Hello Fink. What a rare coincidence." I was casualness itself.

"Hugo! What on earth are you doing here?" Was Michael's surprise genuine? I wasn't sure.

"Having that holiday you advised, old chap." I had one foot on the gangplank, and I was near enough to see fear on E-Woh's face.

"Can we come aboard?"

He seemed to pull himself together.

"What a shame. The port authorities have just given us clearance." He let go of E-Woh and started coiling a heavy rope.

". . .can't miss the tide. Come back tomorrow evening, we'll be back by then."

At last E-Woh found her voice. "It will be longer than that Hugh. We're going to *Dadah*."

I stepped back on the jetty.

"*Ceuta*, Pet. Yes, perhaps the day after might be better."

He touched a switch and the gangplank retreated into the bows with a whirring sound. Then he pushed levers forward and the noise of the engine filled the air. The yacht started to reverse. Oily water splashed our feet.

"See you very soon E-Woh," Linda yelled as the boat roared off into the darkness.

Silently we returned to the car. Sylvie was still asleep. The traffic had thinned out and we were on the mountain road quite quickly. I stopped at the hotel that was my lifeline with Klaus, bringing him up to date with the news of E-Woh and Michael.

When we were nearly at the *finca* I said, "Do you know what *Dadah* means?"

Linda nodded. "It's the Malay word for drugs."

5

LINDA and I returned to the port late the following evening, leaving Sylvie to play with the patron's children. Have you noticed how language is no barrier when children play? Retracing the route we took on the previous night we scoured the marina from East to West, in case Michael moored in a different spot. Half an hour later, outside the Harbour Master's Office, we had to concede that Garsales' yacht was not amongst this lavish display of nautical wealth.

The mistake was in concentrating too much on the yacht and concluding that because of its absence, danger was absent too. Each of us, for our own reasons, kept our minds on the yacht, not yet sufficiently emancipated to give our fears words. Conversely we might have been too relaxed because we did stop for a beer before returning to the car. It was parked in the same spot as before, on the wooden pier at the Eastern end of the marina, and a

Mercedes was right behind it, its bumper an inch from our exhaust.

We stood there saying all the usual things one does in these circumstances. Then we got in and crept forward, then backward, wrenching the wheel until I was covered in a light sweat. Then, through the mirror I watched as two *Seats* roared up boxing us in on either side. I shot out, determined to catch them before they walked away and almost instantly caught the smell of the pack moving in for the kill.

Four men circled me, short and swarthy. They could have been Arabs or dark-skinned Spaniards.

"You no park here, Senor," one said, shoving me in the chest.

As I staggered back against the railings I heard Linda open her door and yelled, "Get back in and lock the doors."

The circle was closing in around me and I tried to anticipate which was coming at me first. I hit one—then felt a vicious cut from a man's ring which landed simultaneously on the side of my head—it was such a neat joint movement by the two of them. My hand came up automatically to my face at the same time as a heavy boot connected with my ribs. As I hit the deck I remembered thinking Klaus would never have been caught like this. Once on the ground boots worked methodically on kidneys, lungs, guts and mentally I was back at Kai Tak where I had thought this sort of thing was over. Those boots really worked me over and the Marquis of Queensberry was conspicuously absent.

Then they were gone and I was being sick over the edge of the wooden planks onto the sand. Linda was sitting beside me holding a handkerchief to my temple, which kept shifting as I heaved.

Finally I heard her voice, which seemed a long way away. "Did you remember to relax?"

It was an old adage in jail, to relax and go with the punches. I shook my head and felt the blood running down my face where they had opened up the scar tissue from the old jail wound. As I tried to sit up my ribs felt as if they were penetrating something vital.

"They want us out of the area," she said.

"Why?" I gasped.

"They haven't broken your legs. They want you to walk away."

A sudden wind blew swirling sand, stinging my skinned face and arms. I lay back on the pier trying to ease the pain in my ribs.

"I bet they've got a consignment of drugs on the way; they wouldn't want us around when they start moving it."

"Then why did they practically drive us out of London?"

Linda collected piles of bloody tissues together and put them in the car.

"They didn't know we were coming to Spain. From their point of view it's the timing that's suspicious; they don't know it's just chance."

The passenger door was open and I had to get myself round the bonnet. My legs buckled at the first step. Speechlessly I nodded towards the back of the car, then leaning heavily on Linda, negotiated the distance with pain shooting through every fibre of my being and fell flat on the back seat.

Linda drove with great care on those mountain roads but by the time we reached the *finca* I was ready to die. She drove the car right up to the front door and it took us both ten minutes to get me out and start my crab-like shuffle towards the bedroom, clutching my ribs all the time as if my entire superstructure was about to give way.

For several days after that I lived on a diet of veganin and milk. Linda moved the alcohol out of my reach. As I drifted between pain and sleep I caught bits of conversation between my wife and child which went like this.

"Better not bother him . . . you know what he's like . . ."

"How *could* he fall down the steps. . . ?"

"I think he was drunk at the time."

Linda bound up my ribs and at the end of the week, I found that I could sit up and take some nourishment.

"I phoned Klaus today," she said as she spooned soup into me. "He thinks we should go back."

"You'll have to do all the driving."

"That's OK. Do you feel up to it? I could take you to Malaga and put you on a plane."

But I had this feeling that we should stay together.

Four days later we were in central France and the pain was receding. Every few hours Linda stopped the car in a quiet place and I struggled out and put one foot in front of another for fifteen minutes to stop my muscles seizing up.

It was in the middle of one of those long afternoons when one feels Boulogne will never appear on the horizon, when Linda's voice wafts over her shoulder.

"You shouldn't complain Hugo . . . pain is nature's way of giving the mind a rest."

I didn't think I had been complaining but I was so bored that I was ready for any diversion.

". . .didn't you find that . . . ?"

The Walkman was firmly in place so I replied, "I was too busy avoiding the goons to indulge in philosophical thoughts."

"I don't mean the ordinary rough stuff . . . I mean in the Special Unit."

A continental lorry passed us on a bend and its speed made me nervous.

"I was never sent there."

"What . . . never?"

"No."

"But didn't Garsales try to get the names out of you?"

"In the beginning . . . then he seemed to lose interest." I felt a sudden stab in the region of my lungs and drew a deep breath searching for symptoms. Nothing happened and idle curiosity returned. "Did you cave in?"

"What?" Traffic was coming at us from all directions.

"I said, did you give him any names?"

"Sometimes . . . but they were mostly dead . . . or people who had left the country."

"Didn't he pitch in when he found out?"

"I don't know if he ever found out. As I told you the nastiness came from boredom; besides I lost track of time after Lyla died."

When we drove into Abbeville on the night before the crossing I said to Linda, "You're a different woman."

"You can get used to anything," she replied.

"I discovered that in Merida. Before that I always felt I had the choice . . . to make my life or take it. Now I wouldn't give Garsales the satisfaction . . ."

We stood looking at each other and I thought, what a pleasing face.

Charles was waiting for us at Dover. I was surprised to see him.

"I've come to stop you going home. You're coming back with me."

"We're not," I replied firmly. "They're tired out."

"No I'm not. I want to go to Uncle Charles house," Sylvie insisted.

"Garsales is hanging round your house," Charles hissed.

We drove in convoy into central London, then on to Chiswick. Sylvie got more and more excited and Linda looked pleased and full of anticipation. I felt really well when I saw Penny standing in the porch, and I tried to remember how long it was since I'd been inside the Winthrope household. She rushed through the garden which was bursting with daffodils and narcissi and gathered us all into her arms.

353

"How lovely, and how *well* you all look, you darling things."

Her small figure was weighed down by a Laura Ashley dress and three little girls brought up the rear like a Greek chorus. Instantly they attached themselves to Sylvie and drew her inside like conspirators.

The seasons seemed to have advanced in that lovely drawing room where every table top and desk was ablaze with bowls and jugs of spring flowers and the flames from a sharp new fire leapt up the chimney. Linda and I wandered over to the French windows and stood staring into the garden, past the stone terrace, at the flowers massed in curving beds and lawns at different levels. Behind an old wall were trees and Chiswick Park.

"Better than Singapore!" I commented as Penny came into the room. "Didn't suit you, did it Flower?" I dropped a kiss on the top of her hair. She pulled a face.

"Who does the garden?"

"Charles. When he's out there the company doesn't exist."

Through the doorway I noticed small figures attached to our luggage.

"I'll do that," I said bravely.

"It's OK. They've got it in hand."

Standing in the hall I watched an efficient chain gang at work. Charles' eldest stood at the top of the stairs supervising. Sylvie was in charge at street level. In between two small things acted as navvies-cum-rollers as they struggled up each step amidst much changing of hands. I sensed their father's orderly mind behind this performance.

Later we had a substantial tea in the kitchen with crumpets and homemade jam and fruit cake and iced sponge *after* a home made terrine and salad with home made salad cream.

"Why didn't you tell me about these Hugo?" asked Linda, holding up a crumpet.

I hung my head, muttering something about important things escaping me sometimes. Penny got up and walked across the teak wonderland in order to replenish the teapot.

"You all look so fantastically fit. Charles why don't we have holidays?"

When the table was a mass of debris the girls scrambled down with something on their minds. With the washing up completed we returned to the drawing room in time to see Sylvie rehearsing the others in a tasteful rendering of the flamenco. Then they retired upstairs to do girlish things and Penny put glasses into our hands.

After the second drink Charles said casually, "Roilo and the agent broke into Garsales' house last night."

I shot up straight, forgetting my ribs. "Say that again!" Charles' disregard for the niceties of the law stunned me. "Have you told Foster?"

"That will come later," he said shortly. "Before that there's some translating for Linda; might as well make a complete job of it."

"But what made you decide on burglary?"

"Difficult to say. I think I woke up one day and thought I'm not going to be shoved around any more. I waited a bit after I heard you were beaten up, just to be sure I wasn't acting in anger. You see, everything seemed to be going Garsales' way and we were being constantly caught on the hop. After E-Woh's comment on drugs I told the agent to concentrate on this constant flow of furniture, much too much furniture for one house. He put more men on the night shift and the result was that the furniture was seen to be loaded back in the vans under cover of darkness."

Linda leaned forward "They were moving the drugs inside the furniture?"

Charles nodded. "Quite. Well, even criminals have to keep some sort of books so I told the agent to look out for documents. As far as the furniture is concerned, that was a bonus. Garsales' men were slinging the stuff into the van like toys, no weight at all."

"Made especially for the purpose?" I interjected.

"Exactly!"

Charles picked up a letter and handed it to Linda. "I'm warning you, a lot of this stuff covers the same ground as the earlier reports, but these papers tie Garsales in with P2 from a legal standpoint."

I stared over Linda's shoulder and there at the bottom of the page was Marcos' fine lawyer's signature. The letter was addressed to *Opus Dei*, care of Banco

Ambrosiano, Milan. It confirmed that his personal representative was Garsales who had authority to direct and control the following companies. There followed a list of concerns all registered in Luxembourg, Liechtenstein, Panama and the Caymans; all set out on fine Malacanong notepaper.

After she had finished translating, Linda said, "I can't understand how this P2 can have any hold in the Philippines. I mean Masonic Lodges are illegal. Cardinal Sin would never . . ." She dried up because of the look on Charles' face.

"Linda, these are powerful and evil men and it doesn't matter what they call themselves. They have survived since 1928 with a rising membership and they have never looked back since they cut their teeth in Spain by bringing Franco to power. Now they are on to the ultimate winner. Total control in every Catholic country in the world. Total power for themselves and their children. And their puppets in all these countries will be men like Garsales."

The room fell silent as we grappled with this enormity.

"But surely this is Italy's problem?"

"It was, but things have got out of hand.

358

The law has never amounted to much in Italy because bribery is a way of life there. All these bombings and assassinations over the last years have been blamed on the Communists, but most have been carried out by P2. Don't forget the Mafia's in it." Charles picked up another bundle of letters.

"This correspondence shows that Garsales has been communicating with them."

Gingerly I took the top letter, which was in English. There was a cheque attached. It was from General V. . . a household name amongst the Filipino military and was for payment for construction equipment. Enclosed were two invoices with identical details itemised, but the second invoice was costed at a much lower figure. The cheque corresponded with the smaller amount. There was a request for *both* invoices to be receipted and returned. At the top of the page was a Swiss bank account number, written by hand. Like the Houston account, General V was getting in on the act. The thought struck me that Houston was one of them too, but I pushed it away as being paranoid.

Charles was watching me. "No, we can't get him for fraud because he's not a British citizen. But the Home Office can report him to interested parties."

I picked up the second letter, which was from a Real Estate office in New York and very carefully worded. It thanked Garsales for his interest in the above mentioned properties and confirmed that the price offered to the company was satisfactory and had been accepted by the major shareholders who were involved in this joint concern. The sting in the tail was to be found in the two addresses; the first, The Crown Building, the second 200 Madison Avenue, New York.

"My God, but this is millions. Even if he's working on commission it's still millions!"

"He'll be buying for Marcos. It would be interesting to know if the money ever reaches it's proper destination."

The third letter heading showed it was from another cronie of Marcos. He handed it to Linda.

"There's not a lot to it. It says if he—Garsales—needs more money in a hurry he's to send a telex saying 'Happy Birthday'."

She looked at the letter again more carefully. "There's a postscript, I think it's a joke."

"Read it."

"Martial Law makes us seriously rich."

Charles shuffled the papers and handed over a memo pad with Garsales' writing on it. He must have written it whilst doodling on the "phone". It said, "The object of fraud is to get money, make it disappear, then spend it."

"Well, we can all verify it's his hand writing."

"He'll go berserk if he ever finds out we've seen these!"

But Charles was confident. "A man like that has plenty of enemies. He'll never be sure it's us. Still, you can see why it was a wise move not to go home tonight."

"Did anyone actually see him near our place?"

"It's not conclusive. One chap swears he saw him, but he fades like a shadow."

"What does he want with us?"

"God knows!"

During this exchange Linda had been

looking through the rest of the stolen papers. Suddenly she let out a gasp. Speechlessly she let a poster unfurl and held it up. In the foreground was Garsales resplendent in uniform. Beside him, but small, his sister gazed up in admiration, against a background of rice fields with a new road slicing through it. And blackly —across the poster were printed the words "WE WILL BE GREAT AGAIN."

A log crumbled and fell in the hearth and we all stared at it. "Why do these peculiar people come into our lives?" Penny asked, not expecting an answer.

My voice sounded unnaturally loud in the quiet room. "But why *me?* Why doesn't he clear off and stop bothering *me?*"

In a tone intending to rationalise Charles replied, "The only thing I can come up with is that you and Linda are the only ones who really know him. Know him for what he really is. If Garsales has delusions of being Number One in the Philippines he has to be seen to be Mister Clean."

Linda cut in emphatically, "We got it all wrong. It's Hugo he's trying to discredit, not the company. It would suit him perfectly if you sold out and quietly returned to Kenya under a cloud. Then, who's going to listen to Hubert Aitkin?"

Charles got up to pull the velvet curtains across the windows. "Just in case you've still any doubts," he said, crossing the room and slotting a tape into the record player. Before depressing the play-back he looked at Linda. "Sorry, Petal. Brace yourself."

Then the tranquil room was full of that voice we knew so well. Startled I looked towards the speakers in the corners because it was as if Garsales was in the room with us. I caught sight of Penny's face suspended with dread, her back pressed into her chair.

The new dictator was practising his speeches, coached by his sister, and there was a power there that I had never heard before. My flesh crept. Cell doors were clanging, and I wanted to yell a warning to McMahon. The words blurred in my ears, but the voice battered on and roared into a crescendo as doors slammed all over the Philippines and the country was sinking and disappearing like Vietnam.

Silently, rigidly, Linda sat with tears

pouring down her face. I got up to put my arms round her but she shot out of her seat as if she couldn't be still. She walked to and fro, her arms tight round her waist. I caught hold of her to stop the walking.

"We must be going."

Penny was saying, "You're not going anywhere!" and I sat down again.

The voice, full of power had got to me, distorting my mind with thoughts of curfews. Then Linda was on her knees beside me.

"It's alright Hugo, it's going to be alright."

I don't know what Charles and I talked about during the night. One part of my mind was aware that the tone of Garsales' voice had triggered off a state of shock, but the other half was crowded with the faces of the prisoners I had left behind. The womenfolk had gone long ago, but not to sleep, I was sure of that. McMahon's boy stood in front of me trying to tell me something in that dialect of his until Charles brought some coffee and a pill. Then I dozed. I awoke when

Charles pulled the curtains back, and sat watching as a new day was born.

Later, we ate bacon and eggs in the kitchen in that sleeping household and a thought grew in my head.

"I want to go and look at that house," I said, putting my knife and fork carefully on my plate.

"Weybridge?"

"Yes."

Charles stood with his back to me, piling plates into the sink.

"Right."

"Charles."

He turned and waited.

"Don't worry. I won't crack up, like David."

It was still early when we arrived at the jewel in the crown of the Home Counties. It was quite deserted and a shroud of mist hovered over its spacious centre. The inhabitants of Weybridge are not early risers.

"We'll leave the car here because it's exposed near the house."

Charles locked all doors of his Volvo and left it in splendid isolation, in the car park.

We loped along lanes, me in my grubby holiday gear, Charles in his city suit, until we came to a "T" junction. We turned right and at the end, facing us, were stone pillars which looked as if once, long ago they had been the entrance to an estate. Here and there were modern bungalows, built on land that had been sold off from time to time. Charles nodded in the direction of the pillars. "That's it," he said.

I stood staring through the opening. I could see nothing but neglected grassland. Deep ruts in the muddy grass wove away to the right, so I assumed the house was in that direction. We stood there for a few minutes considering our next move when the muffled rattle of a milk float wafted on the morning air and slowly came nearer.

As the clatter of bottles grew louder Charles said, "Let's get behind those trees and see if any milk is delivered."

Standing in a shallow ditch behind an ancient oak we watched the milkman slide off his seat and hump a crate of bottles onto his arm. The strains of "The Sting" hovering on his lips slowly ceased, and he stared at us.

366

"Hugo, why are you hiding so conspicuously?" he asked.

Roilo, like the experienced private eye that he was, peered at us in the morning light and held out a hand to ease us out of the ditch.

"We've had a busy night," he said without waiting for an answer. "George is up at the house. There's no one there."

He stuck a thumb into a bottle top and took a swallow, and handed it to me. I finished the milk; Charles refused this sustenance. "What do you mean, busy?" he asked and I tried to remove mud from my trainers.

"We found a body." I blame those old American films for Roilo's manner. "In the lake. George says not to touch it because of identification."

Clearly the incident was going down on his curriculum vitae. Without a word Charles turned and walked through the absent gates and set off in a westerly direction. Clearly, he knew his way to the lake. Personally I would have inched round the wall that surrounded the place but Roilo was adamant that the house was empty.

"They cleared out during the night. We

saw them go," he told me as he strode purposefully beside me.

"Did you recognise anyone?"

He shook his head. "It was too dark and we were too far away, but one could have been a woman."

As we stumbled on the house came into view and, like the pillars, was old and built of stone. The windows had closed blinds giving the place a mute blind look. There was an Edwardian glass-covered way between the house and the garages. I wondered why Garsales had bought such an unattractive pile; he certainly had no eye for gracious living.

Long ago someone had attempted to dig a pond in a natural dip in the land about half a mile from the house. Now a broken tree brought down by a storm drifted quietly on the water, its roots still partially tethered to the bank. Tangled weeds and bull-rushes clung to the trunk and a hand drifted upwards in a final effort to reach the undergrowth. As a wind blew up the hand appeared to be waving. As we got closer I saw that attached to the hand was an arm and a body and a face half submerged in the dark water. Roilo and

Charles dragged it onto the grass, and slowly turned it over. As the neck followed the impetus of the body I saw a vicious wound, too deep to have been inflicted by a fall. Death was forcing a slow pace and it seemed a long, long while before the head came to rest and I was looking at a bloated white face and pale eyes of a man that had been so alive sixteen days ago.

I walked away, my mind suspended, and it seemed a long time before that awful anxiety for E-Woh filled the vacuum. Where was she? Could she be lying like this somewhere else?

When I returned Charles had Michael's wallet in his hand and was stuffing one of Garsales' pamphlets into it. He pushed it back into the dead man's pocket.

"What about the police?" Roilo's voice had lost some of its former confidence.

"Not yet. I'll make a full report later."

"What shall I do?"

"Push him back."

My opinion of my partner's character and ability soared as we stumbled back the way we had come.

"He died the way he lived, dangerously. It'll save me the trouble of sacking him."

6

CHARLES and I went straight to the office when we left Weybridge. He was determined to complete the dossier on Garsales which would accompany his report on Michael's death.

"If I don't let Foster have it at once they will start a conventional murder hunt and all the ramifications of this business will be overlooked."

"He's probably out of the country already."

He dictated for hours, questioning me on all the finer points, and his middle-aged secretary took it all down without batting an eyelid. When the typed up sheets were on his desk he carefully attached each stolen document to the appropriate subject.

"Now go to your office and write a statement about the attack in Spain; describe the men, the yacht and the conversation you had with Michael and E-Woh. Bring it back when you've finished and I'll enclose it with these."

Whilst he was talking he was putting the documents into a large padded envelope and the tapes into a separate one. He sealed the smaller of the two with red wax and signed his name across it.

"What are we going to do about E-Woh?"

He leaned back in his chair and for once, hadn't got an answer.

"What can we do? It's in Foster's hands now. He'll have connections. There's a lot of stuff here, Hugo. He'll get other departments on to it. There is a police guard outside your flat now. Did I mention?"

The sitting room was empty when I got back to the now safe flat, but someone had been watching the television and it flickered silently in the corner. As I watched the news came on, so I turned it up and slumped into a chair. A chap I recognised as the BBC's Far Eastern correspondent was talking to the camera and almost at once the picture changed to Marcos (in powder blue) and Imelda (in evening dress) on the balcony of the Malacanang Palace. In the full blaze of the television cameras they were being privately blessed by the Pope. As the Pope did his thing I was ravaged by a destructive hatred for this creature who was a blueprint for all the Garsales waiting in the wings for their chance.

The pictures in my head swamped the pictures on the screen; weapons unloading from Hong Kong ships on distant islands, whilst tipped-off police waited to arrest anyone in sight and call them Communists. Weapons paid for by the dictator. Assassinations in City Hall which just happened to include Marcos' enemies among the dead. Congressmen killed in church, bombs in the Plaza Miranda, planes hijacked and burned at Manila airport. Thousands of civilians dead, whose only crime was to be there at the wrong time. Sickened, I turned the thing off.

Linda rushed out of the kitchen. "Don't turn it off," she called. "They've found Michael's body."

She turned it on again but somehow it didn't seem to matter. This time yesterday we had been picnicking in France, a world away from this on-going saga. But the dissertation unwound and continued wherever we were like some scenario with no end.

We watched the Manila crowds roaring in the streets, those near the cameras whipping themselves into a frenzy to earn their handouts.

"Ninoy's the only one who can stop him," I said.

"He's having another heart operation."

"Oh God!"

The picture changed to a man with a microphone beside a screened off lake. It was almost a relief. A workman was pushed forward and stood in front of the flapping canvas sheeting looking dazed by his moment of notoriety. Linda turned the sound up.

". . . found this morning by the gardener whilst on his way to the house . . ."

No he had never met the owner, his instructions were left on the kitchen table. Yes, he had a key to the back door. He worked for a firm of contractors and the arrangements were made by phone. How had the owner contacted his firm? The interviewer's attention was distracted for a moment; the gardener's features shifted and settled into the countryman's craftiness.

"Yellow Pages, Sir."

The camera moved on quickly to a member of the Surrey Constabulary.

"We have reason to believe that the dead man was connected with a political group in opposition to the government in the Philippines. It's obvious that the occupants left in a hurry because burnt papers were found in the fireplace. These charred papers correspond with the contents of the dead man's wallet. No—we have no other leads so far."

A phone number was heavily emphasised, which was the local cop shop.

"They'll make a cock-up of it!"

"Michael was blackmailing them."

"Mmm—that's in character."

I'd intended having a shower and returning to the office after lunch but the happenings of the past thirty-six hours suddenly caught up with me and I was too tired to move off the sofa. I wondered briefly where Klaus might be, but driving this thought away was the image of E-Woh's frightened face, constantly on my mind. I tried very hard to think clearly what I should do but the fact that she had been with Michael and Michael was now so definitely dead, undoubtedly murdered, frightened the life out of me. I kept coming back to the yacht but as it wasn't in British waters there seemed nothing to do. Foster could attempt to get a court order in a Spanish court to have it impounded, but Spanish judges were notoriously unhelpful with the bickering about Gibraltar influencing their decisions and the affair could drag on for months. Unless the boat turned up in British waters and came under our jurisdiction we were well and truly up the creek.

I chased these negative thoughts round and round and only one thing emerged. If Garsales had been in England there was very little chance that he still was now that Michael's death was common knowledge. Also he wasn't going to hang about in a Spanish marina when he only had to up anchor and sail away out of *any* country's waters.

Later, I found out that while I was

dwelling on these broody cogitations three people were on the move, although not all together.

Garsales and his sister landed at Orly Airport in the late afternoon and walked out of the terminus. No one attempted to stop them. Interpol had sent out instructions requesting that they should be detained for questioning. The French said we had been laggardly with our paper work and there was no definite evidence against him anyway. Whilst this cock-up was going on the pair of them disappeared into the French interior.

The third absentee was Roilo, who must have scarpered before Michael's body arrived at the mortuary. I didn't blame him because his permit had been out of date for weeks. He phoned as soon as he arrived in New York and said he was waiting for a flight to Boston where he intended looking up the Aquinos. I must admit I thought it was a lot of hot air at the time but a strange thing happened.

Two nights later Cory Aquino gave her first interview on American television and the presenter was Peter Hennessy. She didn't say a lot that was new but we got the impression that she was keeping the seat warm for Ninoy. When asked about his health she said she was forcibly keeping him in bed.

She told the world that all Filipinos were victims under the present regime, but with friends like the American people nothing could last for ever. A petition was being compiled stating Ninoy's intention to run as a candidate in the coming elections and would be forwarded to Manila in the near future. Peter asked her if he had the support of the New People's Army and she turned her lovely smile on him and replied, "Don't be silly! They are people just like you and I. Questions like that obscure the issues. Freedom from tyranny is all that matters and the people are with us."

As Peter brought the interview to a close she held up her hand and looked directly into the camera, saying, "I just ask for your prayers."

Her smile and her yellow frock stayed with us long after the programme was over.

A few days later I was in the local hospital

having an X-ray on my ribs. As I was leaving I bumped into Klaus. He was coming out of a sinister looking department and looked gaunt and painfully thin. He leaned against a wall and his eyes were gauging the length of the corridor.

"Klaus, wait, I'll get a wheel chair! Where have you been? Why didn't you leave a message?"

I was in the grip of a nasty bout of guilt because I'd taken a quick look in his room on our return and when I'd seen his clothes hanging in the cupboard I'd forgotten all about him. Instantly I put my usual remedy into action and pushed him and the chair round to the nearest pub.

When he had a large schnapps in front of him he said, "I was a bit off colour last week so they took me in for a few days. It was unexpected . . ."

The contents of his glass shot down his throat and a few minutes later the old wolfish grin came and went. "I suppose you've come for a checkup? Did they do any lasting damage?"

"Only to my pride."

"How's Linda? Did she talk?"

"Yes, it's all out in the open."

Then I started to tell him about Michael's death and the documents and tapes in Garsales' house. He had heard the announcement of the murder on the radio and dismissed Michael's death as of no consequence, but kept returning to the subject of the papers. He questioned me closely about Charles' statement, looking very thoughtful. Finally he asked about E-Woh.

"There's no news at all, and nobody seems to be doing anything about it."

I watched him anxiously. Somehow Klaus seemed to be my only hope.

He nodded as if that was the answer he had expected, then changed the subject. "Sarah will be here tomorrow."

"Tomorrow!"

"Well, it's not surprising. How would you feel if your daughter disappeared?"

I was to remember that remark. But all I said at the time was, "I'll kill her when she gets back!"

But it was only words—just the silly thing people say when they are full of dread. Then I was lost in thought about how she could have remembered the word *Dadah* from her childhood.

Klaus put his hand on my arm and said "Don't worry. She'll be alright, they're bound to need her."

My mother didn't arrive the next day. Linda fixed up Elaina's room for her, but when I returned from the office she was back in her old flat and had taken Klaus with her.

Linda said, "Don't be churlish, it's only natural."

Sylvie added her twopence worth. "You look as if you haven't been asked to a party."

But I was irritable and felt she could have come round.

"She's too independent!"

"She has to be, she's only got Klaus."

"I thought she was supposed to be worried about E-Woh."

"They're hatching a plan."

"How do you know?"

"I went round this afternoon." Linda was taking off her gloves by the window and a ray of sunlight burst into the room. She had on a new green suit that was the same colour as the trees in bud in the park.

"Why am I never told anything?"

"They'll tell you tonight. They're coming for dinner."

I'd quite cheered up when I heard their footsteps on the stairs. I put on a nice bit of Prokofiev, *Romeo and Juliet*, I thought don't be tactless Hugo and changed it for Paul Robeson singing "It ain't necessarily so, the things that you're liable to read in the bible" and my mother was standing in the doorway taking off a brown suede coat.

I bent to kiss her cheek and she muttered, "Well done."

She seemed thinner than when I'd seen her last. But she's taller than Linda. Perhaps it was because Linda had filled out recently. But her face *was* quite gaunt and her hair swept up on top of her head gave her the same look as that woman in "The Graduate". We hadn't communicated since that phone call. She sat down and fished for her cigarettes, then shot me a look. "Is your hair going grey?" she asked.

I approached the mirror. "I don't think so," I replied coolly.

Linda started pouring drinks rapidly and Klaus handed them round. Making an effort I remarked "You're looking well anyway." She was, thin or not. The dark blue dress and long string of pearls suited her.

"Where's the small Liebchen?" Klaus' was the ultimate in cordiality.

"She's writing a letter to her father in the kitchen," Linda replied.

"Oh God! what does she want?"

"A kitten. She's listing a hundred reasons why we should have one." She turned to Sarah. "There were kittens in the *finca* in Spain."

"No!"

In small matters I'm still the head of the house—very small matters—Sylvie heard me as she came into the room. Wailing she threw the letter on the floor and flung herself at her grandmother.

"I want to come home with you. People can have pets in Kenya!"

When the food had tranquillised us all Sarah said, "It seems we have three problems. First the ups and downs of the company shares." She paused to tuck up a lock of hair that had fallen onto her cheek.

"That's levelled out since Klaus and the Doc bought up the Filipino shares."

"Good, then we can give our undivided attention to shutting up this Garsales for good. Klaus thought he'd kill him but I have persuaded him that that move could bring about a fresh set of problems. So this is what we have come up with. Klaus has a highly suspect friend in Italy. During the past few days he's made endless enquiries and it's now confirmed that the friend is a member of P2. What we suggest is that, through him, we put it about that Garsales is swindling them. The Italians are rather headstrong about that sort of thing."

That was a shot in the arm, I must say. Linda, was full of eagerness.

"What a brilliant idea! but how?" Ma replied "Ah well, that will take some thought," catching sight of Linda's shining face beside her she started expounding on her remarkable good health and the benefits of holidays.

"*Please!*" I interrupted. "What are we doing about E-Woh?" All this tittle tattle!

She stopped at once and behind those controlled eyes I saw a lot of anxiety.

"I should have put her at the top of the

list. You see, something can be done about the first two items, but I don't know what to suggest about E-Woh."

We all subsided and stared at our own particular blank wall. What do you do when your kin disappears?

"Hugh." Klaus' hand was on my sleeve, "I'm going to Rome tomorrow."

"You're not well enough."

He smiled. "They gave me some splendid new pills at the hospital. I must go myself and personally sew the seeds of suspicion. When the rumours get to P2 they will start looking for Garsales and they will probably start with the yacht. After all, they put up most of the purchase money and it wasn't bought for Garsales' private use. Inadvertently they may lead us to E-Woh."

The idea was growing on me but I was still concerned. Supposing he collapsed in some out of the way place? He might never be found.

"Why don't I go instead?"

"Do you speak Italian?"

I shook my head.

"Besides, they wouldn't trust you. No

one would take any notice of you. It's a closed society."

I looked at my mother for help but she only smiled.

"He's made his mind up. He's been glued to the phone for three days. Nothing will stop him now."

The following day was Saturday and it spread ahead like a blank page. I looked at the clock calculating that Klaus' plane would be airborne. I wondered why none of us had thought to ask him when we could expect him back. Like a fool, I had offered to see him off at Heathrow but his blue eyes had glinted with amusement.

"I don't see how they can connect us, Hugh. Only Garsales has seen me and he might not recognise me again. Better leave it that way."

His brain was still sharper than mine. When I was nineteen and untarnished by the blighting effects of reaching forty, it had always seemed that Klaus' mind was functioning in immense strides, way ahead of the rest of us. But unlike my father, Klaus' notions had to have an objective. Whilst my father pursued negative values positively Klaus pursued success positively.

"Let's go for a walk."

I felt too drained to settle to anything. The women folk scrambled to get out into the morning sunshine and when we arrived in Kensington Gardens shoots were burgeoning out of freshly turned earth and the air was new and balmy. Birds sang happily in that unobtrusive way of English birds and it couldn't have been nicer. I picked up a paper from a booth and had a quick look at the front page. A train crash had pushed Michael's death off page one, so I shoved it in my pocket and followed those tripping feet onto the grass.

Along the walks, flower beds blossomed with early tulips and late double daffodils and May trees and magnolias stood guard like sentinels, their pink buds waving in the breeze. But Sylvie had her eye on the Serpentine. The breeze turned into a south west wind over the water and sharp little waves drove the ducks along until they gave up, and scrambled onto the gravel paths. Two inexpert oarsmen rowed like mad and stayed in the same place. The ducks, thoroughly over stimulated by the wind, charged us as we walked along the water's edge, then retreated as our feet got close.

Twenty minutes later we found a bench under a tree and sat there to get out of the wind. Sylvie protested that she wasn't tired but later admitted that her legs were. Linda pulled a copy of the South China Morning Post out of her pocket and showed me an article about the Philippines. Over her shoulder I read that in an attempt to curb corruption the cabinet had decreed that receipts should be given for all gratuities.

In a final search for incident we started the return trip via Rotten Row and settled on another bench to give Sylvie an opportunity to watch the riders galloping by. We were quite near the Prince of Wales Gate now and the park seemed deserted. The occasional car whizzed by purposefully but the change in the weather had driven people indoors. A huge limousine with darkened windows cruised towards us, then pulled onto the grass. Doors opened and black-swathed Arab women descended to take the air. They were obviously from one of the embassies. Sylvie moved nearer to stare at the leather thongs covering their faces. The chauffeur who doubled as a body guard watched her approach and looked menacing. His manner was so hostile that neither of us noticed a bottle green Mercedes pull up behind the car. When it did catch my eye I thought it was some kind of security vehicle connected with the Arabs.

Then the unbelievable happened . . .

A woman in a fur coat got out of the back seat of the Mercedes and left the door open. Idly I waited for her to walk over to the Arab women, but she bent down and put a struggling bundle of fur on the ground. It was a small cat, its little body encased in a harness. The women watched impassively.

Then everything speeded up like an old film that had got out of hand. Sylvie cried out and ran towards the cat that was dancing about fighting its lead. Linda's paper was on the grass and she was sprinting towards the car and her feet weren't touching the ground. With one smooth movement the woman dropped the lead, caught Sylvie under the arms and swung her through the open door. With a retort like a gun the door slammed and the Mercedes shot forward scattering the Arabs. The unseen driver swung the car onto the grass and drove it round in a full circle. By this time I was running and the tyres screamed as they hit the road. I had some idea of throwing myself in front of it but the windows passed my face with inches to spare and my daughter's eyes were wide and her mouth was silently screaming. Rocking dangerously it tore off in the direction of the Alexandra Gates.

All hell broke loose. We both stood screaming at the disappearing car. I rushed at the chaffeur yelling in long forgotten Arabic. He towered over me and answered in some unrecognisable dialect. He rounded on his charges and herded them back into the car. Like lightning he was in the driving seat, reversing onto the road, and breaking all speed restrictions to distance himself from us and the other car. The extraordinary thing was there wasn't another human being in sight. We were alone in that vast park.

A bottomless pit opened in front of us. Linda slumped speechlessly onto her knees, the cat rubbing against her, mewing pitifully. For long drawn out minutes I couldn't move. Then I dragged her to her feet and looked around desperately for a phone box. We stumbled and ran back the way we had come and the cat danced and tripped under our feet. The first phone had been vandalised. We hurtled in the direction of the next red box—then stood staring at the graffiti and the cut wires. Numbly we turned and gazed at the dull green emptiness.

Across the road in the distance were the round towers of the Sheraton Hotel. Speechlessly I dragged Linda towards it. Her sleeve jerked out of my hand and she returned to the phone box. Through the glass the cat mewed soundlessly; she dragged at the heavy door then bent down and picked it up and stuffed it inside her coat.

In nightmares one runs and gets nowhere.

We crossed the road on the edge of the park and dashed down a tiny street into Knightsbridge. Our lungs were bursting. All the cars in London had congregated in that road. The roar of the traffic numbed my mind. Endless time passed before we were across, traffic on our heels, and running towards that space in front of the brown building.

Why is the entrance at the back?

The pounding on the concrete was jarring my ribs and a strange noise was coming from my lungs.

The telephones are behind the lifts and the marble foyer is full of people who never hurry. Dilettantes watch as we hurtle towards those telephones. Americans pointed us out to other Americans as examples of cultural differences and off-duty air crew smiled condescendingly. Linda slumped onto the tiny bench in the booth as I tore open my wallet and found Foster's card.

Slowly the digits went round, slowly it started to ring. With all the time in the world a voice answered.

"Get Foster. *Get him!*"

Quite quickly that controlled voice was speaking in my ear.

"They've snatched my daughter!"

Linda grabbed the phone. "It was Rosana Garsales! Do you hear me? It was Rosana."

391

I had the receiver back and his calm voice said, "Where did this happen?"

"Hyde Park. Alexandra Gate."

"Any witnesses?"

"Only some Arabs."

"Where are you speaking from?"

"The Sheraton."

There was a pause that seemed to go on forever, then a murmur as he talked to someone else. Finally he said "Get a taxi and get your wife home. We'll be there before you. Have you got that Mr. Aitkin?"

Inside the flat I thrust the brandy bottle at Linda and seized the phone. It rang and rang and I was afraid she wasn't there. At last she picked it up. "Mother? Get over here, Linda needs you. No, no, I'll tell you when you get here."

We sat on the sofa and held each other tight and I kept saying "Don't let go, I can't cope if you let go."

The flat is full of people and my mother is dwarfed by men in blue. I take her over to the window because I must tell her before Foster arrives, before she hears any bald statements from the police. A terrible thing happens as the full impact hits her. She crumples before my eyes and sits down quickly. The lines on her face etched by the African sun deepen and the tiny scar I haven't noticed for years starts to twitch and she keeps on saying, ". . . not again . . . not again . . ."

There was only one woman police constable and she sat next to my mother. When the CID man started questioning Linda she got up and sat next to her. He spoke in a drone, his tone repetitious, blocking out our infectious emotions, holding our urgency at arm's length, making a nonsense of our headlong urging to lose no time.

He positioned another colleague with a pad behind the sofa. The man was in civilian clothes, which should have made him more human, but didn't.

"Chief Superintendent Foster has gone to the scene of the incident, he will be here shortly. In the meantime we'll go over it in detail. Mr. Aitkin, listen to your wife carefully and tell me if she overlooks anything?"

God, I hate that tone! Why can they

only do their job when humanity is at arm's length?

"Exactly where were you in the park when the incident occured?" I'll kill him if he says "incident" again! "Was there some trouble between you when your daughter ran away?"

She didn't run away. Oh shit.

"Why did she run towards a stranger? A cat? A *cat!*" clearly they hadn't covered child psychology at Hendon. I sat back willing Foster to arrive.

"The woman. How tall was she? What was she wearing? Was she English?"

"Inspector, I know who she is, I told Mr. Foster. Her name is Rosana Garsales. I knew her in Manila."

Linda was shaking with the effort to get this man on the right track. I gave her a cigarette, watching the tremor as her hand tried to connect with the flame.

"Are you absolutely sure, Madam?"

"Absolutely."

He turned to me. "Did you recognise the woman, Sir?"

"I've never met her."

"But you knew of her when you lived in the Philippines?"

"No, I had no contact with her. I didn't know this man had a sister until my wife told me."

"Do you know anyone else who has come in contact with her?"

"My cousin Roilo." Linda answered quickly, attempting to justify herself, although heaven knows why she should.

"Is he available for questioning?"

"He's in New York."

There was a pause while the inspector had a mouth to ear communication with his opposite number behind the sofa. We sat there waiting to be cleared of the crime of our daughter's disappearance and willing Foster to turn up. Then it started up again.

"Mr. Aitkin, describe this woman."

"She's about five feet, five inches."

"About the same height as your wife?"

"Yes. She was wearing a fur coat."

"Hair?"

"The coat had a hood; I couldn't see her hair."

"Anything else?"

"I wasn't close. I was sitting on a bench. My wife was closer."

Reluctantly he turned back to Linda as

if, in some way her answers were of less value than mine.

"Mrs. Aitkin, tell me the circumstances in which you came to be acquainted with this Rosana Garsales."

Linda shot me a horrified look and I braced myself to fend him off. At that moment there was a stir as the men in blue mentally came to attention and Foster's presence filled the room. He stood there divesting himself of his overcoat and taking everything in. Our interrogator hurried over and conversed in low tones during which time he watched Linda. Foster came over to us, waving the WPC into the kitchen for tea and sank down onto the sofa with obvious relief. I felt he was giving Linda time to adjust as he reconfirmed that there was no one else except the Arabs in the vicinity. He muttered about them hiding behind diplomatic immunity, before turning to Linda.

"You have no doubt at all about the identity of this woman?"

"Inspector Foster, if I had the slightest doubt I would tell you, to help you get my daughter back."

He put his hand on her's and squeezed.

"Right, we'll get Special Branch on to it. But first I'll have the tea."

We returned to the questions and answers. The car, the registration plates, unusual markings, clean or mud stained? Then Sylvie: age, colouring, distinguishing marks, health? Did she require any medication? A photograph. Each question triggered off pain. Our voices rose. We argued about details. At one point we were shouting at each other about the colour of her tee shirt. It was then that Foster came and sat between us and quietly pulled the strands of the law together. He studied the rawness in our faces. "Conserve your energy. It's only just beginning."

The wall in the garden was mentioned . . . police on the front door, access, a van down the road, the telephone, *the telephone!* Where was Sarah? I got up to look for her, then heard her voice on the extension in the bedroom. I returned to convoluted words about ladders, phone tapping, more tea. Then they were gone.

Ma cooked an omelette. Engineers unscrewed the phones and asked odd questions into the mouthpiece. There was shift changing and quiet knocks on doors and the police woman suggested we lay on the beds.

I jerked up in bed and my heart was jumping with fear because we had slept. It was very dark. I looked at Linda. Her arm was thrown up on the pillow and she was lying on her back breathing stertorously. In another room a door closed quietly as they do in old houses. It's the police woman, I thought before remembering a conversation between her and a constable and the outcome had been that the force took up position *outside* during the night.

The door to our bedroom was open, as I like to leave it, but last night the policewoman had shut it and I had been too tired to call her back. Even then I wasn't too perturbed because Ma was in the spare room and I know she looks in on us when things aren't good.

The lights were out but there was a glimmer from the windows because we had forgotten to pull the curtains to and I could see the outline of someone sitting in Linda's chair. Even then I thought it was Ma.

As I put my hand out towards the light

switch a woman's voice said, "Pull the curtains." It was a voice I didn't recognise.

I did as she said and as I turned back from the windows I caught sight of perfectly enamelled nails connecting with the lamp on the table beside her. I stared at a woman in a black trouser suit and thought, she's shorter than I expected. Her face was lush with those exaggerated Polynesian cheekbones like ripe peaches. There was a small clatter as she pushed dark hair out of her eyes and a bracelet glinted. Her pupils were so large they were swallowing me up—and there was excitement—and a slight cast—and only one other person had that cast—Garsales!

"The phone's bugged, I suppose?"

Her voice was like molasses, rich and out of place, like orchids that grow wild in Asia.

She was looking past me and her tone was amused, jeering.

"Linda, there you are. I've seen you looking worse."

Linda was tying the cord of her dressing gown and her voice was neutral, and distant. "I knew you'd turn up."

Disappointment crept into Rosana's

face. "I thought you'd be hysterical. Have they given you some pills?"

Linda ignored this. "How did you get in?" she asked and I was astonished at her calmness.

"I said I was your cousin. I was so overwrought and concerned for you that they let me in." A malicious grin flickered across her face.

"Well, now you're here, spell it out."

Rosana's face became petulant and I could see she was thwarted because there was going to be no emotional outburst.

"Get me a drink. You're not going to do anything heroic whilst we've got your blessed kid."

I slurped some whisky into a glass and she caught my hand with that beguiling smile I'd found infectious in another decade. I jerked it away as if it had been slimy and crustacious.

"Hugo," she bent towards me, intent on fascination and her features slipped into hurt sadness. "I know it is a terrible thing to take your child, but, put yourself into our shoes. Our hand was forced. Kidnapping isn't so unusual at home. You understand our ways. Just a few little things to settle. Then she will be back with you."

For a moment I was lulled, and I clung to the idea that something could be worked out, as it had before.

I jumped as Linda shouted, "Words! Words! what about Michael? Are we going to get him back, and E-Woh?"

An unrestrained wildness sprung into Rosana's face.

"Keep out of it, you pathetic nothing! Who cares what you think! Keep your mouth shut!"

Astonished I watched exaggerated emotions chasing each other across her face. Out of the corner of my eye I saw Linda bracing herself against this onslaught that was not new to her . . . only to me . . . But during that time Rosana had got a grip on herself. She leant towards me confidentially, shutting out Linda.

"Hugo, Jamie needs you. There is no time to waste. Everything is in place for the coup, but he is obsessed with this idea that you must be beside him when he appears on the balcony at the Malacanang Palace. He sees you as his mentor, his talisman and nothing will change that."

For a moment she looked moody as if she was not as sure as her brother. "For years he has read the history books, studied the methods of take-overs and the characters of men who become leaders. And the outcome of all this study is that the men who last—the leaders who influence—must convince the world that they are a force for good; and to do this they must have an Englishman beside them as happened in India, in Jordan—to set a seal, to lend credence, to gain respect. Hugo, think of the drama! You too will mesmerise an immature electorate!"

She had worked herself up to a frenzy of excitement and I felt speechless with the folly of it all. How had I got entangled with this madness?

"It might be a bit of a laugh. And when he's established, I end up like Michael?" I had to humour her.

"Rubbish! He loves you like a brother! After all, he never hurt you in jail." Eyes wide with her own logic. "He could have picked any Englishman in Manila. He chose you." The silence in the room was electric—"As for Michael, he let us down.

He would have sold us out to the highest bidder. What else could we do?"

Casually, I asked, "Where's E-Woh?"

Carelessly she replied "She's on the boat, of course."

"With Sylvie?"

"Naturally."

"Where is the boat?"

She laughed shortly. "I'm not that stupid!"

Trying to regain her confidence I said, "You're saying that when I was arrested, Jamie picked me?"

"That's what I've been trying to tell you. It's been planned for years." I saw how desperate she was to convince me, to get me on her side.

"And if I throw in my lot with you, Sylvie and E-Woh will be returned?"

"Exactly!"

Her eyes were melting with promise—which snapped off instantly as I asked, "And Linda?"

"She stays here. She's too many contacts in the Philippines. We can't spend all our time watching her." But there was more than that. Fear for Linda filled me as I watched the undisguised hatred on her face. My God, she's jealous of her!

A thousand manoeuvres chased through my mind.

"How do you intend . . . ?"

A sudden rattling of door keys at the front door interrupted me.

Rosana leapt to her feet. "Who's that?"

"I don't know, perhaps my mother."

Slowly the door of the sitting room opened and an old man shuffled in, I heard her breath exhale with relief.

"Oh you're awake. I couldn't sleep so I thought I'd come round to see if there's any news."

The gun in Rosana's hand disappeared back into her trouser pocket as Klaus moved forward. Seemingly unaware of a third person he slowly unbuttoned his coat and laid it over a chair.

When he turned he said, "Oh, I'm sorry, you have a friend. Please excuse me."

Rosana rose to the occasion. "I was just leaving." She walked to the door her hand raised in a casual wave. "I'm sure everything will be alright. I'll be in touch tomorrow."

For a full minute no one spoke. Then Linda's questions came flooding out.

"How did you know? How did you get past the police?"

"Sarah phoned me. I got on the return flight." He held out his arms to her.

"And the police?"

"Oh, they knew someone was here. They thought it just the thing for me to take a look."

Out of the corner of my eye I saw my mother rush out of the kitchen. She had him in her arms and his head was resting tiredly on hers.

"At least I know what she looks like now, both of them," he said as if it was a consolation.

7

S HE didn't "see us tomorrow"—or the next day—or the one after.

Nothing happened for a week. A week made up of days when the four of us never left the flat, taking it in turns to sit by the phone or rest on the beds. We were never still for long. We jumped and twitched at unexpected sounds, and stood on the balcony to escape from the tension and suspense.

A post office van remained in the street and engineers dug a hole in the pavement and erected a small tent around it. Sometimes they forgot to switch off the connection and one could hear them murmuring about their flexitimes and complaining about the damp. I yelled at them to give their attention to their work and they informed me in flat monotones that lights flashed when there was an incoming call, Sir.

Uniformed police stood at the front door endlessly checking the girls as they came and went to work and scruffy plain clothes men hid behind bushes in the garden.

On the fourth day I gave Foster an explicit and unreserved rundown on my opinion of the metropolitan police force. My words were well chosen but my vocal chords gave out and I sat down when my wife and mother appeared. Foster waited for my fury to abate then in moderate tones, which enabled him to keep going longer than me, explained the niceties of police procedure.

"From what you are saying Mr. Aitkin, I conclude that your chief complaint is that we didn't arrest Miss Garsales when she left this flat. We had no leads at the time so it was essential that an avenue was left open for the kidnappers to contact you. A kidnapping is a pointless exercise if the perpetrators can't communicate with the family."

"Don't waffle," I interrupted rudely. "You lost her!"

"Our psychiatrists have identified a pattern," he continued, as if I hadn't spoken. "And that is that the first forty-eight hours are crucial because the villains must stay in the vicinity until they have made contact. This is their most vulnerable time, they must stay when all their instincts are urging them to put a healthy distance between themselves and the—"

My teeth on edge, I waited for him to say incident.

"Occurrence. After forty-eight hours they are agitated. They may change to another safe hiding place, which isn't easy with a child, and makes it harder for us to trace them. On Saturday night we took a calculated risk. In the darkness she seemed to fit your wife's description."

He went over to the phone; speaking to the engineer I only caught the word amplifier. Rosana's fruity voice echoed eerily round the room: "*Kidnapping isn't so unusual at home. You understand our ways. Just a few little things to settle. Then she will be back with you.*"

Foster replaced the receiver and you could have run the National Grid off our tension. Klaus' face was like granite as he stared out of the window. Sarah's eyes flickered round the fixtures and fittings.

"Have you been listening to our conversations?" she asked.

"Only when unauthorised persons are present, Mrs. Aitkin."

"How do we know that?"

"There's a small light under the instrument when it's on."

He picked up the whole telephone and held it up. A red light stared back at us.

As the days passed and nothing happened, Foster took to talking to Klaus instead of me. There was no question of leaving the house because Foster was afraid of further kidnappings. Linda was very silent. She sat stroking the cat. When she spoke she always seemed to say the same thing.

"Give them time. They're trying to wear us down."

Charles came round every evening, asking if there was any news and shoved papers at me, which I signed without reading. One day he said he was thinking of sending the girls to the country. It was then I realised the ramifications of Garsales' actions.

"You're in no danger Charles. This madness started in Manila."

"But didn't end there. I had a chat with Foster; he was noncommittal, said he couldn't rule out anything, Garsales isn't your run-of-the-mill criminal."

"Did he say what they are doing?"

Charles shook his head. "Very cagey. The Philippines are a bit off the beaten track for your average cop. It seems like a stalemate."

"He said they were bringing in Special Branch."

"Well, they're not going to broadcast it if they have, are they?"

I stretched and rubbed the back of my neck trying to relieve the bunched up muscles. "They are driving me mad with their convoluted Hendonese talk. Talk about limited! They aren't taking into account that Garsales was a cop himself! He's one jump ahead of them. I know it!"

The phone rang and I was across the room in a flash, but it was one of the engineers saying they were disconnecting for ten minutes whilst they replaced the tapes. When I turned back to Charles he was coiled in his chair and there was sweat on his forehead. The interruption galvanised him into jerky conversation.

"You know, I can hardly remember what he looks like. The more I think about it the more ordinary he seems. Just another bloke in a business suit. I spend hours trying to conjure up first impressions, on the tarmac at Kai Tak, but the only thing I come up with is dark curly hair and a face in the shadows."

As I listened to him it dawned on me that I too had a different picture of Garsales these days. Since this horror had happened I always saw him in his cream gaberdine uniform; and I could smell that authority, that power.

"You know me Hugo. At the time it was papers, details, working towards an agreement. I couldn't allow myself to think in terms of personalities. It was you and Linda, Linda and you. Getting you both out, what ever the cost. Then later, when the press made him out to be a good guy, I was glad to push him under the carpet, so to speak, and concentrate on Michael.

Taking off his jacket he chucked it on a chair and reached for the gin. Charles has this habit of tearing off his clothes when stressed and, over the years, I've come to gauge his degree of trauma. Top shirt button—irritation, tie dragged off—frustration, but when the jacket went it was

411

synonymous with reaching for a gun or bursting into tears.

"What sort of bloke was he in jail?"

"Unpredictable, changeable, always charming, but when he was violent he made my blood run cold; there was no feeling. He didn't relate to others and all one could do was keep one's head down and wait for it to pass."

"I just can't come to terms with the way he treated Linda. He could have stopped all that."

"It was a different culture. It's hard to describe. One becomes brain washed. It was of no importance to him, especially if it was a woman. He hardly noticed it. Sometimes he looked surprised if I started ranting."

"How is she bearing up?"

I didn't answer; in spite of everything Linda seemed to have reserves that I hadn't got.

"Come and look."

Quietly we walked towards the half-open door of Sylvie's bedroom. Linda lay on the child size bed in an old track suit, lost in blessed sleep. The cat, curled up on her chest seemed to be guarding her.

He opened his eyes and watched us, but when we didn't go in, dropped his head on his paws and dozed.

Back in the sitting room Charles asked, "And the other two? How's Klaus?"

The manoeuvre was repeated and we stood looking at Klaus who was lying on his back as sick people do. The flesh on his face had drained away sharply and his cheek bones were very prominent. Beside him, on top of the bedclothes, her eyes wide in enquiry, lay my mother. I shook my head in what I hoped was reassurance, but she slid off the bed and her black slacks and pullover were covered in blanket fluff. Silently she closed the door and stood waiting.

"Just going Sarah. Do you want Penny to get anything?" He asked the same question every evening.

We stood there racking our brains. Finally she said, "The police woman's doing the shopping."

"Aspirins? Throat tablets? Cigarettes? Booze?"

Ma and I shook our heads. "We're on the wagon until something happens."

Charles attempted a laugh, "Never

413

thought the day would come when you lot went temperance." He hugged Ma and muttered, "No joke not being able to go out." Attempting a positive note to end on, he said, "Remember what Shen San used to say—the banquet always ends."

The door clicked behind him.

"Coffee?"

She nodded and we went into the kitchen. She put the kettle on and I went to the fridge for milk. As I closed the door I noticed a grubby teddy bear stuffed between the fridge and the wall. I pulled it out and put it on the kitchen table and we both sat staring at it. My hands were sweating as I picked up the mug.

Carefully, I said, "I don't want to hear all the emotional stuff. Just tell me, what did you do?"

"Do?"

"When Sophie disappeared."

For a long time she didn't answer, "It's not the same, you've got the law behind you."

"*It is the same!* They aren't doing anything."

Her fingers were bony round the mug. "Hugo, one pushes these things away, I can't remember. You will, too, when this is all over."

"But it's *not* over," I grabbed her wrist. "*Think!*"

She was trying very hard. "I was always alone. I knew there were others because the Governor said so, but I never saw them, never knew who they were until the end."

"Start from the beginning."

She seemed relieved at a direct question. "Oh, at the beginning I bribed everyone in sight, right from the first day. Then your father got fed up with it and only let me shop where they took chits. But later Dad sent me money."

My sister in her pram, not in her pram, and my father counting the cost of a kidnapping! Career first—family a long way behind.

"Knowing the language was my great bonus. I'd have got nowhere without that. You haven't that problem."

"No."

"You see, I had to find out who had stolen her. You know."

I struggled to find the right questions about this thing I had pushed away all my life; this thing that had caused a lifetime's distress, driven them apart, and made me side first with one, then the other.

"Describe what happened when you located this Mustapha character."

Her spoon rattled in the mug. "There's no time for personal likes and dislikes when one comes to that stage. He became besotted with me and I had to put up with it, but that was my strength."

That's not something a son wishes to dwell on in relation to his own mother.

"When you catch up with Garsales you go along with him. Bury your feelings until they don't exist. If he wants you to become his closest friend you become his closest friend—the first person he turns to —and you believe it. You open up a new dimension in self control." She took a cigarette out of the packet and tried to light it, then laughing at herself said, "You see, it doesn't last. In fact it disappears as soon as the need for it has passed."

My attempt at being a hard man dissolved and I dropped my head on my hands, "Did you kill him?"

She laughed shortly. "I didn't pull the trigger if that's what you mean, but I didn't stop those that did. It always *felt* as if I did. I was desperate to do it but when it came to it, I don't know; there's something pathetic in the worst people." She rubbed her forehead as if she'd developed a headache. "Don't tell Klaus I didn't actually kill him. He thinks it was a wonderful act of vengeance."

"The old Hun, never had a cautious thought in his life!"

She put her hand on mine. "Something will happen soon. It always does."

"It's six days."

"It was two years for me."

"Do you think Linda's alright?"

Firmly she replied, "She's alright. She's been through more than you, so she's got greater reserves and she's making it work for her. Whatever happens I shall stay with her."

I got up to make another cup and said, "We're not like other people are we?"

"I suppose it's not in our blood," she replied.

We sat in chairs and dozed for the rest of the evening. We never switched the television on now because we were always

417

listening. The new drugs made Klaus sleep a lot. Linda lay on Sylvie's bed practising some sort of relaxation or meditation she'd learned in prison. But I had a superstitious fear of the prone position because there is something primeval about lying down; one's faculties are too relaxed and weakened and things catch one unawares.

But near midnight when the front door buzzer shrilled and the telephone rang and there was a constant hammering on the door, my weaknesses were still there although I wasn't lying down. My heart pounded, my legs wouldn't move, my mouth dried up until it was devoid of saliva and my mind cried out for valium. Sarah got to the front door first and a huge cop filled the doorway. Linda slowly put the phone down as he moved to one side. Shaking, shivering in the jeans she had been wearing in Spain, was E-Woh. A gust of cold air swept into the sitting room. Choking on her sobs she threw herself into Ma's arms. Linda flew across the room— the phone swinging on it's chord—and the three of them stood hugging and kissing like something in a Greek fresco. A pain started to throb in my head. Suspended, they turned and stood staring at me.

"What is it? It's Sylvie, she's . . ."

E-Woh said, "She's alright."

"Then what are you all staring at?"

"You called her Shen San."

In a daze I stared at them, then said weakly, "Rubbish!"

We piled pullovers and blankets on her. The brandy bottle was out and the cop found glasses. He allowed himself to be persuaded to have a small one, but took his cap off as a concession. For some reason this struck me as being hilariously funny. I fell about with mirth and he gave me a startled look. I pulled myself together. "Where did you find her?" I asked.

"She was wandering in the park near the event of the kidnapping."

I looked at her properly and for the first time saw how much weight she had lost. Her hip bones stuck out and her stomach had a caved in look.

"When did you last eat, Fink?"

Childishly, she started to cry again and threw her arms round my neck and I stood there talking nonsense and smoothing her wet hair. When she finally slowed down I asked, "Chips?" and she nodded vigorously.

There was an undignified rush for the kitchen but I insisted on cooking E-Woh's first supper myself, for two reasons. Firstly, because it gave me time to adjust my face—to make the fixed smile more natural and to hide my bitter disappointment that it hadn't been Sylvie. And secondly, because it delayed the heart wrenching searing information that was going to change hands.

Female chatter waned as I advanced with chips and eggs on the largest plate I could find in the kitchen. Like a starved waif in a Victorian melodrama E-Woh held out her arms for the food—and it was then that I saw it. Pricks like a rash all over the inside of her arms; only for a moment, then the sleeves slipped back as she took the tray. With great care I sat down and looked around but the others hadn't noticed. I watched her wolf down the food, determined to say nothing until that nourishment was inside her. When the plate was empty Linda got up to make a gallon of coffee and Sarah went to tell Klaus.

Carefully I started. "Have you come straight from the yacht?"

"Yes."

"In Spain?"

"Yes."

"How did you get here?"

"I don't know, I woke up out there." She nodded past the trees in the general direction of the Serpentine where a huge moon hung in the sky.

"And Sylvie's on the boat too?"

She nodded but seemed agitated. I watched her closely and noticed she was twitching and trying to conceal it.

"Look E-Woh . . . if she's dead tell me now before the others come back . . ."

Tears . . . tears . . . more tears. "She's not dead—just very frightened, especially when I left . . ."

"Why did they let you go?"

"To give you this." She rummaged in her pocket and brought out a tape in a paper bag.

My hand was out when the cop yelled, "Don't touch it Sir—it's got to be checked." God, I'd forgotten he was there.

Carefully he placed the whole thing in a large envelope. By this time E-Woh's twitching had become a convulsive shuddering and I caught him as he made for the front door.

"Get the police doctor."

Then I sat beside her and held her hand and we waited.

The doctor arrived in a quarter of an hour and E-Woh had one more injection and was asleep before her head touched the pillow. Two hours later Foster arrived and Klaus rallied. Foster put the tape on his recorder and switched it on saying, "He's mad of course." Klaus had a pad and pen and listened as if his life depended on it. My mother's face was blank and I remember thinking that she had never heard his voice. She jumped when it started, then there was nothing to show what she was thinking. As for me, a dreadful weariness overcame me as once again, reality slipped away.

"Hugo . . . you must be thinking all kinds of bad things about me. How can I convince you that not for the world would I have brought this anxiety on you without

an excellent reason. The world is the reason Hugo. The world is at stake.

Have you considered the tremendous power we will wield together? Have you thought of the level of influence we can exert on other leaders when we have the Philippines under our control? We shall not be as ordinary men, hampered with the smallness of things.

Consider, every day of our lives, with one word, one stroke of the pen, we shape the order of millions, alter the course of millions of lives, manipulate the very sun in the skies.

Hugo, there is no power like total authority. Autocracy is the pinnacle of being. With you beside me I can stand on the balcony at Malacañang and say I am the state.

The world has taken a wrong turning. Who thought of this limiting thing called democracy? The mob is feudal . . . littered with tin men. You and I Hugo, are gold men. The cheering masses beneath the balcony are puppets, creatures to be led by the nose—to be held in the hollow of the hand—to bend to one's will, to turn *around our little finger, and to keep under our thumb.*

Hugo, believe me, the herd want to be ruled, want to be told what to do; then they are free to occupy themselves with daily trivia.

The world waits for us to take the reins. It waits for our example. It is all there for us to grasp.

Garsales' voice went on and on. I looked around at the others, at their battered stunned faces and felt pity for them. That voice like other voices in history—but this time impinging on *their* lives. What ever happened to normality? I caught Linda's eye and for a second she creased into an ironic grin before the anxiety returned. Foster switched off the cassette without turning the tape over.

"I think we'll all be vigilant with our votes in future," he commented.

I had to fetch a glass of water before I could ask, "What does he want me to do?"

How can I describe the combined relief when I asked that question?

"He wants you to return to Spain." Foster's voice was carefully non-committal.

"Are there instructions on the other side?"

"Yes."

"I want to hear them."

"I'm afraid not. They will be forwarded to the appropriate quarters."

Sarah was twisting her bracelet round and round.

"Why can't I hear them?"

"The matter is out of my hands Mr. Aitkin." Foster had locked and bolted his face.

Ma's neutral tone drifted across the room. "Perhaps you could *tell* us what's on the other side." Her voice suggested that only the most uncivilised man could refuse. "We have to adjust Mr. Foster. It will have an adverse affect on my son and daughter-in-law if they feel that information is being withheld."

Foster struggled with officialdom and his natural humanity.

"Your granddaughter will be returned to her mother when your son is on the yacht; or conversely she may accompany him back to the Philippines."

A kind of moan escaped from Linda which, because she was so still, came as a shock. Klaus sat down beside her, his arms round her shoulders.

"He would prefer Sylvie to return to her mother because he sees women as an impediment to progress."

"What are you advising us to do?" Klaus' voice sounded more teutonic than I'd heard for years in this suspense filled atmosphere.

"It's still a waiting game Mr. Werner. The people who are trained for this kind of thing will take care of it."

At that moment I *knew* with a blinding clarity that we would never see Sylvie alive again if that course of action was put into effect. If Garsales was caught he'd take everyone with him. If he lost the war, no one else was going to win it. Foster was stuffing things back into his briefcase with less than his usual methodical procedure. When he had finished he turned to all of us.

"You all know the ramifications of this man's actions. It's no longer one family's tragedy. He will be trapped and caught providing there is no outside interference."

When he got to the door he turned to

me with an expression that made me understand why the younger generation called them the filth. His voice was flat and purposeful.

"I must warn you against taking any independent action. The consequences would be wide-spread."

"What time is it?"

Ma was opening the curtains on a thin, sunless dawn filtering through the windows. Why do people always want to know the time when they are grasping for normality? Life depending appointments, hospital waiting rooms, courtrooms; everyone must isolate the hands on a man-made contraption on these occasions.

"Early."

Later, weak chatter comes from E-Woh's room, and I think how vulnerable we all are at dawn.

They talked to each other in low voices, dividing and re-grouping like figures in a shadow play. Their eyes drift and settle on my face, then look away. I open the doors onto the balcony, trying to think my own thoughts, and soak up the morning air.

When I return to the sitting room Klaus

is on the phone. He is speaking fluent Italian and the old command is back in his voice. For a second I wonder what we really know about him. He could be a member of P2 himself. How does he know such people? Who can you trust? And does it matter? Only a child.

Sarah came over with a cigarette. "He's on to some thing," she said, holding my hand tightly.

Klaus puts the phone down "The yacht's on a circular course between various North African ports, then Naples, returning to Southern Spain. The trip takes two weeks including refuelling."

I leap on the telephone and lift it up. There is no red light.

"I bet they heard."

Linda dashes to the window and peers into the street.

"They're changing shifts. There's a new team."

I pace about clinging to the one clear thought in my head. "I'm going."

There is a collective sigh of relief. Ma tips the contents of her handbag on the table and starts sorting pounds from Kenyan shillings. Klaus goes to his room and returns with a wad of lira and I find Spanish pesetas left from our holiday. I fetch a calculator and start counting.

"Sod it! Why have we never got enough money?"

A kind of buoyancy infects us. Klaus produces a grip and I stuff in tees shirts, underpants and a spare pair of jeans, shaving things and soap. Then—joy of joys—I come across some forgotten travellers cheques.

Later, feeling foolish, we gathered in the bathroom and turned on the taps.

"How do we know those engineers didn't bug the place?"

"They don't have to be connected to the phone, do they?"

"I read they could put one in an olive."

"We haven't any olives."

"Don't be silly!"

"Perhaps they want Stumblebum to make a break for it . . . then they can follow him."

"E-Woh, get in the kitchen and make me some sandwiches!"

"What time will you go?" Linda sat on the edge of the bath.

"When the girls come back from work, then I can merge with the commuters."

"I've got some overalls—you can put them over your clothes. And these." Klaus hands me some tinted spectacles.

Later I went to bed to catch up on my neglected sleep and I lay there thinking of questions I should ask E-Woh. But Linda slipped in beside me and her warmth sent me to sleep.

I'm only half a person without her, I thought as I drifted off.

At four tea appeared, and with it nervous anticipation.

At half past four I said to Ma, "If it all goes wrong take Linda back to Kenya."

"It won't," she said, giving me a mighty hug, "and I shall be by the phone until you get back."

When I came out of her room Klaus waylaid me. "Once you make contact try to get to a phone, just a few words to pin point your position." He seized my shoulders in a continental embrace.

Then it was time. I said to Linda, "Do your trick."

She walked into the hall and opened the front door.

I heard her say, "Constable, would you mind getting a cork out of a bottle of wine for me? I can't move it and Hugo's strained his wrist." There was an age to wait before I heard them go into the kitchen.

Seizing the grip from under the coats I was through that door in a flash and racing up the stairs towards E-Woh's flat. Opposite her door was a cupboard containing workmen's tools. I grabbed some heavy wrenches then leaned against the door inside her room trying to stop my heart palpitating because I had forgotten to check if her door was locked before leaving our flat. When I'd recovered I started dragging on the overalls and crammed on a cap and put on the glasses. Then I opened the door an inch and waited until I heard a noisy bunch of Filipinos at the front door.

Mostly the girls use a back staircase that had been for servants, but sometimes they use ours which is carpeted. I listened and heard their feet clattering and made a dive for the next flight upwards towards the landing under the eaves where the two staircases join. Standing on the landing looking down the stair well I could see the front door was wide open and a group of beauties were surrounding the new cop like bees around a tall blue flower. Noisily I clattered down the carpetless stairs like a workman with his mind on knocking-off time. The grip was very heavy.

Shrieks of laughter distracted him and I held the grip open impatiently for his inspection. He glanced at the spanners and wrenches on a dirty bit of sacking and nodded, his mind taken up with who was entering rather than leaving the building. I pushed past their backs and banged down the stone steps into the street waiting for the voice of authority to call me back.

Once among the home going crowds I walked briskly. I didn't run. Slowly the distance increased. At the bottom of the road I stepped onto a bus which was going to Victoria.

Later . . . much later . . . I was on a coach leaving for Barcelona.

8

IT took me a week to cross Spain.

You should have gone via Madrid, I hear you say. Well, you may be right, but there were many reasons why I didn't rush helter skelter back to that marina. The main reason I took my time was that I wasn't in the necessary frame of mind to take on Garsales. Consider if *your* daughter had been snatched. Would you be nerve ridden? In my shoes would you be backing away from an encounter with her kidnapper? In other words, would you have lost the necessary grip on yourself? And why Barcelona, I hear you say? Why not, when Foster and minions were hot on my heels. The simple answer is it was the first coach to present itself.

Then there was Klaus' information that the yacht was on a two week trip and I had to assume that the Italians were up to date with that news. But more than that the minutiae of Garsales' characteristics were coming back to me now that I was out of England. The one he had always used most effectively was to keep people waiting thereby reducing them to a bundle of nervous anticipation.

So here I am, Klaus' grip making indentations in my hand, the endless autoroutes of Barcelona sweeping past, and the thirty-eight hour journey nearly over which is no mean feat when one is an indulged member of the middle classes. Buns and sweet drinks by the wayside in the middle of the night may fortify waiters returning to their homeland but had done little to sustain me against the lurches and judders and intake of diesel fumes.

As the new white roads dissolved into old black streets and buildings I rehearsed my impoverished Spanish. *"Un cuarto para una persona"*, and thought I'd got it as we thundered under a cavernous ceiling into the bus terminus. The driver dragged on a joy stick and the doors crashed open and we all floundered towards the exits like sailors who had been too long at sea.

The streets in this part of the town haven't changed since Franco's heyday. At three in the morning the sight of the Guardia Civil, guns to hand and patent

434

leather caps shining in the street lights would not have surprised me. As it was an old crone who was half heartedly sweeping the pavement outside a doss house waved me in and I thought well, this is not the time to be looking for a four star. On the other side of the bead curtain a dangerous Spaniard smiled when I said my piece and threw a key on the counter and jerked his thumb at the stairs. Upstairs doors sagged on hinges and empty rooms contained similar beds. As I was dropping off there was a hammering on the door and pesetas changed hands. I slept for fifteen hours.

A nagging pain awoke me with instructions to find food. I dragged myself down a corridor and found a cupboard with a tap high on a wall. Cold water shocked the living daylights out of me and I slipped on the slime under my feet. I changed into my clean jeans and tee shirt and stuffed my travelling outfit into Klaus' grip.

The early evening sun shines on some tables on the pavement. I sit down and dredge up Linda's Spanish.

"*Una tortilla y un vaso de leche.*"

The girl says "*Que?*" and flicks at the table with a dirty cloth. I wonder whether to leave but surprisingly an omelette stuffed with many Spanish commodities arrives—also a glass of milk that had never seen a cow.

The pain went as soon as I'd drunk the milk and I unwrapped the cutlery in a meagre paper napkin and addressed myself to the seven inch cake on my plate. Interesting potatoes appeared entwined in onions, tomatoes and garlic and small things that looked as if they should be in shells. Ten minutes later I sat back and considered which way was south.

I got to know Barcelona rather well that evening. Finally I got out of the city and found myself on an unlikely road with some sort of paddy fields between me and the sea. Continental lorries thundered by. A local bus with Valencia on the front passed me and I let it go thinking economy must commence. This was a mistake. The lorries swept up the sand on the road and hurled it in my face; two hours later the landscape looked exactly the same. Unable to stand the stinging grit I stood by the edge of the road on a tuft of dried weeds and stared across at the mountains. Why not the direct route to Andalucia? It was summer. Somehow I could do it. In my ear Linda said don't be silly. The dry gale was addling my wits. I had to have a drink before I decided. A tatty café on the other side of the road caught my eye. As I stepped towards it there was a mammoth screaming of brakes and a massive vehicle came to rest inches away.

A stocky figure scrambled out of the cab and shoved his face into mine. Tattooed mahogany arms waved and a torrent of gutteral abuse heated up the atmosphere. I gave him his head. What else could I do? Gradually rage turned into questions; questions into place names. When he said Alicante I nodded violently and scrambled onto the huge wheel.

This Spanish son of the soil was not a man to let a little thing like language barriers get in his way. He ascertained my nationality, then discussed football. Real Madrid and Manchester United brought a glow to his face; other continental teams —particularly the Italians, a hawk and spit of gigantic proportions out of his window.

At Tarragona people from the camp sites played vigorous football on the sands in the moonlight and some of the traffic turned off for Rheus. We shared sausage and garlic between wads of bread, before I dropped off to the tune of football results.

The streets widened into *avenidas* in Valencia and neat school girls hurried home. Students lounged under street lamps energetically discussing this and that with faces that were in their prime. We turned inland and the road climbed into the hills. By now I was beginning to catch his drift and, as we swooped through darkened villages he pointed to a hillside dotted with lighted villas and managed to convey that this was land given to Germans (spit!) by Franco for their help in the Civil War. After much lurching on bad roads he put me down on the diamond squares of the promenade that was Alicante and went off whistling the Internationale.

I had a glass of wine and some tapis in a bar; had a useful conversation with some English hippies who asked me what work I did. I told them it was clerical but quite rewarding and they told me how to get Social Security whilst on holiday. I slept on the beach that night.

My face was burning with the sun and

fresh air when I awoke and I started to feel fitter. Bright and early I stood on the road near a sign for Motril and raised my thumb. A farmer with a load of tomatoes encouraged me to perch among his crates, then dropped me off fifteen miles along a dirt track. As he disappeared one thing was clear. I wasn't on the road to Motril. There was only one way so I started walking.

As I trudged along away from the sea the countryside became undulating with small copses and tree covered hills in the distance. Above these, high on the skyline, snow tipped sierras. Because we'd stuck to recognised routes when on holiday I wasn't prepared for the desolation and lack of population and I walked for hours without seeing a soul. When the sun was above my head I climbed off the road and sat on the edge of a wood under the trees eating some cheese and an apple.

Unlike the human populace the country-side was full of singing birds and small animals. A polecat fought with a lizard in a glade and finally caught it behind its neck. With amazing energy she dragged it backwards over rocks to a burrow where tiny kittens howled and shrieked with excitement. Eleven minute catlets fell on the corpse and tore at it like jungle predators. The mother cat smelt a fox prowling and hustled and tumbled her brood back indoors.

All the occupants of that woodland, previously in hot pursuit of foodstuffs, were suddenly anxious, looking nervously over their shoulders. A mother bird, frantically stuffing food into the gaping mouths of her young looked upwards in fear. Following her gaze I saw a fallow deer watching from a hillock. When she saw me she took off on spindley legs and her kid followed copying her movements. This communal panic distressed me. What a business this life is!

A wind blew up in the afternoon and there were spots of rain in the air. The terrain grew wilder and more desolate and I began to think I'd done the wrong thing. I should have made for Madrid and gone south by train. Then I had a vision of Foster linked to a giant computer checking on my money movements, particularly my credit cards.

Does a computer give instant

information if one used a Gold Card or is one's privacy respected as a bonus to members? To block this pointless train of thought I put on my Walkman and listened to Prokofiev's First Piano Concerto. My trainers tripped along at an encouraging pace until the music came to a slow movement and the clouds gathered over the hills shutting out the sun. Then the slow music became trieste piano notes . . . lost daughter music . . .

I came to a mountain village with high old walls and black garbed women who turned their backs when I tried to converse. A village where a stranger still spelt danger.

I sat by an empty fountain in the middle of the square trying to think where I was going wrong. I took off my shoes and studied my blisters, looking up when a man yelled at the women, calling them to order. Suddenly it clicked; I was being too polite, asking instead of demanding; too much of the *per favors* and *muchas gracias*.

A tinkling sound filled the air and a solitary boy with a flock of goats drifted round a corner. He had a leathery cane in his hand which he flicked, first left, then right, on the haunches of his charges with the nonchalant skill of experience. I decided to try out my notion. When he drew level I held my hand up sternly.

"*Agua*," I demanded in a voice of authority.

For a second he looked surprised, then unscrewed a floppy sack-like container and held it out. Quelling civilised pleasantries I took it and tipped it up. Nothing happened. Sensing a peasant's trick, I frowned. He came forward and held up the bottom and the water spurted out like sherry from an Andalucian jar. It tasted of spring water bubbling over rocks, innocent, untouched by human hand and I couldn't resist a grin. Shyly the boy replaced the stopper, smiled and went on his way.

Replacing my shoes I walked across to the one bar which had a closed sign up and hammered on the door. When the owner surfaced I strode in with a complete lack of grace and bawled, "*Comida!*"

I sat down on a wooden bench. He stood at the kitchen door and yelled for the hired help, then slammed a bottle of red in front of me. Anxious to please, the lady rushed in with a quart of soup and a whole loaf which she hacked up at the table. When the last morsel of potatoes and cabbage had disappeared she returned with chips and a piece of meat cooked to a crisp. Later she ventured nearer and stood watching as I cleaned my plate with a piece of bread. I frowned and she fled back to the kitchen. I find these cultural exchanges interesting.

The next day I was back on the road. I stopped thinking. One foot in front of the other, my eyes on the distant Sierras. Images of Sylvie kept drifting into my mind. Like a mirage she danced ahead of me, dust swirling round her legs, turning, calling, but always too far away.

Sometimes I felt Linda at my side. At one o'clock each day I shut the world out of my mind and thought about her, because we had arranged to do this. It was like tuning into the Walkman, comforting, reassuring, strengthening.

It was during one of my rest periods that I heard it. I must have dropped off because Ma was telling me something urgently—shouting at me soundlessly. I was trying to retain the dream, as one does, but the noise grew louder and more insistent.

I stood up and looked back along the winding road, following the steep gradient, and there, tearing it's guts out, reversing on mountain corners, was a huge lorry; the first vehicle since Alicante. I hurled myself over the ground, sliding on the shifting earth and fell into the middle of the road. Slowly—oh so slowly—it ground to a halt.

It is pitch black in Granada and I'm at another bus terminus. Provincial Spaniards with canvas luggage sit in rows on torn vinyl benches and look as if they would give a lot to be back home. When the sign goes up for Cordoba we all strain forward, then slump back exhausted with the concerted effort. The performance is repeated each time a bus departs.

Two hours pass. I get up and try and decipher the timetables stuck on the walls in between the flashy bull fight fixtures. Printer's ink trails dishearteningly down the sheet obscuring the times to Malaga. I stand at the glass doors staring at the buses waiting in their bays but can't read the

444

destinations in the weak yellow light. I return to the waiting room.

At dawn the Malaga bus trundled into the departure bay and there is an undignified rush for seats. Passengers surge forward jostling, and there is a different look in their eyes from an English queue. Doors concertina behind a mass of humanity and my claustrophobia returns. I gag on the smells of old thirties clothes as we weave through the early morning traffic and people hang on to straps above my head.

Time passes. The temperature rises and the terrain becomes flat. A woman of enormous girth beside me unwraps her garlic sausage and offers me some. Her well spaced stumps smile good naturedly when I decline. I try to open the tiny window above my head. I think of the meticulous way we kept to our own space in jail.

Then something happens which distresses me. The land stretches away on all sides barren and desolate. In the middle of nowhere is a bus stop and a woman and a boy stand there waiting. The bus judders to a stop, the doors swing open, and the boy jumps onto the bus as if the journey is a common occurrence. As he passes down the aisle towards two seats behind the driver I notice that he is fairer skinned than the Spanish children—bright and happy—and the woman looks like his grandmother. He is confident, chirpy, and about nine years old.

Something is wrong amongst the passengers. A frisson of latin alarm jumps from Spaniard to Spaniard and a young woman across the aisle screams and covers her baby's eyes. As the boy takes his place, men at the back of the bus stand on seats to get a better view. The woman starts chatting to the driver. She digs into her bag and gives the boy a banana. He strips off the skin and leans sideways to slide open the window. As the yellow skin falls to the ground I have a clear view of the left side of his face. One eye pulled down towards a multi-scarred lip . . . eyelid taught with tension . . . a protrusion below the eye in the middle of his cheek could be a nose but was a lump . . . obscene mounds of unrelated tissue stuck out at grotesque angles like fingers. The right side of his face has the perfect bloom of youth.

A young man standing near the front can't contain his curiosity. In a harsh dialect he calls out questions and everyone leans forward to hear the woman's reply. The boy listens as if he's heard it all before and turns back to the window without much interest. Then the bus falls silent and Spaniard turns to Spaniard with pagan dread in his eyes. At the next bus stop there is an undignified rush for the exit and the bus continues towards Malaga . . . empty.

I sit there hating the whole human race. The incident left me wretched and exhausted. All the strain since I got on the coach at Victoria gathered into one enormous heap and I knew I had to have some sleep before I started looking for Garsales. I got off the local bus at a bleak mountain village near Ronda and found a bed in a white-washed cottage . . . and slept.

Six days after leaving London I was in Algeciras. Gibraltar rose out of the Mediterranean wrapped in a morning mist. I could see the broken coastline of Africa on the horizon. The white road looped out of the town in an easterly direction and it was there I started hitching. A BMW, pristine in its newness stopped almost immediately and an Englishman, kitted out to match the car, leaned across to open the door. He pointed out all the optional extras and boasted about his splendid lifestyle as we sped along. He told me about his accountant in Gibraltar and his money safely stashed away from Her Majesty's Tax Inspectors. But interspersed in this conversation was a vacuum and a longing to be back in the commercial jungle. Later he suggested we went to his golf club for lunch, and like the sponger I had become, I was tempted to accept. I compromised and agreed to eat with him at a restaurant on the coast. At least I wouldn't be stuck miles off my route.

Like a good hitcher I wolfed down the food and he told me things he would never have confided in London. When we were on the third bottle of wine he asked me to take a packet to England and backed up his request with a convoluted story about being the victim of the Immigration Laws. I told him I'd been in prison and wasn't the right person to ask. He didn't seem surprised and when I was back on the road it struck me that he hadn't asked my name.

I floundered along the cliff tops that afternoon. The urgency seeped away and I stood staring down at the sea curling frothily over the rocks. It was so light after the medieval gloom of central Spain. The tide drew the water from the white sand gently, as if it was required elsewhere, and there was no shingle at all. If Sylvie had been there I would have told her that we were Romans and this was the perfect place to build a fort and a forum to remind us of home.

But this was the bottle talking. When the wine was out of my body the sand turned to rocks and painful gravel plagued my feet, and I noticed ancient sandwiches and coke bottles besmirching Camelot.

Distances are always greater than one allows for in Spain, so it was evening as I climbed along the beach to the west of the marina. The lights from the port twinkled in the distance and wealthy voices echoed across the sand as I drew nearer. I could see the ships' masts on the skyline. The movement of shipping in and out of the harbour was not allowed after dark, so I settled in between two rocks on the other side of the road from the Harbour Master's office and waited for the dawn. The sea lapped gently in the distance and I slept fitfully. I lay there thinking and planning how I was going to cope with Garsales. At that moment I would have given almost anything to phone home, but the thought of the red light recording everything stopped me. One call from Foster and the Spanish police would appear guns blazing. One thing was certain—Garsales wouldn't go down alone.

9

THE following day I scoured every inch of the Marina but the yacht wasn't there. Every few hours I returned and rechecked with the same results. I walked down back streets, not attempting to hide, and smelt chickens rotating on rotisseries. Buying one I returned to my lair on the beach. The thing that was worrying me was that, now that I was back, I couldn't remember what the yacht looked like. All these millionaires' toys looked alike; some had sails, some not. All had impressive radar equipment over the bridge. It was idiotic of me not to have questioned E-Woh more closely.

I sat with my back to the rocks and blew my brains trying to recall the technical data Spalding had read out to me. With blinding clarity I remembered the leather on his desk, the colour of his tie, the quantities of walnut, but everything else was blocked out because of my preoccupation with the price. Aimlessly I stared at Spaniards in black berets fishing from the rocks, reeling in lines and placing small fish in baskets.

Twin Deutz Marine Diesel Engines. The words were suddenly there. What was the use of that when I wasn't going to get a look at any engines? Perhaps all boats of that size had these engines. It was white, but then so were nearly all the others. I hadn't even noticed a flag. If only I could phone Linda.

That was the first day.

On the second day, after a going over with cold water in the toilets behind a beach café, I called in at the Harbour Master's office. He was wearing a lot of black patent and had the look of an official who did rather well from his clients at Christmas time. I shoved the mooring ticket at him and started "*Donde-ing?*"

He scowled and his eyes drifted over my clothes, then turning to his slave he muttered words in a voice guaranteed to confuse a foreigner.

"*Habla Vd. ingles?*"

He looked at me again, then walked out of the room. Helplessly I turned to the skivvy and took out my wallet. Terrified she shot out of the office. I stood on the pavement shaking with fury.

I walked along the beach near the water trying to exhaust myself so that the anger would go away. Then I checked the boats. After that I drifted round the lanes and inspected the second homes, heavy with hibiscus and bougainvillaea, of men slaving in Amsterdam and Frankfurt to keep the gardener in the lifestyle to which he had become accustomed. I came to the casino which had been boarded up and fenced off since our holiday and read a huge placard which said that a company called Les Jardins du Paradis was converting it into a summer palace for a Riyadh Sheik. Vicious alsatians strained at ropes and I moved off niftily. Then I checked again.

In the afternoon when it was too hot to walk I sat on the rocks and wondered how I was going to get to a phone when I located him. I didn't eat that day.

On the third day I rummaged through my things like an old tramp and stared at my last few pesetas. My morale was getting dented; this life of a beachboy wasn't suiting me. Whilst tramping through Spain like a latter day Laurie Lee my mind had been occupied with aching muscles, pained feet, hunger, but I could keep going because I had an objective.

I checked the boats, then waited outside the bank for it to open. Like a fugitive I crept in and cashed a travellers cheque. With money in my pocket I sat at a pavement café table and drank cup after cup of coffee. The caffeine got to me and I started to feel truculent. Sod you, Garsales . . . stop buggering me about! You wanted me . . . so come and get me!

I walked round the back of the shops and watched thin waiters humping crates of food into dark kitchens. Ice dripped down their backs and I hoped savagely that all the shitty residents of this worthless corner of Europe would be writhing with food poisoning before the day was out. Then I walked along the eastern beach, kicking up sand near Latins annointing indolent bodies with Ambre Solaire. Cowardly eyes looked at me with loathing. High pitched protests followed me in foreign tongues. Further on the beach was desolate and empty and never ending like the coast of Africa.

That creature in the marine office reminded me of the goons in government premises in Manila and I wondered for the thousandth time how I had got into all this. I thought of Linda waiting by the phone . . . my mother's white face . . . my terrified sister . . . and, at the moment, if he had been there, I would have killed Garsales.

Worn out with anger, I stared back at the port I couldn't leave and, in the distance behind the car park, the cinema.

Defeated I stumped back the way I had come and, half an hour later, stood staring at the posters in a variety of languages. I finally located a matinée showing a James Bond film in English that afternoon and sat on the ground in the shade waiting for the place to open.

Three hours later I woke as a middle-aged Englishman stumbled over my feet. I looked around and saw the last of the audience making for the exits. He turned to make a tight lipped comment to his wife and I gave her my best smile but she turned away. It was then I realised I looked, and probably smelt, like a hippy. I waited until the place was empty before leaving.

Wandering through the crowds, delaying the awful prospect of another night on the beach, I started to examine the contents of the shops. Boots for small feet made from dying competitors of the bull ring. Casual wear from Paris sold by elegant women with built in contempt. A *demi-tasse* of demi froth with a croissant for *only* five pounds—a sparsely patronised bar for the English with flat beer and uneasy customers.

I drifted into a gift shop tarted up like an Eastern bazaar and started to paw through the stock wondering how I had got through forty-one years without all these things that other people just had to have. Having exhausted black lace and garish befrilled garments I made for a staircase with pictures of flamenco dancers on the walls and arrived at a balcony which doubled as a second floor. I flicked on my lighter to get a better look at the paintings crowded around the walls because the electricity was at a particularly low ebb that evening.

I felt a premonition—a sort of fore-boding—so I didn't jump when he called out.

"Hugo . . . my friend . . . my old vagabond . . ."

He stood in the shop doorway and the street lights glinted on his curling hair. His healthy tan was immaculately clean under the Pierre Cardin navy tee shirt. Laughing, he waved me down the stairs and Spanish heads turned to watch all this camaraderie. Then his arm was round my shoulders and we plunged into the mêlée of strollers and I could smell that bloody aftershave.

"Sylvie?"

Reassurances . . . please . . . even if it's not true . . .

"She's fine—having a ball—a holiday." His muscular arm squeezed, convincing me that there had been no tears, no fears.

"E-Woh said she was upset."

"Oh women; they live on their emotions!"

I was half way to believing it.

He stopped. "Let's have a drink before we go back." His eyes had forgotten

Sylvie. He stepped back "Hugo, you're filthy." He seemed quite shocked.

"Well what do you expect! It was no joke getting away," but I could see he wasn't going to listen to details. "I want to see her now."

"Just as you like," but he was disappointed.

We were walking up the western jetty now and Garsales was relaxed and delighted at the arrival of his company. He strolled ahead calling to me over his shoulder. Near the Harbour Master's office, he disappeared down an alley. I stood there in the poor light, my heart pounding, and reaching out to the walls on either side, thinking it was another trick. They were damp with condensation and smelt of urine. A torch shone and Garsales was waving me on.

As I emerged from that noxious place a blaze of lights dazzled me and a white ship rocked gently in it's own yacht basin.

"All lit up to welcome you."

His face glowed with pride. Up the gangway onto scrubbed decks and I was looking across the Med towards my beach.

I realised that anyone with binoculars could have seen me.

"Why did you leave me stewing on that bloody beach?"

"Had to be sure you were on your own, Hugo."

A Filipino arrived with a tray of steaming coffee and a bottle of brandy and arranged it carefully on a glass coffee table bolted to the floor with expensive brass fittings.

Garsales slumped into a wicker armchair and said "I knew you'd come. Rosana said you wouldn't, but I knew you would. I know you better than she does."

How to describe the look on his face? Bland, unaware of consequences, infectious enjoyment.

"Where is she?"

"Rosana?"

"No, Sylvie." I walked towards the rail and leant on it with my back to Garsales. I could no more drink that coffee than swim under water without oxygen and I was afraid of it showing on my face. I could feel myself slipping into the master-slave relationship of the jail. I had to struggle against it, and maintain the fiction of the friendly boss. That matey, quizzical manner perfected over the years.

"In her bunk, of course. Where did you think she'd be at this time of night?"

He seemed genuinely surprised at the question. With as much command as I could muster I started to walk towards the companion way which I presumed must lead down to the other decks.

"Come on show me the way."

Over my shoulder I heard him protesting, "Hugo, you're being unreasonable. There are many points to discuss. I'm behind schedule."

The lower decks were seedy, not at all in keeping with the splendid exterior. We arrived at what I would have thought were crew quarters and Garsales hammered on a steel door. A catch clicked on the inside and he turned a handle with a locking devise in it. A frightened Filipino girl backed away to make room for us in the small cabin.

There were two single bunks in that place. That's it—just the two bunks. On one of them was Sylvie sleeping heavily. I stepped over the steel hatch and knelt on the bare floor beside her. Her head was on a canvas pillow and her arm was thrown up above it. Small droplets of perspiration covered her forehead and the room smelt of sickness.

"Sylvie baby . . . it's Papa."

Her eyelids flickered but she didn't open her eyes. Her arm slowly came up round my neck, then fell away again. My head was on the pillow beside her and I could feel the heat from her body.

"She's ill. She's very hot!"

"Just a childish thing. She'll be fine in the morning."

I bent forward and smelt her breath. It was sweet and I tried to push away my fear.

"You've drugged her! You sod! Can't you control a child?"

I seized her arm and stared at the pinpricks. Pinpricks like E-Woh's.

"Only a tiny whiff whilst we're in port. It will have worn off tomorrow."

"You always had to use a hammer to kill a fly!"

I could feel his anger rising but he seemed to make an effort to control it.

"Stay with her tonight. Sleep in the other bunk."

"She needs sponging to bring the temperature down."

He snapped something in Tagalog at the girl and pushed her into the corridor. They stood there arguing and I heard her voice rising in protest. There was a sudden soft crack as flesh hit flesh, then a sharp scream which ascended then descended as it had in jail. Minutes later she returned with a basin of water and a sponge. Her lip was like an oozing red doughnut.

The rocking movement of the boat awoke me and I sat up sharply looking for the porthole but there was none. It was an inside cabin and I hadn't noticed it on the previous night.

Sylvie was lying on her back, bedclothes kicked off, and a stertorous snore made her chest rise and fall at an alarming rate. I picked her up, wrapped her in blankets, and kicked on the door; all in one shocked movement. Her head fell on my shoulder and I twisted my neck to look at that grey face.

Jesus Christ! Linda! Help me!!

Running footsteps. A tiny Chinese with a miniscule forehead stood in the doorway.

"Bring orange juice and *hot* coffee at once. And leave that bloody door open."

I walked to and fro like a thing possessed. "Sylvie—wake up—*wake up* childie."

Her eyelids flickered, "I thought I dreamed . . ."

Too heavy they fell shut.

Holding her in my arms I stood in the corridor bawling, "Consuella or whatever your name is, *come here!*"

Flapping a tea towel she came running, her cheek a purply mess.

"When did she last eat?"

"Not for a long time, Sar."

"*When?*"

Her voice sank to a whisper. "Not since the young lady left." She looked behind her nervously.

The orange juice and coffee arrived. I sat her on the bed and spooned it in, her head lolling against my shoulder.

"Don't want it."

She kept on sliding down. The woman stood there and watched and I felt like hitting her myself.

The stertorous noise had stopped. Her skin was cold and clammy.

"Just the juice."

"Don't want it."

"Petal—please open your eyes."

She tried . . . she really tried.

Over my shoulder I snapped, "Go and get a boiled egg, four minutes!"

Fatalistically the Filipino stood there. "No eggs—we got no eggs."

"Then bring soup."

"She will be sick."

"Then bring a bloody bowl!"

She was sick, but she was better afterwards.

Leaning against the bulkhead she smiled weakly. "Did E-Woh get home?" she asked.

"Yes, she's fine."

She started to slide down again and I blocked her descent with the side of my legs. Gamely she gave the soup another try.

"Why did you take so long coming?"

"Come on! I'm here now, aren't I?"

I'm going to kill you Garsales . . . so help me J.C.

I sat beside her for three hours nudging her awake when she went limp. The

Filipino brought bottled water and she drank a drop each time her eyelids flickered. She grizzled, pleading for sleep, and I had to let her for ten minutes until the next sip. Gradually the unhealthy grey was tinged with a trace of pink, the clammy skin warmed.

The airless cabin, somnambulant rythmical noises from the engines, and the tension of the past ten days caught up with me. My head kept nodding and falling forward on my chest. Resisting the urge to lie down beside her, I compromised by putting my feet on the other bed. Even in this twisted position I managed to sleep until a small voice woke me. "Pa, I want to see the sea."

I picked her up, wrapping a blanket round her, and got her into place so that she didn't keep slipping down over my hip. How light she was. And yet her legs seemed to have grown longer. In the passageway the ship rolled and I used one hand to grab a rail. She slipped again and I had to stop to jerk her up and thin arms crept round my neck. Once, during our progress, I caught hold of a door handle and, out of momentary curiosity, turned it. It was locked. I tried others. They were all locked. We staggered up perpendicular stairways and I had to sit down. The widening corridors had double doors leading into saloons and a lounge; I could see this through the glass windows. But the entrances to these public rooms were boarded up with large planks criss-crossing each other. We never saw any crew during that journey.

After negotiating the last companionway we came out on the bridge where Garsales was standing at the wheel studying his charts. His eyes lifted for a moment.

"I told you she'd be alright," he said before returning to his instruments.

Breathless—my feet apart to keep my balance—I said, "I'm going to kill you!"

His face flickered with amusement. "No you're not."

"What makes you so sure?"

He looked at Sylvie and replied, "You'd have to put her down."

I glowered. "Just don't turn your back on me!"

The Filipino girl brought a deck chair and we sat aft out of sight of Garsales. She returned every hour with juice and mineral water. Gradually the sun and fresh air worked and my little girl sat with her thumb in her mouth holding her own head up. At lunch time she drank some more soup and wasn't sick again. Later I suggested that we construct a bed in the deck chair but her arms were round me like a vice and she was having nothing to do with the idea.

In the afternoon she started to get agitated. With mounting horror I watched as E-Woh's symptoms started. She scratched her arms, and her legs. Her nose started to run and she cried in a weak grizzle.

"It hurts . . . it hurts."

Her white chest grew a bloom of red blotches. Garsales strolled round the deck and I bawled, "You've turned her into a junkie, you sod!" But his eyes had a flat look which pre-empted trouble and all he said was, "All this fuss over a child. You were supposed to help not hinder. Take her back to the cabin."

He said something to a passing crewman and we were hustled back.

Below decks I demanded the Red Cross box and the man returned with a rusty contraption that hadn't been opened for years. I rummaged through the dusty bandages and iodine and found some aspirin. I dissolved two in the mineral water and she kept it down. We walked up and down the corridor with the Walkman over her head listening to the doleful singing of Julio Inglesias. Later, as it grew dark, we lay on the bunk and I felt her fingers stroking my cheek.

"You need a shave Pa."

On the following day she wasn't sick. She poured with diarrhoea, but she wasn't sick. The shakes started again in the afternoon. I'm not sure whether it's because I'm prepared for it, but it's not so severe as yesterday. She wants the music on all the time and it has to be Julio Inglesias. I found some more cheerful tapes but it has to be those melancholy Spanish tunes. So help me, if we get out of here, I'll never listen to that Church fella again!

Days pass. She's getting better.

"Pa," a small voice calls from the bathroom, "there's no paper." My child is sitting on the toilet looking vulnerable.

"You're going to eat potatoes for supper," I say sternly as I wash her bottom. Knickers are soaking in the wash basin. "There you are you'll have to go without until they're dry. Keep your skirt over your knees."

She bursts out laughing and does a funny walk—skirt pulled down to her ankles.

We walk round the decks to strengthen her legs. When she's tired she lays on her bunk with the Walkman over her head— her expression subdued and absorbed and mouths soundlessly, "Don't be long."

On the fifth day, with no explanation, we were locked in the cabin. It happened in the morning before I had been on deck so I had no idea if we were in a port or still at sea. Listen for the engines you fool! They were quieter as if Garsales was negotiating a difficult route. Suddenly they cut out completely and I heard the whirring sound Michael had used to pull the gangplank from the jetty. The boat started to rock as boats do when they are in harbour.

Nothing happened for an hour. There were odd calls in the distance but too muted to recognise. I heard donkeys making that long drawn out sound as they called to each other. It was very claustrophobic. Sylvie listened to her music quietly as though this occurrence wasn't new to her. As the hours passed the cabin heated up like an oven. I dozed fitfully. We were getting hungry.

At five o'clock when the heat started to subside there was a thudding of feet on the decks above and gruff Arab voices yelled instructions to each other. Then a clanging in the bowels of the ship as if something metal was being taken on board. The boat juddered and keeled as a heavy object fell and voices were raised. Metal banged against metal sending shudders of movement through the bulkhead. Then it stopped.

An hour later it started up again, but much nearer this time. I looked up at the ceiling and thought, they are storing cargo in the state rooms. Suddenly there was a sickening crash as if a guide rope had snapped and I heard Garsales' voice raised in fury.

I was pouring the last drop of mineral water into a cup for Sylvie when the engines started up. We were both weak with lack of food. I yelled and kicked on the door. It opened almost at once and

Garsales stood there and for a moment I was astonished because I thought he never left the bridge.

"We've had no food all day."

His face had that thunderous look of fury that meant something was thwarting his plans. He yelled up the passageway for the girl then swiped at her viciously as she stood there. Sylvie shrunk against me and started to cry.

He swung round and glared at her. "Shut up or you'll get another jab! I can't stand crying children!"

He turned to me and snapped, "On the bridge in half an hour."

But we got some food.

Swathes of fog wafted off the sea and hung in clouds over the decks. I heard a telex chattering, its staccato sound eerie and out of place. The engines were rotating slowly and the ship made almost no progress. As I climbed the last steps to the bridge I heard someone tear a sheet of paper; a moment to read it and the ball of crushed paper sailed over my head and dropped overboard.

Garsales was swearing under his breath,

then lapsed into silence. He stared through the glass at the nothingness ahead. I moved up behind him.

"What's the cargo?" I asked.

He didn't answer and his expression was withdrawn.

As if I hadn't spoken he said, "The child leaves at the final port of call. That will be in a day or so, if the weather lifts."

"She can't travel alone. Who's going with her?"

"Rosana can go with her." His interest was minimal, and waning as I watched his face.

"She'll be terrified of Rosana." The words were out before I could control them. "Jamie." My gorge rose as I used his Christian name. "Look at it from my point of view . . . when she is safely back in England I can settle down to do some constructive work. I can see you have too much on your mind, but until she is back with her mother I can't concentrate."

I saw his face change and respond to the metaphorical hand held out to him. He sighed.

"Hugo, she goes with Rosana or she goes over the side." My heart gave a sickening lurch. "I'm sorry—but that's how it is. I can't stand children, their noise distracts me. You've just said yourself you can't work with her around. I can't allow any distractions at this crucial point."

"I do understand. Where are we making for?"

"Italy." He turned and smiled. "That was quite smart. What are you going to do with that information, Hugo?"

"What should I want to do with it? We're partners, aren't we?"

When he looks like this his face is so transparent. He wants it to be so. His mind is like a piece of machinery that has been set to function wrongly. Once in a while he'll look bewildered as if there's something there he can't quite comprehend. Then the anger flares to blot it out. Why can't I manipulate him? How does he retain the upper hand with his warped intellect?

"Will Rosana be waiting for us in Italy?"

"Yes." He checked various dials, then pulled a lever. The engines roared, slowly picking up speed, nosing and displacing the fog.

"The cargo will be transferred to another ship near Naples. When that's done the child can go."

"Good." I forced confidence into my voice. "Now that's settled what can I do to help?"

The last of the hardness seeped away and guileless eyes shone. He slapped me across the shoulders.

"That's my Hugo!" Like a schoolboy in cahoots with a fellow conspirator.

I smiled back, and for a second it was almost genuine. With terrible shame I thought of Linda and knew with awful certainty that I was going to kill him like a rabid dog at the first opportunity.

"This country ... founded on four hundred years of Spanish pride ..."

I am taking down a speech for Garsales. He is still behind the wheel because he trusts no one else with the navigation.

"All the bar girls will go."

"You want me to put that in?"

I wondered how he could manage with so little sleep.

"Say rewarding work will be found for

them in Mindanao, or somewhere else that seems suitable."

Hoards of child prostitutes on cat-walks in bikinis hiding their under developed chests . . . crowds sitting with numbered cards round their necks . . . canned music . . . little things trained to silence for the perverts . . .

"But there are 350,000 hospitality girls in Manila. How will you cope with numbers like that?"

I've done it again!

Garsales swings round towering with animosity. "Don't use that word! Hospitality. Those creatures are filth . . . filth! They must be weeded out! My people will *not* degrade themselves for R & R troops as if they are inferior beings! We will start afresh without them."

"I thought you liked the Americans," I said mildly.

"Trash! That's why I left Chicago." Then more moderately, "One or two in Washington are useful. Put in something about the purity of the line."

"And our line will become great again."

What did it matter what I wrote? Caligua would forget it or cross it out. He continued, whipped up in front of an imaginary mob.

"—recruiting illiterates who have never held cash in their hands by provincial governors and similar bureaucrats for Big City prostitution will be eliminated."

He switched the wheel onto automatic pilot and stood behind me reading.

"That's good Hugo, really very good."

"How will you do it, Jamie?"

"It's so simple, amazingly simple. Firstly—" He stopped, lost in some impossible dream. "No—I'll tell you everything when we leave Naples."

He lit a cigar and smoke rings curled round his head. Then, unable to resist the temptation to confide he said, "The first action will be to have hundreds of thousands of pesos printed."

I wrote, "The currency will be immediately reinflated."

"When the populace see how much money is available they will be encouraged to inform against citizens who do not conform to our code. Grades will be allotted and wages will be paid in accordance to information received."

He put his hand over my scribbling pen

476

and said modestly, almost with humility, "I'm proud of this scheme, Hugo. Other dictators have terrified their people into a manageable state. I, on the other hand, am going to give them a purpose, an aim. Those that really work will find their wages increased by many hundreds per cent."

Speechlessly I wrote: "Wages will be well ahead of inflation."

He was still watching me. "What do you think of it?"

"It's original."

That satisfied him. "Yes—it's not been done before."

He moved to the next subject. "Hospitals and schools will be equipped with the finest technological equipment and staffed only by people with the best Western degrees."

"Hospitals and schools will be an example to the world. Where will you find these people?" Had he forgotten that the population of the Philippines was equivalent to Great Britain?

"The world's best will apply for the privilege, Hugo."

477

"The cream of academia will be welcome in Camelot."

I was so tired that the words were jumping about on the page. I put the pen down and rubbed my eyes.

"When will this fog clear?"

Garsales turned to a Filipino sitting by the radio receiver with headphones over his head and asked something. The man flipped switches and garbled crackling noises errupted. He brightened at the man's answer and turned on gigantic windscreen wipers and peered into the night.

"The wind will blow up at dawn, that will clear the fog. We'll be there late tomorrow."

"Then what?"

"We dock at a berth reserved for us next to the cargo ship that will take this lot to the Philippines."

"Is it ammunition?"

He smiled secretly. I thought, this cargo is your baby, something very special.

"It's not ammunition . . . that's already there . . . delivered directly from Libya."

"Libya!" My pretended awe wasn't far

short of the real thing. "That must have been some project!"

"On the contrary, we don't need a lot of ammunition. There are other ways."

"So you keep saying. How can you have a revolution without guns? Are the military with us?"

But the curtain had come down and he didn't answer me.

That was one of the longest nights of my life. When I said I was going to check on Sylvie he started on a whole new line of conversation. When I admitted to fatigue he sent for coffee. Finally I got the message that whilst Garsales wanted to talk we stayed on the bridge. I drank three cups and decided to make the most of the moment.

"Michael showed me a manifest." This was not true, Foster had shown it to me. "I must admit I couldn't see the connection between the different items; for instance there was a load of reactors and some empty steel drums. What do we need those for?"

His face darkened at Michael's name. "That shit!" He shrugged. "Still he didn't do much damage—just held things up. I was glad of an excuse to get rid of him."

"What did you need him for in the first place?"

He looked at me pityingly. "Hugo—you're naive. For a second generation entrepreneur you're thoroughly naive. Traders don't always want to be paid in money. They want commodities. To do this you need a go-between. That was Michael's job."

"And your commodity is drugs."

He shrugged, "A satisfied customer returns."

"Thus the house in Weybridge?"

He nodded. "In the furniture. Neat, wasn't it? Michael's idea as a matter of fact. He was good at that kind of thing. It could have gone on for years if he hadn't aspired to ideas of his own."

He considered this for a minute before asking, "It's all come out now, I suppose?"

I nodded.

"Oh well, it served its purpose."

"Why did you pick England? Doesn't seem your place somehow?"

"Well I was there, wasn't I? Thanks to

you for fixing me up with a job. Then, working in the city I discovered that London was full of Michaels—all falling over themselves to provide me with the documents I required. Anything can be arranged in the city."

I walked over to the fog streaked glass.

"So the drums and reactors were shipped directly to the Philippines? The fog's lifting," I said casually.

"Yes. You'd better get below for a few hours. We've a busy day tomorrow."

I looked at him sharply but the shutters had come down . . . Garsales had shut up shop.

Reaction set in when I was back in the cabin. My scruffy kid was sound asleep. I lay on my back trying to slow down my racing thoughts. What would the Empire Builder do? Some swift action on the opponent's carotid—or simply talk his way out of it and walk away. Charles? Charles would never have got in so deep in the first place. Charles is a great anticipator; he sees things coming. The Doc? I warmed to the thought of the Doc. He was the easiest of all. With no thought of self

481

he'd have had a knife in Garsales' ribs and be dead with his final heart attack. That left Klaus—and I didn't know about Klaus.

Supposing I thought of a way to clip Garsales' wings, would we spend the rest of our lives looking over our shoulders for other members of P2?

Finally I slept and dreamt I was playing football in the Coliseum. My team consisted of Charles and the Barcelona lorry driver, who spent a lot of the game on his knees praying to Moscow. At the other end of the pitch the opposing team advanced in their thousands led by their centre forward . . . Garsales.

10

FOG slows life to almost a halt. It creeps into the brain and suspends mental activity and one is aware of it before casting an eye on the elements. The moment I woke I knew it was still there.

The Filipino crew didn't like it any more than I did as they scampered in and out of the dense greyness with averted faces. By now you know that there's no such thing as a complicated Filipino mind. It's all there on the surface. As seamen, surely fog was a common occurrence, not a cause for agitation? Of course not. Therefore it had to be the cargo: a cargo that could be inflammable, combustible, unstable, and would not take kindly to a collision. The hours limped by. We seemed to be drifting in circles.

In the afternoon, whilst dozing, I awake to that mind shattering silence that means the engines are off. I rush up on deck and watch as a weak sun lifts the fog. It starts to roll away on a light breeze. An hour later we nose our way through shallow water towards desolate mud flats. Dredgers in the distance deepen the seabed at the entrance to a harbour. We are certainly *not* in Naples.

I race back to the cabin to fetch Sylvie, to show her terra firma and find her struggling valiantly with shoes and socks. It breaks my heart to see how slow she is— as if everything is an effort. I try not to carry her any more, but our walks often end with her crying with fatigue. Today was an exception and with legs banging my knees, I lug her up on deck.

We have docked beside a decrepit cargo boat lying low in the water and we are so close that a gangplank could be put across between the two ships. This seems strange because, as we leant on the rails looking across the enormous expanse of dockyard, there is almost no other shipping to be seen. In front of our berth are acres of new white concrete and in the distance huge gates with small buildings in their shadow that look like offices. Mounds of bricks and rolls of wire are dumped in heaps at intervals near the sea wall. What we appear to be looking at is a half-completed wharf that might one day be a considerable harbour.

I had decided that everyone had knocked off for the day when a scruffy looking seaman wearing a captain's cap squashed flat on his head, jumped off the cargo boat and shinned up our gangplank. He ignored us and grasped the rails of the companionway leading to the bridge and levered himself upwards, feet hardly touching the steps. I could hear the murmur of an exchange between him and Garsales which was in a monotone. Ten minutes later they emerged and clattered down to the hold in a great hurry.

When the light started to fail at about six o'clock we were escorted back to the cabin and after a skimpy supper, the catch on the lock clicked and we were in there for the night. Time at sea is a slow business for the noncombatants, but in dock it grinds to a complete halt. That night I prowled around the cabin like a caged animal.

When the Chinaman arrived with our breakfast coffee I asked him to look at the drainaway in the bathroom and managed to stuff a piece of torn handkerchief into the aperture opposite the lock. After speedy ablutions we were back on deck.

Workmen were filtering through the gate swinging bottles in their hands and calling to each other as only Italians do. A group of surveyors—superior with their tripods—were busy with people to see, things to do, places to go. Dock officials arrived in cars, leaving them behind the gates and entered the harbour board offices then re-emerged with clipboards.

The sun which had had a watery quality about it up to now, became hot on our backs and yesterday's puddles started to steam. Loading machinery attached to haulage equipment was driven up to the two ships and winches whirred and rose into the air. Garsales and the freighter captain stepped onto the wharf and stood watching, hands over their eyes. A crane towered overhead. Something about the positioning of the crane didn't please Garsales. He yelled at the driver who inched it closer to our boat. Still dissatisfied he elbowed the man out of the driving seat and took charge of the controls himself. There was a mind blowing grinding as the arm of the winch sailed overhead and hovered over the decks. Seagulls rose into the air screaming as the rest of the unloading machinery clattered into action.

A bird swooped over our heads as the cook threw a bucket of refuse into the water, caught something, and flew off with it in its mouth. Other gulls hurtled towards it and there was a mid-air tussle for the food. Head thrown back, Sylvie watched, stepping onto the gangplank to get a better view. The overhead battle continued and a swarm of birds joined in. Hand on the rail—turning this way and that to watch the fighting birds—she moved down one step at a time until she was on the wharf.

Quickly I looked round at the hive of activity but no one had noticed. Wooden crates covered the jetty now and I saw that she had moved behind a large square one, effectively shielding her from the crew's line of vision. The noise from the various winches was becoming intolerable. I waved at Garsales' crane trying to indicate that we were strolling round the harbour wall. He was high in the air raising a heavy wooden box. For a second I caught his eye and he lifted his hand. With false confidence I put my feet on the gangplank and strolled down to join my kid.

Innocuously we walked round the packing cases and crates. The flat ones must have contained guns but the larger ones could have had anything in them. There was no sign of metal drums. I looked back at the activity and was in time to see a man, hands in the air steadying a crate, overbalance and fall into the hold. Garsales heaved on an enormous brake and hovered like a bird of ill omen shouting at the crew.

We meandered slowly round the sea wall and the fresh air found every crevice in our lungs and the ground didn't rock. A workman rotating a concrete mixer by hand smiled at Sylvie and indicated that she could have a go. She was shy and turned to me to see if it was alright, but soon got excited as the wet grey stuff slipped into the huge bucket.

I stood staring into the distance, dreading the return to the yacht, when I noticed that the surveyors had moved closer and were taking photos of the boats.

Garsales was shouting again trying to stop them. The novelty of the concrete mixer waned and we moved off in the direction of the gate and sat on the harbour wall to watch a group of dockers busy with their paraphernalia. One of them took a packet of smarties out of his pocket and held it out to Sylvie—I remembered being surprised that one could buy smarties in Italy. Then I caught Garsales' eye and he was waving us back to the ship. I took Sylvie's hand and took a step in his direction when someone grabbed the back of my shirt.

"Hang about, don't go near the freighter or the yacht."

I swung round to see who'd spoken but the Italians had moved away and were winding cables onto a round wheel. Irresolute, I stared back at the chaos as the men started loading the cargo into the freighter; then the most extraordinary thing happened. Garsales had stopped his contraption and was trying to control a group of dockers who were swarming all over the freighter. If I hadn't been staring directly at the boats I would have missed it.

Moving like trained circus performers—like a swarm of lemmings—the men threw themselves into the sea. At that instant there was an almighty explosion and people were flying through the air. I saw Garsales because he had further to fall. Like a trapeze artist, spread-eagled, he seemed to be falling in a controlled way and I expected him to get up and walk away. Like a starfish he lay spread out on the concrete.

There were more explosions and millions of pieces of debris shot into the air, descending slowly in the shimmering heat haze. Hands grabbed us from behind, and brought us crashing to the ground, shielding our heads. When the explosions stopped and the hand was removed from my head I looked up and there was no yacht, no freighter, and no Garsales.

In disbelief I stared, looking for running men carrying the wounded, but there was no sign of life.

Then we were being hustled from hand to hand and shoved through the gates and it was all done with such speed and competence that later I could never remember a single face.

Workers' cars were parked in a haphazard fashion on the waste ground. A man picked up Sylvie and raced towards a Lancia with its engine running. Confusion —dust—stumbling, I fell into the back seat and Sylvie is hurled onto my lap. The car is moving and the doors aren't closed. Like a contestant in a Grand Prix the driver slews across the dirt and rocks onto the roadway. I close my eyes and take a deep breath. When I open them the man sitting next to the driver has swivelled round. "Well done Hugo," he says.

Sylvie shrieks with delight and throws her arms round his neck. My reactions seem suspended. To my ever lasting shame I thought, why Klaus?

I sat silently in the back of the racing car as it tore along deserted roads and tried to dredge up words. I knew it was shock— reaction, but I couldn't act on it. Sylvie was not so afflicted. She asked endless excited questions but I couldn't take in a word. I only spoke once during that first hour when I saw a car hurtling along behind us.

"Klaus." I touched his shoulder and his eyes followed mine.

"It's only the surveyors. They're ours."

Sylvie struggled into the front seat and was sitting between Klaus and the driver. Threads of conversation drifted back to me.

"Has she been there all the time?"

"She never moved."

"Is E-Woh there too?"

"Yes, and Nana."

"All this time?"

When he nodded she turned round and said to me, "Oh Papa, aren't they good?"

If I'd been a dog I would have howled. Finally, I asked, "Where are we going?"

The car sped through a tunnel and came out again on the coast road. Cedars clung to the cliffs growing at acute angles battered by the winds.

Klaus' voice said, "There's a villa in about twenty minutes."

"How did you manage it?" I asked.

"P2 want Garsales out of the way. When they found out about the cargo they got the sailing dates out of the Libyans. It was so inflammable they only needed a small explosive."

"Suppose we had been aboard?"

He shrugged. "As far as they're concerned—hard luck. But Foster fixed the surveyors. They would have rushed the yacht."

"Those dockers?"

"P2, infiltrated by the Italian Secret police. That's why we were in such a hurry. We didn't know who would get the upper hand."

"What was the cargo?"

"Drums containing phosphorus oxychloride, potassium floride, and sodium cyanide." Klaus' voice was precise, the voice of an industrial chemist.

"Cyanide!" I couldn't cope with that emotive word.

"Yes, they are precursors. Mixed with pesticides, and there's plenty of that in the Philippines, they convert into very efficient nerve gas."

"*Nerve gas!*"

"Nerve gas. He's got this madman's idea that he's going to immobilise the population while he takes over. What he doesn't understand is that it produces different types of nerve gas, all with differing effects. He's a liability now to his former cronies, so it's curtains for Garsales."

My brain went totally blank. I knew I should tell Klaus about that optical illusion on the wharf, but before I could speak the car behind roared passed and shot ahead. When it was almost out of sight it turned onto a dirt road and disappeared. When we caught up with it the driver followed and I saw a villa set well back from the road. We skidded to a halt beside the other car and stepped out into a silent desolate countryside.

Klaus held up a hand detaining us and the surveyors gathered in a cluster round the front door.

They disappeared inside, then returned calling, "Don't touch the windows."

Red quarry tiled floors—faded—unswept—sparse furniture—chinks of light through closed shutters. No impression left by its owners. A telephone with one of the men talking in rapid Italian. Klaus listens, then draws me away from Sylvie.

"He's disappeared. I can't imagine how he survived that blast."

My heart stops, then races to catch up.

"Could he be in the water? What do we do?"

I look at Klaus for the first time. His clothes hang off him as if he'd bought them in a jumble sale. His face is jaundiced.

"I must get on to Foster."

"You know about the Weybridge house?"

He nodded. "Foster went through it with a fine toothcomb when you left." He picked up the phone. "We've got to get Sylvie out." Turning to her he asked, "Are you ready to talk to your mother, Liebschen?"

She was beside herself with excitement and I had to walk away in case the line didn't connect. Disappointment like that I could not face.

"*Mama?*" Sick with relief I sat down abruptly.

The room was alive with excited shrieks. I moved closer to hear the distant muted sounds of relief. Slowly I allowed myself to think of Linda again. I don't know how long it was before Klaus held out the phone to me. High pitched voices shrieked

495

Hugh, Hugo, and my mother's voice said "*Wait! E-Woh Wait!*"

I had trouble with my voice, but on the second attempt managed. "Hello, Flower."

"Oh Hugo," Linda said.

"She's as fit as a flea, darling girl."

"Fitter than we were?"

"On my life!"

Then E-Woh snatched it and I'm saying in a gabble, "*You* won't be going on that yacht again . . . Klaus has blown it up!"

Then Ma, and I'm saying, ". . . aren't we a bother . . . aren't we a bother? . . ." and she says "I knew you'd do it" over and over again.

Half dead with the emotion of it all Sylvie and I sat slumped in a chair as Klaus spoke to Foster. Businesslike and serious they went on and on.

The phone was in my hand again.

"I'm delighted to hear the news, Mr. Aitkin," said Foster, and it sounds as if there's a chance that he's going to overlook my exodus . . . not that I care. "It sounds as if our chap has got away." (*Our chap!*) "Once he's on his feet he'll try to replace those chemicals but he won't succeed because the Italian authorities will keep him boxed in—that is, with your help, Mr. Aitkin." There is a question mark in his voice.

There was a pause before he continued. "You can be sure that for once the police and P2 are in agreement; no chemicals will come Garsales' way. You can be sure of that."

When I didn't answer he said, "Mr. Aitkin are you going to help us? You are the bait!"

"Foster, we must get Sylvie out."

"No problem if you follow my instructions."

My mother's voice was back. "Klaus can bring her back. Hugh, how is he?"

I look across the room and see him palming pills into his mouth.

"Not good."

Foster says urgently, "Mr. Aitkin, are you willing to stay?"

"So long as Sylvie's out of the country."

Klaus took the phone from me. "Sarah, I'm staying. Hugo can't speak Italian." I could hear my Ma's cry of despair.

I retreated to my chair and listened to the room reverberate with fierce German. I am faintly surprised that Foster speaks fluent German.

We are in the kitchen eating platefuls of spaghetti and sweating because of the closed windows. The atmosphere is heavy with the smell of garlic. The surveyors' elbows knock mine and three bottles of chianti disappear. Two of them start to wash up methodically. "Flight 346 tonight. Rome twenty-three ten," Klaus says.

"Are you taking her?" I stare across the table at Sylvie who is busy eating.

"No, Linda is coming for her."

I put my hands over my face and mutter. "Too dangerous."

"Four men are with her disguised as passengers. They're on their way now."

Dully I watched the expresso bubbling on the stove. "You should go back Klaus. You've done enough."

He shakes his head. "But we haven't finished yet, Hugo. Don't worry about Sarah . . . She has this way of anticipating trouble." The nearest he has ever come to criticising Ma.

We are back in the car and the driver outdoes himself in a frenzied ballet dance of driving to get us to Rome airport. Sylvie is asleep across my lap and I am not alone in my fear of Garsales anticipating our moves because Klaus' back is rigid in front of me. It is dark by the time we reach the outer suburbs of Rome but the traffic is dense in this city where no one ever goes home. Horns blare as we accelerate first right, then left around protesting vehicles. Policemen on white plinths in the middle of the street blow their whistles then shrug their shoulders and turn away. Sylvie's body grows hotter and heavier and the night air blows stiflingly through the windows.

On the autoroute to the airport caribinere join us on motorbikes and Sylvie wakes up. She sits up looking lost, as children do at night in foreign countries and asks, "Where are we going?"

"You're going home duck. Tomorrow night you'll be sleeping in your own bed."

"Are you coming too?" But she doesn't

like it and sits twisting her hair as she did when she was a baby.

A motorbike draws level and the policeman ducks his head to look in the window. Satisfied he roars off taking his place as leader of our escort. My daughter has gone rigid with apprehension. As the street lights circle into the car, die away and return, her eyes are on me dark with fear.

"You're going to leave me again!"

"Sylvie." The car sweeps up in front of the terminal.

"Mama will be on the plane. She's come to fetch you."

We are hustled through the checks with unaccustomed speed. Latin eyes watch us as we carry and drag the wretched, sobbing child to her destination.

Through the glass the plane stands ready for take-off, doors wide for the last small passenger.

"Sylvie . . . Klaus and I will be home in a few days . . ."

Comments about being a big girl are unheeded. I stand there helplessly on the tarmac and stare into the darkness, gazing at that empty space that is the door into the plane. A stewardess and four businessmen hurry towards us. Sylvie buries her face in my jacket. Suddenly there is a scuffle at the top of the steps and Linda shoves someone aside.

"Sylvie!"

The arms round my waist slacken and she listens like a little animal as the voice echoes again across the tarmac.

"Sylvie!"

Turning, she starts running, pushing past the stewardess, dodging round the businessmen who had fanned out and were trying to catch her. Dimly in the airport lights I see her climbing the steep steps. The stewardess follows at a fast clip. Unseen hands tug her inside the plane and the businessmen pull at the doors. For a second, before they close, I see my womenfolk silhouetted in the doorway.

As the aircraft rises into the air Klaus and I walk away.

11

WHEN we got settled in the hotel reaction hit me and a terrible depression set in. Klaus slept intermittently in the next bed; I'd promised Sarah I'd stay in the same room. In the early hours he lay like a dead man, never moving. Then he became restless, throwing his limbs about as the toxaemia raged in his body, and calling out in German. Supposing he drifted into a coma? What should I do? Where would I start? The hours dragged by before I finally slept with the sound of the aircraft in my ears.

I woke with a start and discovered a third party sitting on Klaus' bed talking quietly. The midnight blue outside was lifting in the sky and my watch said five o'clock. Klaus eased himself up on the pillows and the man reached for his dressing gown. Quiet Italian, muted, my comprehension limping behind.

Klaus noticed I was awake. "Hugh, I'm

so sorry to disturb you. They've arrived, everything is in order." He reached for his menthol cigarettes.

I gave up trying to translate and my muscles relaxed with the thought that if I died they would be alright. This quiet exchange lulled me back to sleep because when I woke again the man was gone. Klaus held out a cup of coffee.

"Only the last half inch, Hugh," he said. As always the waking Klaus was very different from the sleeping Klaus, but I saw his pills open by his bedside.

"What did he say?"

"He's still alive."

"How do they know?"

"Some of their men saw him being carried to a car. It got away! The Italians have been checking hospitals all night, with no results. They must have got him to a private clinic." My hands were shaking, I reached for one of Klaus' menthol cigarettes. He walked to the window and stood staring out.

"They are watching the airports for Rosana. She can't be far away if he's badly wounded. Our only hope is that she will lead us to him."

503

"What do we do now?"

"Wait."

The word struck a death knell.

"I'm not good at that," I said.

Klaus gave me a sharp look and I felt ashamed that he had seen my weakness—or more to the point, that I'm no good at hiding it. To cover it I add, "The trouble is I'm not absolutely sure of anything anymore."

"Nobody is. People waste their lives concealing their feelings and putting a face on for the rest of the world, instead of tackling and eliminating the cause."

"I'm too dependent on others, the thing my father warned me against. To be honest Klaus, I only got through those two years in prison because of the strengths of the people I was with." His face became set and angular when I mentioned the empire builder.

"Who is to say David was right? Just because of an accident of birth one does not have to accept values blindly."

Out of habit I found myself reacting against the implied criticism.

"You are good with people Hugh—David wasn't. His aloofness was a wall that distanced him from others. He wouldn't have asked for help if he was dying. I remember him annihilating one with a look, and that's not something to be proud of."

I turned away feeling that this conversation was disloyal, and then remembered when I too had been the recipient of that look.

"Have no respect for the authority of others, for there are always contrary authorities to be found."

"Who said that?"

"Bertrand Russell your fellow countryman. He also said, '*Do not fear to be eccentric in opinion, for every opinion now accepted was once eccentric*'."

"And you believe that?"

"Of course, one can't go through life putting one's feet in the footsteps of others unthinkingly. Never discourage thinking, Hugh, and you will be bound to succeed."

"That's a sobering thought!"

There was a slightly uncomfortable pause during which I took the decision to have a shower. When I was dressed I said

I was going for a walk. Klaus went back to bed.

Nothing much happened for five days. I phoned home every evening, walked and tried to keep out of the bedroom so that Klaus could rest. On the fifth day the Italian was leaving when I returned.

"There's been a development," Klaus said. "Rosana arrived on the morning flight from London." He swallowed his black coffee in a gulp. "She gave those peasants the slip! What do you think of that?"

"How could that happen? You said they had the airports staked out!"

"She flew Alitalia—first class—the fawning sycophants let her through."

"Klaus! Calm down! Surely they were on the lookout for her?"

I gave him some more coffee. Gradually he relaxed and an extraordinary story of an elegant woman in furs and a blonde wig emerged. She was the first off the plane and the half asleep official at Passport Control only noticed the Manila stamp in her passport when she was through "Nothing to Declare". He yelled to a colleague who grabbed her and was left with a fur coat in his hand. A porter tried to stop her as she sprinted for a taxi but she threw the wig in his face. I sighed and thought of the hard men at Heathrow.

On the eighth day Klaus said, "They are cashing cheques."

"What! Both of them?"

He shrugged "Who can tell? Some are signed by Rosana, some by Garsales. The signatures are identical."

"A cheque needs an address if it's cashed by a foreigner!"

"False, and always in big cities."

The faces of the detectives became grimmer. The tantalising trail led nowhere. But one thing was certain. They had money and the cheques were for exceedingly large amounts.

As suddenly as it had started it stopped and there was an uneasy feeling of deadlock. We were all waiting for cause and effect to manifest itself.

Some days later I was walking around the outside of the Coliseum, bored out of my mind and mentally crossing Rome off my list, when I came across a group of youths snorting cocaine. Under the arches I saw another group—and another—and another. Fascinated I watched as a carabiniere strode towards them. They observed his approach without concern. The officer remonstrated gently—gesticulated—then turned as if his attention had been caught by something else. The boy next to him slipped a packet into the policeman's pocket. The carabinier's attention returned; he patted his pocket absently and strode off.

Intrigued, I continued towards a street market where I intended buying a pineapple for Klaus. I was turning the fruit over in my hand, wondering how to detect a ripe pineapple when the bloke behind the stall got agitated and excitable. He yelled in a country dialect and pointed to an alley across the street.

A group of housewives in black aprons spread across their ample stomachs, backs towards the pavement, were snorting amateurishly behind their hands.

I decided on a drink before returning to the hotel so, pineapple in hand, I made for the Via Vendotti. The pavement cafés were in an uproar. Socialites passed the stuff to businessmen accompanied by shrieks of laughter. Strangers engaged other strangers in conversation and, bemused, walked away arm in arm. All reserve had vanished as if it never existed. It was all rather like the four minute warning. What really rattled me on the return journey was the sight of a group of priests near the Vatican with Pepsi cans in their hands, holding lighters under them, sniffing!

I rushed up the stairs and found Klaus in front of the television.

"You're never going to believe this—"

He didn't bother to look round. "It's all over the country."

"I can't believe it!"

"Garsales is increasing his capital."

For two weeks there was chaos. In Milan work deteriorated to such a degree that factories closed. In Forli *all* the men waiting for work in the square were worse for wear. Schools closed, hospitals were full. In any other country a State of Emergency would have been declared. For two weeks Italy was closed. Then the supply dried up and the population crept back to work. But in every office and canteen someone was missing. Carried away by an untried novelty some had burnt holes in their brains, burst their arteries, asked too much of their hearts. Klaus said P2 were calling it Garsales' Revenge.

Impatience was killing me. Three weeks of nothing except that Italy had gone to hell and come back; a fate they richly deserved for sheltering these people, and allowing this evil to prosper. Klaus spent his days on the phone and our conversations consisted of "Have they traced him?" and "Nothing."

But one day he was pacing the room waiting for me.

"They've traced him to a private clinic in Civitavecchia."

I leapt at the large map of Italy pinned to the wall.

"Civitavecchia! It's not far from Rome, on the coast. I went there once when I was a child."

Klaus was standing behind me. He said "Yes," and that one word told me something was wrong.

"What's the plan?" I wasn't having it!

"He's left. He'd gone before they arrived."

"Oh Christ!"

"Those two will get in touch with you. I *know* it!"

Klaus was having most of his meals in the room now. I was finishing my dinner in the restaurant that evening when a waiter came up with a folded note on a silver tray. The florid writing jumped out at me as I read. "He wants to see you". I followed the waiter's gaze to an empty table.

I shot upstairs because I couldn't wait for the lift, and held the note out to Klaus. He read it and dropped it on a table.

"Good! It won't be long," he said. His taciturn manner was getting on my nerves. Then I looked at him more closely and saw that he had deteriorated in the past hour. His breathing was laboured, speech an effort, his supper untouched on a tray. Thank God Sarah couldn't see him.

"Klaus, I've got to get you home, and I mean now. No more delaying."

He shook his head and pointed to the

pills beside the bed. I fetched a glass of water and gave him two capsules. We sat silently waiting for them to work. After a while I stood up and walked to the window trying to surmise how Garsales would get in touch. As I turned Klaus was surreptitiously swallowing another two. I got him back into bed and he sort of shrank and took up very little room. His eyes closed immediately.

I took a turn round Saint Peter's Square before turning in and watched well-fed priests drinking and smoking in the cocktail bars and I could have cheerfully frog-marched one of them back to Klaus and demanded a miracle. The awful inevitability of his death dogged my feet. I found myself at the top of the steps of Saint Peter's and nearly fell over a bony friar in a brown robe eating bread and a bit of cheese under an archway. He smiled and his eyes were burning with faith. As I drew level he murmured a blessing and in a confusion of languages started to tell me he had received a special dispensation to visit the Holy City. His Order was poor so he had walked from his monastery high in the Alps and held up horny feet. He was no worldly intellectual living off the poor so I sat beside him and dredged up some schoolboy Latin. Before I left I gave him some lira to light a candle for the dying.

In the lobby, in our pigeon hole was another note. It said, "Tomorrow. The Forum. Nine-thirty."

It happened again. When I awoke he was standing by the window drinking in the rosy light of the dawn giving new life to another day. It seemed an imposition to disturb him. I wanted to do something for him, but what?

"Are you ready for coffee?"

"Good . . . good." But he didn't move, just stood there watching as the sun edged the night away.

When I'd poured the coffee he took a sip, leaving the rest. This upset me because Klaus and black coffee were synonymous. I looked at my watch, and couldn't delay it.

"It's today."

There is a certain look on a dying man's face when he is trying to think like a fit man. The inner struggle seemed interminable.

"What time?" he asked eventually.

"Nine-thirty, the Forum."

"Ahh."

I had to ask him. "Where can I get a gun?"

"No." His expression closed the subject.

"Klaus, I'm not going to be taken again."

He shook his head, staring at me, willing me to see it his way.

"Not like that . . . his friend."

Whilst I was putting on my anorak he took something out of his dressing gown pocket and held it out. It was tissues rolled into a ball.

"What's this!"

"Pepper, trust me."

I looked away embarrassed. When I looked back he was smiling. He swallowed hard and a complete sentence took me by surprise.

"When they search they won't bother with a bit of paper, cigarettes on top, a minute's advantage."

I flung my arms round those thin shoulders muttering, "Old Hun."

As I moved into the corridor I heard,

514

"Watch, Hugh . . . watch him all the time."

Ancient lawns . . . Grecian colonnades . . . broken pillars lying on their sides . . . calm with the dignity of age.

I had a guide book in my hand. I looked for the auditorium and squinted at the print, then caught sight of Klaus' jade ring on my finger, "just for luck, Hugh".

In the sunlight a plaque:

THE ARCH OF TITUS AD 81

To commemorate the victories of Vespasian and Titus over Jerusalem.

What was that duo after, I wondered? What ramifications motivated you? I sit on a low wall near the pathway leading up to the Forum and light a cigarette. American voices startle me. Two young people, eyes glazed with too much culture, haversacks heavy on their backs, drift by discussing rates of exchange against the dollar.

It was a relief when the black hood came down over my head . . . just afraid the cigarette would ignite it. I'm being pushed and pulled and there is gravel under my feet. I go limp to show I'm not resisting.

A tight hand urges me into a car, and I am expiring under the hood.

The hum of the engine—the movement of the car—and hands holding my wrists together with wiry strength.

The hood is suffocating me. I growl and struggle with the hands. The hood is jerked off and I'm blinded with sunlight. My lids open a centimetre and I catch sight of the sea glittering with prisms of refraction.

Rosana sits beside me. I can't equate her with the strength in those hands. She sits very straight, knees crossed, and there is a gun in her hand. With great style she raises it to my forehead and pulls the trigger. A fraction of my life passes before me, then there is a click.

She laughs, enjoying my stricken expression. "That's a warning! Don't double-cross *me* or there will be a bullet in it next time!"

I stare back and see no flicker of liking today.

"I've never double crossed you or Jamie."

"Crap! You can fool him, but you don't

fool me." The fury on her face is not the controlled variety.

"Why don't you get out? Lead your own life. You could disappear in America."

"Jamie is my life!"

"Then what do you want me for?"

"I am about to tell you."

She lights a cigarette, holding it between thumb and first finger, puffing in a continental way.

"Jamie has this idea that he can replace the lost cargo with something equally effective. You know and I know this is a dream. The Opus people are re-organising, eliminating enemies. They will never deal with him again. If we act quickly we can get him away, but there's no time to waste."

"That still doesn't explain why you need me. You could arrange that yourself."

I'd put my finger on her weakness; her eyes slid away and her voice became less strident. "He won't listen to me."

Then in a flash . . . the family change of mood . . .

"Why does he have this misplaced faith in you?"

Why indeed! It seemed better to change the subject.

"Where are we going?"

Moodily she smoked. "You'll see."

I recognised Civitavecchia because we'd had breakfast there once when I was young. That was the year when I thought my parents might get together again. It's not a big port but the small liners that cruise between the various Mediteranean countries are white and gleaming. Now I know that they are no different from any others and it was just the eyes of childhood. We circled round the back of the town and there were many new half finished white buildings making it look like Egypt.

The hood is replaced.

Minutes later the car stops and I am thrown on the ground and thoroughly searched. One to you Klaus. More shoving and pushing and I am covered in sweat before I fall sprawling over an entrance. The heat turns to shade. The hood is dragged off.

The first thing I notice is the smell of sulphur. I am in a huge silo with enormous ceilings supported by iron girders.

Brilliant sunshine and black shadows distort my vision, but there are massive containers everywhere.

I stumble forward as that voice says, "Oh Hugo, you're back. Good, come over here."

In the distance, at the end of this barn, a white flame hangs in the air. Then I see a bunsen burner, a test tube waving in the flame, and Garsales sitting at a bench. For a moment he is distracted and stares down at Petri dishes. I look into corners behind shadows, but we are alone.

He swings off his stool and comes towards me, then stops in a ray of sunlight and I gasp in horror. The left side of his face is a mass of supurating blisters; his eyelids so inflamed that they seem to be sticking together. Both eyebrows so scorched that he has a lopsided look.

"Good God! Did that happen when the yacht blew up?"

Rosana's voice behind me says, "He did it himself with these stupid experiments!"

"Shouldn't you have it looked at? What are you doing?"

"He's making mustard gas." Rosana's

voice was derisive and when I looked back at him the thunderclouds were gathering.

"Nothing of the sort! Don't talk rubbish! It's far more spohisticated than mustard gas!" His powerful voice reverberated and echoed around the girders.

"Garbage! Why don't you leave it to the experts. You're always getting sidetracked!"

I held my breath at this onslaught. Rosana had made the mistake of moving too close. He grabbed her hair and slowly brings the test tube towards her face. She screamed.

"Don't do it!!" I don't know which of our voices penetrated his brain, but he moved it away and replaced it in its wooden holder.

"Your tongue will be the death of you!"

He returned to his bench and stood with his back to us.

Sobbing hysterically, Rosana threw her arms round his back in a frenzy.

"Jamie, I'm sorry, trust *me*." She jerked her head in my direction.

"*He's* the one that blew up the boat and destroyed the cargo! *He's* the one who nearly killed you!"

He turned round rocking her in his arms. I felt sick with shock. His face was full of calm understanding.

Quietly, patiently, he explained to a loved child, "That is not true Rosana, Hugo is my friend."

She let out a wail of exasperation. "Then *who* did it?"

"P2 of course. You know they are always fighting amongst themselves. They wanted the cargo for South America. Now they can tell them there was a slight accident with an inflammable cargo."

Transfixed I stared at this metamorphosis. They stood, crooning in each other's arms, oblivious of me. I walked towards an aperture in the wall and gazed at the sea and sand. Fishermen were mending nets, sailors painting their boats. Nothing could be more normal.

Garsales is by my side. "Take no notice, Hugo, it's the strain, that's all." Then, as if she has been on a visit, "Did Sylvie get home alright?"

I grunt something, then ask, "Why did you want to see me Jamie?"

"To discuss the revised plans, of course."

Instant alarm. Rosana shouts, "Don't tell him anything Jamie!" His hands are round her face. Cupping it he looks into her eyes like a lover.

"Rosana, consider, if you were right he would be back in England now."

Then he returns to his stool, waving me to a seat beside him and mutters under his breath, "Women! They bring nothing but trouble." Rosana has wandered outside and I nod with heartfelt agreement.

"Come on, tell me the facts before she comes back. What are you going to replace the gas with?"

"I'm negotiating for some portable missiles. I've made an offer for them."

"What about transportation."

"They're coming by sea from South America. The ship will be diverted when the price is fixed and continue to the Philippines."

"When will it arrive?"

"It's already quite near. Three Opus men are bringing the cargo as a gift for the Paymaster. There's been a financial misunderstanding. It's a sweetener to soften the blow of some missing shares in a bank that P2 has underwritten."

"Are you sure Opus will sell?"

"Oh they'll sell."

"Where will it land?"

"Decisions like that aren't taken until the last minute."

He was still fascinated by his test tubes and picked one up waving it through the flame.

"Where's it coming from?"

"Uruguay."

"What's the name of the ship?"

He paused. "It's better not to ask questions like that."

I tried hard to think of an innocuous remark, then, to my astonishment, he says, "I want you to take a message to the Vatican."

He smiled at my surprise. "As you see, I'm not able to go myself."

Once more it's all an adventure. Serous fluid oozes from the blisters as he scribbles on a pad. He puts the note in an envelope and I'm saying, "Jamie, I've got to get a sterile bandage for your face."

There is a sudden scuffle in the doorway.

Rosana and three men, all with guns, stand there.

"The place is swarming with police. I told you not to trust him!"

The four of them move towards me, converging in a circle and I think I've been here before! They block the way to the exit. The aperture is too small and too close to Garsales' test tubes. They are in the centre of the silo now. Caribinere fill the doorway, but hesitate when they see my plight. Garsales' face is transfixed with anger. I move away from him, knocking against the bench. Rosana moves closer. Over her shoulder I see someone struggling through the police with a gun in his hand.

"Klaus!"

It's incredible, impossible! She swings round and fires into the crowd. At the same time I fling the pepper into her face. It misses but lands in the eyes of one of the men as he moves closer. He screams and Rosana turns back in disbelief as his hands cover his face. Carefully, she levels her gun at me.

A bullet ricochets off an iron strut and she starts to fall. She won't accept that she has been hit. Her hand comes up to her chest and she stares at the blood. Slowly, in silence, she continues her journey to the ground.

Like a wounded beast, cornered and distraught Garsales shoves the bench out of the way and seizes her in his arms, pressing her to him as if to stop the bleeding. In a paroxysm of grief, a weird sobbing fills the silo and all movement is suspended.

I look away as if it's wrong to witness such grief and see the spilt contents of the test tubes bubbling and burning a path across the floor.

In a dream—on that beautiful morning—I see a handcuffed Garsales disappear dully through the door with a posse of policemen, like a minor criminal.

That night—sitting beside the stretcher, the plane's engines lulling us into a kind of sleep—I took Klaus home.

Epilogue

1983

IT is nearly two years since the end of that family madness. Who knows if it would all have happened if they hadn't been there to encourage each others excesses.

The note to the Vatican led to the arrest of three priests—all high ranking and all connected with the Vatican Bank.

The Italians from Uruguay, hotly pursued by the CIA, were picked up when they docked at the small port near Naples. In an attempt to avoid several lifetimes of imprisonment they sung like birds and their confessions led to a mass round up of the high and low in the land.

During these activities Garsales awaits trial in the Regina Coeli jail. He refuses all food because of fear of poisoning and only drinks bottled water which he opens himself. Occasionally they force-feed him. The law grinds exceedingly slowly on the Continent and many months pass as the Examining Magistrates get their act together and I make the journey between Heathrow and Rome too often.

We are a strangely subdued family. E-Woh clings to my mother and rarely leaves Nairobi. As she matures the resemblance to Shen San fades. She studies Mandarin and talks vaguely of going to China with VSO. She has no interest in European life.

Klaus' will to live slowly drifted away as the worst of the Opus criminals were arrested. He died at five o'clock on a Tuesday holding Sarah's hand on the verandah of our house in the Ngong Hills.

His last words were, "Now David and I are equals."

I've lost the trick of watching death with equanimity so I'm selfishly glad I wasn't there to witness Sarah's grief . . . but glad she has E-Woh. I often hear him laughing with my father.

Charles and Penny have another baby, a boy this time. Like two pillars of the community, we are reorganising the Group. We have moved the various divisions into the country and recruited young people who work competently and comfortably in idyllic conditions and receive a chunk of shares each Christmas. They eat their lunch in the grounds and I take my dog to the office. Spalding helped considerably and we are selling the headquarters in London to pay for it.

Charles says, "You only have to motivate people . . . as David motivated me."

The Doc waits in Hong Kong for his country to be a democracy again and Roilo keeps him in touch with the various factions in New York. He adds coloured pins to his maps and says, "Ninoy will do it . . . wait and see."

And Linda . . . you are wondering about Linda . . . My wife has such marvellous qualities. When Sylvie and I were away she wrote an article and sent it to the papers. They asked for more and now her features are gathered together in a book called *Letters from a Political Prisoner*. I am very proud.

Last night she told Sylvie the story

about the Merchant of Baghdad who sent his servant to the market for grain. There, Death brushed against him in the market place.

He said, "Master, Master, lend me your horse so that I may ride to Smyrna, for Death jostled me in the market place."

When the man had ridden away the merchant sought out Death and asked, "Why did you jostle my servant in the market place, for he is a good man?"

Death replied, "Sir I did not jostle him. I accidentally brushed against him in surprise because tonight I have an appointment with him in Smyrna."

She notices me listening and smiles. "Only a brush, Hugo, only a brush." Love, like life, is so good when you nearly lose it.

Sylvie has turned into a quiet child. She likes to be with us, but is shy of strangers. She prefers the company of her pets to people and sometimes talks of being a vet. I don't know what she thinks any more.

There is a final incident. I was called to Rome for Garsales' trial. It is a sunny morning, the pavements newly washed with rain. I decide to walk to the court as a private celebration because it is the last time. Sirens storm past causing pandemonium, followed by a posse of police on motorbikes. Slowly, a large limousine cruises by and I recognise the Chief Magistrate in his robes in the back seat. Almost unnoticed in the rear, the prisoner's Black Maria.

Out of nowhere come three gunmen who shoot the Magistrate to smithereens —his body half in, half out of the car door. A Latin frenzy erupts as the entire police force surges towards him. The Black Maria, unnoticed, unattended, until someone in the crowd sees the dead driver, the rear door hanging open—another body, bloody on the pavement.

Opus Dei is not about to have their people in the dock.

In the same week Ninoy was killed, but you know about that.

But now I've plucked from the memory a rooted shadow. On Saturday we approached the first part of our Sabbatical in Africa. At Heathrow the reporters waited.

One called, "How's the family, Mr. Aitkin? Are you happy now?"

I grin and reply, "The wife argues with me . . . the kid gives me lip . . . yes we're very happy."

A landrover waits for us in Cairo. We shall drive south across the Nubian desert, then along the verdant parts of the country until we reach Khartoum. Don't tell me it's a mistake to go back: I've allowed for it. Then I shall show Linda and Sylvie the house where I was born . . . the house by the Nile where Sarah didn't get her daughter back.

After that, it will all be behind us.

"HUBERT AITKIN, Chairman of the *Aitkin Textile Group*, left London today with his family for Kenya.

He is taking a well earned rest after the astonishing but now happily resolved events surrounding the kidnapping of his daughter.

Charles Winthrope, Vice Chairman, will run the company during his absence—a position he was made familiar with during Mr. Aitkin's unfortunate imprisonment in a Filipino jail.

The businessman's life is indeed a precarious one when three years of one's life is passed, first as a political prisoner, and second as the father of a kidnap victim."

GUIDE
TO THE COLOUR CODING
OF
ULVERSCROFT BOOKS

Many of our readers have written to us expressing their appreciation for the way in which our colour coding has assisted them in selecting the Ulverscroft books of their choice.

To remind everyone of our colour coding— this is as follows:

BLACK COVERS
Mysteries

★

BLUE COVERS
Romances

★

RED COVERS
Adventure Suspense and General Fiction

★

ORANGE COVERS
Westerns

★

GREEN COVERS
Non-Fiction

FICTION TITLES
in the
Ulverscroft Large Print Series

The Onedin Line: The High Seas
Cyril Abraham
The Onedin Line: The Iron Ships
Cyril Abraham
The Onedin Line: The Shipmaster
Cyril Abraham
The Onedin Line: The Trade Winds
Cyril Abraham
The Enemy   *Desmond Bagley*
Flyaway   *Desmond Bagley*
The Master Idol   *Anthony Burton*
The Navigators   *Anthony Burton*
A Place to Stand   *Anthony Burton*
The Doomsday Carrier   *Victor Canning*
The Cinder Path   *Catherine Cookson*
The Girl   *Catherine Cookson*
The Invisible Cord   *Catherine Cookson*
Life and Mary Ann   *Catherine Cookson*
Maggie Rowan   *Catherine Cookson*
Marriage and Mary Ann   *Catherine Cookson*
Mary Ann's Angels   *Catherine Cookson*
All Over the Town   *R. F. Delderfield*
Jamaica Inn   *Daphne du Maurier*
My Cousin Rachel   *Daphne du Maurier*